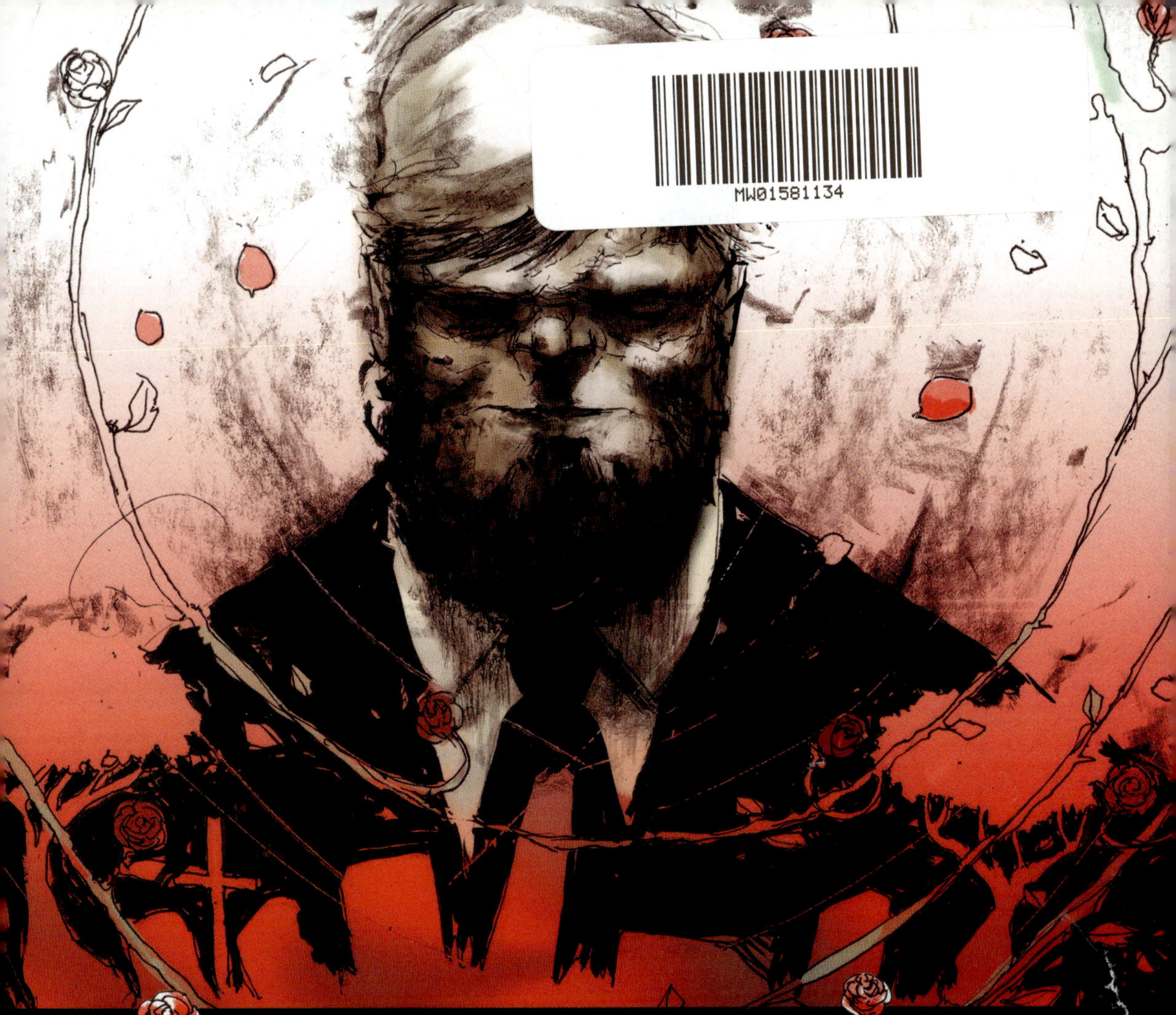

PROOF™ BLUE FAIRIES

CREATED BY **ALEXANDER GRECIAN & RILEY ROSSMO**

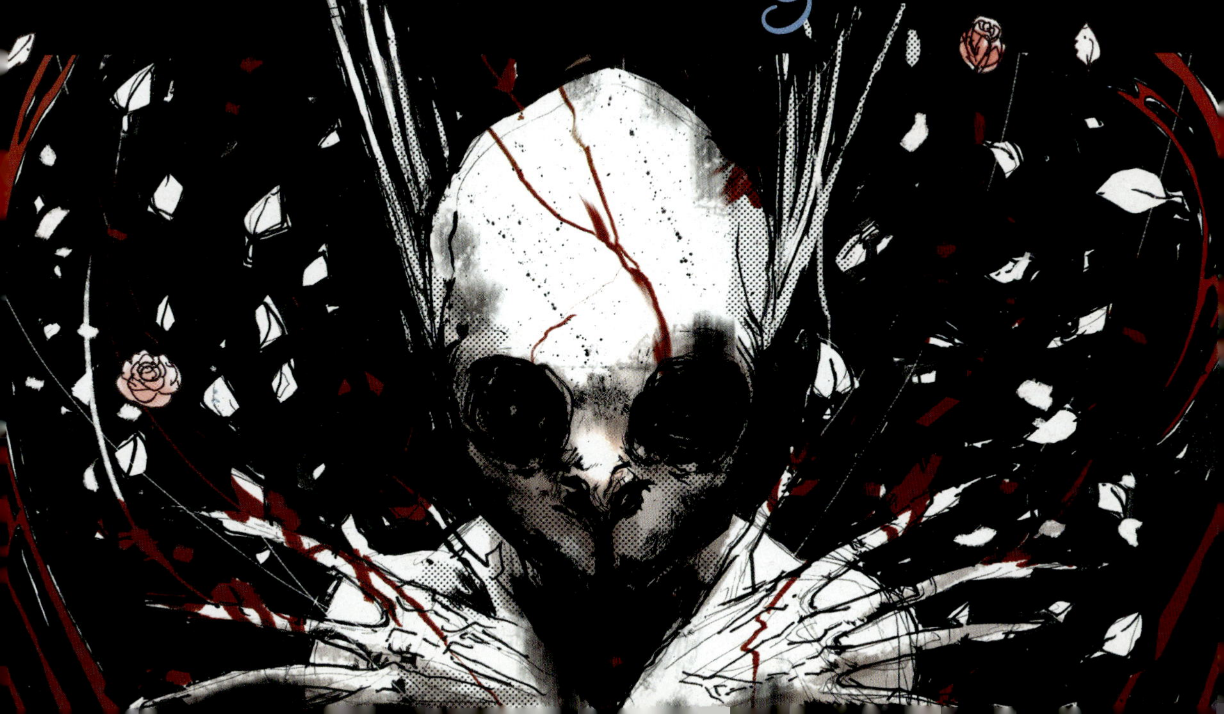

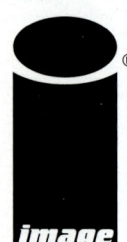

IMAGE COMICS, INC.

ROBERT KIRKMAN chief operating officer ERIK LARSEN chief financial officer TODD McFARLANE president
MARC SILVESTRI chief executive officer JIM VALENTINO vice-president

ERIC STEPHENSON publisher TODD MARTINEZ sales & licensing coordinator BETSY GOMEZ pr & marketing coordinator
BRANWYN BIGGLESTONE accounts manager SARAH deLAINE administrative assistant TYLER SHAINLINE production manager
DREW GILL art director JONATHAN CHAN production artist MONICA HOWARD production artist
VINCENT KUKUA production artist KEVIN YUEN production artist

www.imagecomics.com

PROOF BOOK 5: BLUE FAIRIES
ISBN: 978-1-60706-348-3
First Printing

Published by Image Comics, Inc. Office of publication: 2134 Allston Way, 2nd Floor, Berkeley, CA 94704. Copyright © 2010 Alexander Grecian and Riley Rossmo. All rights reserved. Originally published in single magazine format as PROOF #24-28. All rights reserved. PROOF™ (including all prominent characters featured herein), its logo, and all character likenesses are trademarks of Alexander Grecian and Riley Rossmo, unless otherwise noted. Image Comics® and its logos are registered trademarks of Image Comics, Inc. No part of this publication may be reproduced or transmitted, in any form or by any means (except for short excerpts for review purposes) without the express written permission of Image Comics, Inc. All names, characters, events and locales in this publication are entirely fictional. Any resemblance to actual persons (living or dead), events or places, without satiric intent, is coincidental.
For information regarding the CPSIA on this printed material call: 203-595-3636 and provide reference # EAST – 70302.
International Rights Representative: Christine Meyer (christine@gfloystudio.com)
PRINTED IN THE U.S.A.

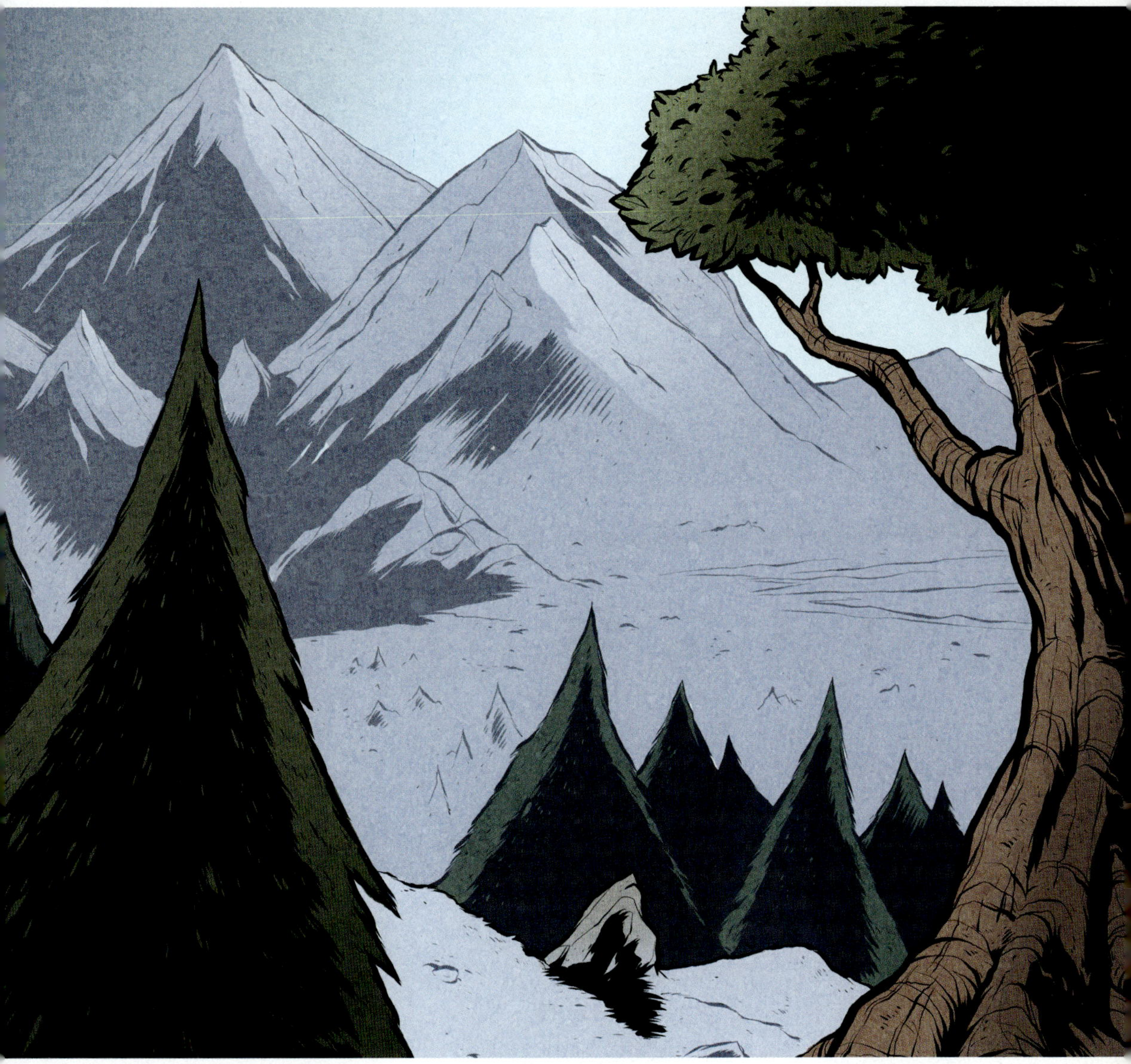

WRITTEN BY
ALEXANDER GRECIAN

ART BY
RILEY ROSSMO & DAVE CASEY
CHAPTER ONE: *Aftermath*

DAVE CASEY INTERLUDE ONE: *1977*

PAUL FRICKE INTERLUDE TWO: *Lodged*

CHRIS GRINE CHAPTER TWO: *The Blue Fairy*

RILEY ROSSMO & DAVE CASEY
CHAPTER THREE: *Who Killed the Dover Demon?*

Lettered using the Blambot font Jack Armstrong.

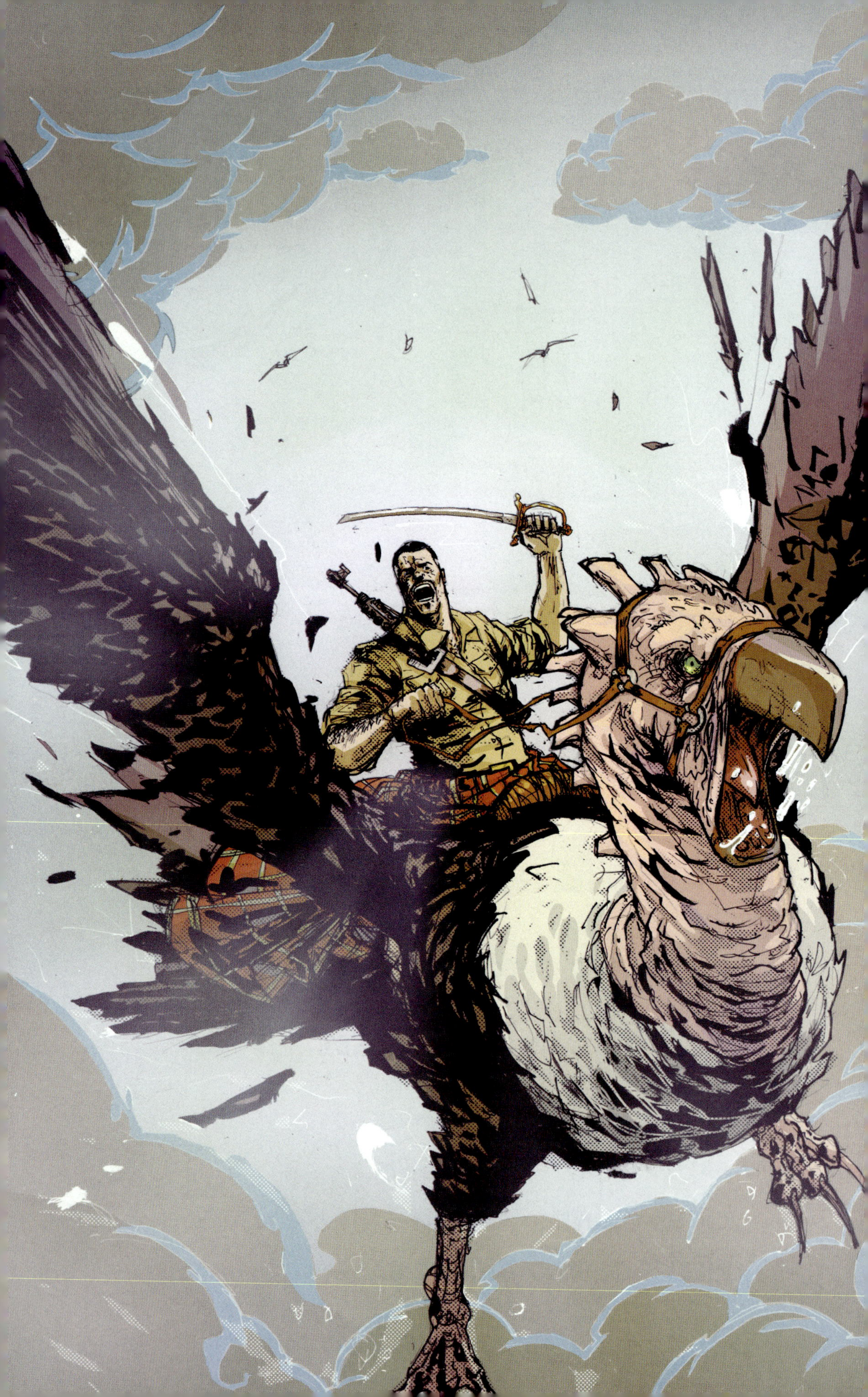

CHAPTER ONE

AFTERMATH

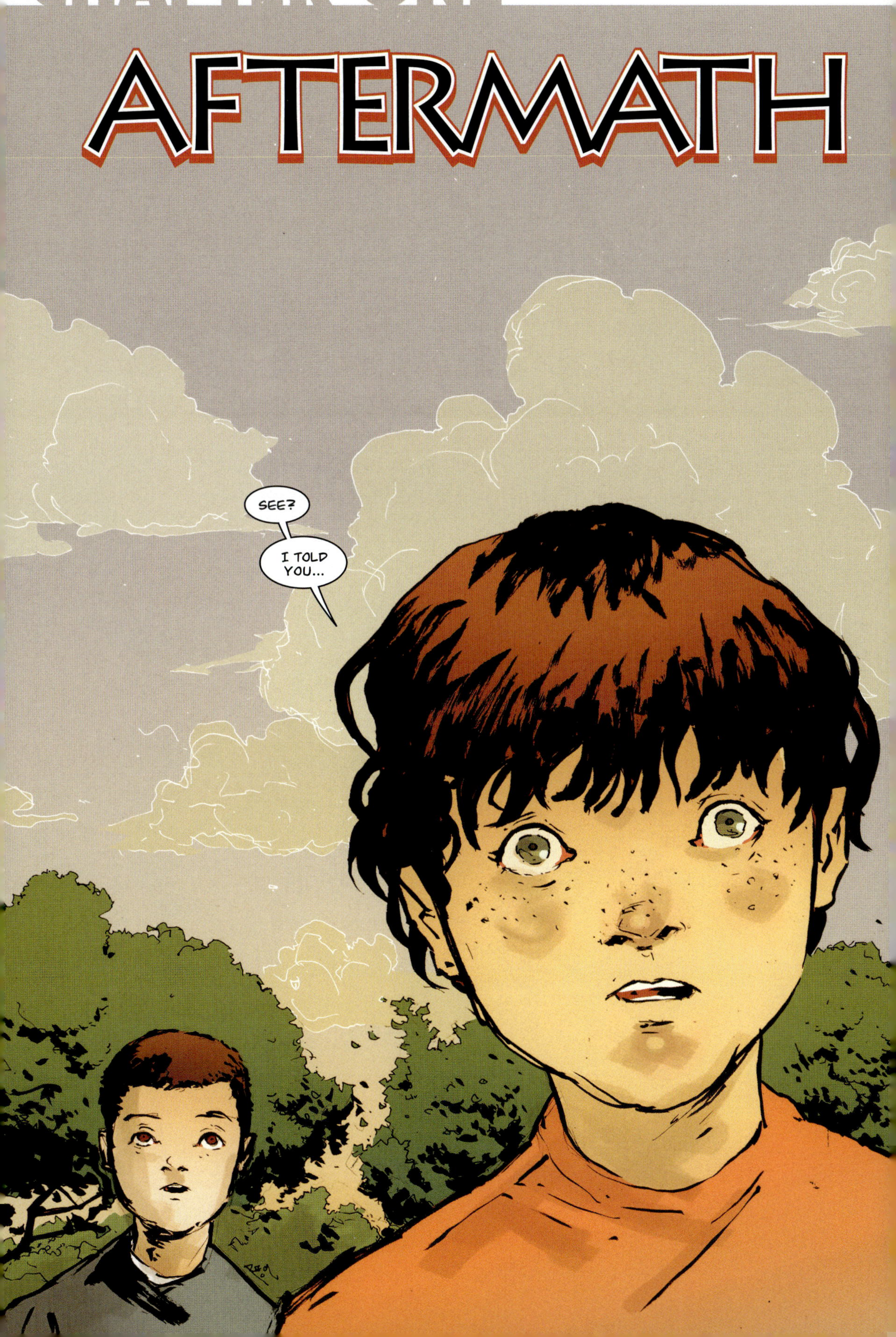

SEE?
I TOLD YOU...

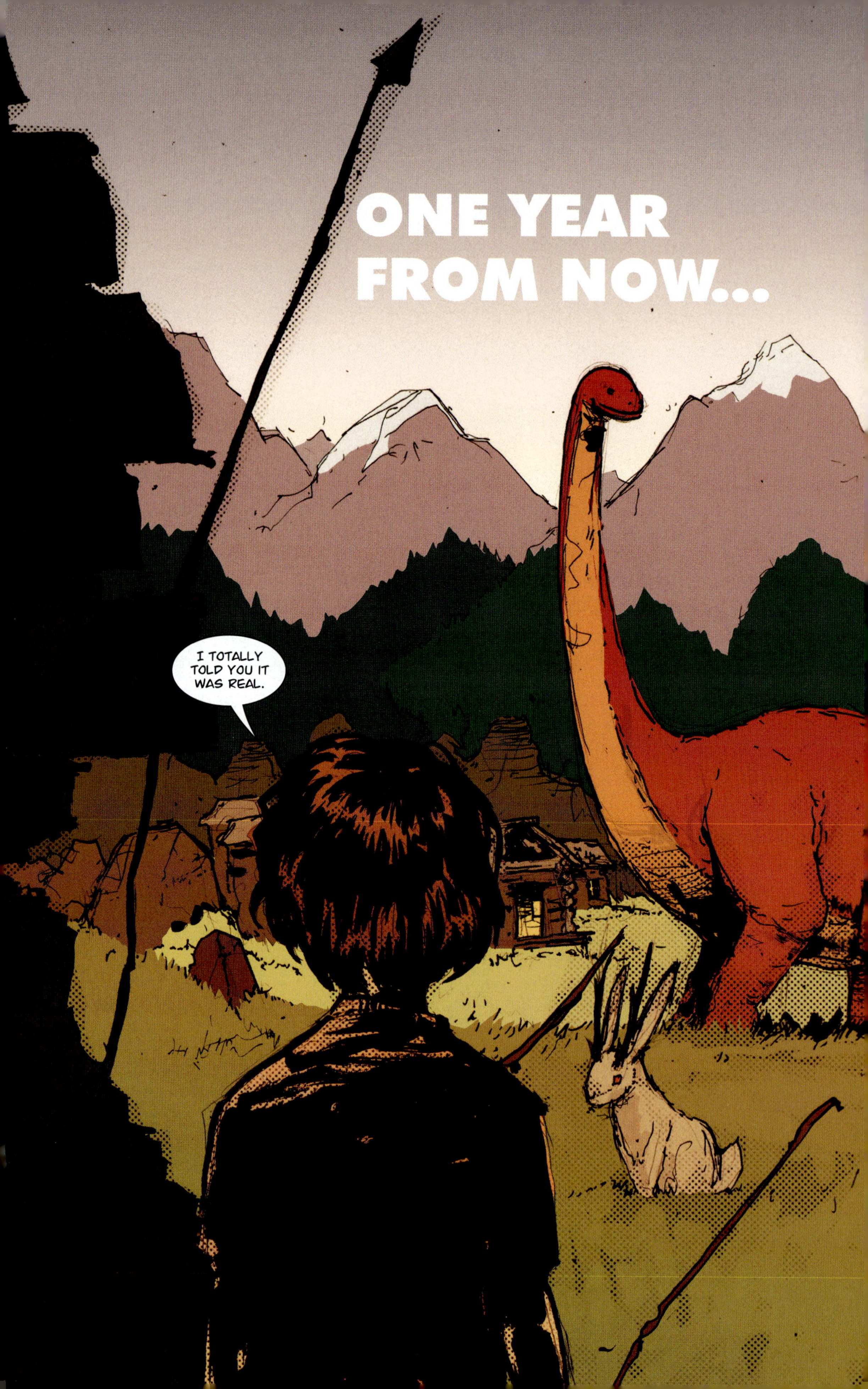
ONE YEAR FROM NOW...
I TOTALLY TOLD YOU IT WAS REAL.

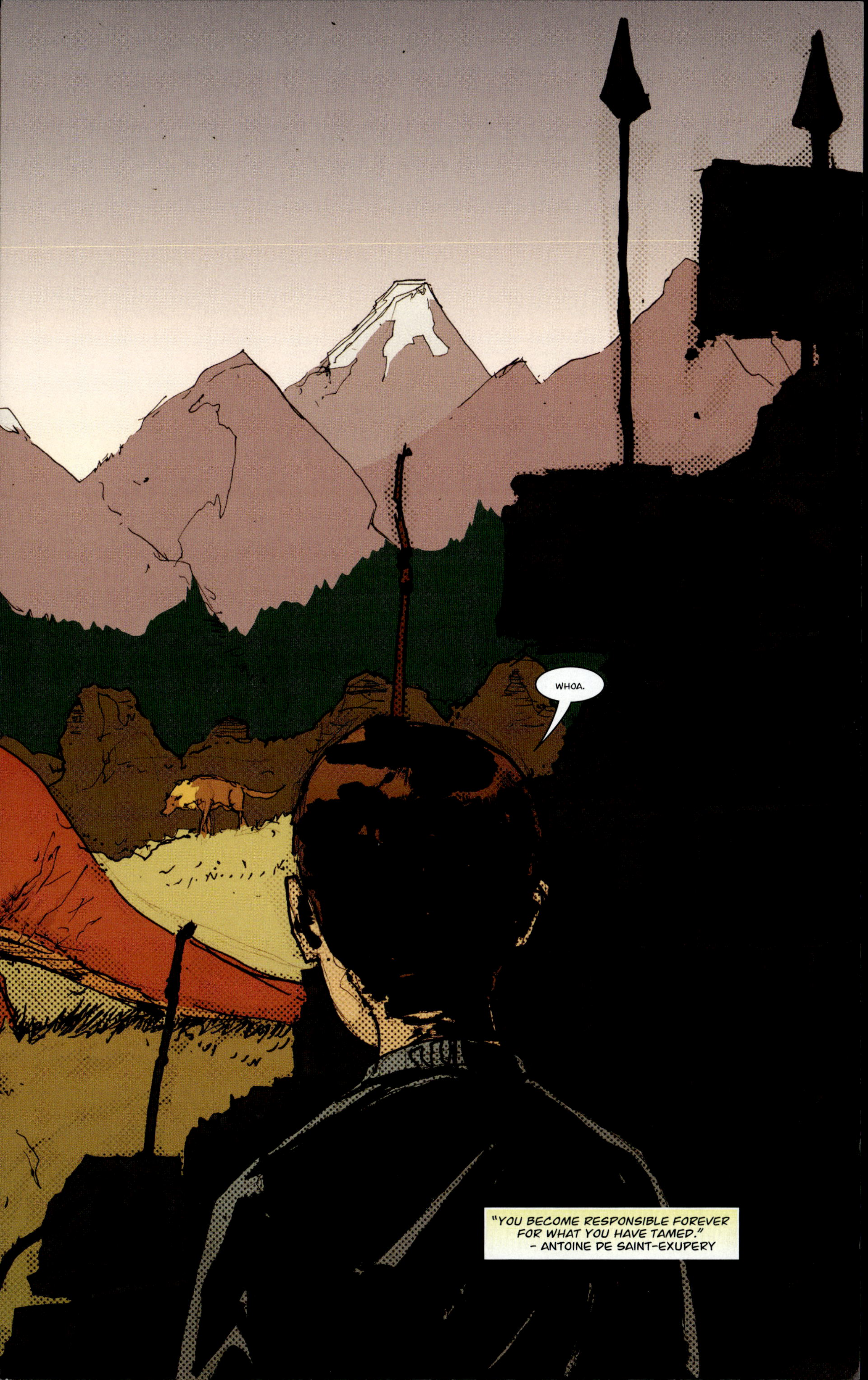
WHOA.
"YOU BECOME RESPONSIBLE FOREVER FOR WHAT YOU HAVE TAMED."
- ANTOINE DE SAINT-EXUPERY

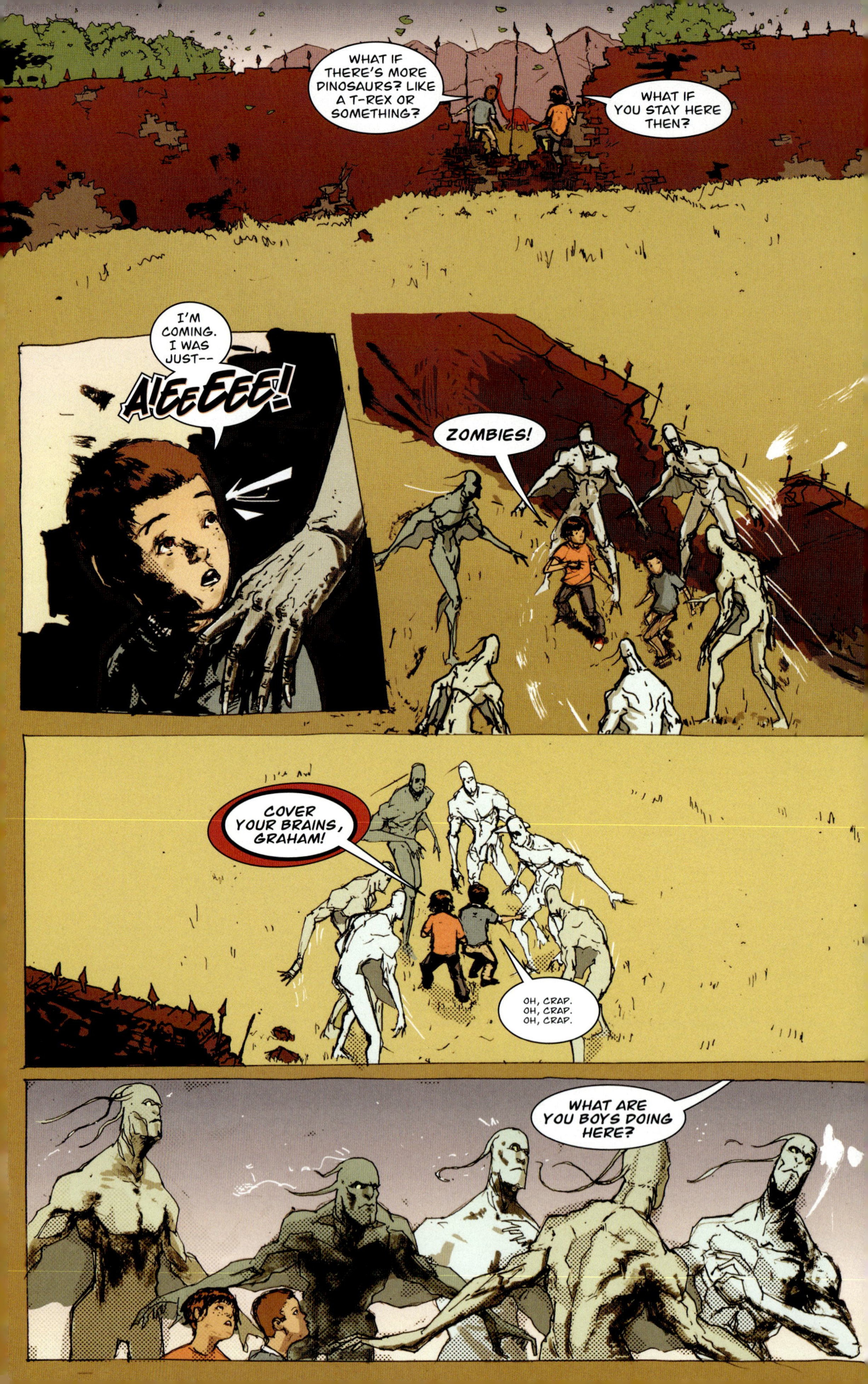
WHAT IF THERE'S MORE DINOSAURS? LIKE A T-REX OR SOMETHING?
WHAT IF YOU STAY HERE THEN?
I'M COMING. I WAS JUST--
AIEEEEE!
ZOMBIES!
COVER YOUR BRAINS, GRAHAM!
OH, CRAP. OH, CRAP. OH, CRAP.
WHAT ARE YOU BOYS DOING HERE?

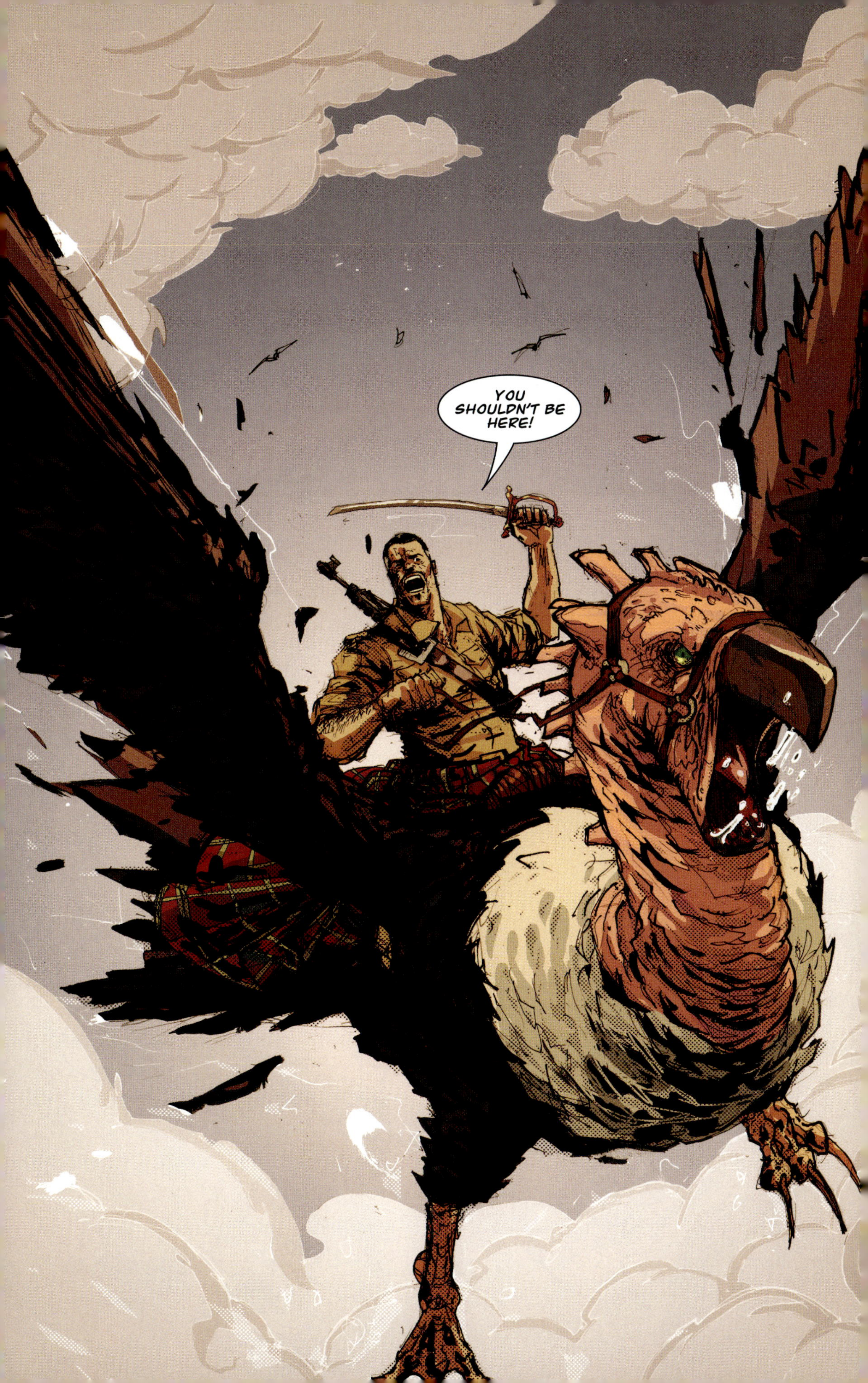
YOU SHOULDN'T BE HERE!

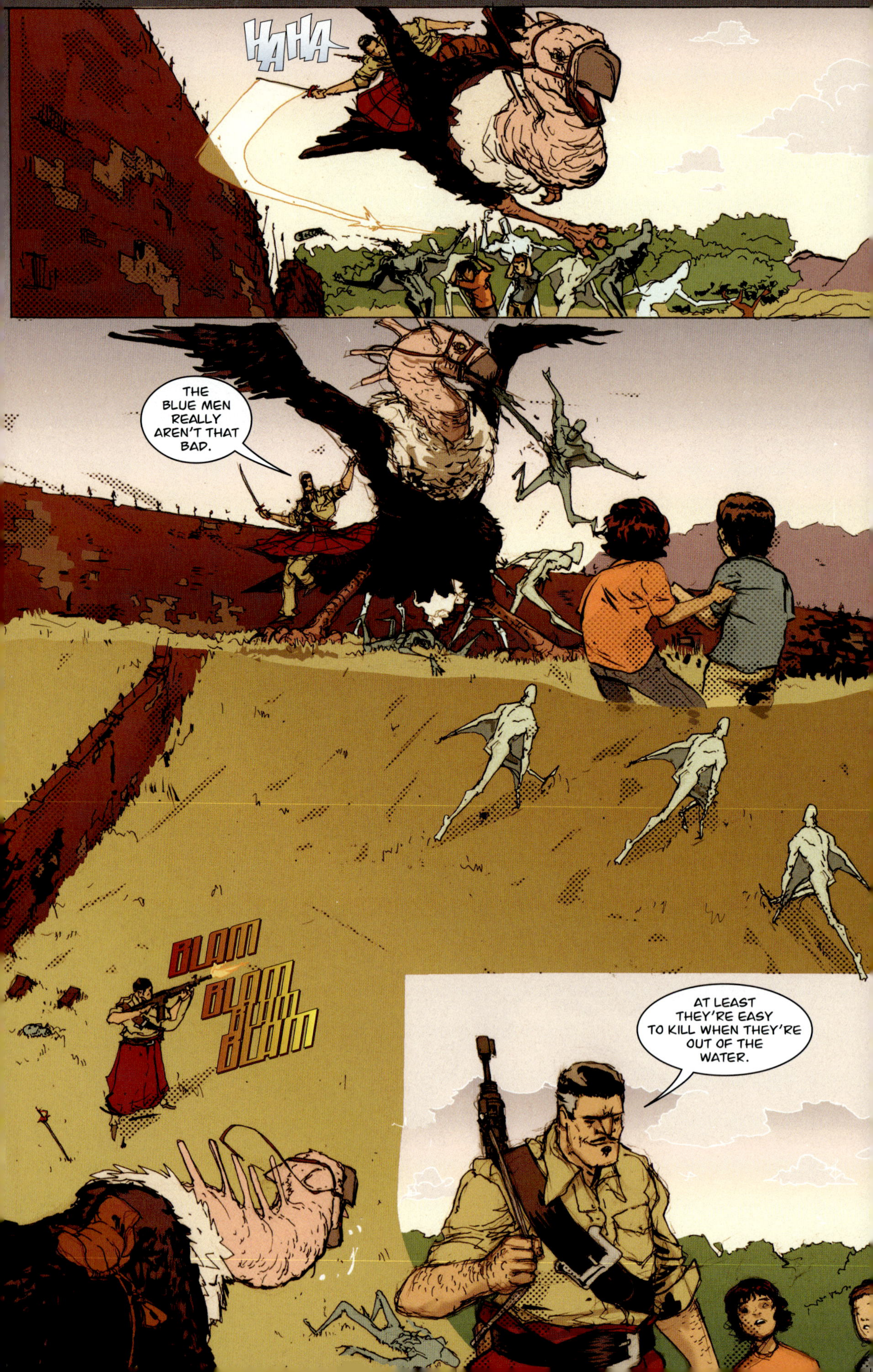
HAHA
THE BLUE MEN REALLY AREN'T THAT BAD.
BLAM
BLAM
BLAM
BLAM
AT LEAST THEY'RE EASY TO KILL WHEN THEY'RE OUT OF THE WATER.

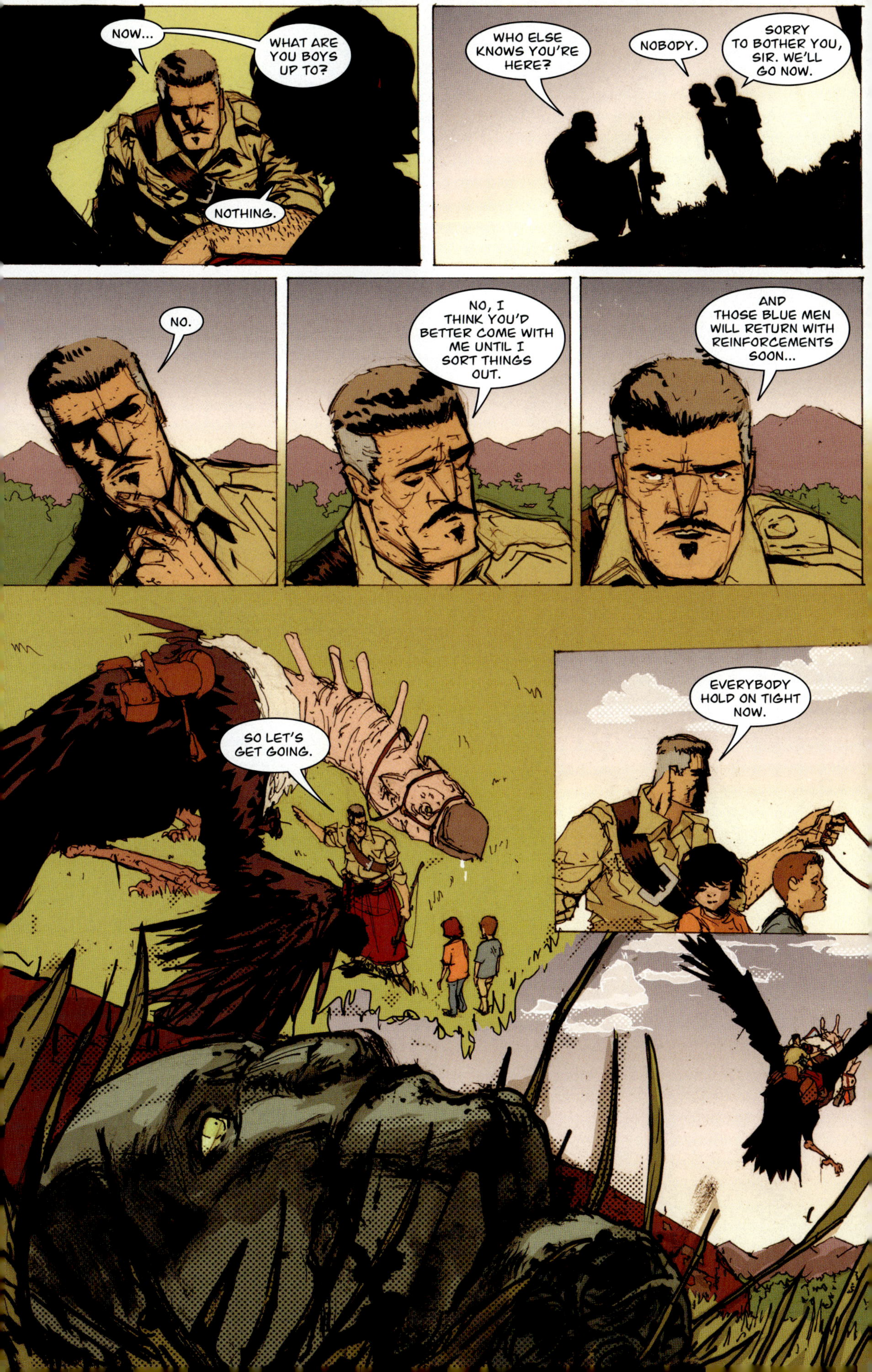
NOW...
WHAT ARE YOU BOYS UP TO?
NOTHING.
WHO ELSE KNOWS YOU'RE HERE?
NOBODY.
SORRY TO BOTHER YOU, SIR. WE'LL GO NOW.
NO.
NO, I THINK YOU'D BETTER COME WITH ME UNTIL I SORT THINGS OUT.
AND THOSE BLUE MEN WILL RETURN WITH REINFORCEMENTS SOON...
SO LET'S GET GOING.
EVERYBODY HOLD ON TIGHT NOW.

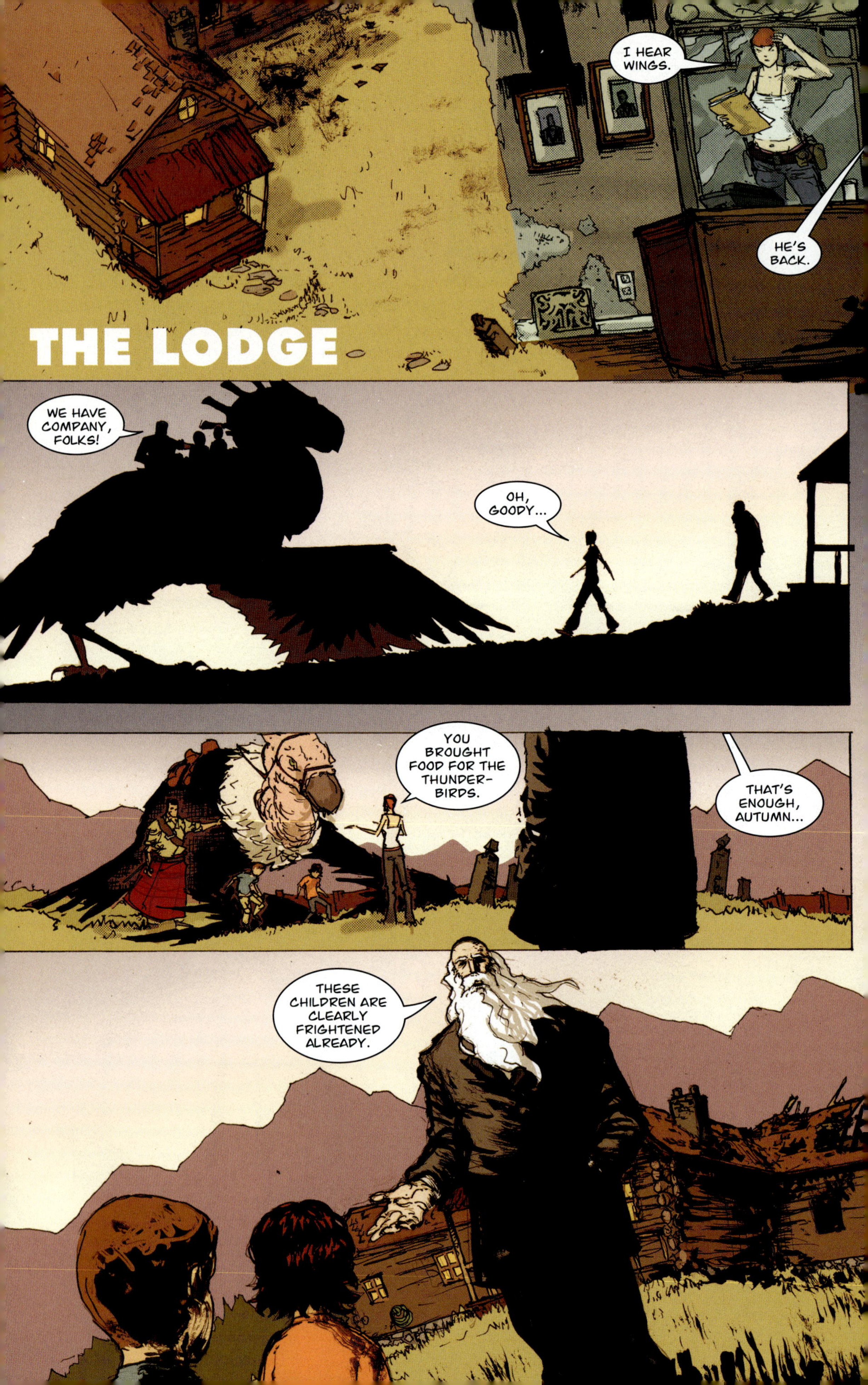
THE LODGE
I HEAR WINGS.
HE'S BACK.
WE HAVE COMPANY, FOLKS!
OH, GOODY...
YOU BROUGHT FOOD FOR THE THUNDER-BIRDS.
THAT'S ENOUGH, AUTUMN...
THESE CHILDREN ARE CLEARLY FRIGHTENED ALREADY.

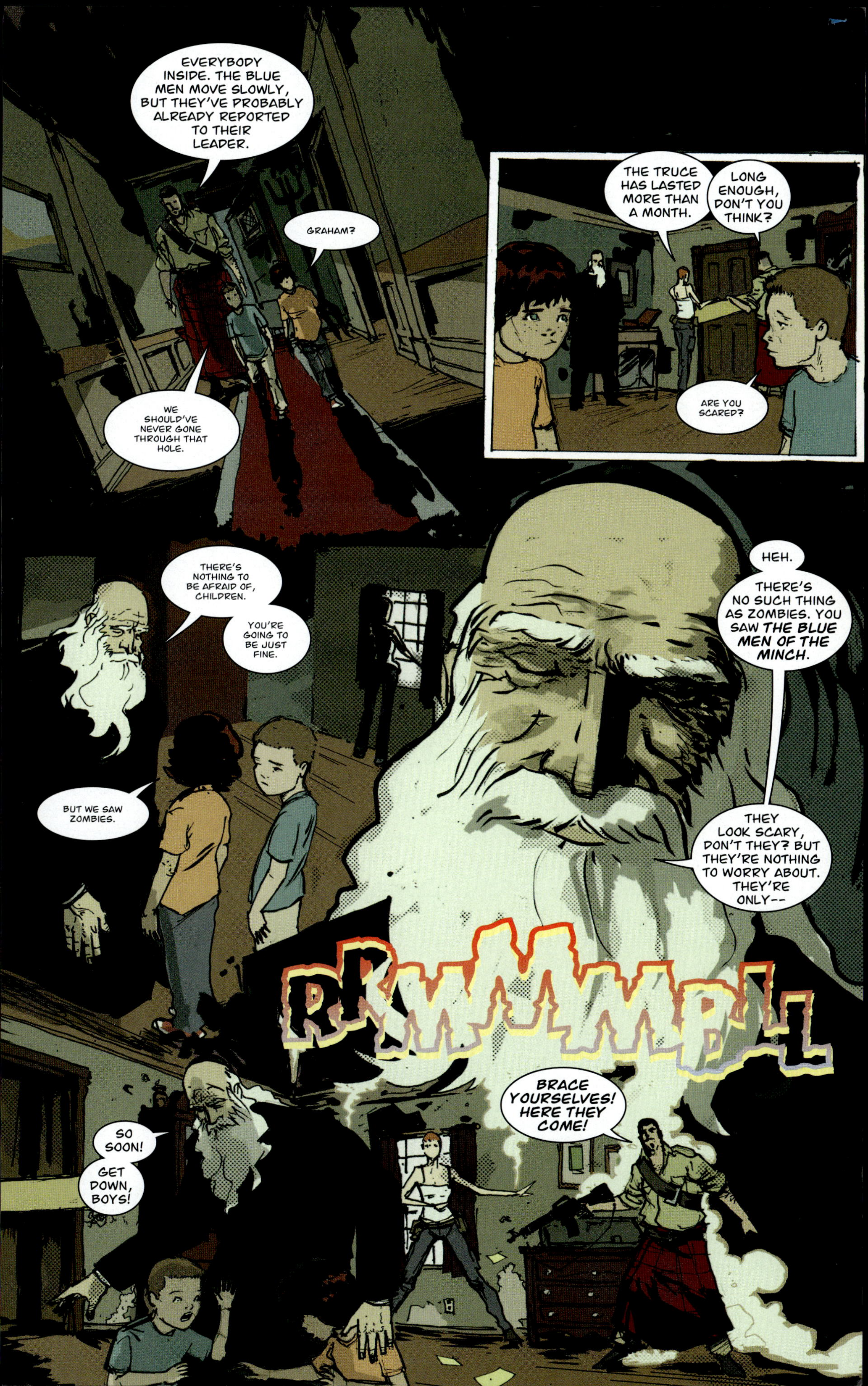
EVERYBODY INSIDE. THE BLUE MEN MOVE SLOWLY, BUT THEY'VE PROBABLY ALREADY REPORTED TO THEIR LEADER.
GRAHAM?
WE SHOULD'VE NEVER GONE THROUGH THAT HOLE.
THE TRUCE HAS LASTED MORE THAN A MONTH.
LONG ENOUGH, DON'T YOU THINK?
ARE YOU SCARED?
THERE'S NOTHING TO BE AFRAID OF, CHILDREN.
YOU'RE GOING TO BE JUST FINE.
BUT WE SAW ZOMBIES.
HEH.
THERE'S NO SUCH THING AS ZOMBIES. YOU SAW ***THE BLUE MEN OF THE MINCH.***
THEY LOOK SCARY, DON'T THEY? BUT THEY'RE NOTHING TO WORRY ABOUT. THEY'RE ONLY--
RRWWMMPHL
BRACE YOURSELVES! HERE THEY COME!
SO SOON!
GET DOWN, BOYS!

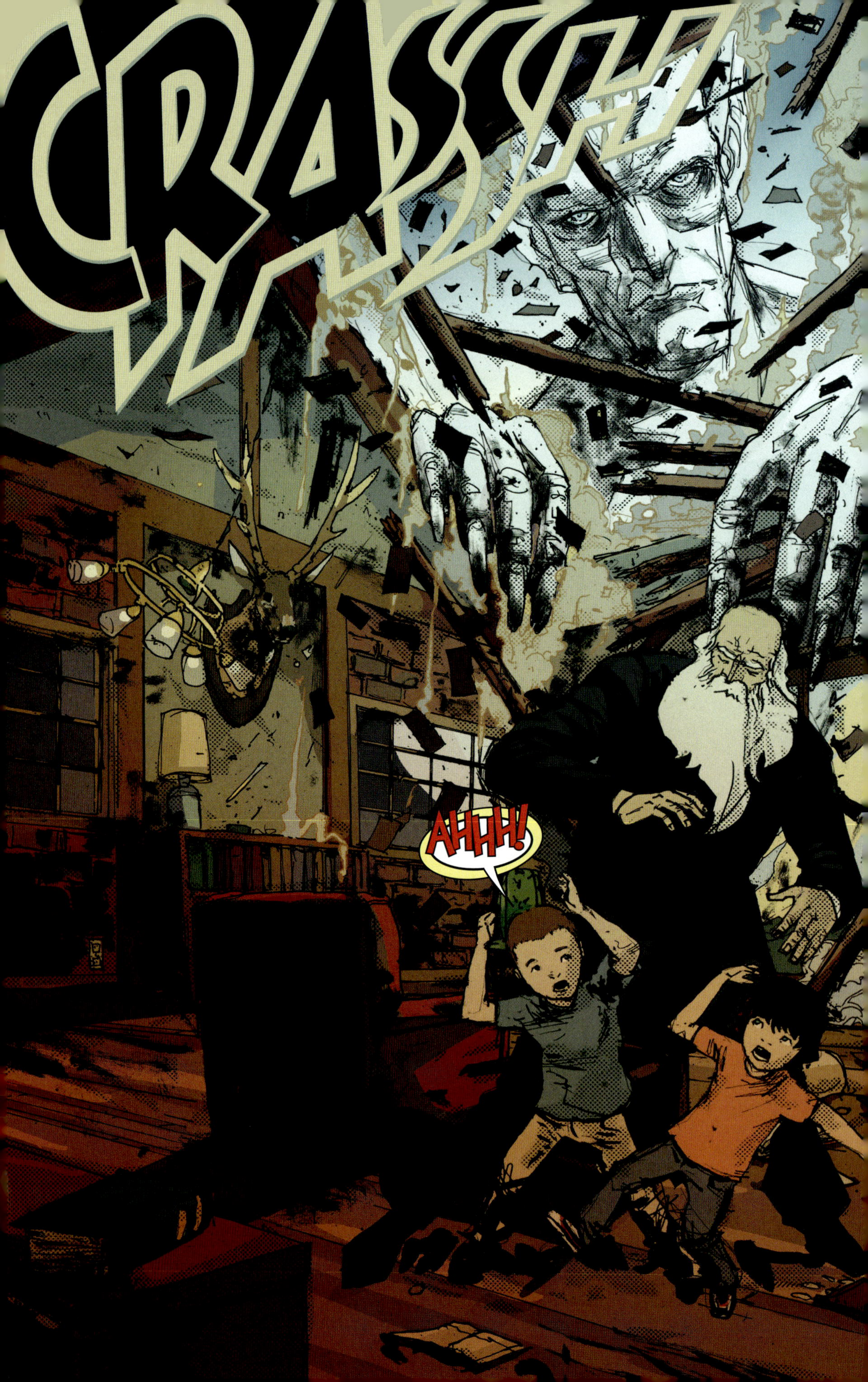
CRASSH
AHHH!

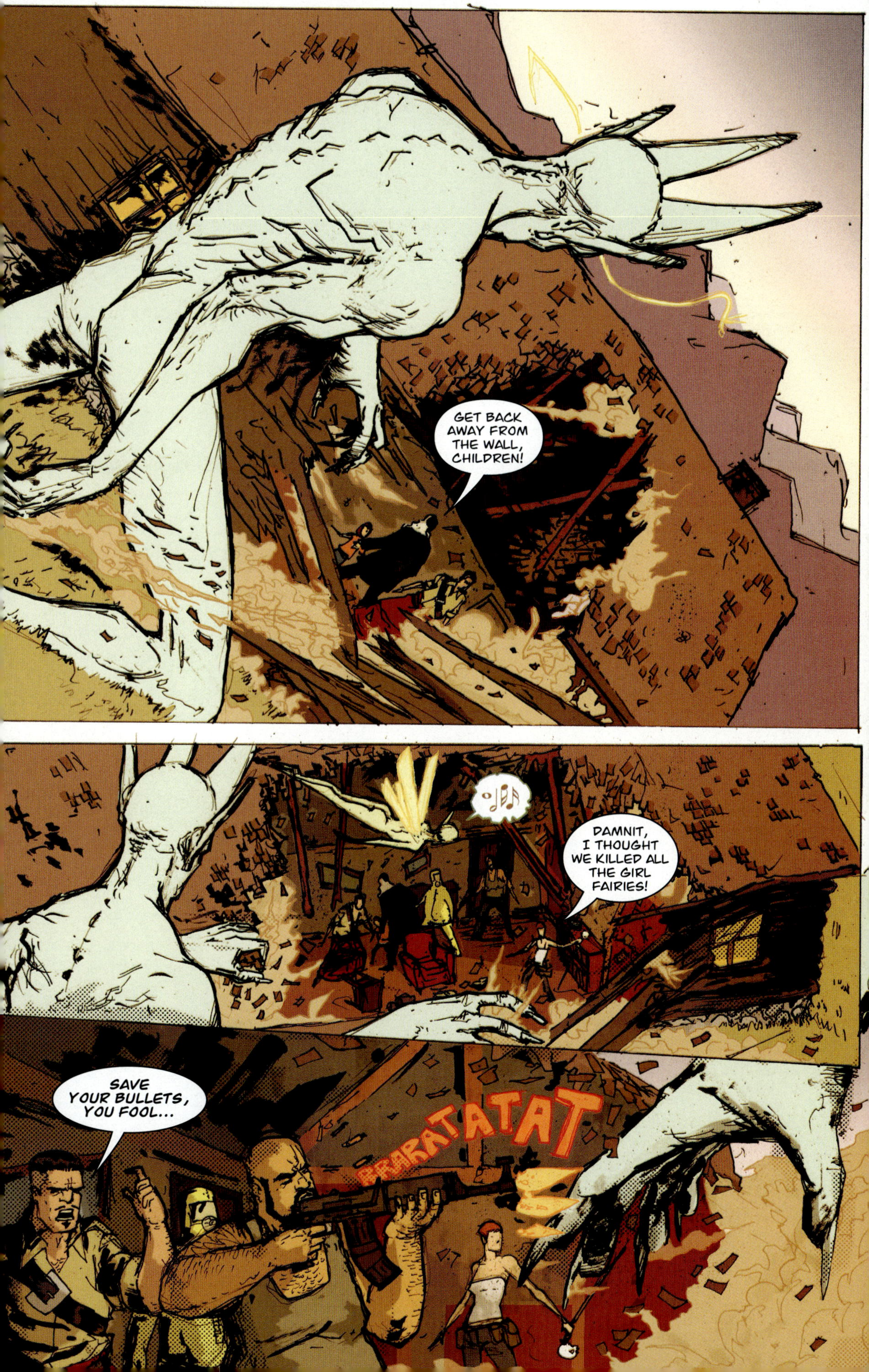
GET BACK AWAY FROM THE WALL, CHILDREN!
DAMNIT, I THOUGHT WE KILLED ALL THE GIRL FAIRIES!
SAVE YOUR BULLETS, YOU FOOL...
BRARATATAT

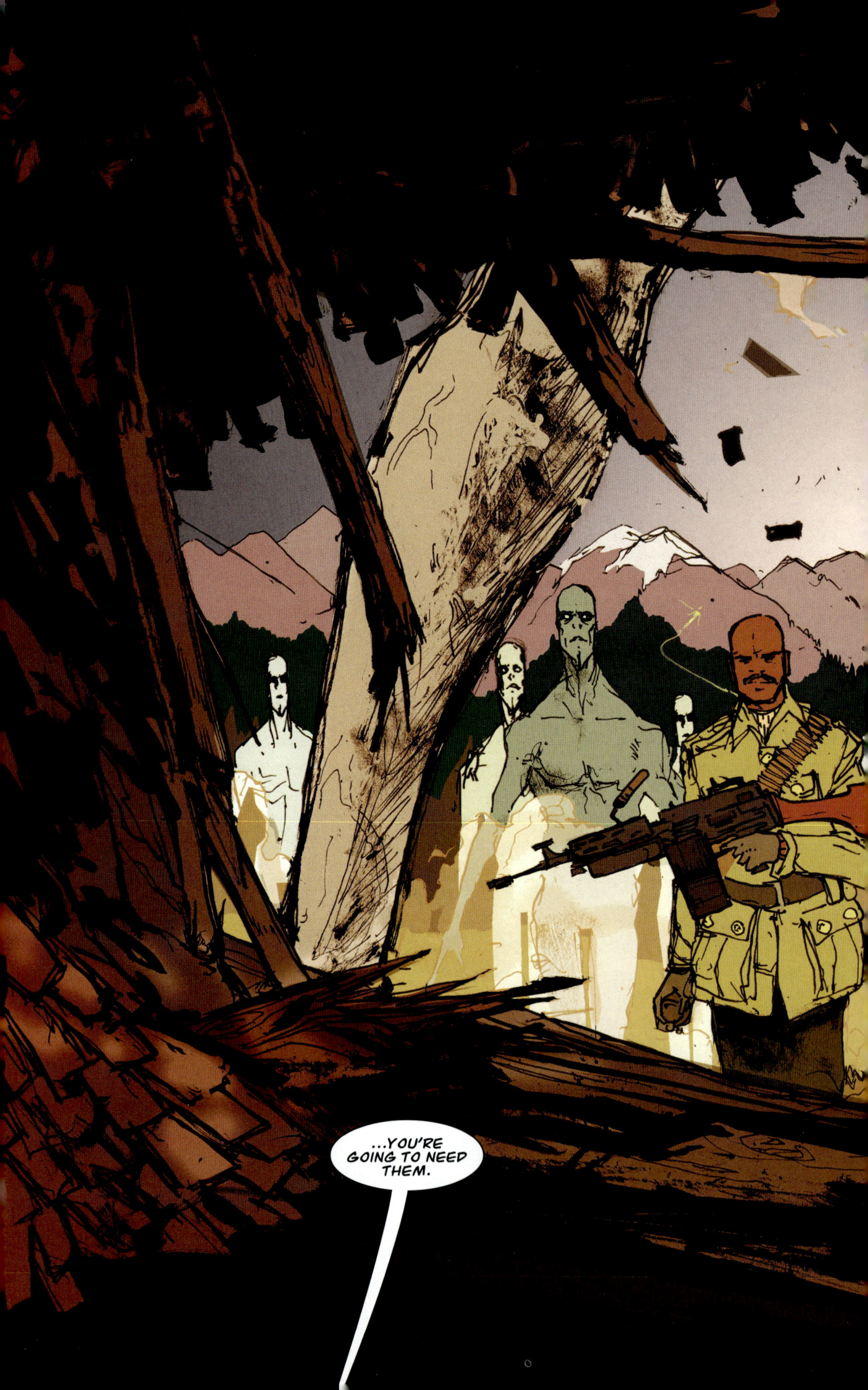
...YOU'RE GOING TO NEED THEM.

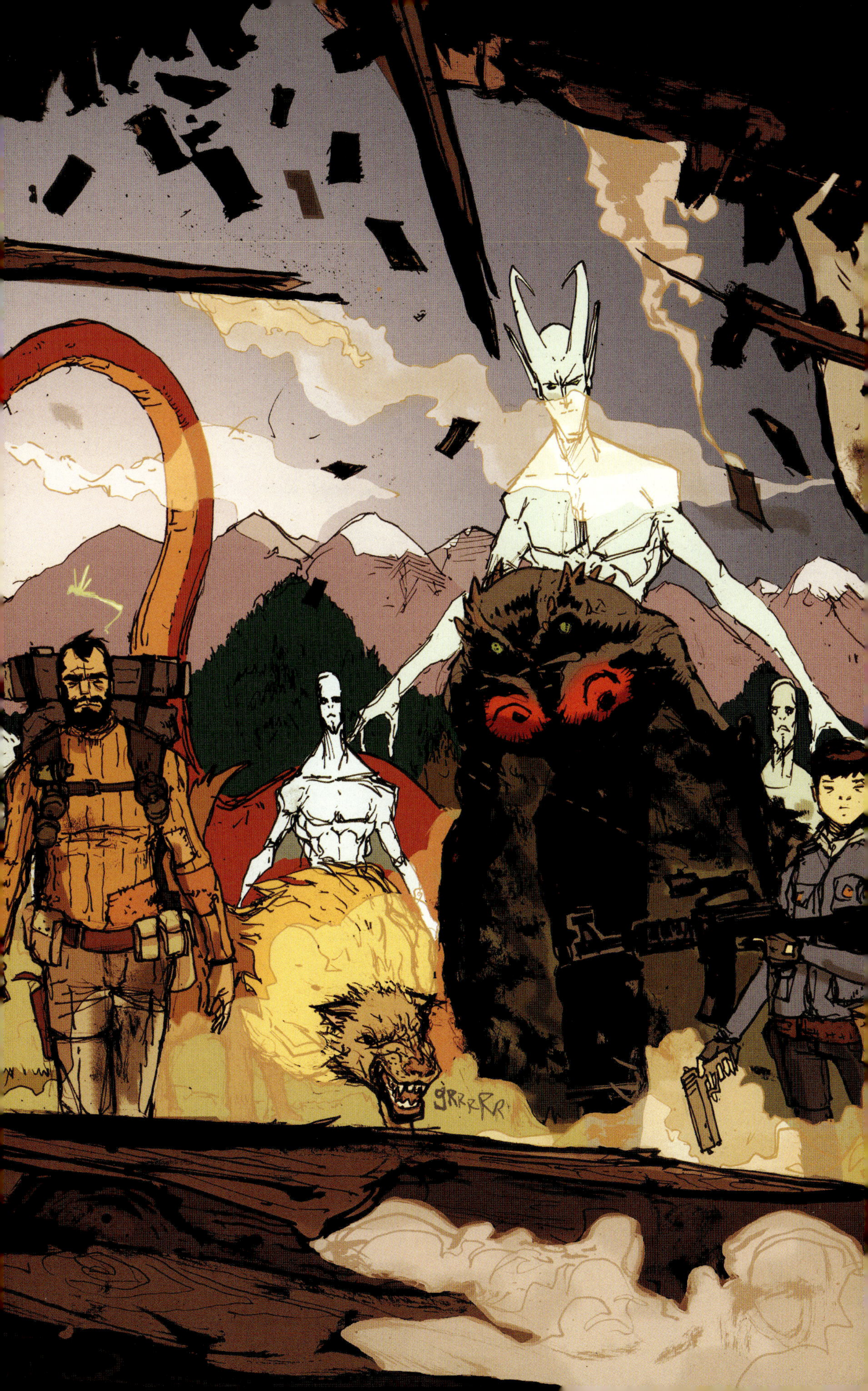
GRRRRR

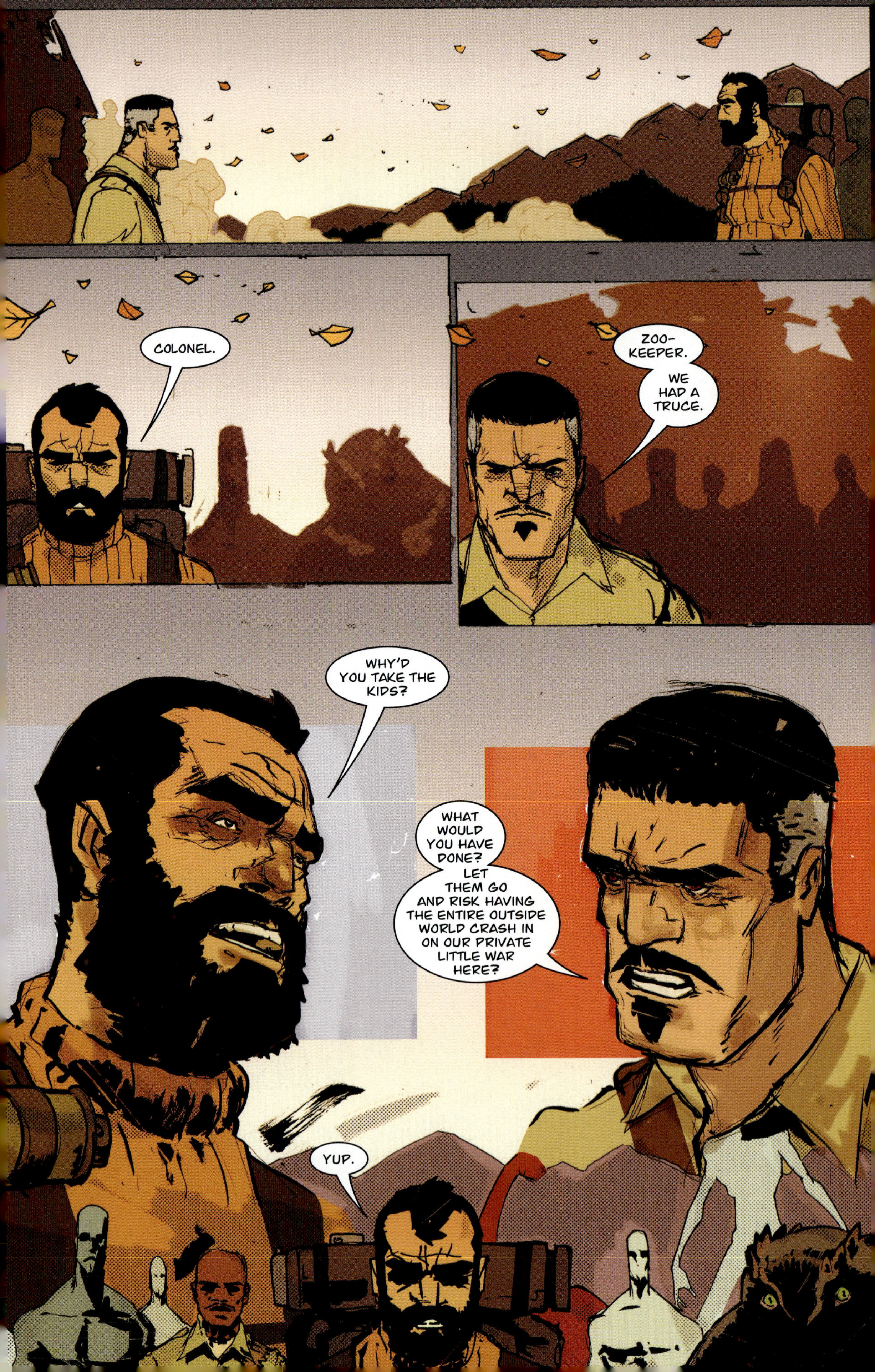
COLONEL.
ZOO-KEEPER.
WE HAD A TRUCE.
WHY'D YOU TAKE THE KIDS?
WHAT WOULD YOU HAVE DONE?
LET THEM GO AND RISK HAVING THE ENTIRE OUTSIDE WORLD CRASH IN ON OUR PRIVATE LITTLE WAR HERE?
YUP.

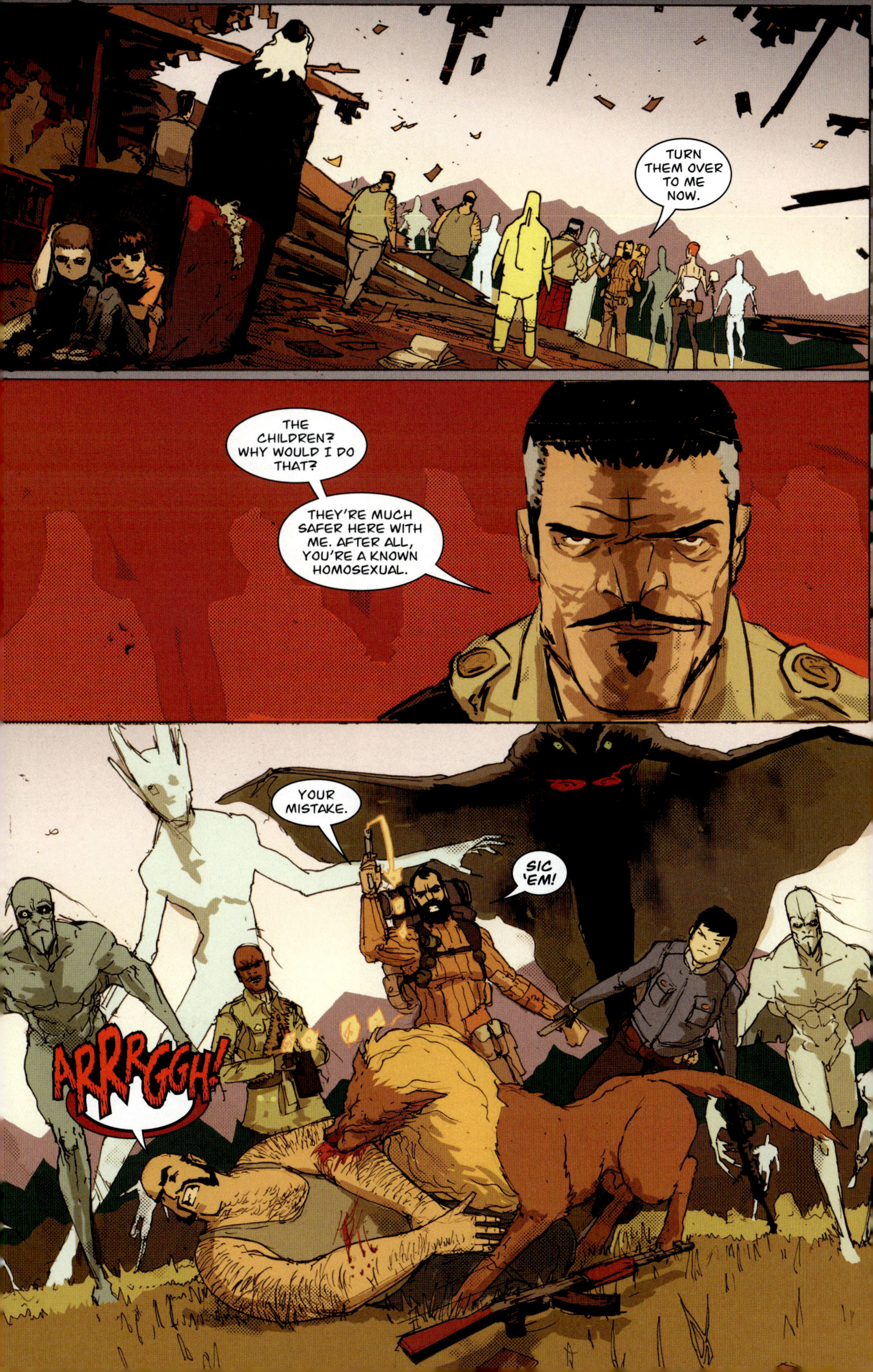
TURN THEM OVER TO ME NOW.
THE CHILDREN? WHY WOULD I DO THAT?
THEY'RE MUCH SAFER HERE WITH ME. AFTER ALL, YOU'RE A KNOWN HOMOSEXUAL.
YOUR MISTAKE.
SIC 'EM!
ARRRGGH!

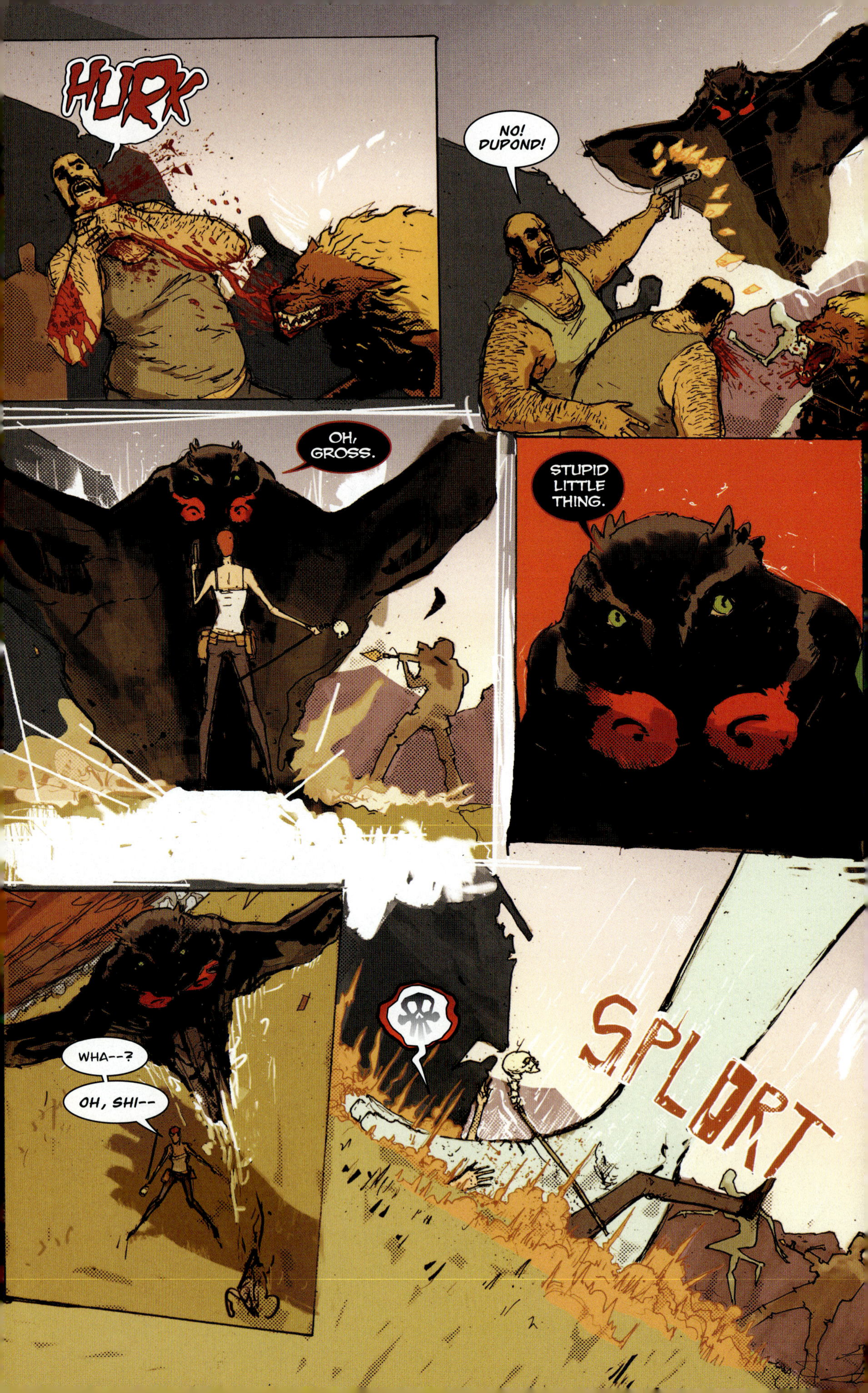
HURK
NO! DUPOND!
OH, GROSS.
STUPID LITTLE THING.
WHA--?
OH, SHI--
SPLORT

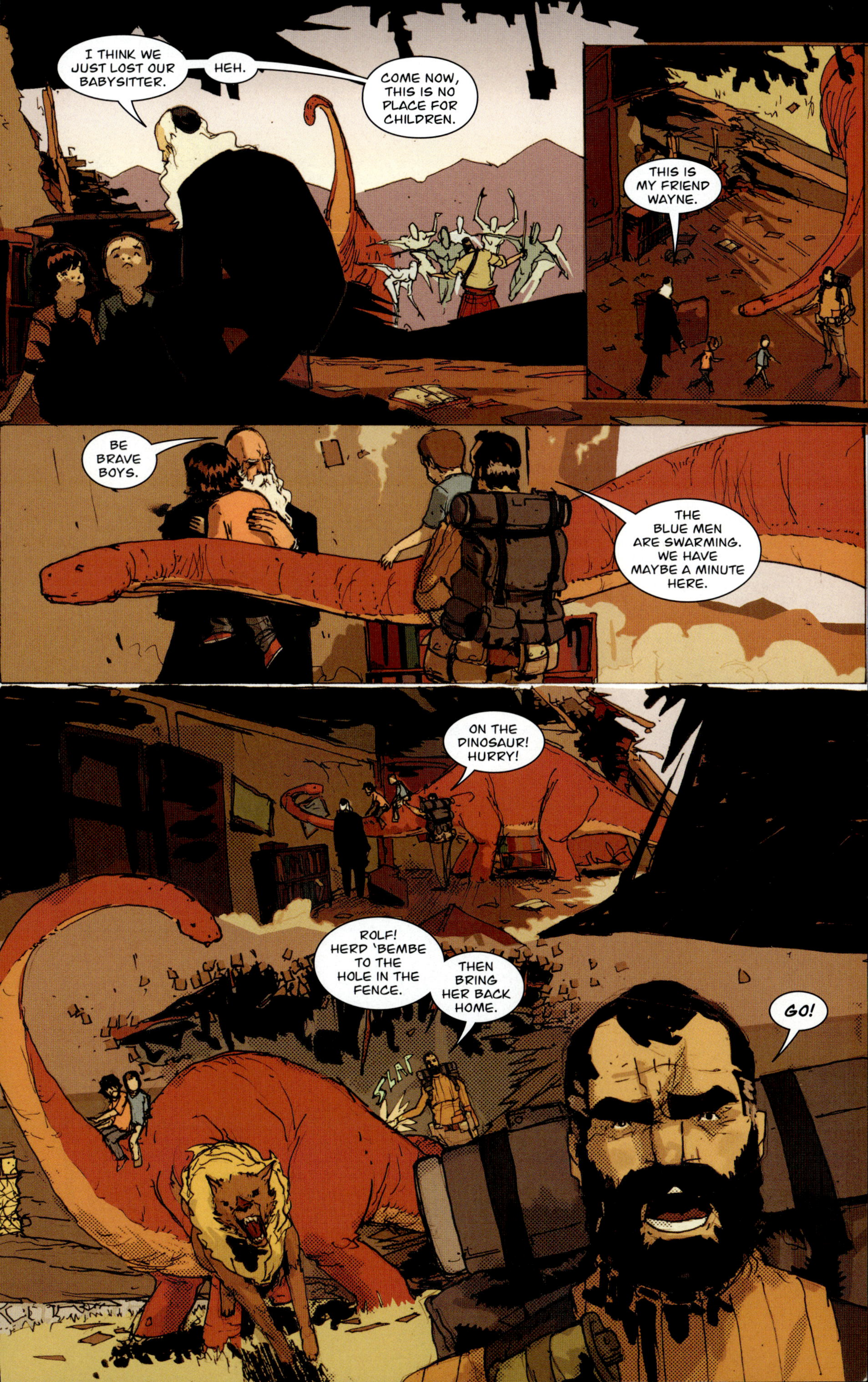
I THINK WE JUST LOST OUR BABYSITTER.
HEH.
COME NOW, THIS IS NO PLACE FOR CHILDREN.
THIS IS MY FRIEND WAYNE.
BE BRAVE BOYS.
THE BLUE MEN ARE SWARMING. WE HAVE MAYBE A MINUTE HERE.
ON THE DINOSAUR! HURRY!
ROLF! HERD 'BEMBE TO THE HOLE IN THE FENCE.
THEN BRING HER BACK HOME.
GO!
SLAP

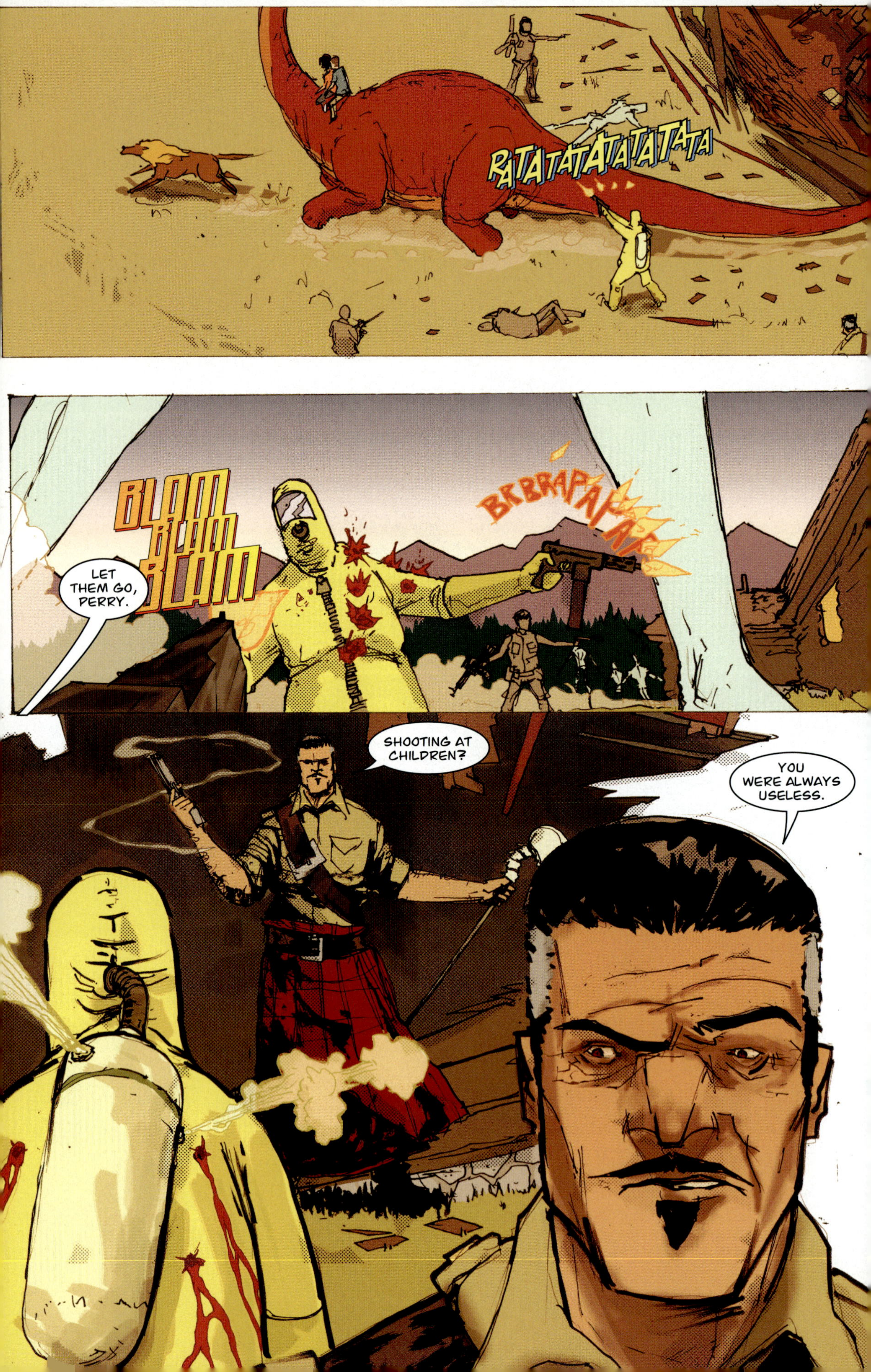
RATATATATATATATA
BLAM BLAM BLAM
BRBRAPAPAPA
LET THEM GO, PERRY.
SHOOTING AT CHILDREN?
YOU WERE ALWAYS USELESS.

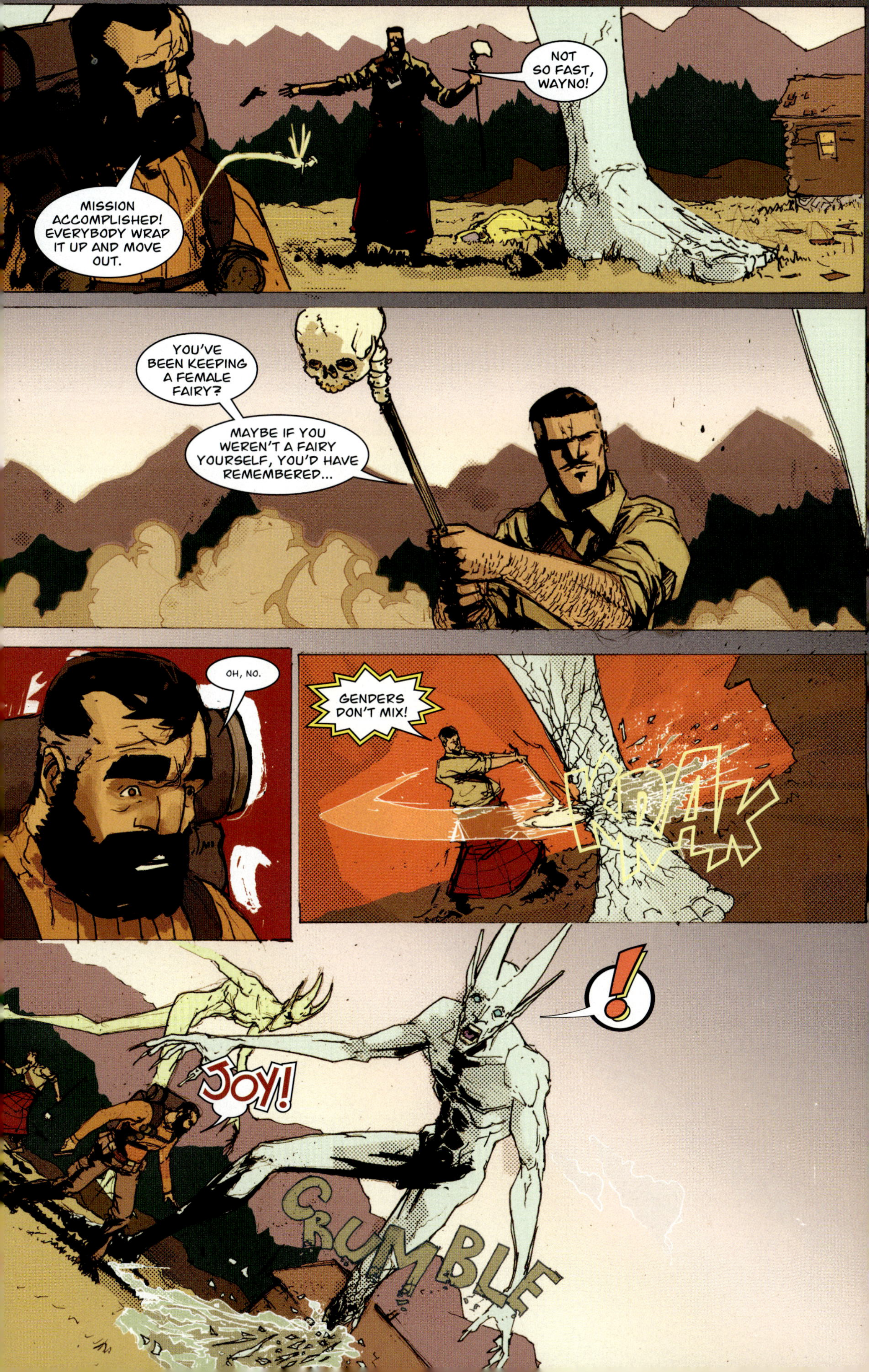
NOT SO FAST, WAYNO!
MISSION ACCOMPLISHED! EVERYBODY WRAP IT UP AND MOVE OUT.
YOU'VE BEEN KEEPING A FEMALE FAIRY?
MAYBE IF YOU WEREN'T A FAIRY YOURSELF, YOU'D HAVE REMEMBERED...
OH, NO.
GENDERS DON'T MIX!
!
JOY!
CRUMBLE

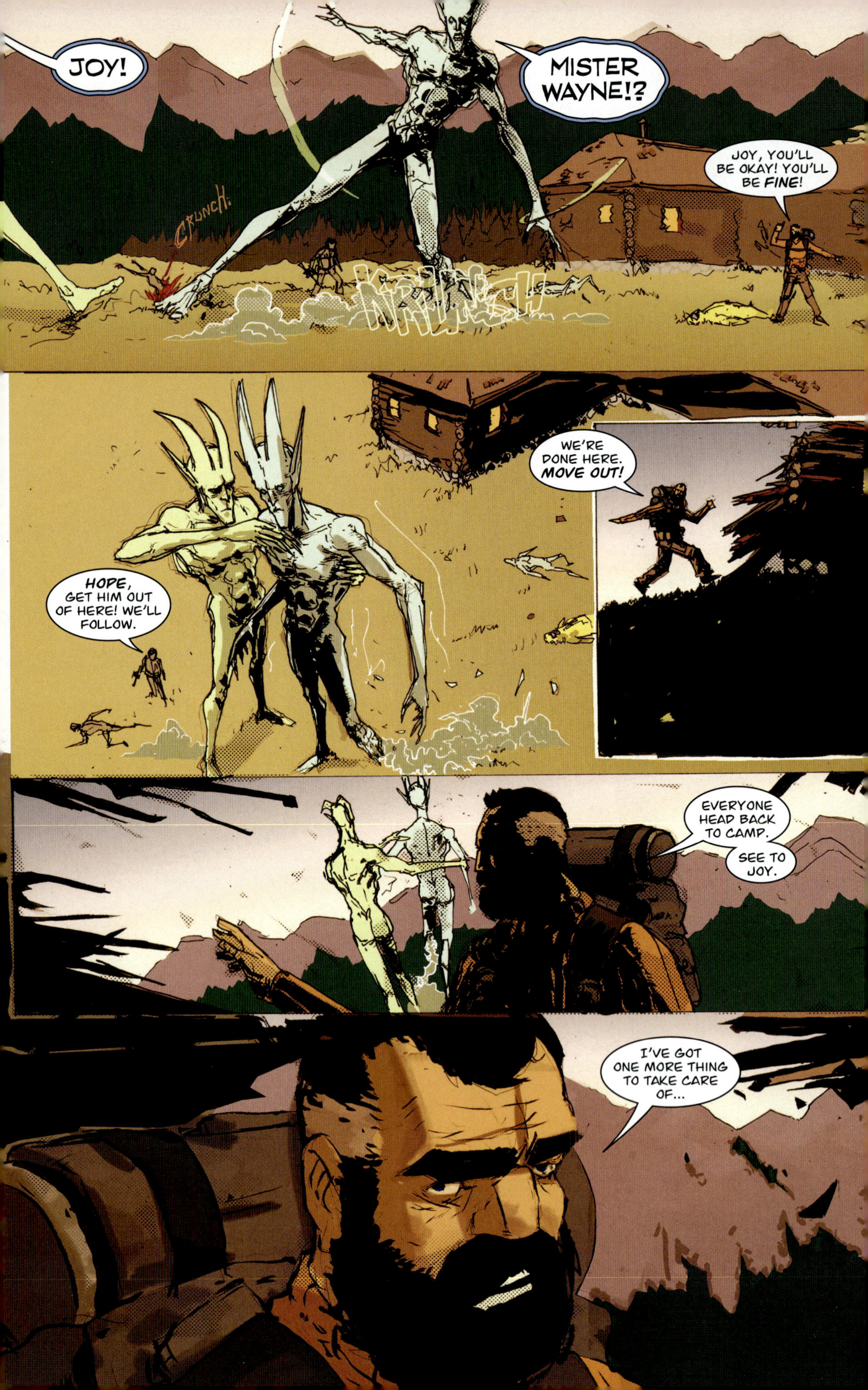
JOY!
MISTER WAYNE!?
JOY, YOU'LL BE OKAY! YOU'LL BE FINE!
CRUNCH
HOPE, GET HIM OUT OF HERE! WE'LL FOLLOW.
WE'RE DONE HERE. MOVE OUT!
EVERYONE HEAD BACK TO CAMP.
SEE TO JOY.
I'VE GOT ONE MORE THING TO TAKE CARE OF...

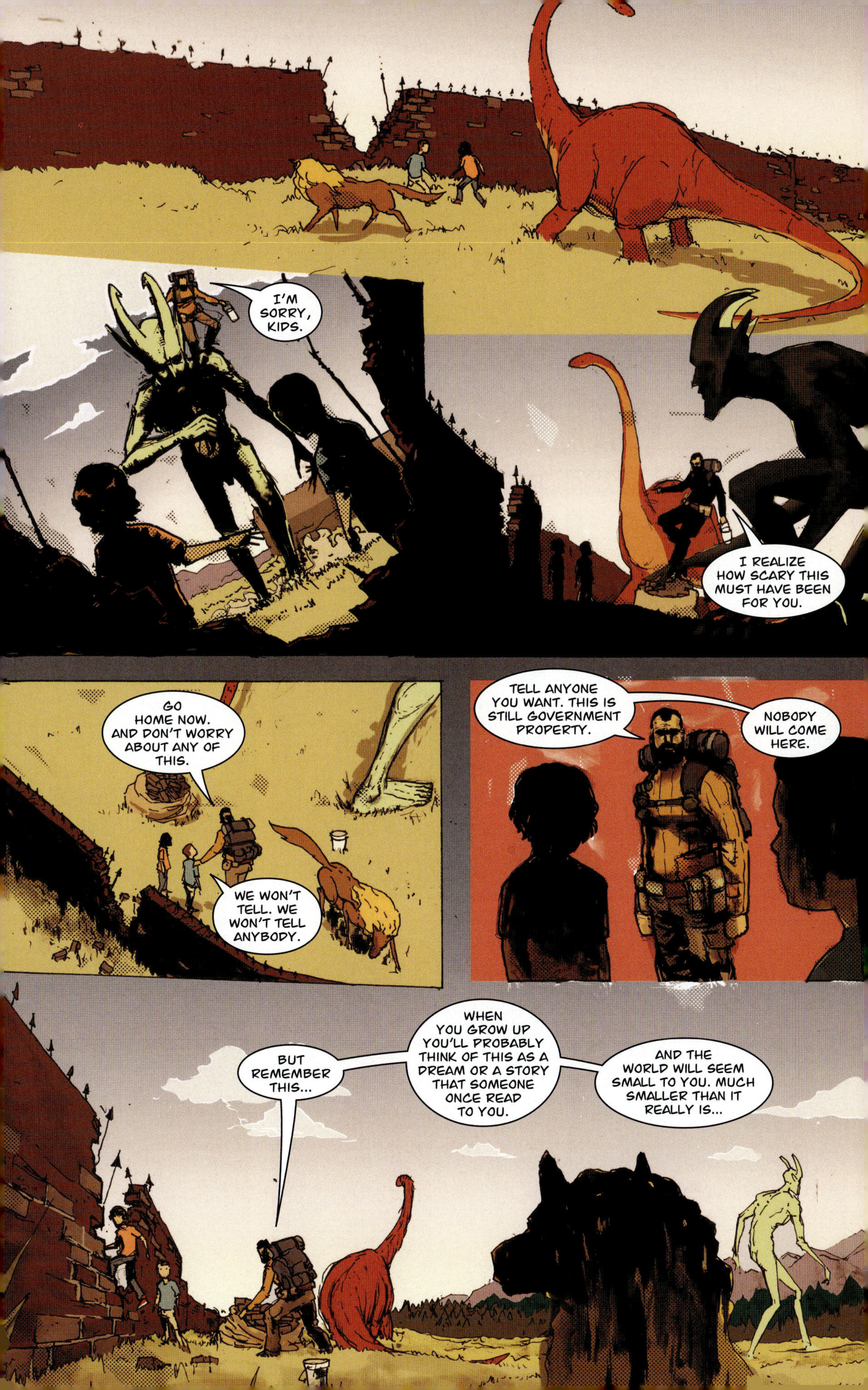
I'M SORRY, KIDS.
I REALIZE HOW SCARY THIS MUST HAVE BEEN FOR YOU.
GO HOME NOW. AND DON'T WORRY ABOUT ANY OF THIS.
WE WON'T TELL. WE WON'T TELL ANYBODY.
TELL ANYONE YOU WANT. THIS IS STILL GOVERNMENT PROPERTY.
NOBODY WILL COME HERE.
BUT REMEMBER THIS...
WHEN YOU GROW UP YOU'LL PROBABLY THINK OF THIS AS A DREAM OR A STORY THAT SOMEONE ONCE READ TO YOU.
AND THE WORLD WILL SEEM SMALL TO YOU. MUCH SMALLER THAN IT REALLY IS...

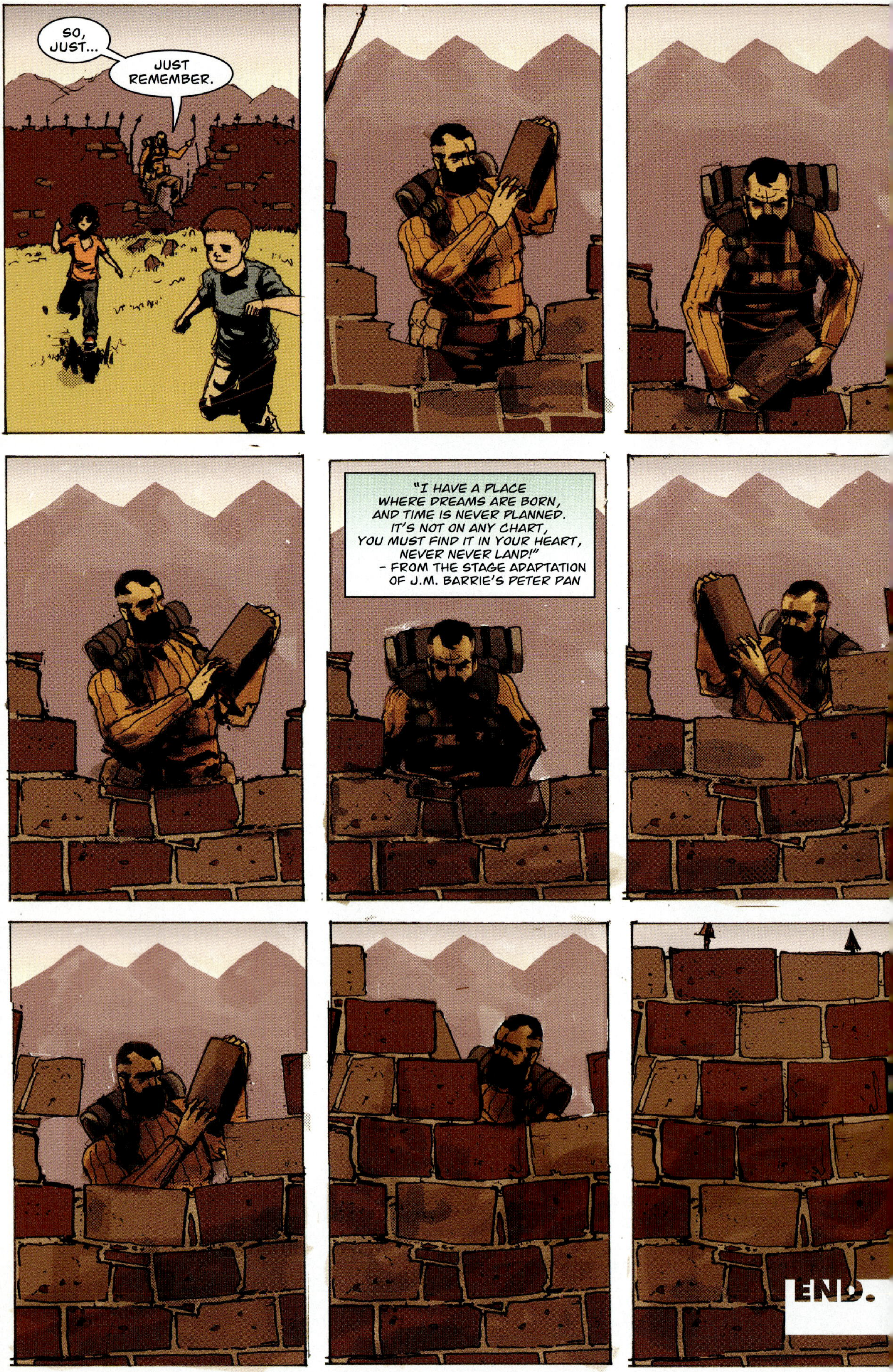
SO, JUST...
JUST REMEMBER.
"I HAVE A PLACE WHERE DREAMS ARE BORN, AND TIME IS NEVER PLANNED. IT'S NOT ON ANY CHART, YOU MUST FIND IT IN YOUR HEART, NEVER NEVER LAND!" - FROM THE STAGE ADAPTATION OF J.M. BARRIE'S PETER PAN
END.

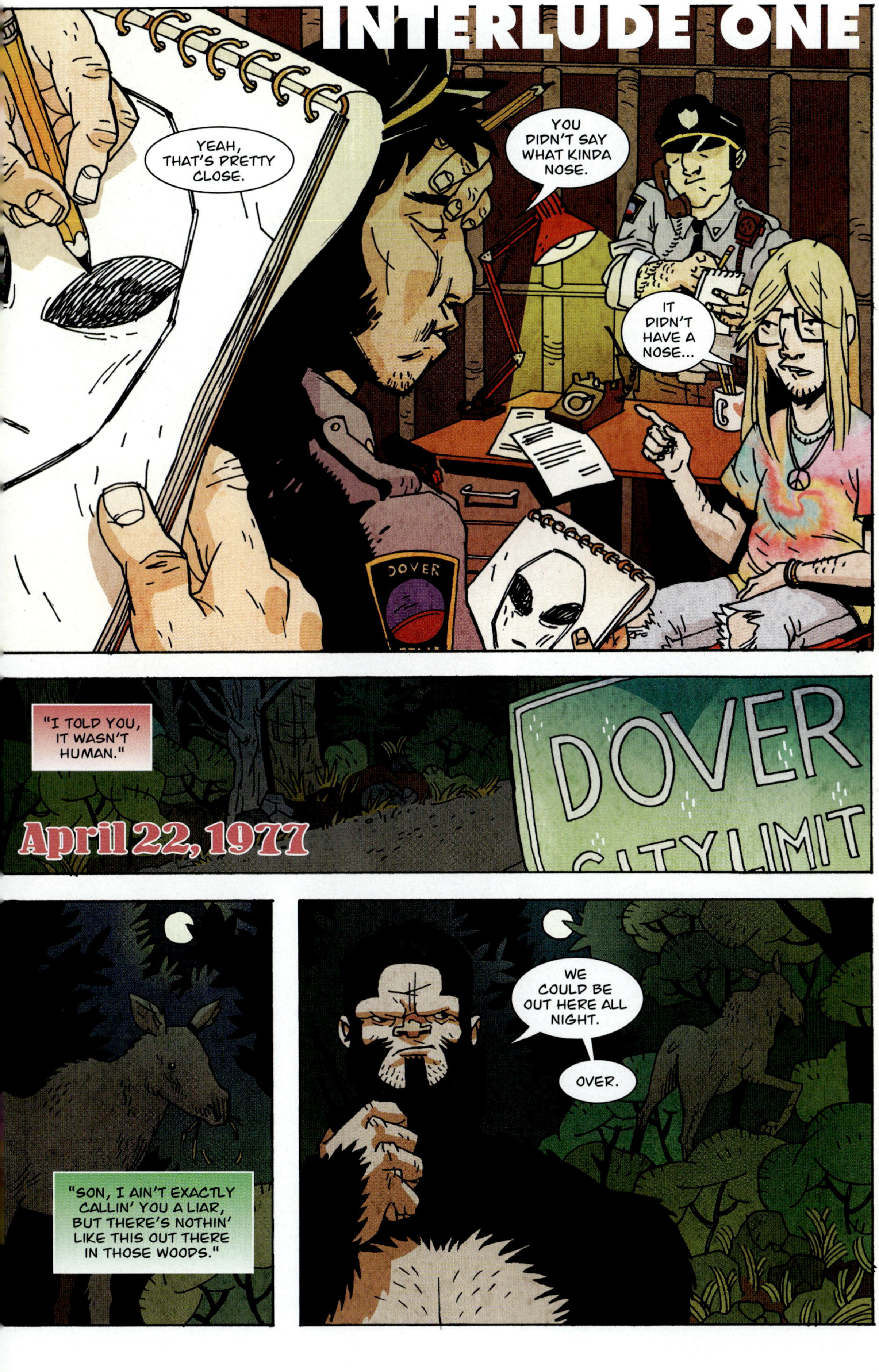
INTERLUDE ONE
YEAH, THAT'S PRETTY CLOSE.
YOU DIDN'T SAY WHAT KINDA NOSE.
IT DIDN'T HAVE A NOSE...
DOVER
"I TOLD YOU, IT WASN'T HUMAN."
April 22, 1977
DOVER CITY LIMIT
WE COULD BE OUT HERE ALL NIGHT.
OVER.
"SON, I AIN'T EXACTLY CALLIN' YOU A LIAR, BUT THERE'S NOTHIN' LIKE THIS OUT THERE IN THOSE WOODS."

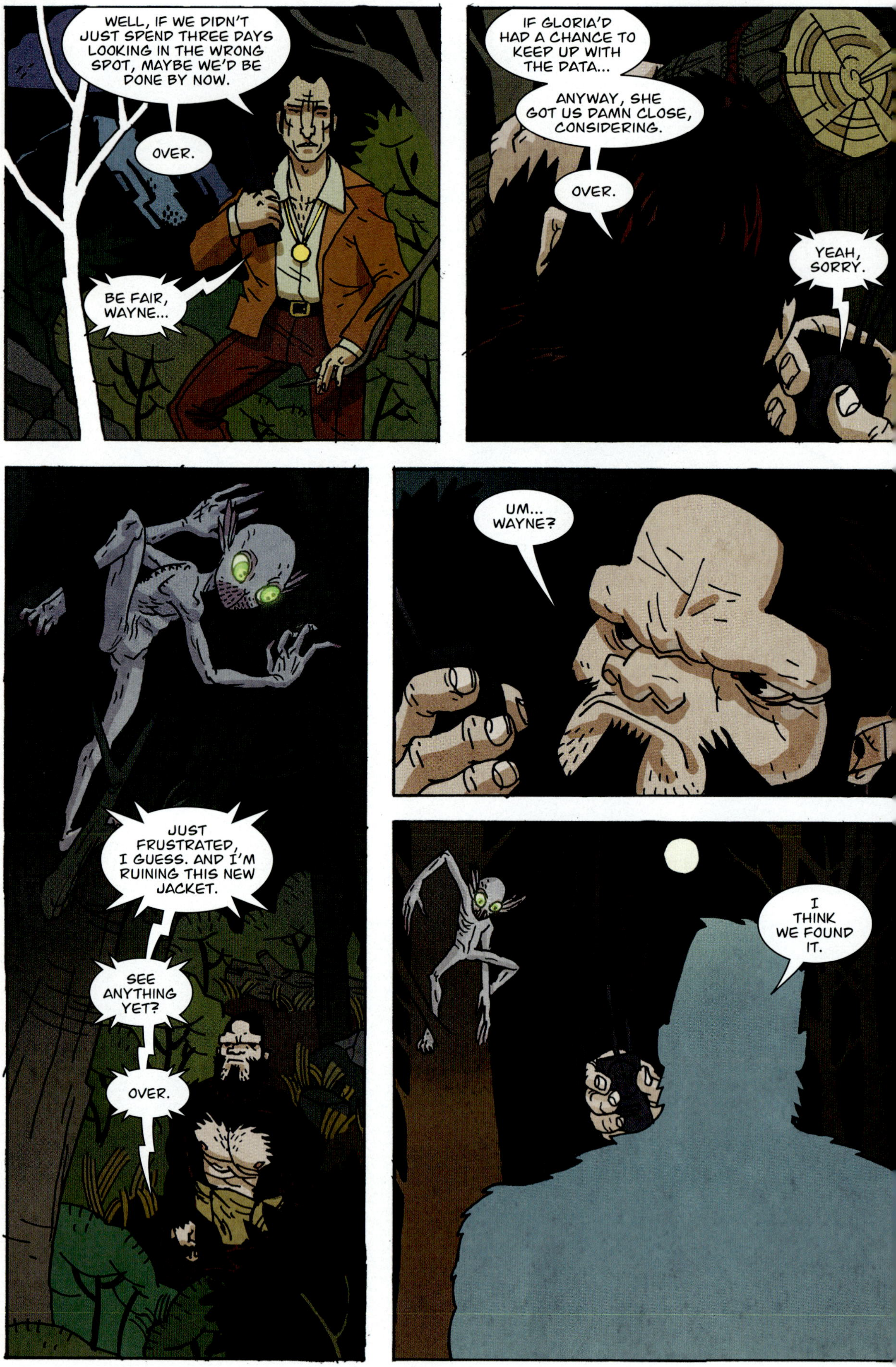
WELL, IF WE DIDN'T JUST SPEND THREE DAYS LOOKING IN THE WRONG SPOT, MAYBE WE'D BE DONE BY NOW.
OVER.
BE FAIR, WAYNE...
IF GLORIA'D HAD A CHANCE TO KEEP UP WITH THE DATA...
ANYWAY, SHE GOT US DAMN CLOSE, CONSIDERING.
OVER.
YEAH, SORRY.
JUST FRUSTRATED, I GUESS. AND I'M RUINING THIS NEW JACKET.
SEE ANYTHING YET?
OVER.
UM... WAYNE?
I THINK WE FOUND IT.

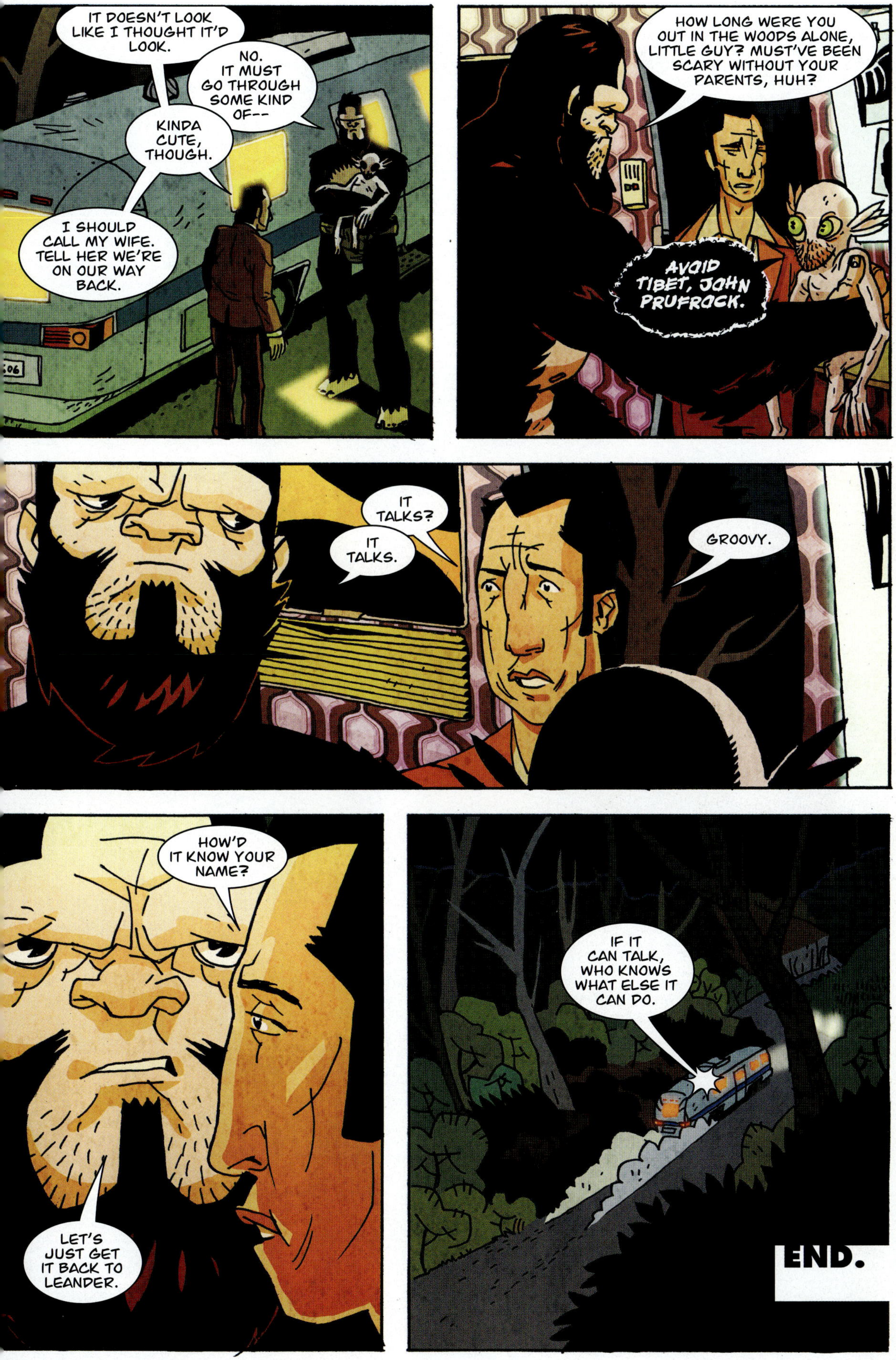
IT DOESN'T LOOK LIKE I THOUGHT IT'D LOOK.
NO. IT MUST GO THROUGH SOME KIND OF--
KINDA CUTE, THOUGH.
I SHOULD CALL MY WIFE. TELL HER WE'RE ON OUR WAY BACK.
HOW LONG WERE YOU OUT IN THE WOODS ALONE, LITTLE GUY? MUST'VE BEEN SCARY WITHOUT YOUR PARENTS, HUH?
AVOID TIBET, JOHN PRUFROCK.
IT TALKS?
IT TALKS.
GROOVY.
HOW'D IT KNOW YOUR NAME?
LET'S JUST GET IT BACK TO LEANDER.
IF IT CAN TALK, WHO KNOWS WHAT ELSE IT CAN DO.
END.

INTERLUDE TWO

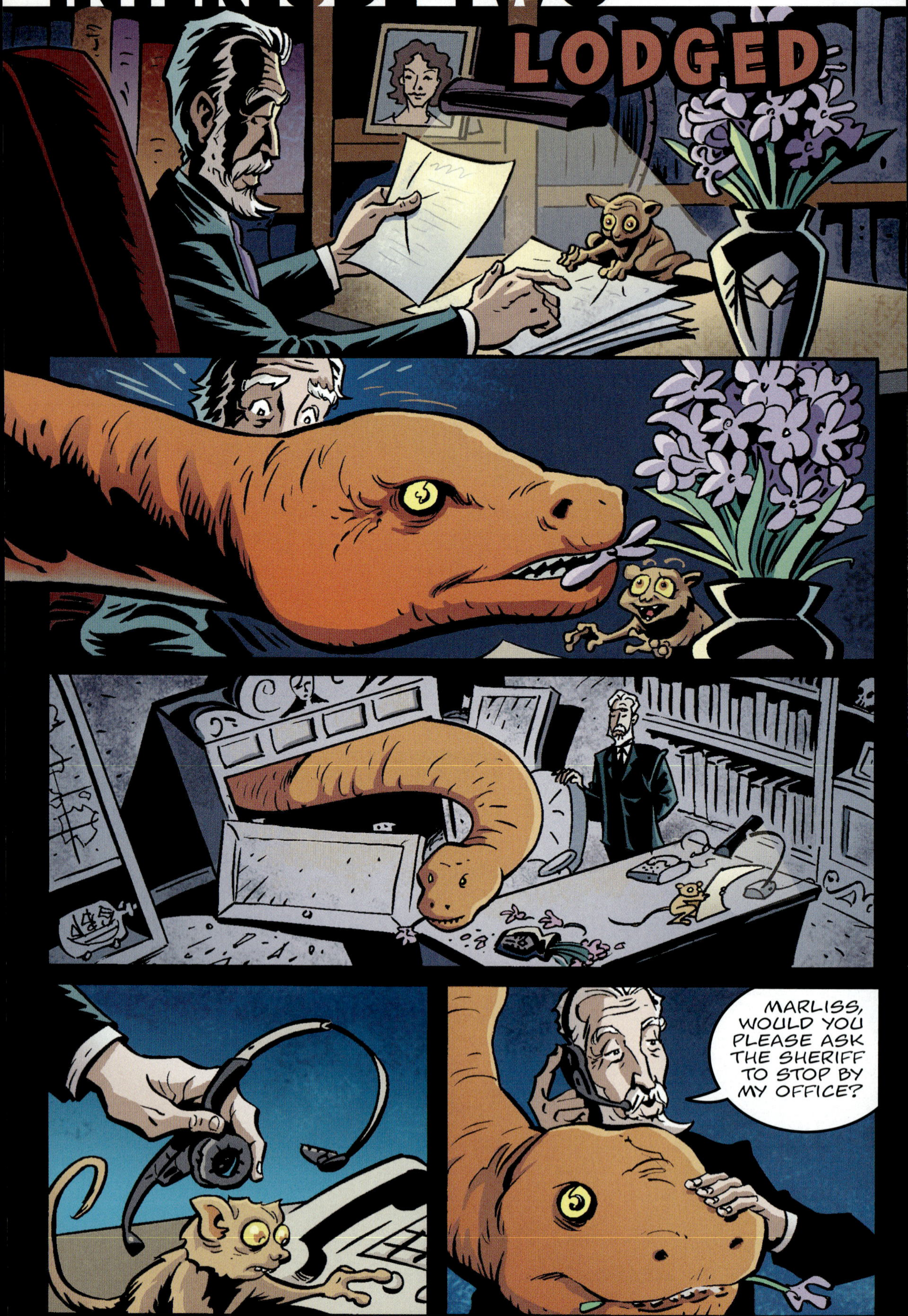
LODGED
MARLISS, WOULD YOU PLEASE ASK THE SHERIFF TO STOP BY MY OFFICE?

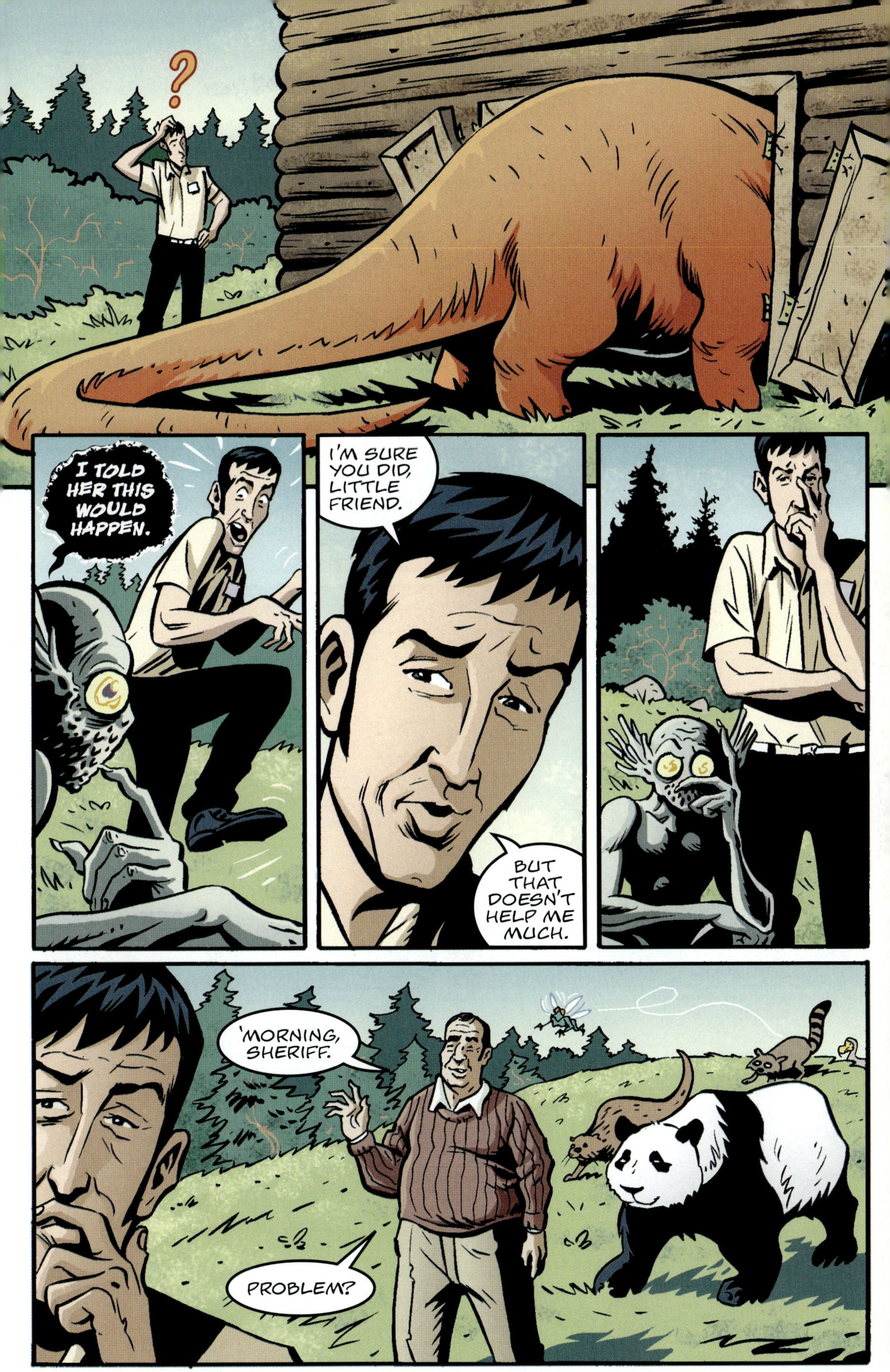
?
I TOLD HER THIS WOULD HAPPEN.
I'M SURE YOU DID, LITTLE FRIEND.
BUT THAT DOESN'T HELP ME MUCH.
'MORNING, SHERIFF.
PROBLEM?

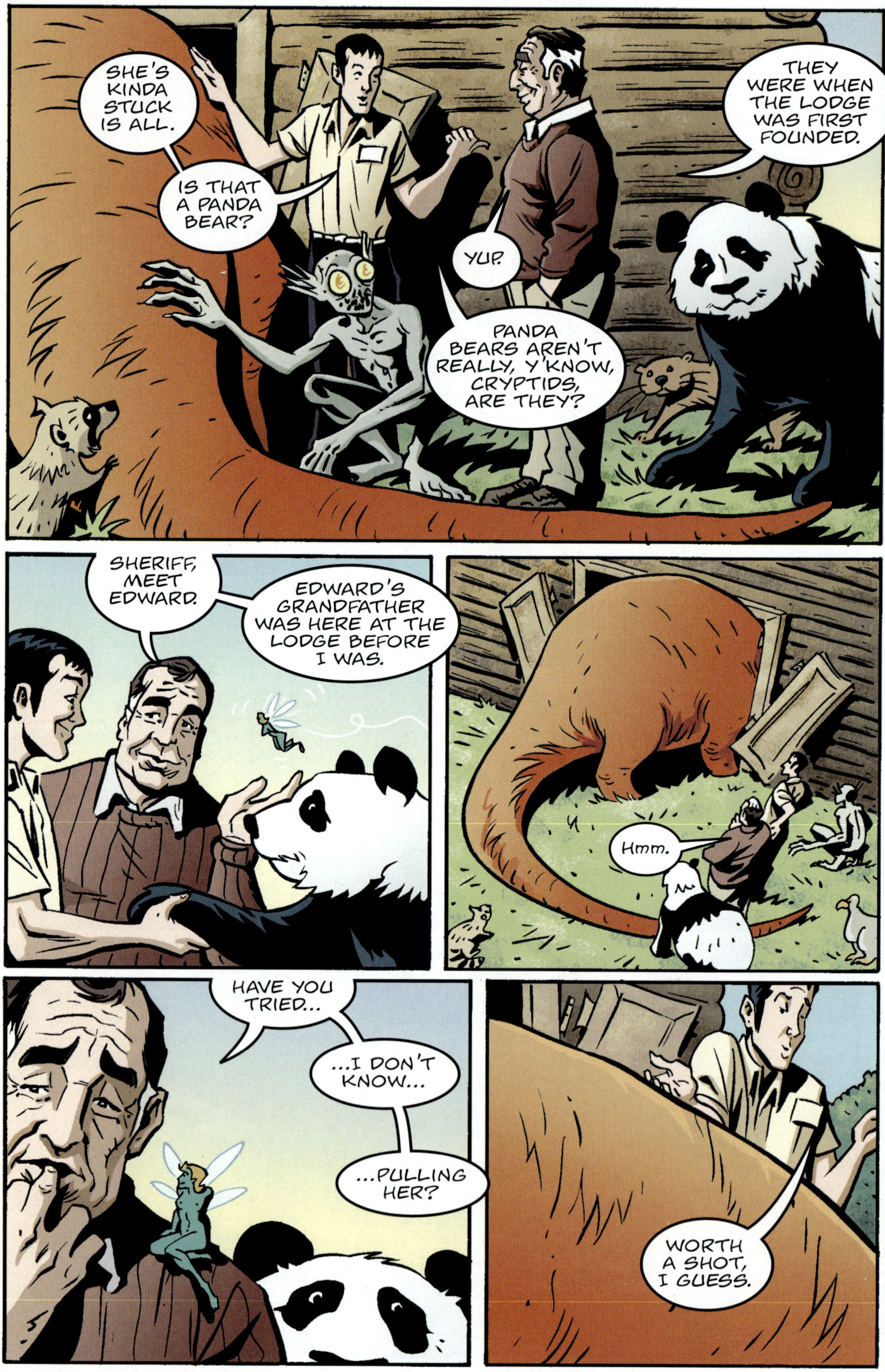
SHE'S KINDA STUCK IS ALL.
IS THAT A PANDA BEAR?
YUP.
PANDA BEARS AREN'T REALLY, Y'KNOW, CRYPTIDS, ARE THEY?
THEY WERE WHEN THE LODGE WAS FIRST FOUNDED.
SHERIFF, MEET EDWARD.
EDWARD'S GRANDFATHER WAS HERE AT THE LODGE BEFORE I WAS.
Hmm.
HAVE YOU TRIED...
...I DON'T KNOW...
...PULLING HER?
WORTH A SHOT, I GUESS.

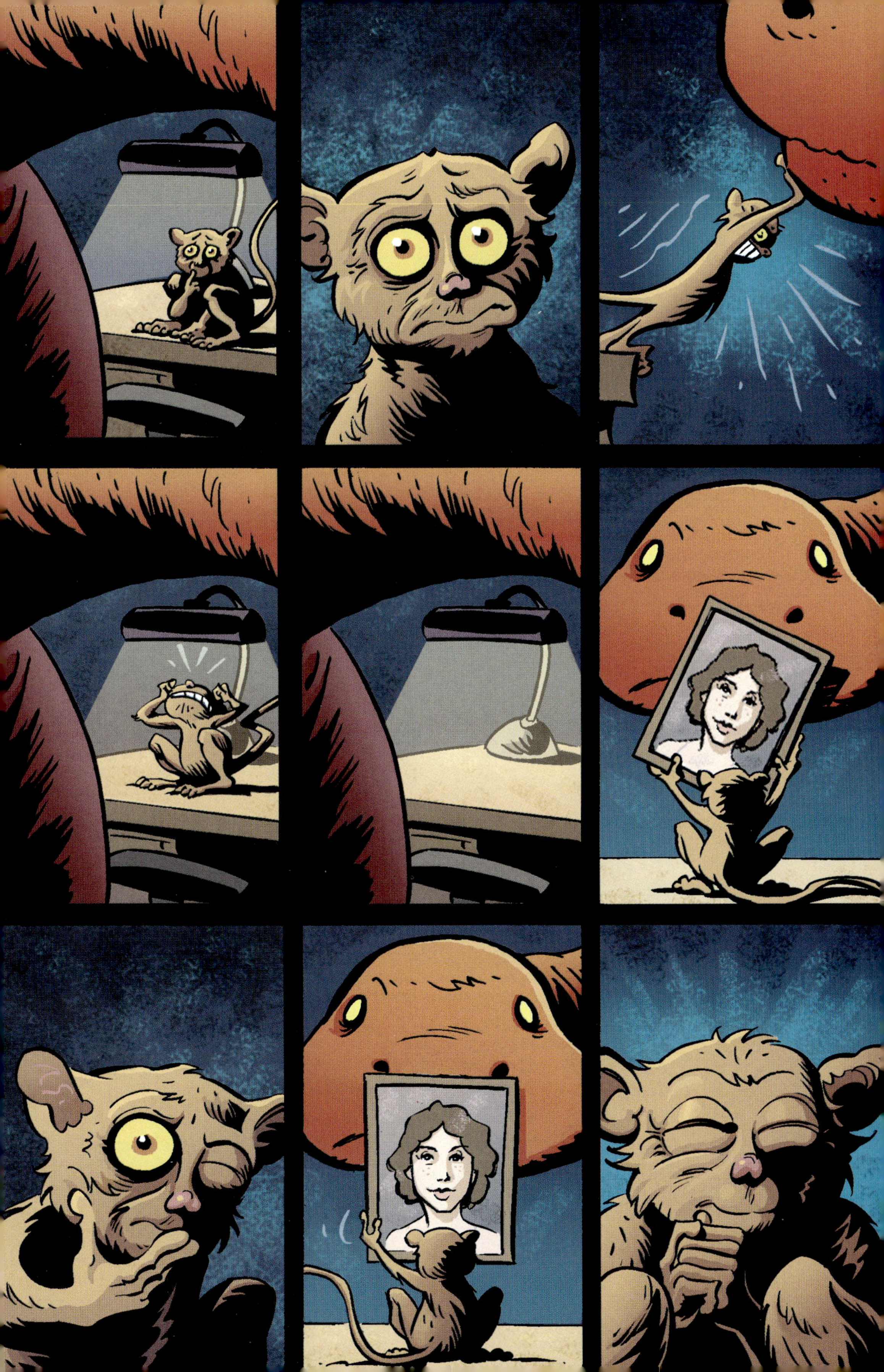

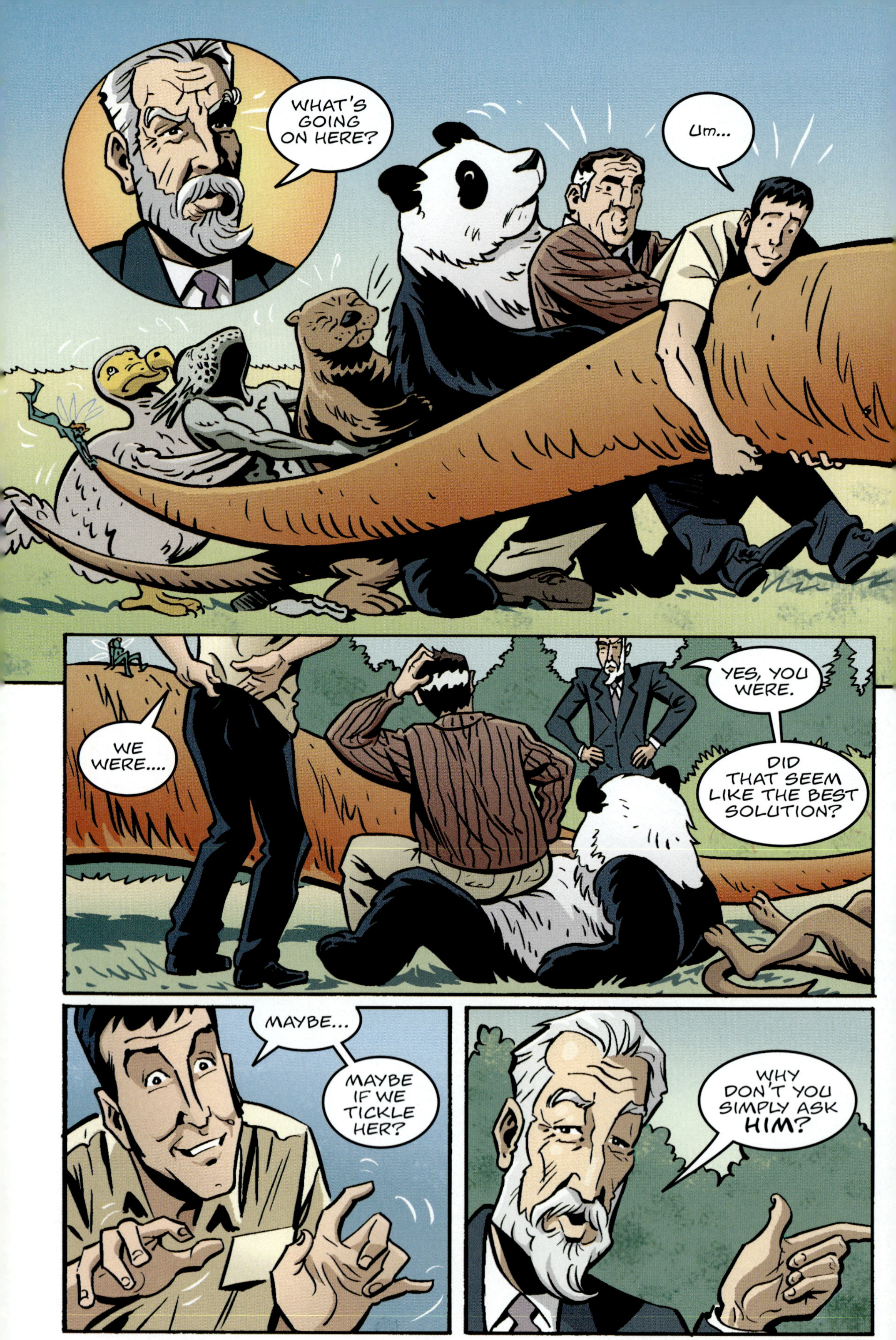
WHAT'S GOING ON HERE?
Um...
WE WERE....
YES, YOU WERE.
DID THAT SEEM LIKE THE BEST SOLUTION?
MAYBE...
MAYBE IF WE TICKLE HER?
WHY DON'T YOU SIMPLY ASK **HIM**?

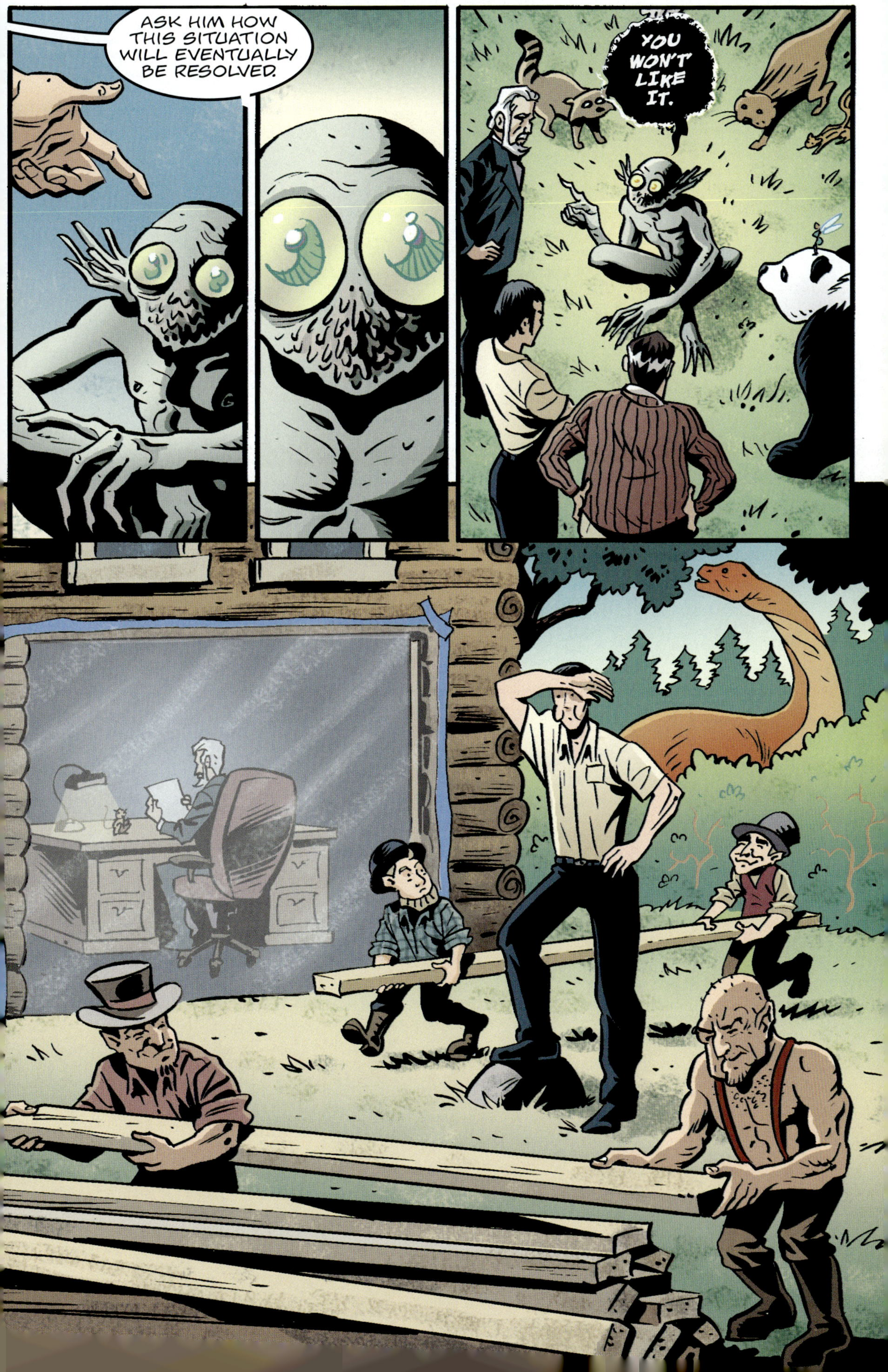
ASK HIM HOW THIS SITUATION WILL EVENTUALLY BE RESOLVED.
YOU WON'T LIKE IT.

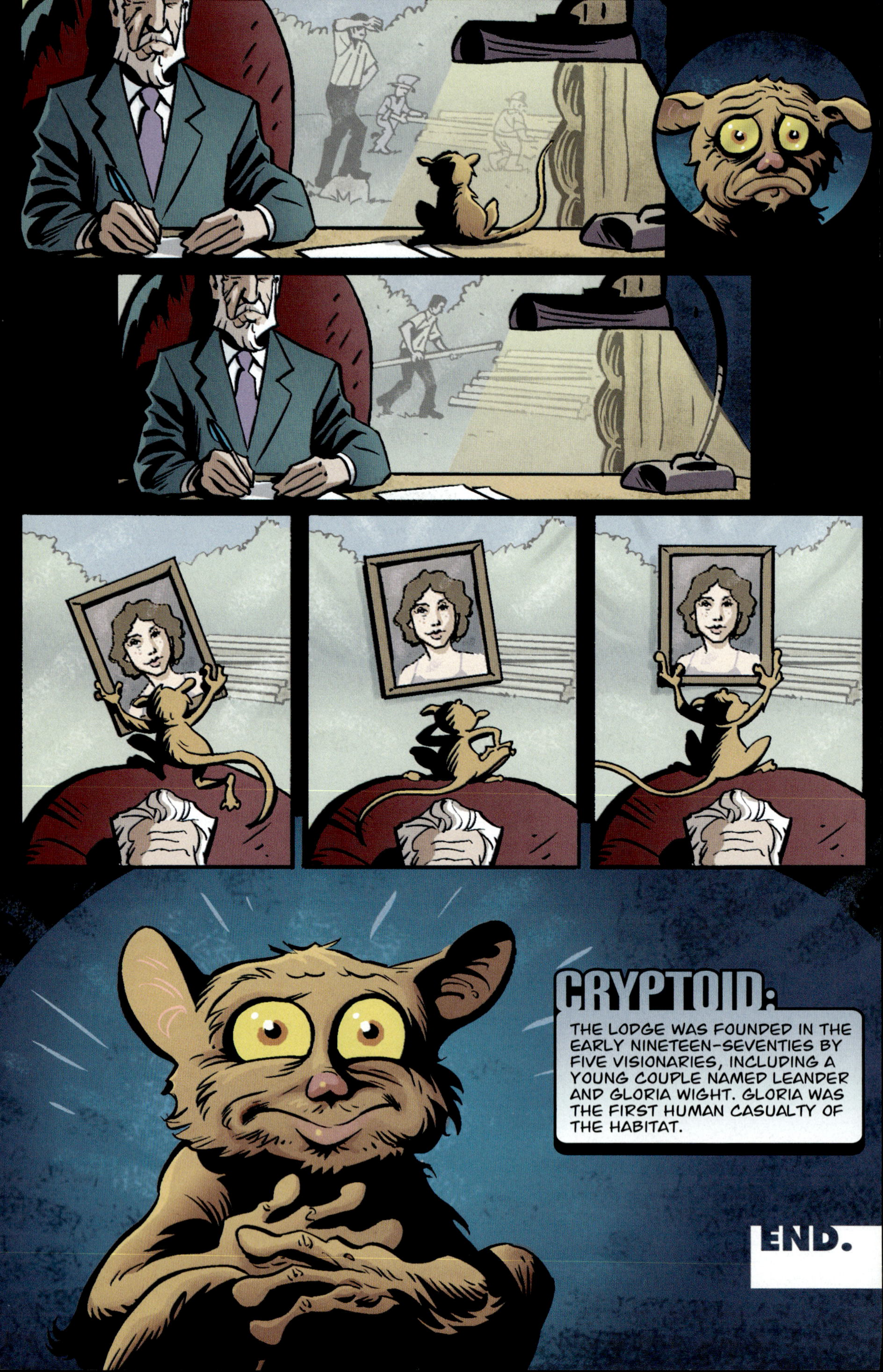
CRYPTOID:
THE LODGE WAS FOUNDED IN THE EARLY NINETEEN-SEVENTIES BY FIVE VISIONARIES, INCLUDING A YOUNG COUPLE NAMED LEANDER AND GLORIA WIGHT. GLORIA WAS THE FIRST HUMAN CASUALTY OF THE HABITAT.
END.

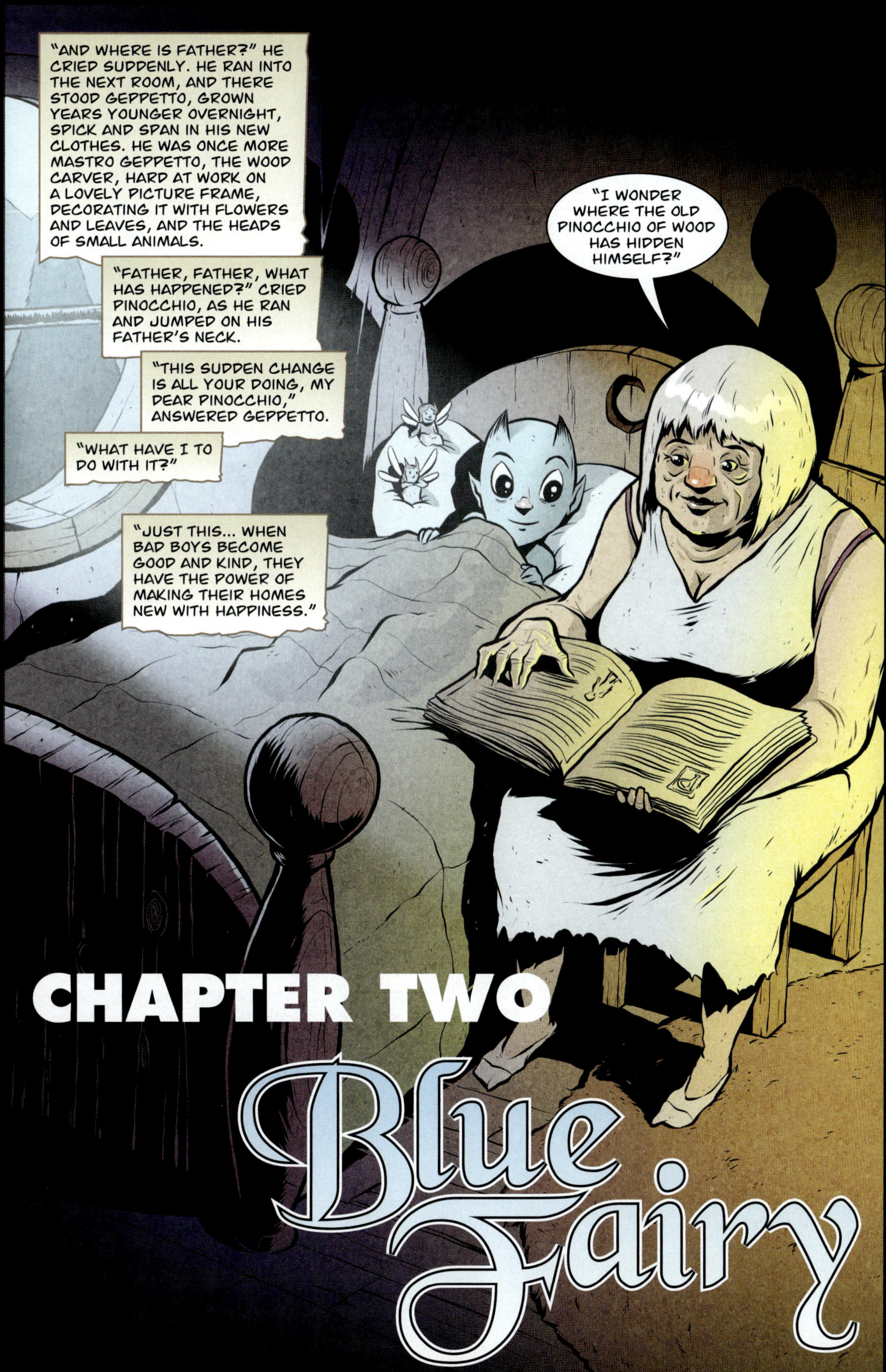
"AND WHERE IS FATHER?" HE CRIED SUDDENLY. HE RAN INTO THE NEXT ROOM, AND THERE STOOD GEPPETTO, GROWN YEARS YOUNGER OVERNIGHT, SPICK AND SPAN IN HIS NEW CLOTHES. HE WAS ONCE MORE MASTRO GEPPETTO, THE WOOD CARVER, HARD AT WORK ON A LOVELY PICTURE FRAME, DECORATING IT WITH FLOWERS AND LEAVES, AND THE HEADS OF SMALL ANIMALS.
"FATHER, FATHER, WHAT HAS HAPPENED?" CRIED PINOCCHIO, AS HE RAN AND JUMPED ON HIS FATHER'S NECK.
"THIS SUDDEN CHANGE IS ALL YOUR DOING, MY DEAR PINOCCHIO," ANSWERED GEPPETTO.
"WHAT HAVE I TO DO WITH IT?"
"JUST THIS... WHEN BAD BOYS BECOME GOOD AND KIND, THEY HAVE THE POWER OF MAKING THEIR HOMES NEW WITH HAPPINESS."
"I WONDER WHERE THE OLD PINOCCHIO OF WOOD HAS HIDDEN HIMSELF?"
CHAPTER TWO
Blue Fairy

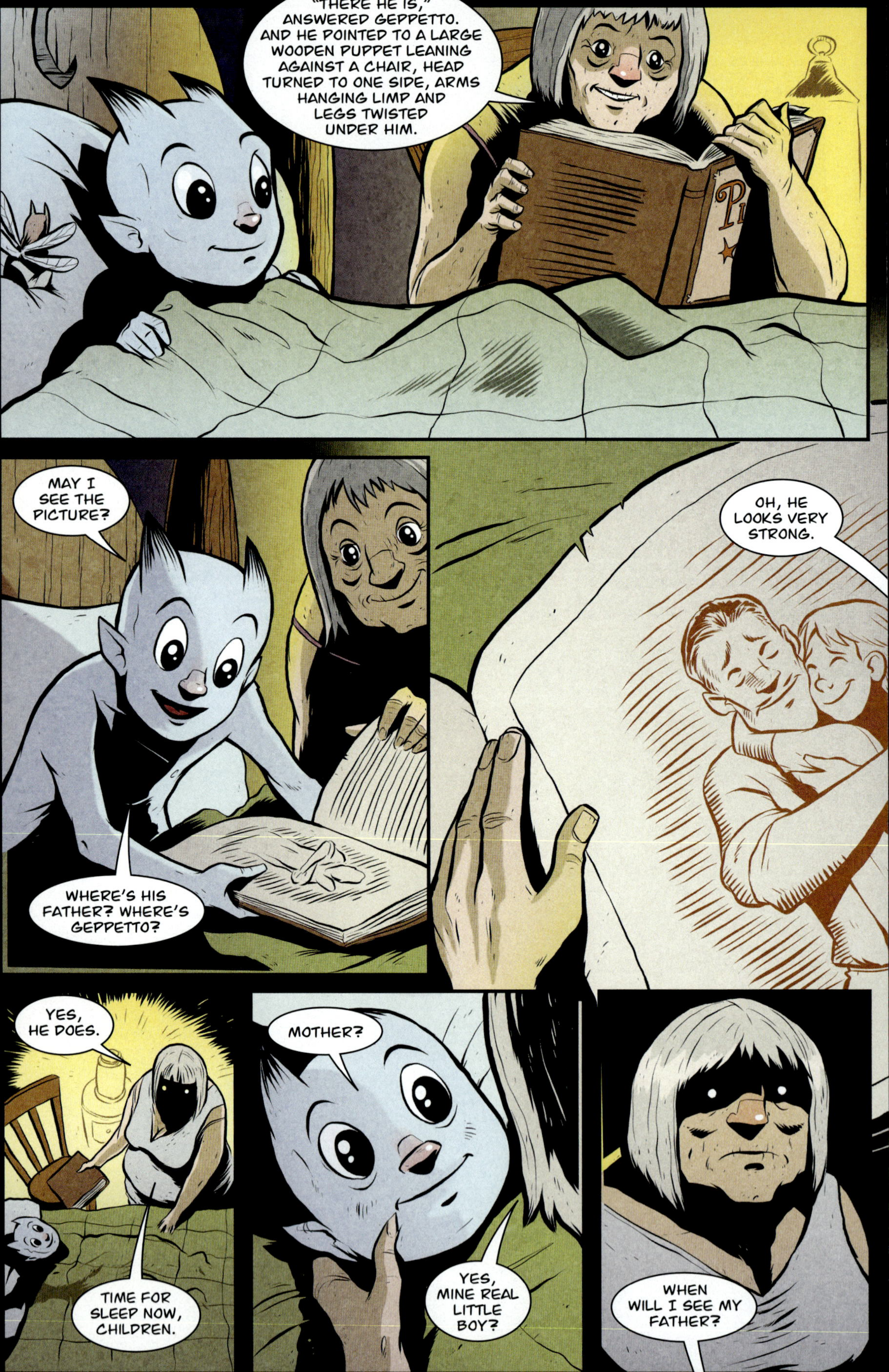

"THERE HE IS," ANSWERED GEPPETTO. AND HE POINTED TO A LARGE WOODEN PUPPET LEANING AGAINST A CHAIR, HEAD TURNED TO ONE SIDE, ARMS HANGING LIMP AND LEGS TWISTED UNDER HIM.
MAY I SEE THE PICTURE?
WHERE'S HIS FATHER? WHERE'S GEPPETTO?
OH, HE LOOKS VERY STRONG.
YES, HE DOES.
TIME FOR SLEEP NOW, CHILDREN.
MOTHER?
YES, MINE REAL LITTLE BOY?
WHEN WILL I SEE MY FATHER?

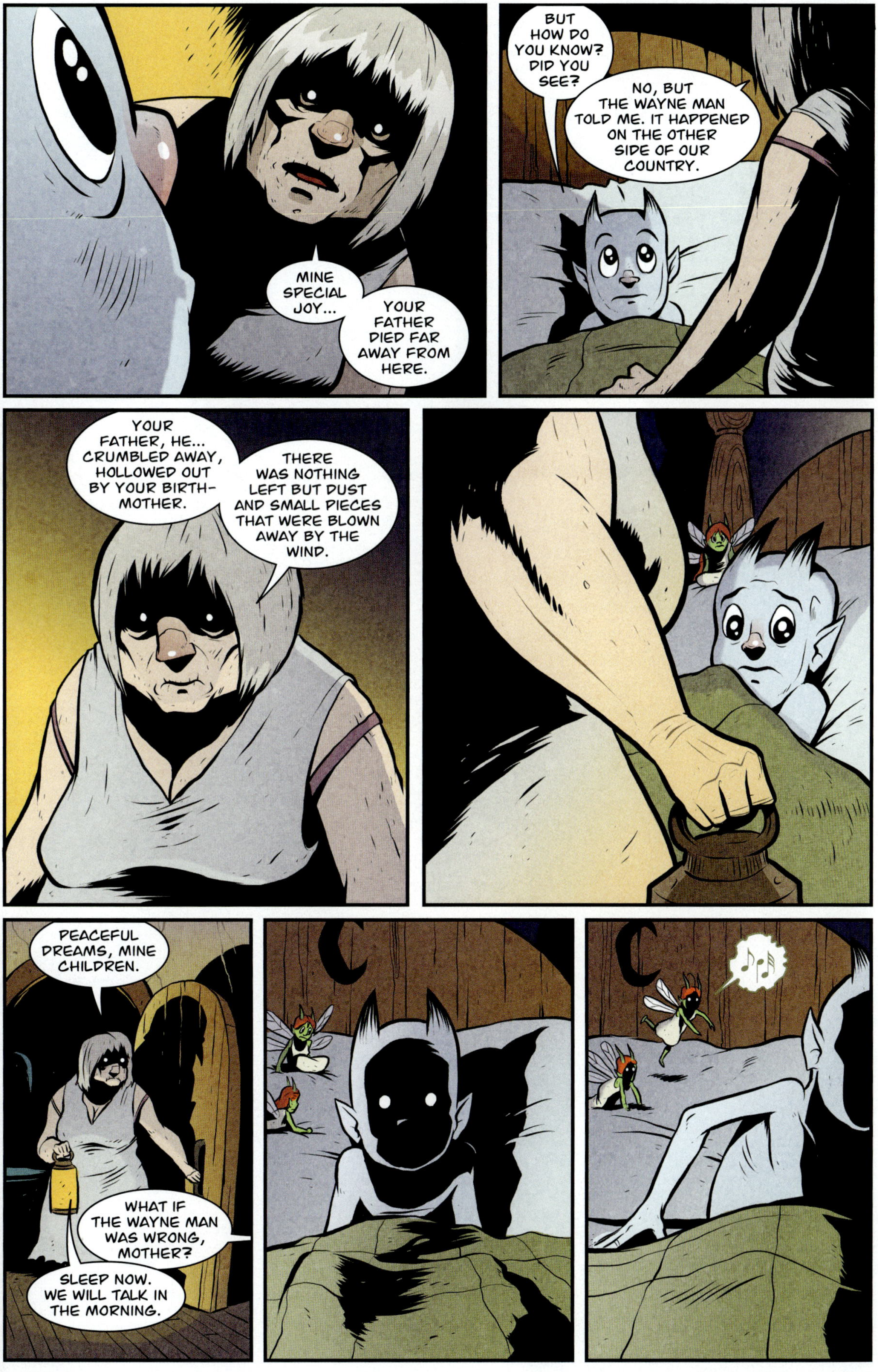
MINE SPECIAL JOY...
YOUR FATHER DIED FAR AWAY FROM HERE.
BUT HOW DO YOU KNOW? DID YOU SEE?
NO, BUT THE WAYNE MAN TOLD ME. IT HAPPENED ON THE OTHER SIDE OF OUR COUNTRY.
YOUR FATHER, HE... CRUMBLED AWAY, HOLLOWED OUT BY YOUR BIRTH-MOTHER.
THERE WAS NOTHING LEFT BUT DUST AND SMALL PIECES THAT WERE BLOWN AWAY BY THE WIND.
PEACEFUL DREAMS, MINE CHILDREN.
WHAT IF THE WAYNE MAN WAS WRONG, MOTHER?
SLEEP NOW. WE WILL TALK IN THE MORNING.

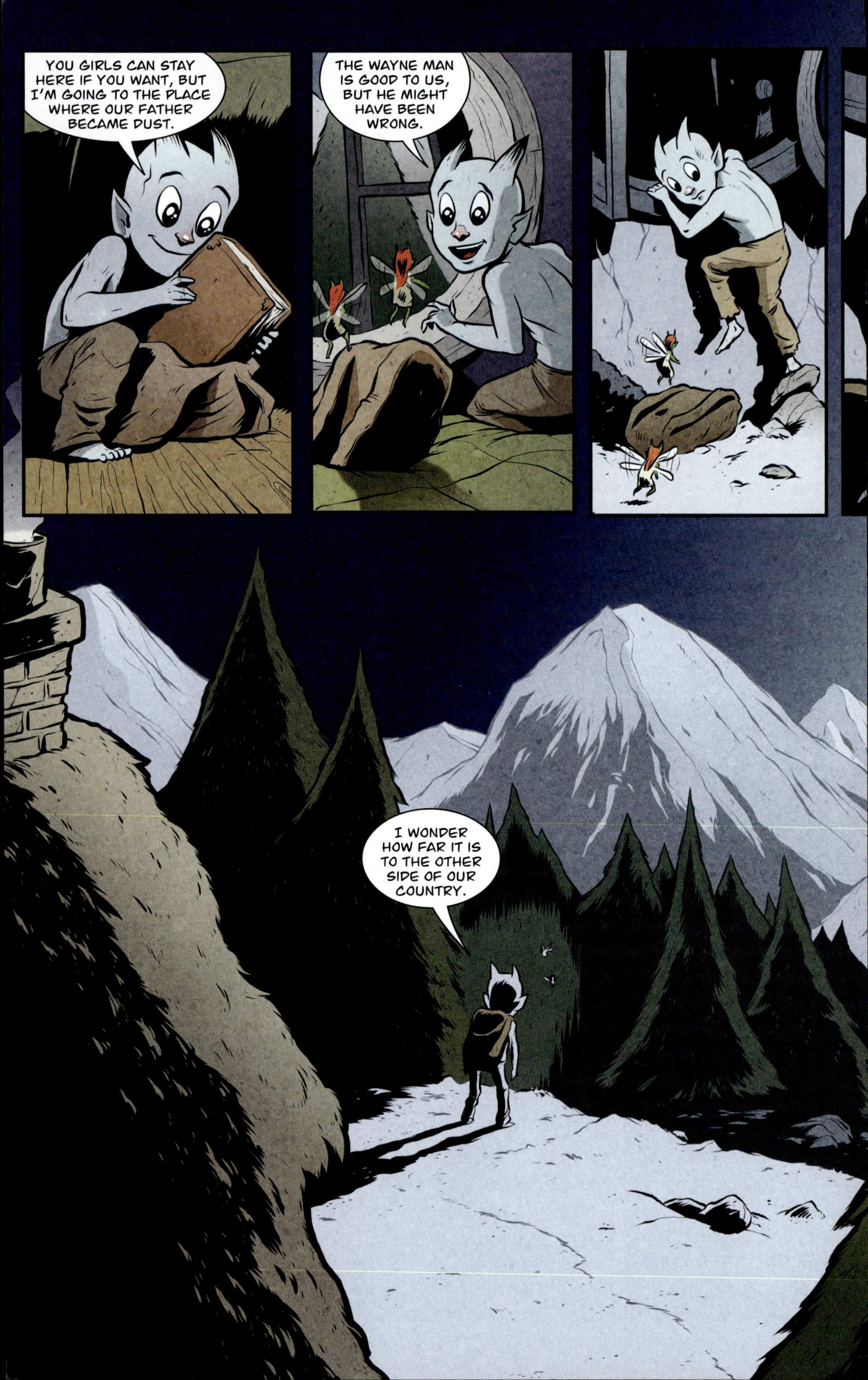
YOU GIRLS CAN STAY HERE IF YOU WANT, BUT I'M GOING TO THE PLACE WHERE OUR FATHER BECAME DUST.
THE WAYNE MAN IS GOOD TO US, BUT HE MIGHT HAVE BEEN WRONG.
I WONDER HOW FAR IT IS TO THE OTHER SIDE OF OUR COUNTRY.

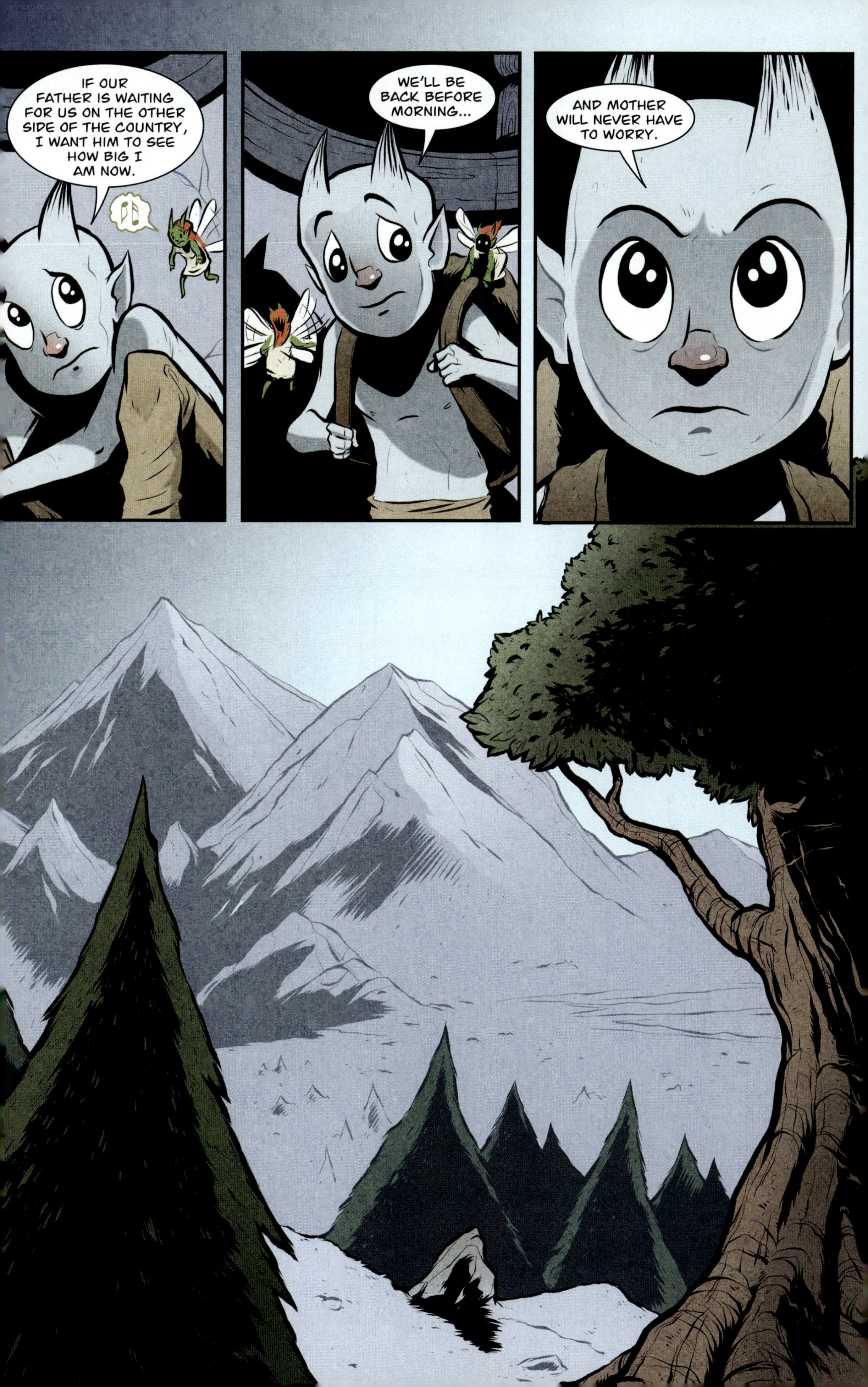
IF OUR FATHER IS WAITING FOR US ON THE OTHER SIDE OF THE COUNTRY, I WANT HIM TO SEE HOW BIG I AM NOW.
WE'LL BE BACK BEFORE MORNING...
AND MOTHER WILL NEVER HAVE TO WORRY.

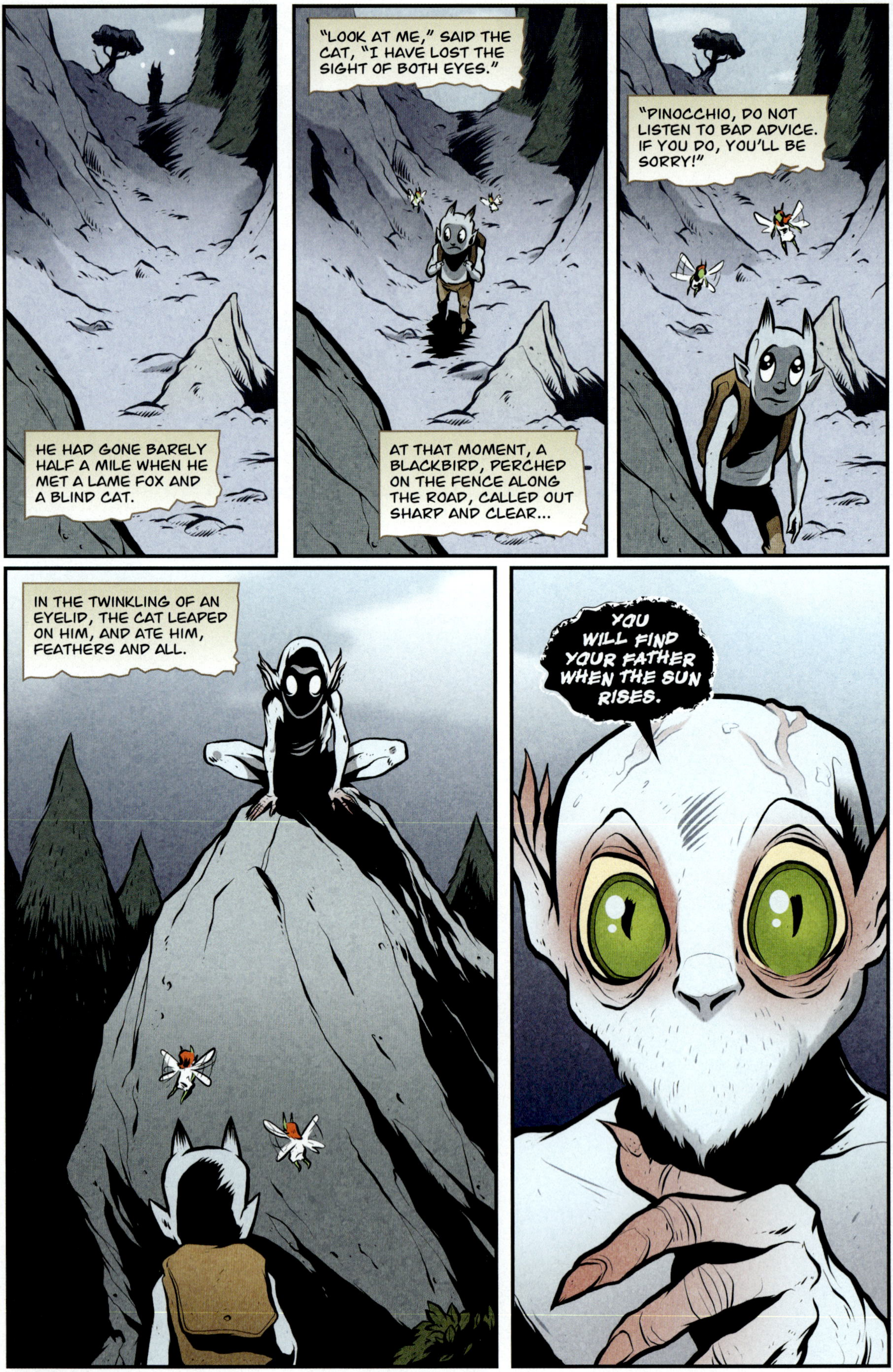
HE HAD GONE BARELY HALF A MILE WHEN HE MET A LAME FOX AND A BLIND CAT.
"LOOK AT ME," SAID THE CAT, "I HAVE LOST THE SIGHT OF BOTH EYES."
AT THAT MOMENT, A BLACKBIRD, PERCHED ON THE FENCE ALONG THE ROAD, CALLED OUT SHARP AND CLEAR...
"PINOCCHIO, DO NOT LISTEN TO BAD ADVICE. IF YOU DO, YOU'LL BE SORRY!"
IN THE TWINKLING OF AN EYELID, THE CAT LEAPED ON HIM, AND ATE HIM, FEATHERS AND ALL.
YOU WILL FIND YOUR FATHER WHEN THE SUN RISES.

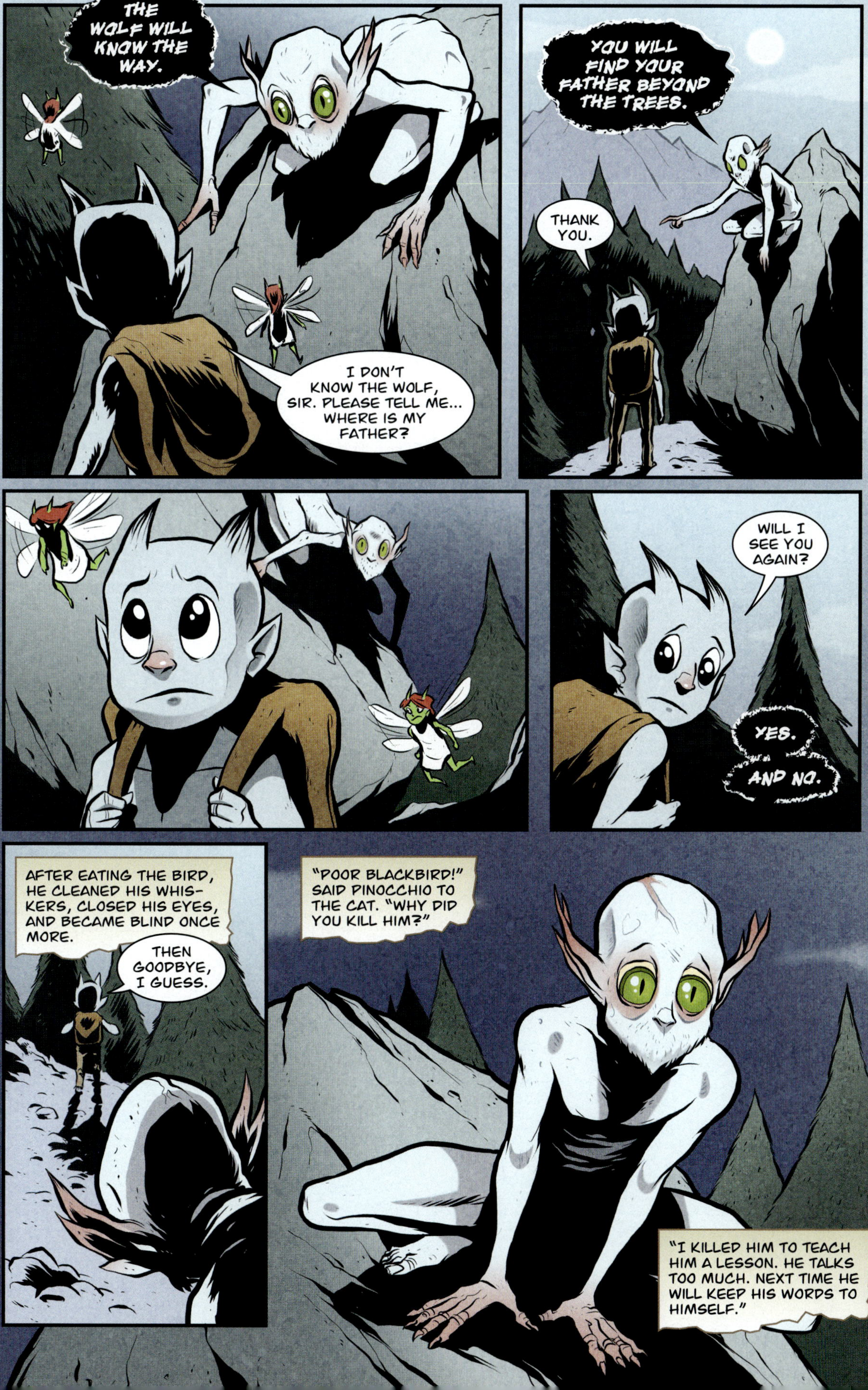
THE WOLF WILL KNOW THE WAY.
I DON'T KNOW THE WOLF, SIR. PLEASE TELL ME... WHERE IS MY FATHER?
YOU WILL FIND YOUR FATHER BEYOND THE TREES.
THANK YOU.
WILL I SEE YOU AGAIN?
YES.
AND NO.
AFTER EATING THE BIRD, HE CLEANED HIS WHISKERS, CLOSED HIS EYES, AND BECAME BLIND ONCE MORE.
THEN GOODBYE, I GUESS.
"POOR BLACKBIRD!" SAID PINOCCHIO TO THE CAT. "WHY DID YOU KILL HIM?"
"I KILLED HIM TO TEACH HIM A LESSON. HE TALKS TOO MUCH. NEXT TIME HE WILL KEEP HIS WORDS TO HIMSELF."

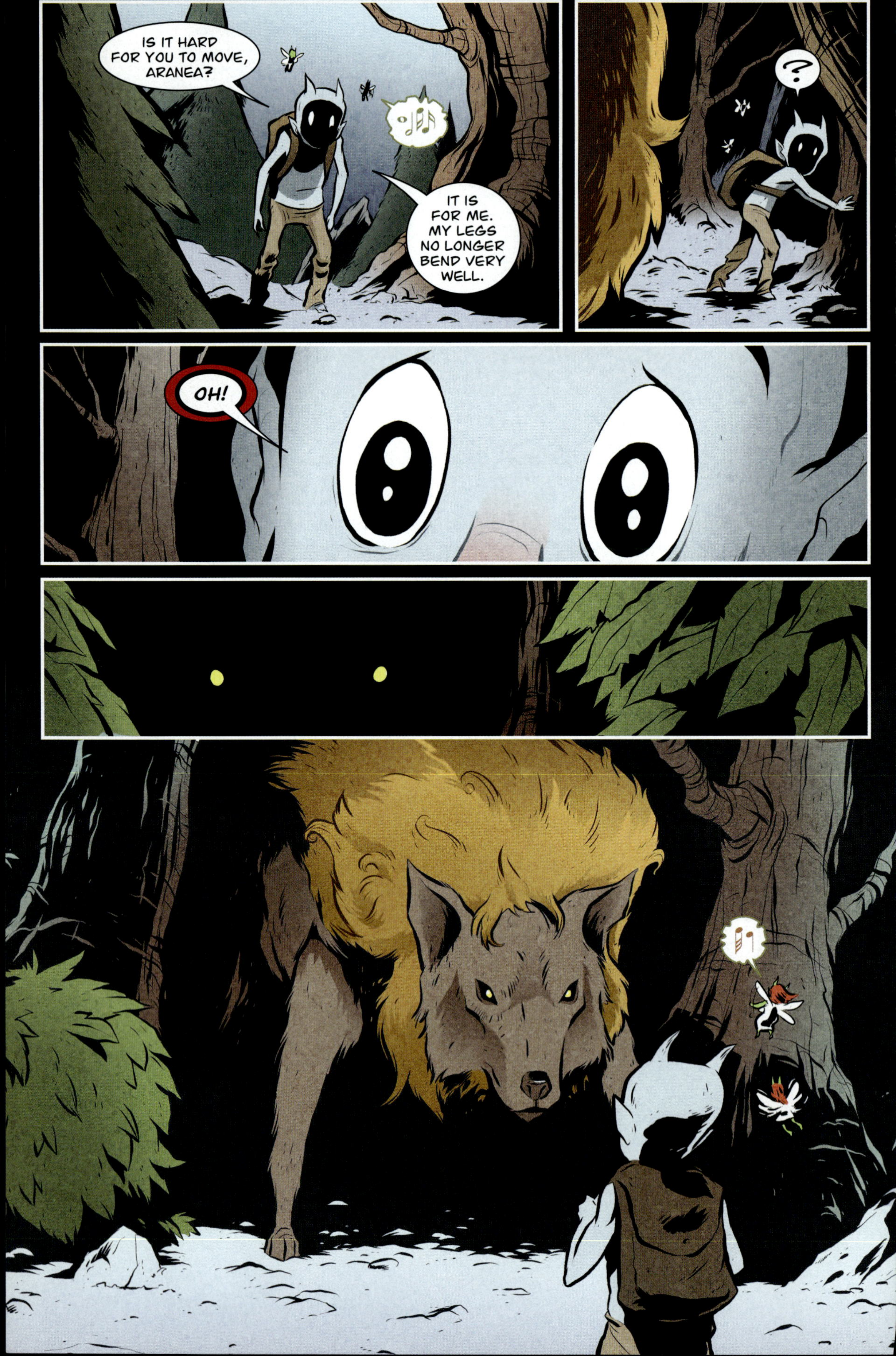

IS IT HARD FOR YOU TO MOVE, ARANEA?
IT IS FOR ME. MY LEGS NO LONGER BEND VERY WELL.
?
OH!

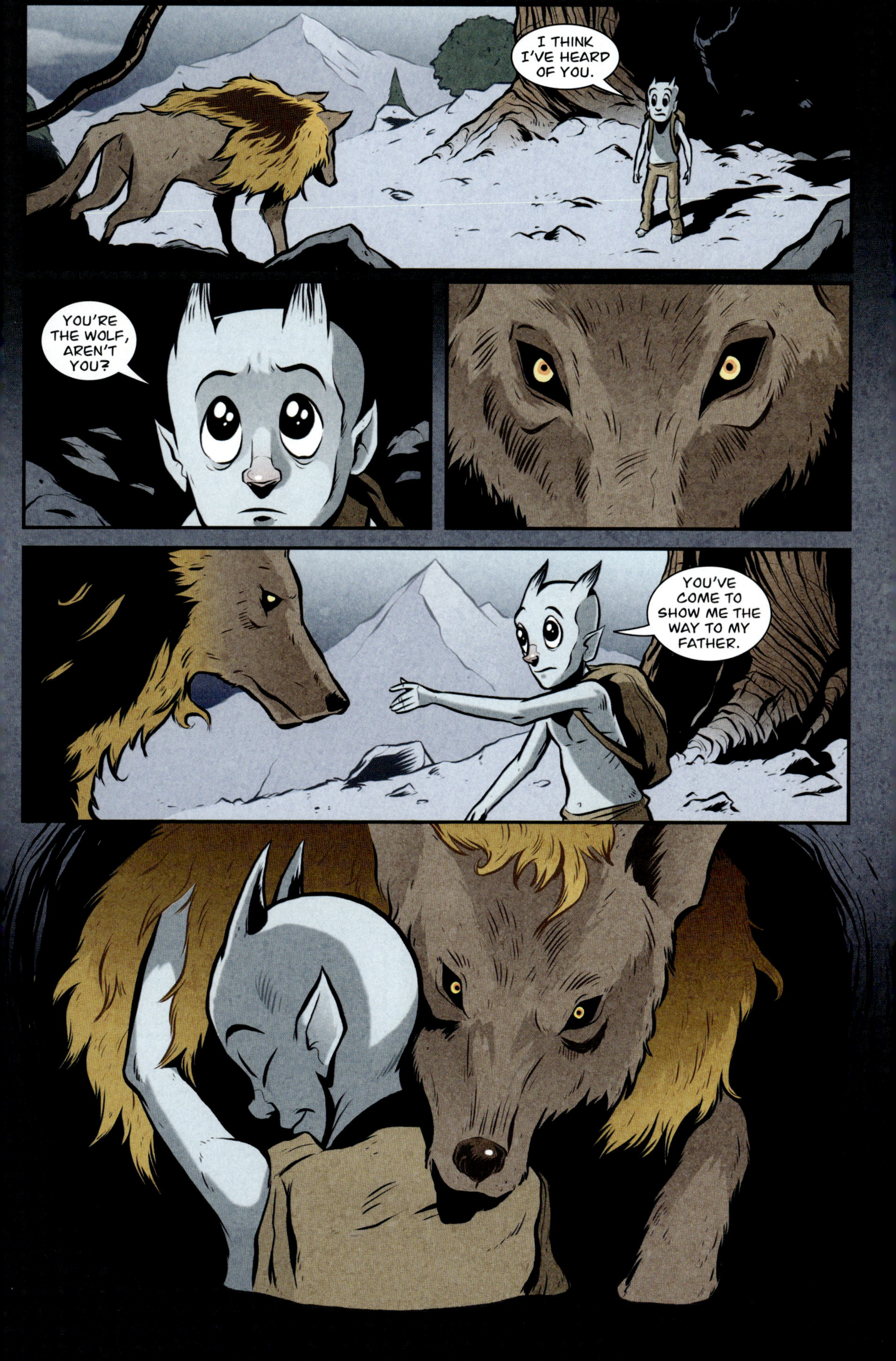
I THINK I'VE HEARD OF YOU.
YOU'RE THE WOLF, AREN'T YOU?
YOU'VE COME TO SHOW ME THE WAY TO MY FATHER.

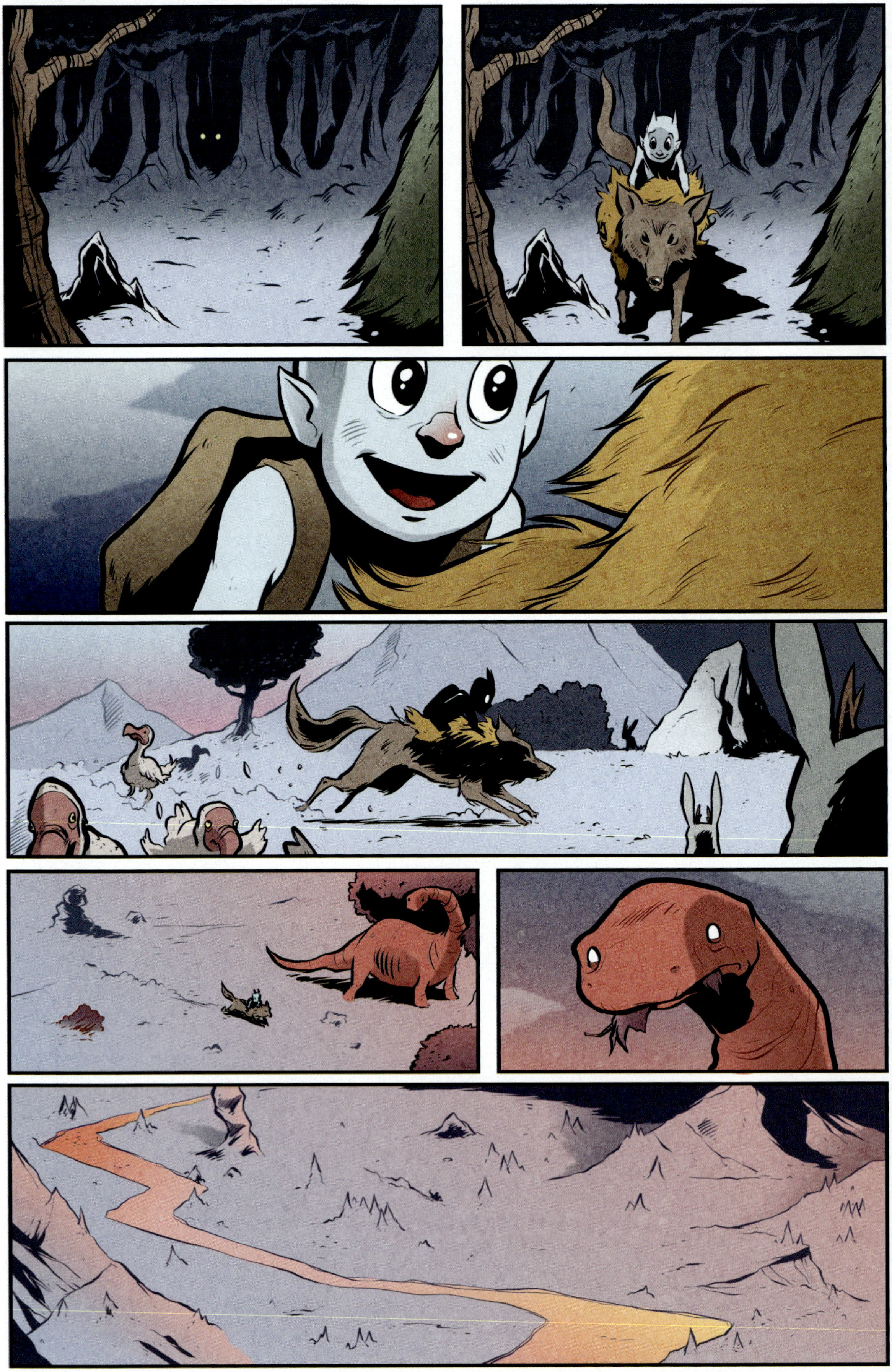

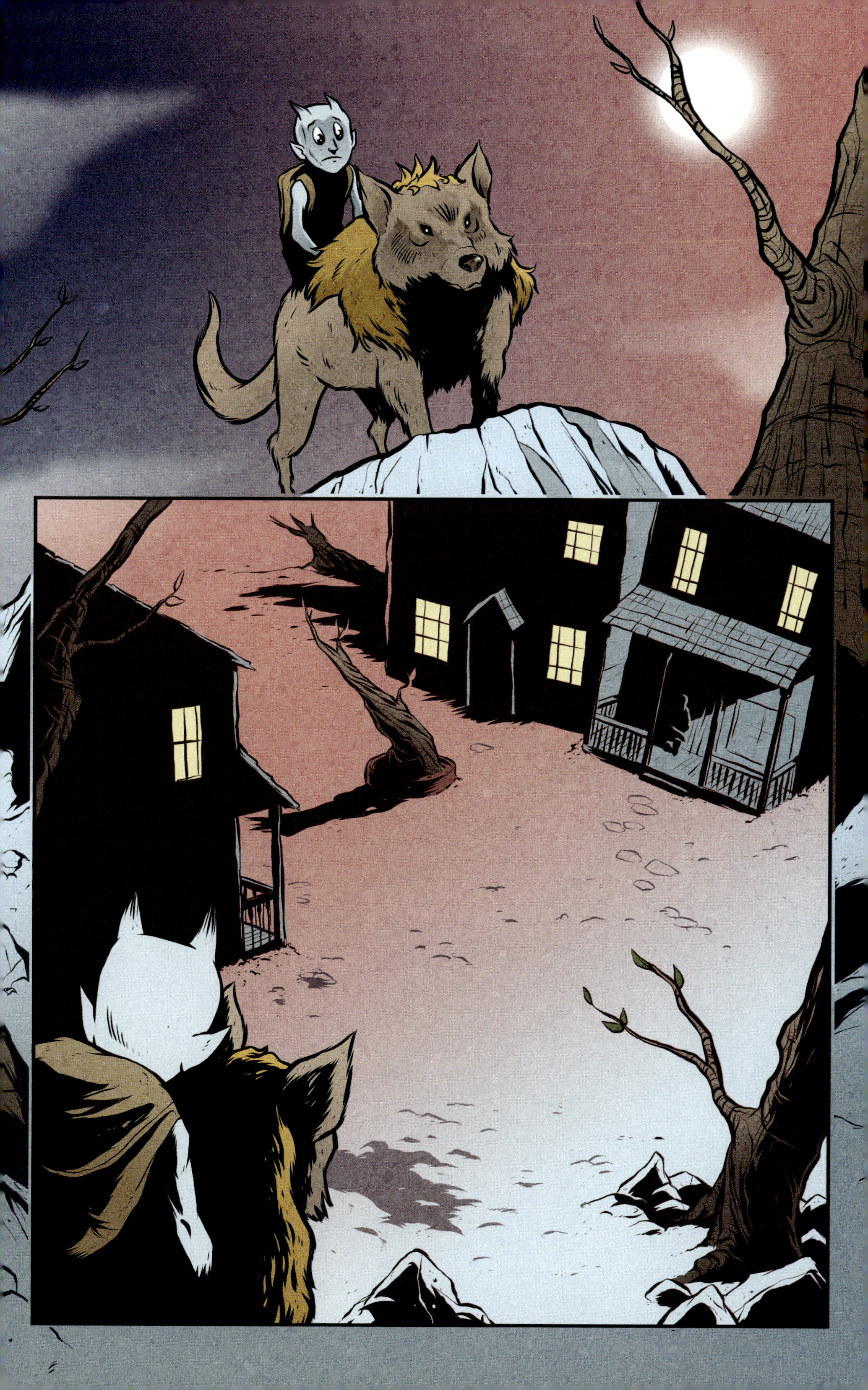

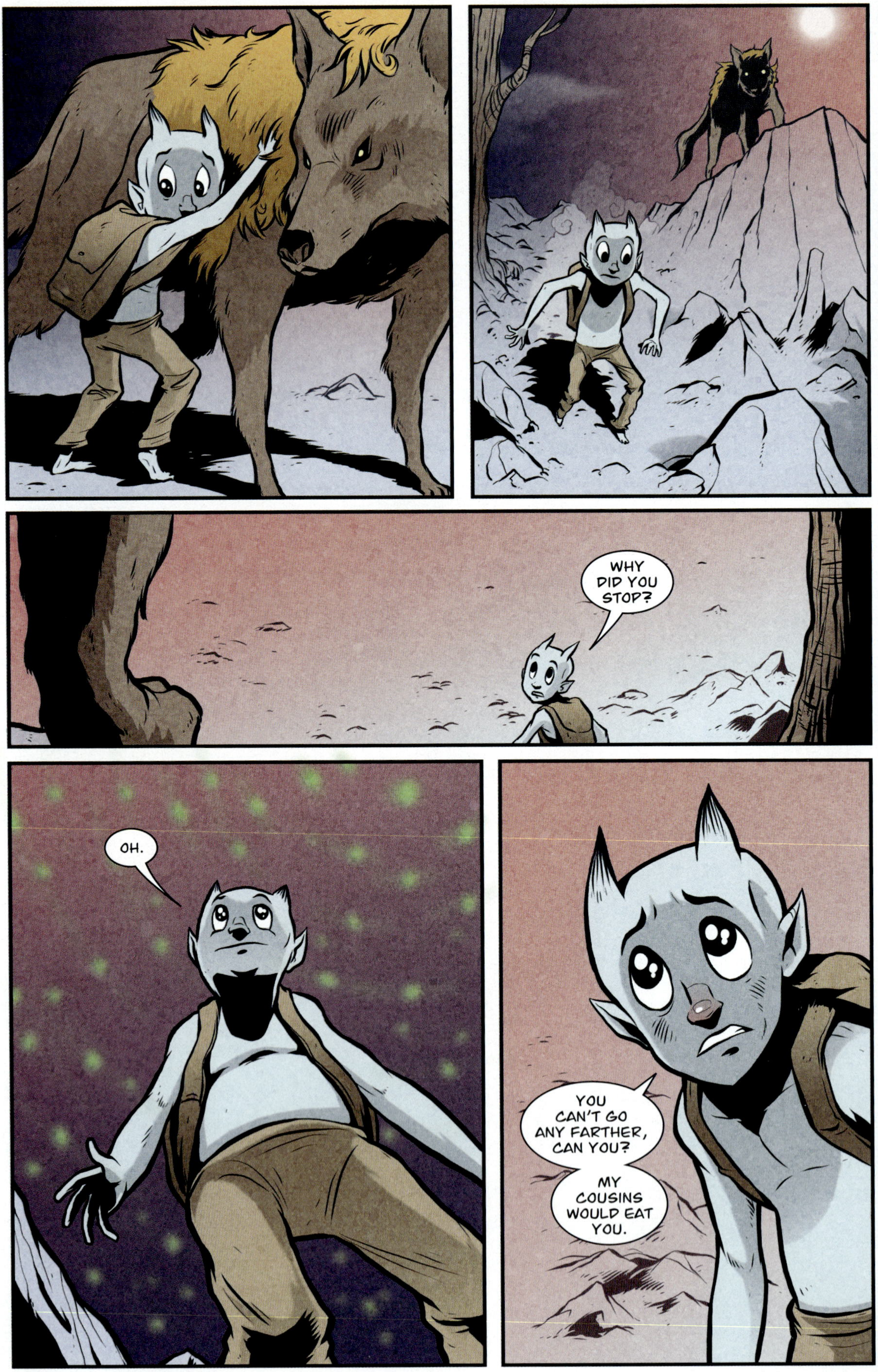
WHY DID YOU STOP?
OH.
YOU CAN'T GO ANY FARTHER, CAN YOU?
MY COUSINS WOULD EAT YOU.

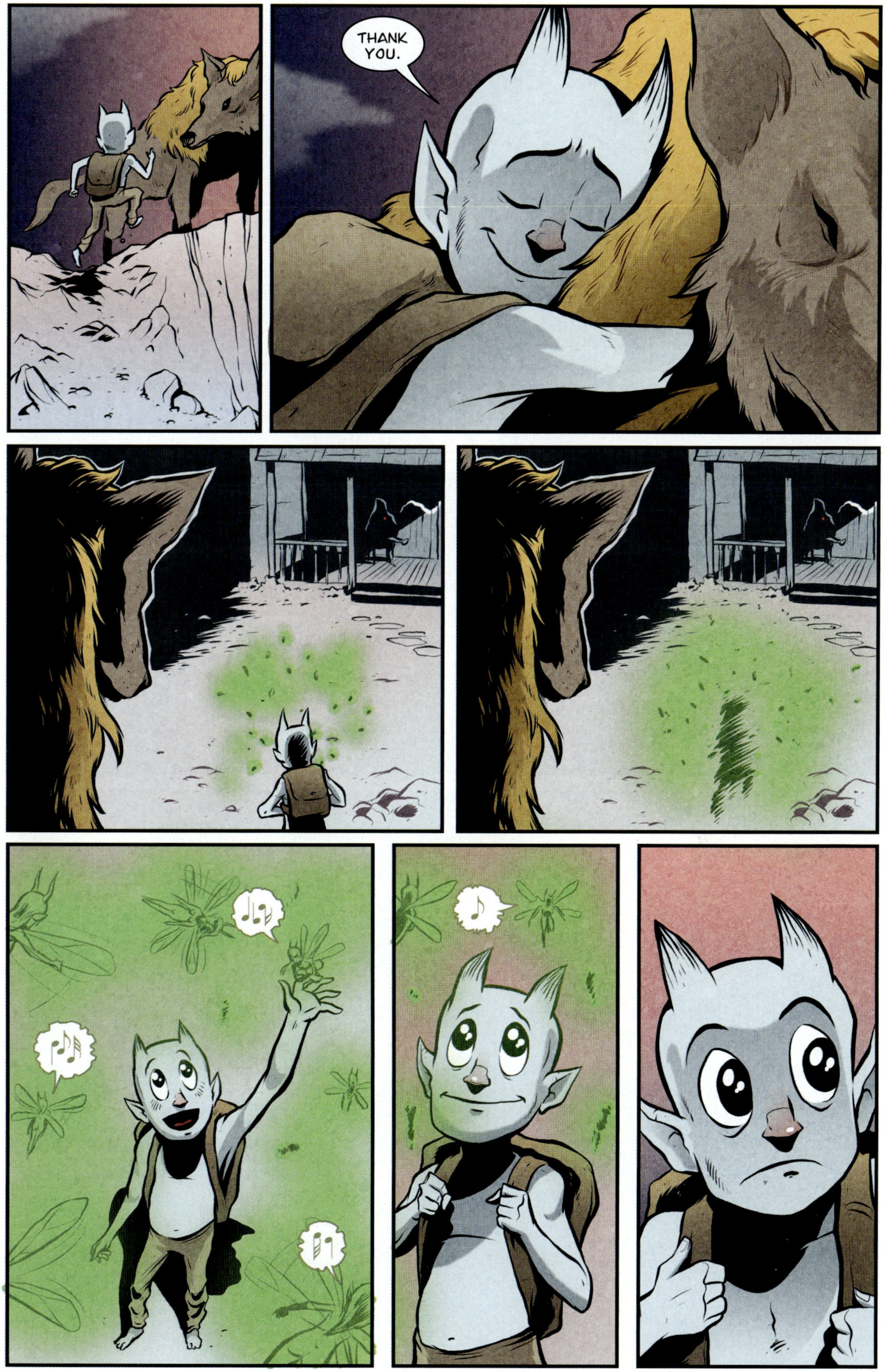
THANK YOU.

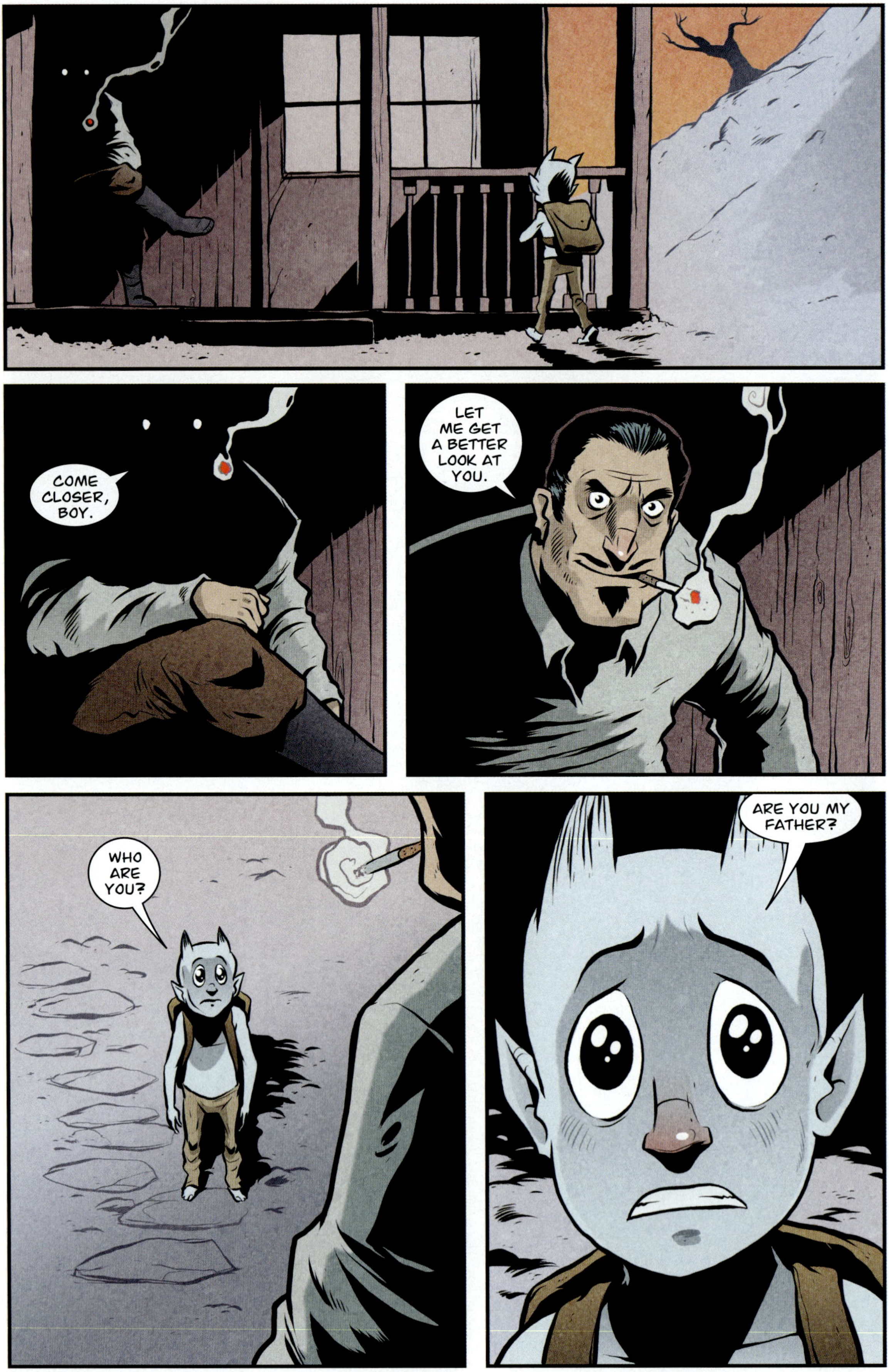
COME CLOSER, BOY.
LET ME GET A BETTER LOOK AT YOU.
WHO ARE YOU?
ARE YOU MY FATHER?

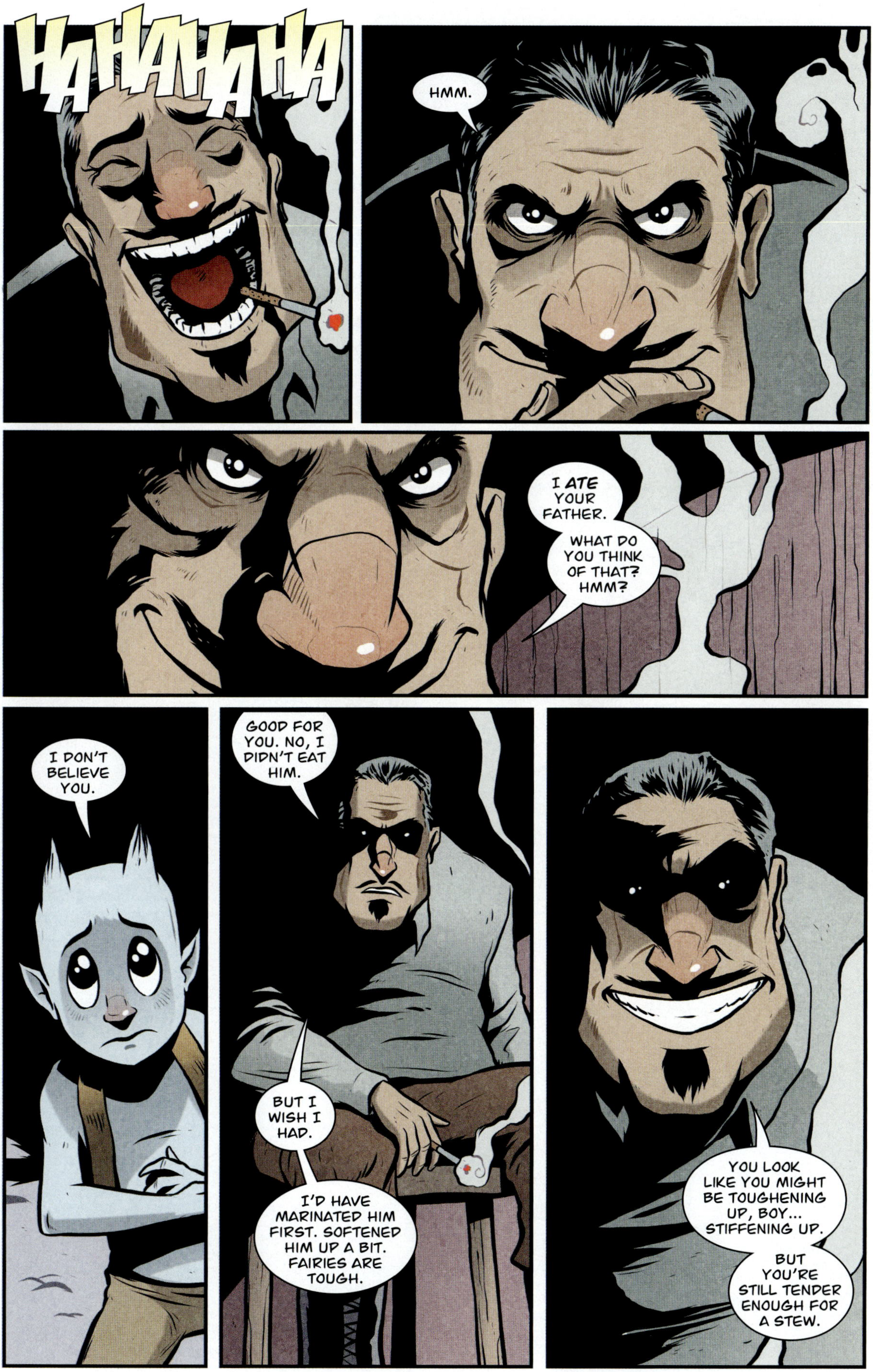
HAHAHAHAHA
HMM.
I ATE YOUR FATHER.
WHAT DO YOU THINK OF THAT? HMM?
I DON'T BELIEVE YOU.
GOOD FOR YOU. NO, I DIDN'T EAT HIM.
BUT I WISH I HAD.
I'D HAVE MARINATED HIM FIRST. SOFTENED HIM UP A BIT. FAIRIES ARE TOUGH.
YOU LOOK LIKE YOU MIGHT BE TOUGHENING UP, BOY... STIFFENING UP.
BUT YOU'RE STILL TENDER ENOUGH FOR A STEW.

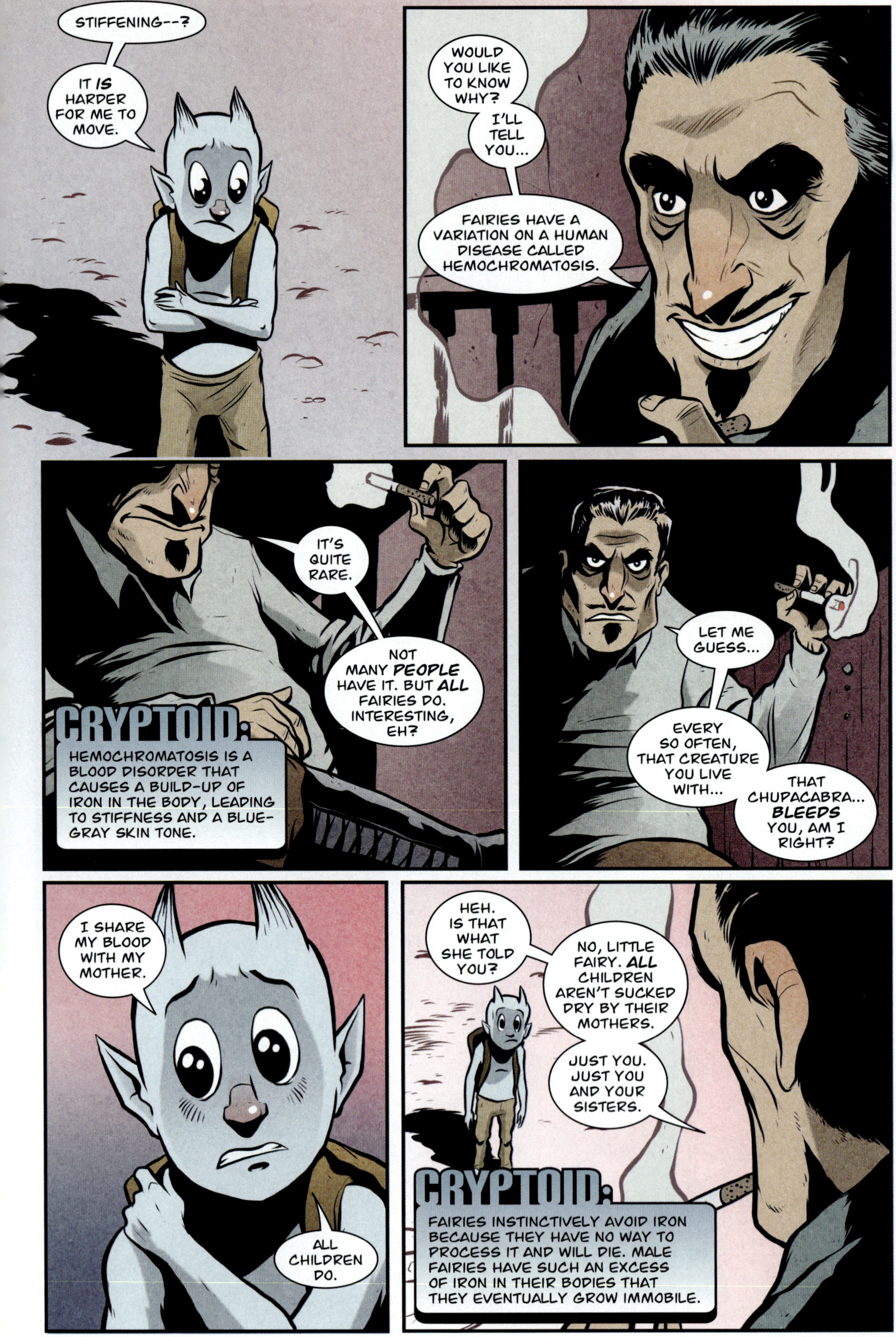
STIFFENING--?
IT IS HARDER FOR ME TO MOVE.
WOULD YOU LIKE TO KNOW WHY?
I'LL TELL YOU...
FAIRIES HAVE A VARIATION ON A HUMAN DISEASE CALLED HEMOCHROMATOSIS.
IT'S QUITE RARE.
NOT MANY PEOPLE HAVE IT. BUT ALL FAIRIES DO. INTERESTING, EH?
CRYPTOID:
HEMOCHROMATOSIS IS A BLOOD DISORDER THAT CAUSES A BUILD-UP OF IRON IN THE BODY, LEADING TO STIFFNESS AND A BLUE-GRAY SKIN TONE.
LET ME GUESS...
EVERY SO OFTEN, THAT CREATURE YOU LIVE WITH...
THAT CHUPACABRA... BLEEDS YOU, AM I RIGHT?
I SHARE MY BLOOD WITH MY MOTHER.
ALL CHILDREN DO.
HEH. IS THAT WHAT SHE TOLD YOU?
NO, LITTLE FAIRY. ALL CHILDREN AREN'T SUCKED DRY BY THEIR MOTHERS.
JUST YOU. JUST YOU AND YOUR SISTERS.
CRYPTOID:
FAIRIES INSTINCTIVELY AVOID IRON BECAUSE THEY HAVE NO WAY TO PROCESS IT AND WILL DIE. MALE FAIRIES HAVE SUCH AN EXCESS OF IRON IN THEIR BODIES THAT THEY EVENTUALLY GROW IMMOBILE.

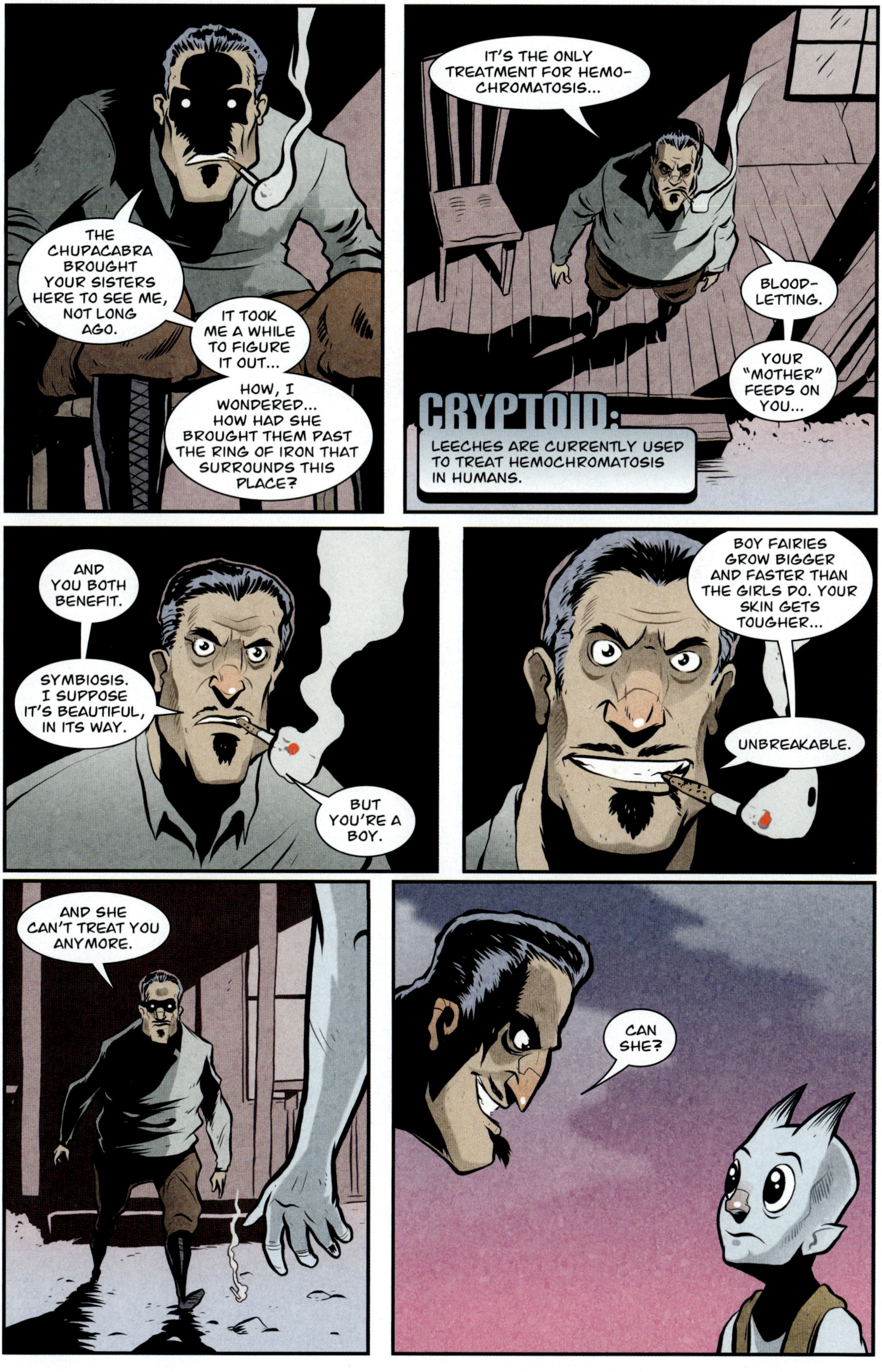
THE CHUPACABRA BROUGHT YOUR SISTERS HERE TO SEE ME, NOT LONG AGO.
IT TOOK ME A WHILE TO FIGURE IT OUT...
HOW, I WONDERED... HOW HAD SHE BROUGHT THEM PAST THE RING OF IRON THAT SURROUNDS THIS PLACE?
IT'S THE ONLY TREATMENT FOR HEMO-CHROMATOSIS...
BLOOD-LETTING.
YOUR "MOTHER" FEEDS ON YOU...
CRYPTOID:
LEECHES ARE CURRENTLY USED TO TREAT HEMOCHROMATOSIS IN HUMANS.
AND YOU BOTH BENEFIT.
SYMBIOSIS. I SUPPOSE IT'S BEAUTIFUL, IN ITS WAY.
BUT YOU'RE A BOY.
BOY FAIRIES GROW BIGGER AND FASTER THAN THE GIRLS DO. YOUR SKIN GETS TOUGHER...
UNBREAKABLE.
AND SHE CAN'T TREAT YOU ANYMORE.
CAN SHE?

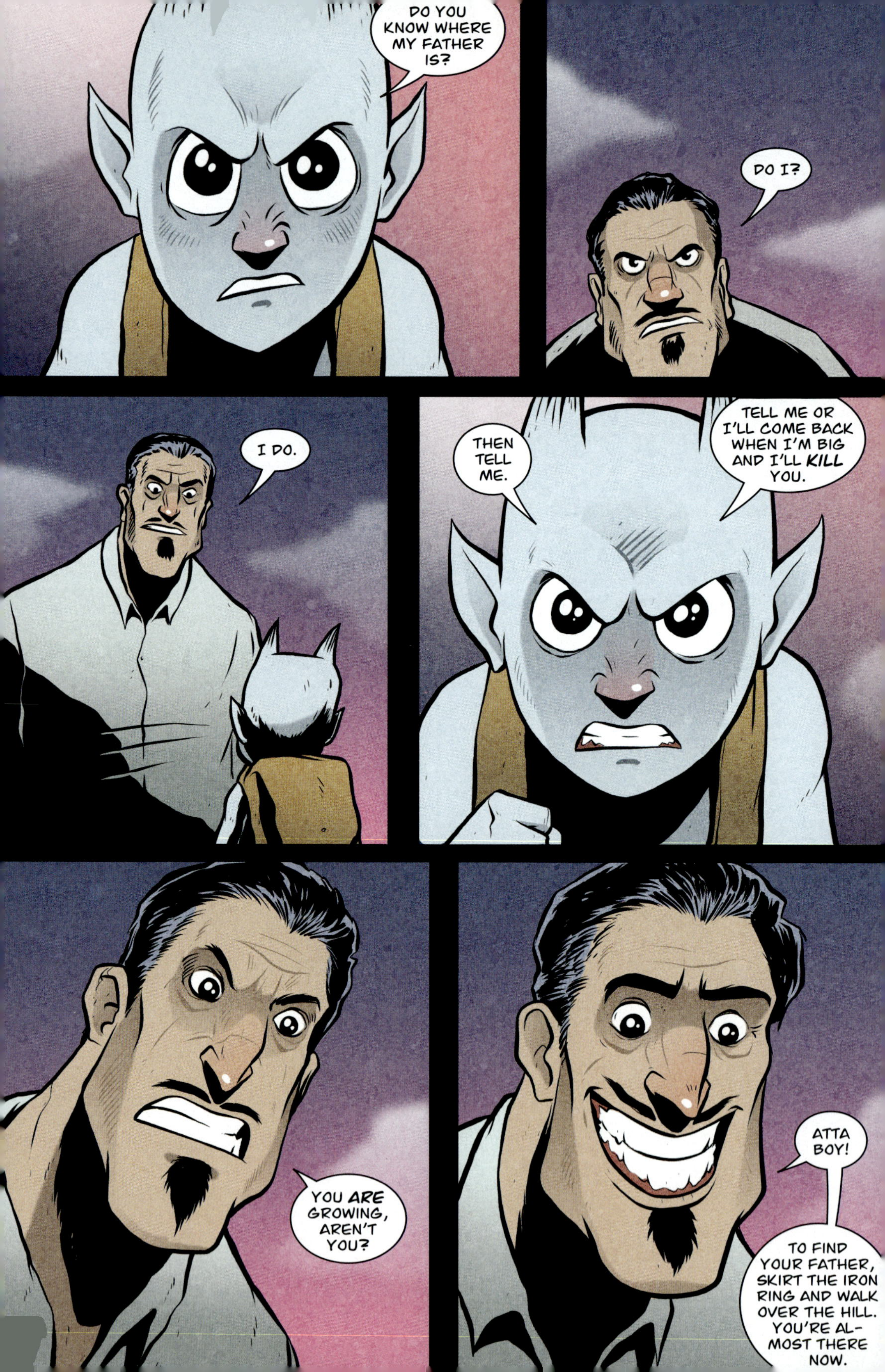
DO YOU KNOW WHERE MY FATHER IS?
DO I?
I DO.
THEN TELL ME.
TELL ME OR I'LL COME BACK WHEN I'M BIG AND I'LL **KILL** YOU.
YOU **ARE** GROWING, AREN'T YOU?
ATTA BOY!
TO FIND YOUR FATHER, SKIRT THE IRON RING AND WALK OVER THE HILL. YOU'RE AL-MOST THERE NOW.

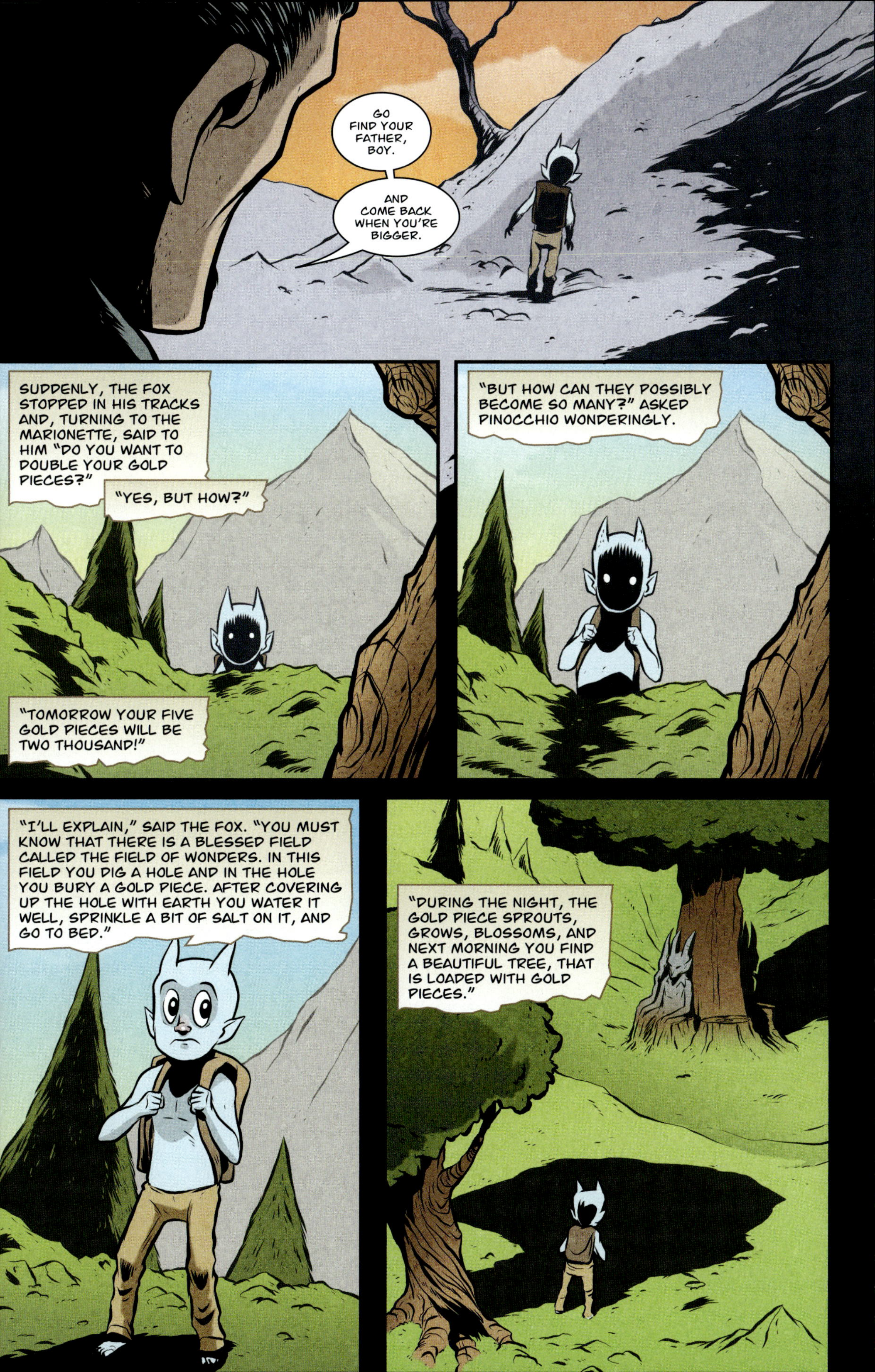
GO FIND YOUR FATHER, BOY.
AND COME BACK WHEN YOU'RE BIGGER.
SUDDENLY, THE FOX STOPPED IN HIS TRACKS AND, TURNING TO THE MARIONETTE, SAID TO HIM "DO YOU WANT TO DOUBLE YOUR GOLD PIECES?"
"YES, BUT HOW?"
"TOMORROW YOUR FIVE GOLD PIECES WILL BE TWO THOUSAND!"
"BUT HOW CAN THEY POSSIBLY BECOME SO MANY?" ASKED PINOCCHIO WONDERINGLY.
"I'LL EXPLAIN," SAID THE FOX. "YOU MUST KNOW THAT THERE IS A BLESSED FIELD CALLED THE FIELD OF WONDERS. IN THIS FIELD YOU DIG A HOLE AND IN THE HOLE YOU BURY A GOLD PIECE. AFTER COVERING UP THE HOLE WITH EARTH YOU WATER IT WELL, SPRINKLE A BIT OF SALT ON IT, AND GO TO BED."
"DURING THE NIGHT, THE GOLD PIECE SPROUTS, GROWS, BLOSSOMS, AND NEXT MORNING YOU FIND A BEAUTIFUL TREE, THAT IS LOADED WITH GOLD PIECES."

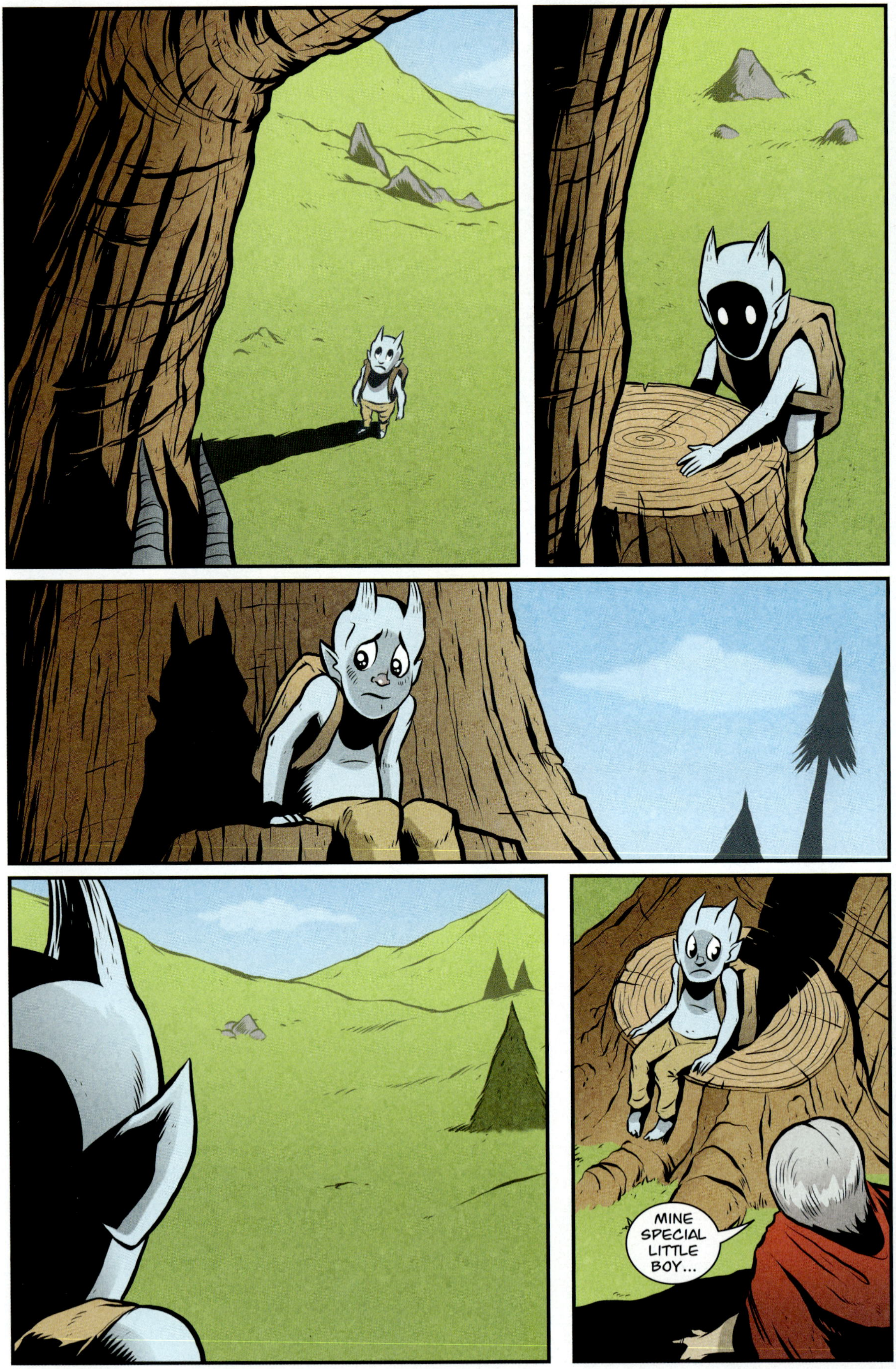
MINE SPECIAL LITTLE BOY...

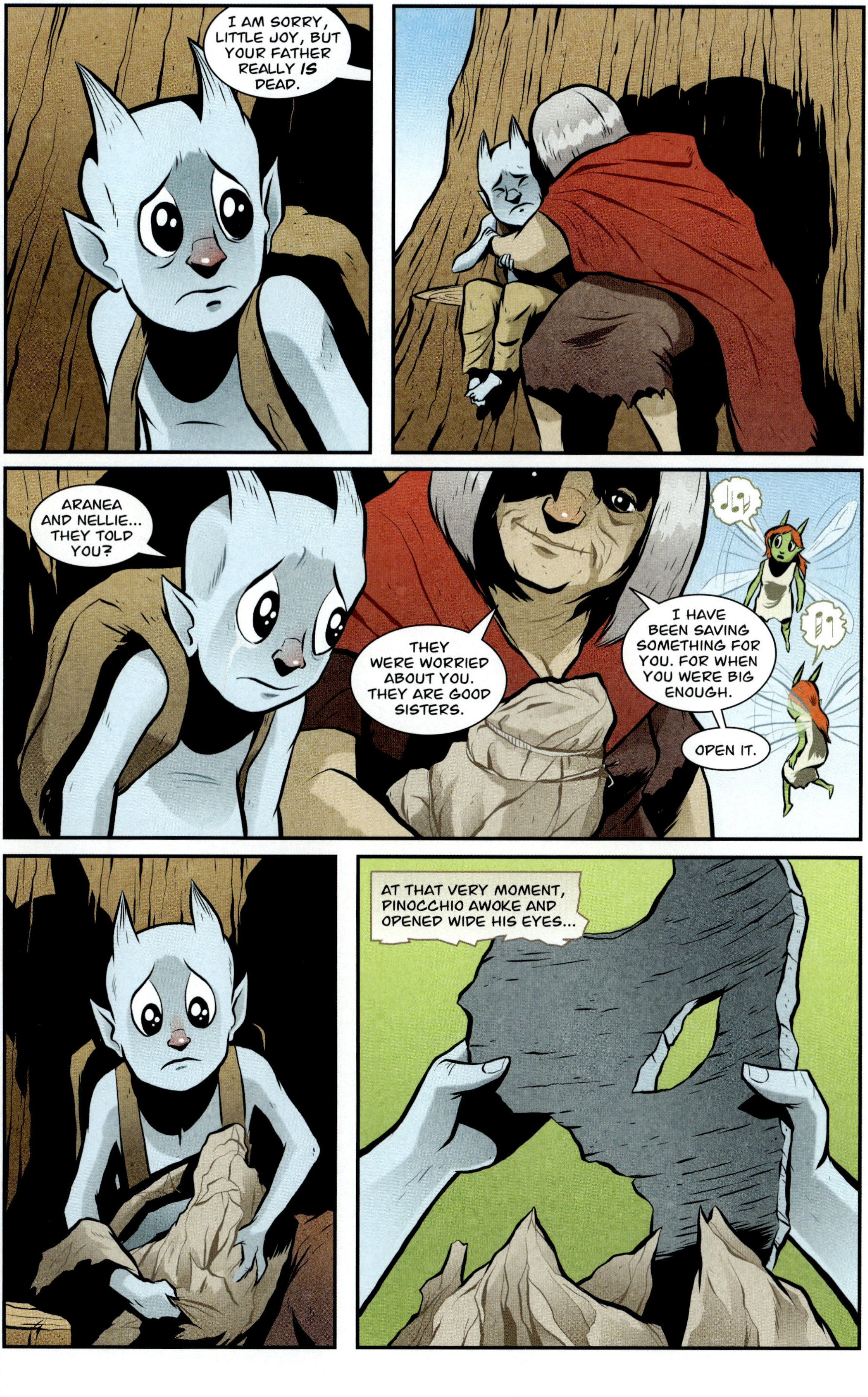
I AM SORRY, LITTLE JOY, BUT YOUR FATHER REALLY *IS* DEAD.
ARANEA AND NELLIE... THEY TOLD YOU?
THEY WERE WORRIED ABOUT YOU. THEY ARE GOOD SISTERS.
I HAVE BEEN SAVING SOMETHING FOR YOU. FOR WHEN YOU WERE BIG ENOUGH.
OPEN IT.
AT THAT VERY MOMENT, PINOCCHIO AWOKE AND OPENED WIDE HIS EYES...

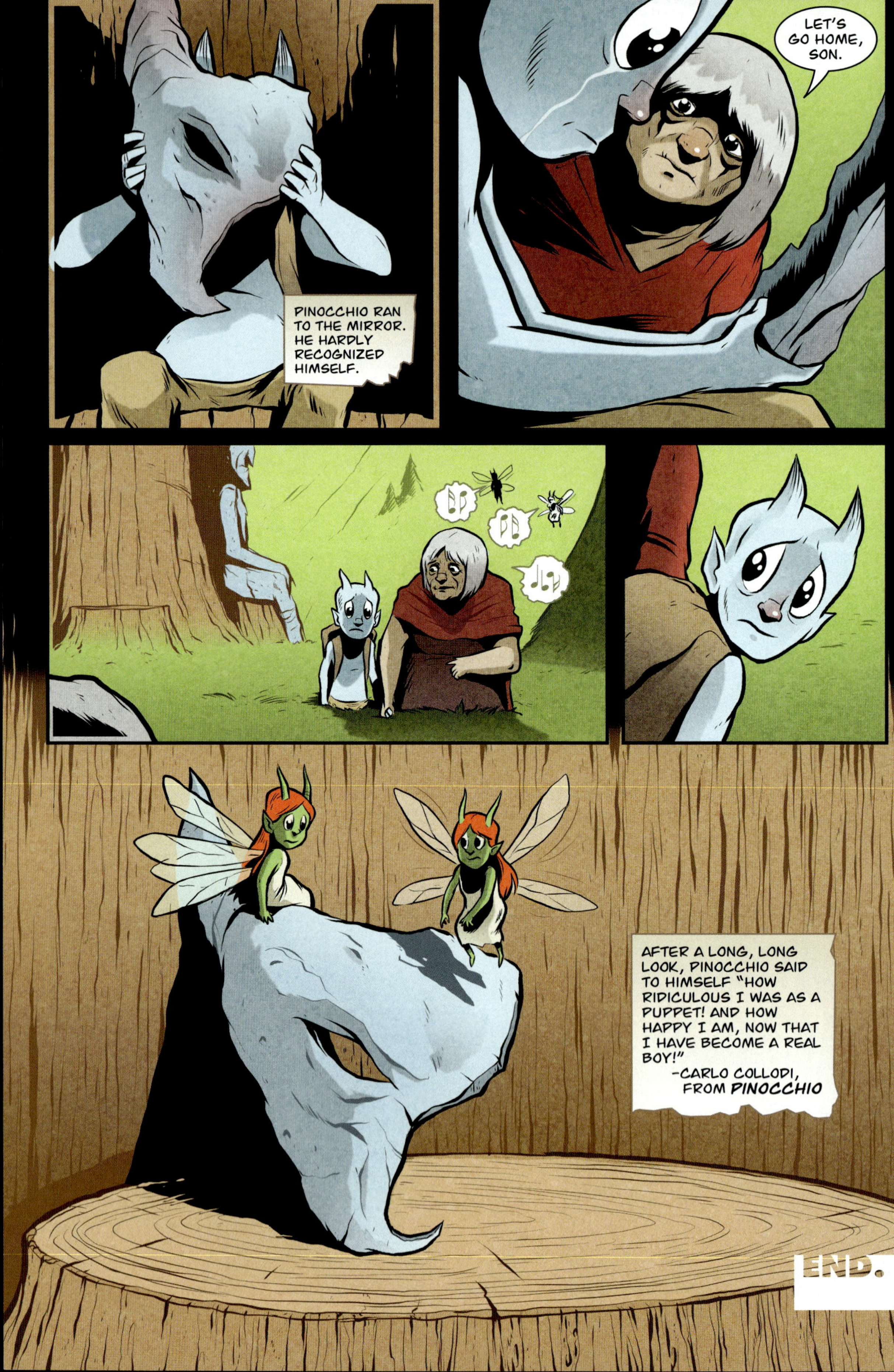
PINOCCHIO RAN TO THE MIRROR. HE HARDLY RECOGNIZED HIMSELF.
LET'S GO HOME, SON.
AFTER A LONG, LONG LOOK, PINOCCHIO SAID TO HIMSELF "HOW RIDICULOUS I WAS AS A PUPPET! AND HOW HAPPY I AM, NOW THAT I HAVE BECOME A REAL BOY!"
-CARLO COLLODI, FROM PINOCCHIO
END.

DING
DONG

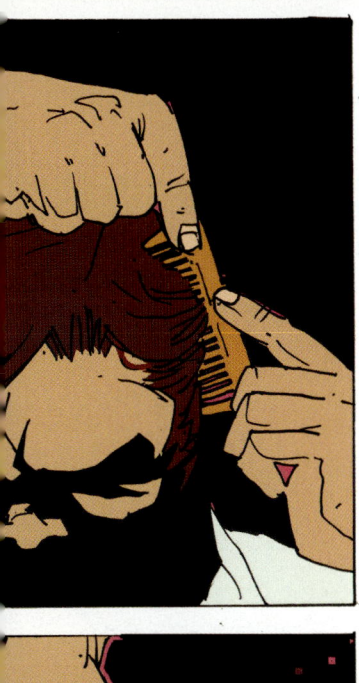

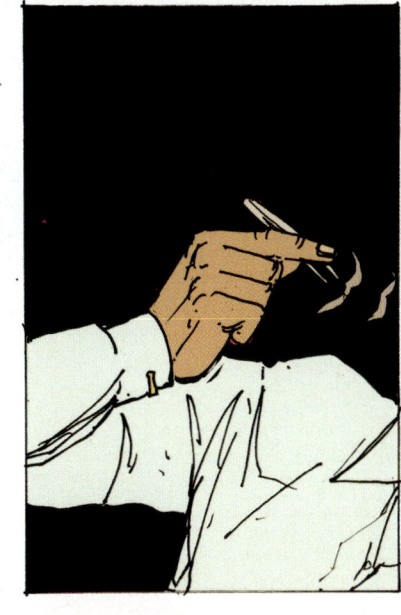

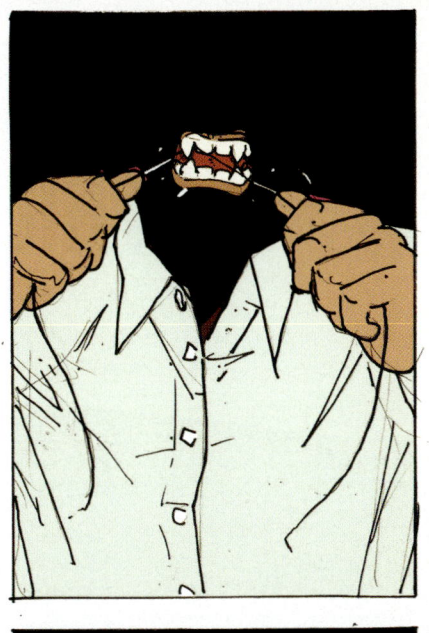

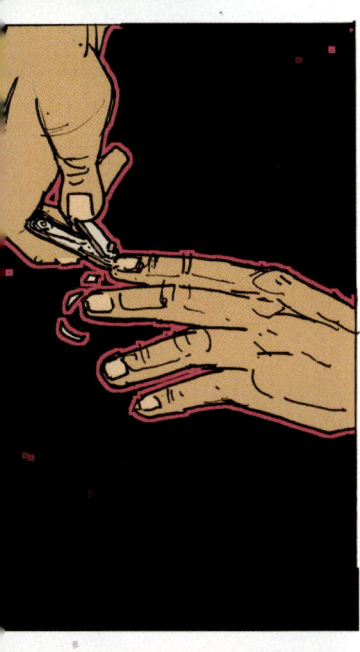

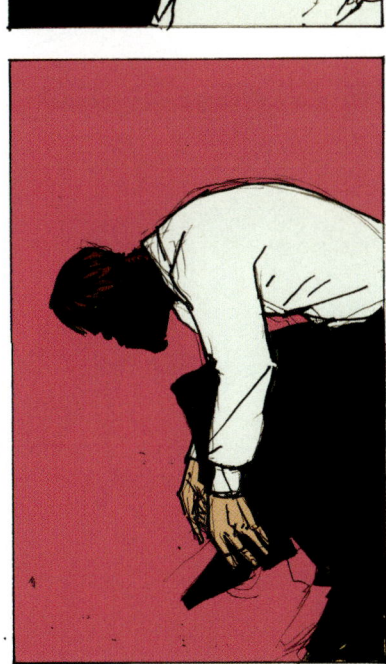

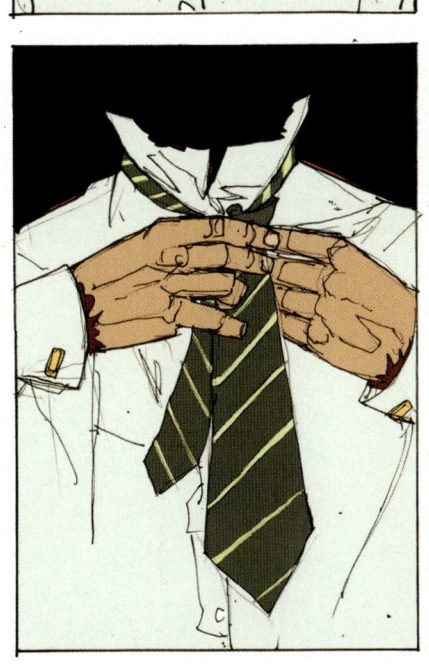

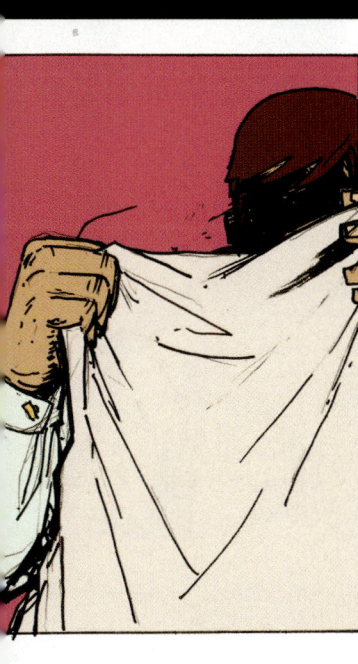

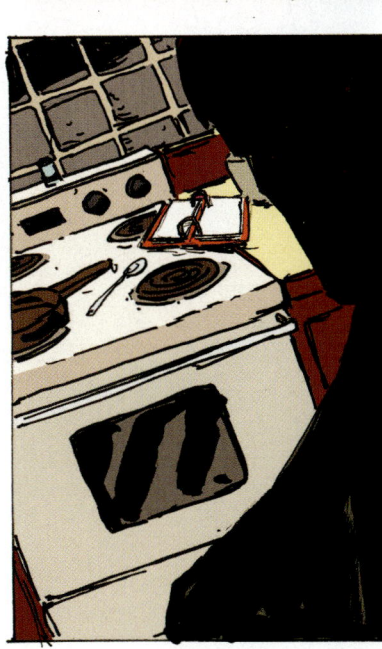

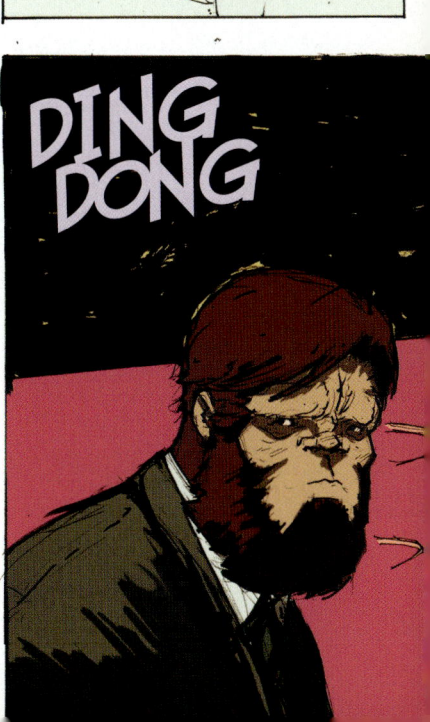

CHAPTER THREE

WHO KILLED THE DOVER DEMON?

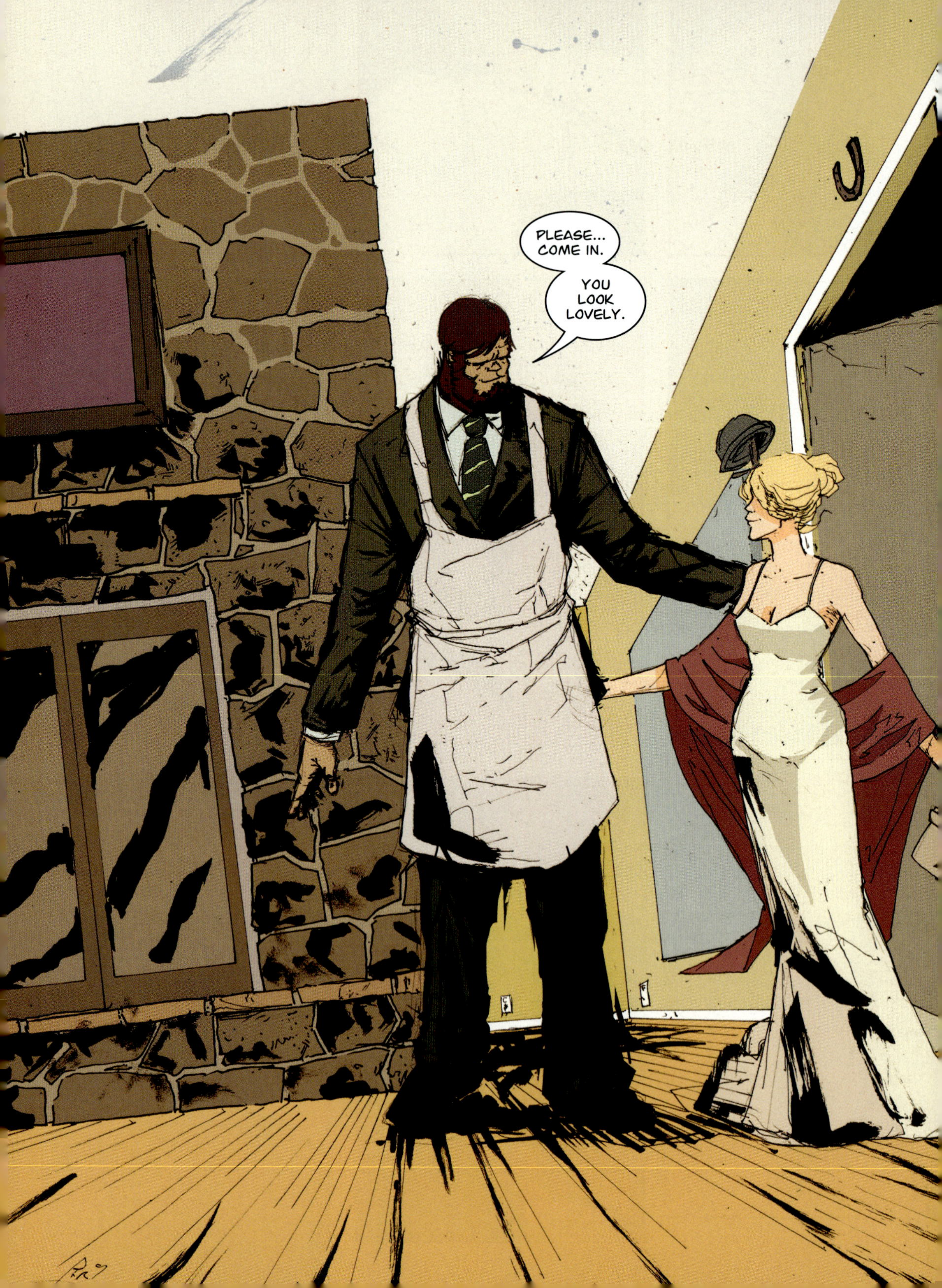
PLEASE... COME IN.
YOU LOOK LOVELY.

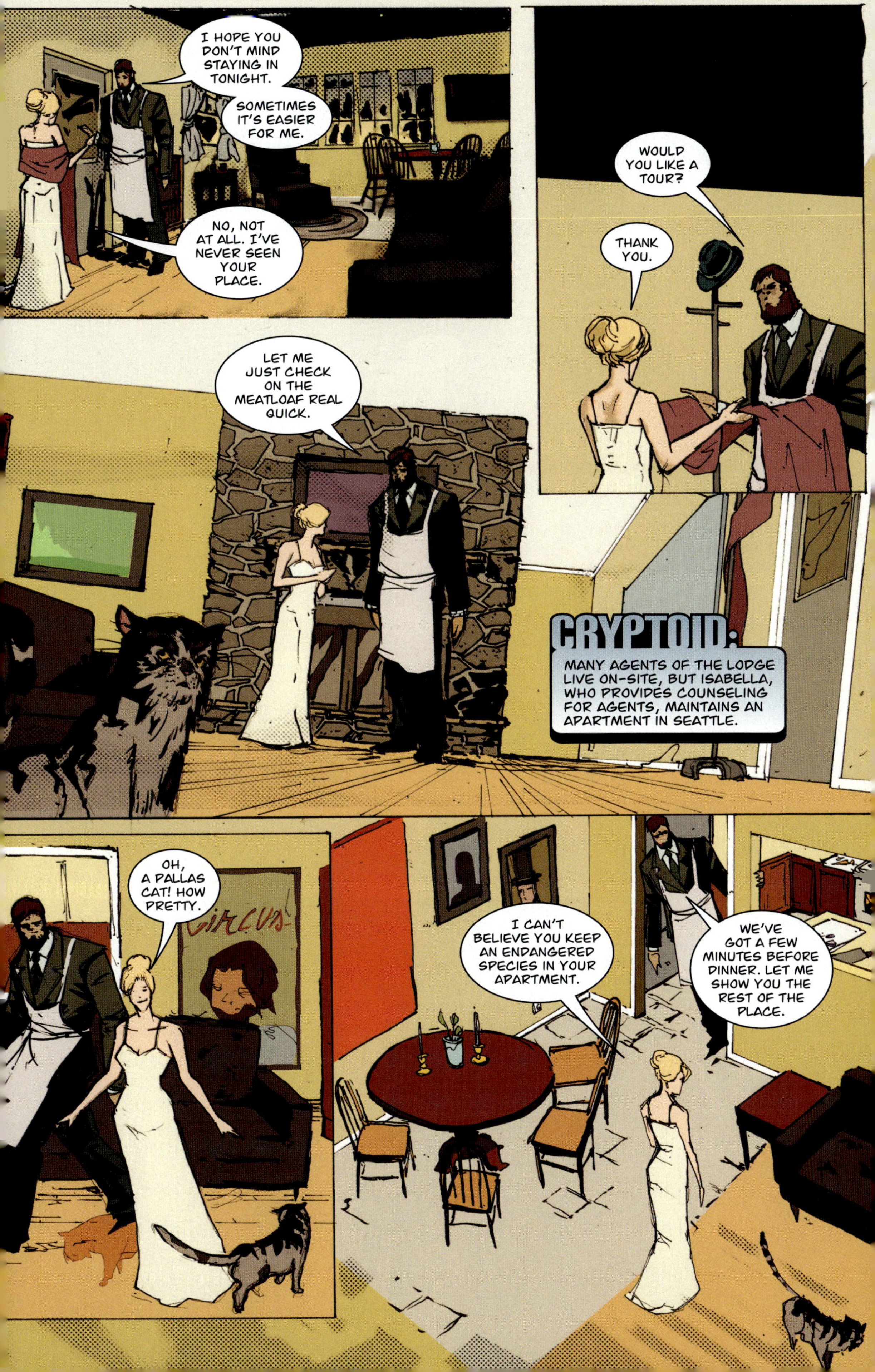
I HOPE YOU DON'T MIND STAYING IN TONIGHT.
SOMETIMES IT'S EASIER FOR ME.
NO, NOT AT ALL. I'VE NEVER SEEN YOUR PLACE.
WOULD YOU LIKE A TOUR?
THANK YOU.
LET ME JUST CHECK ON THE MEATLOAF REAL QUICK.
CRYPTOID:
MANY AGENTS OF THE LODGE LIVE ON-SITE, BUT ISABELLA, WHO PROVIDES COUNSELING FOR AGENTS, MAINTAINS AN APARTMENT IN SEATTLE.
OH, A PALLAS CAT! HOW PRETTY.
CIRCUS
I CAN'T BELIEVE YOU KEEP AN ENDANGERED SPECIES IN YOUR APARTMENT.
WE'VE GOT A FEW MINUTES BEFORE DINNER. LET ME SHOW YOU THE REST OF THE PLACE.

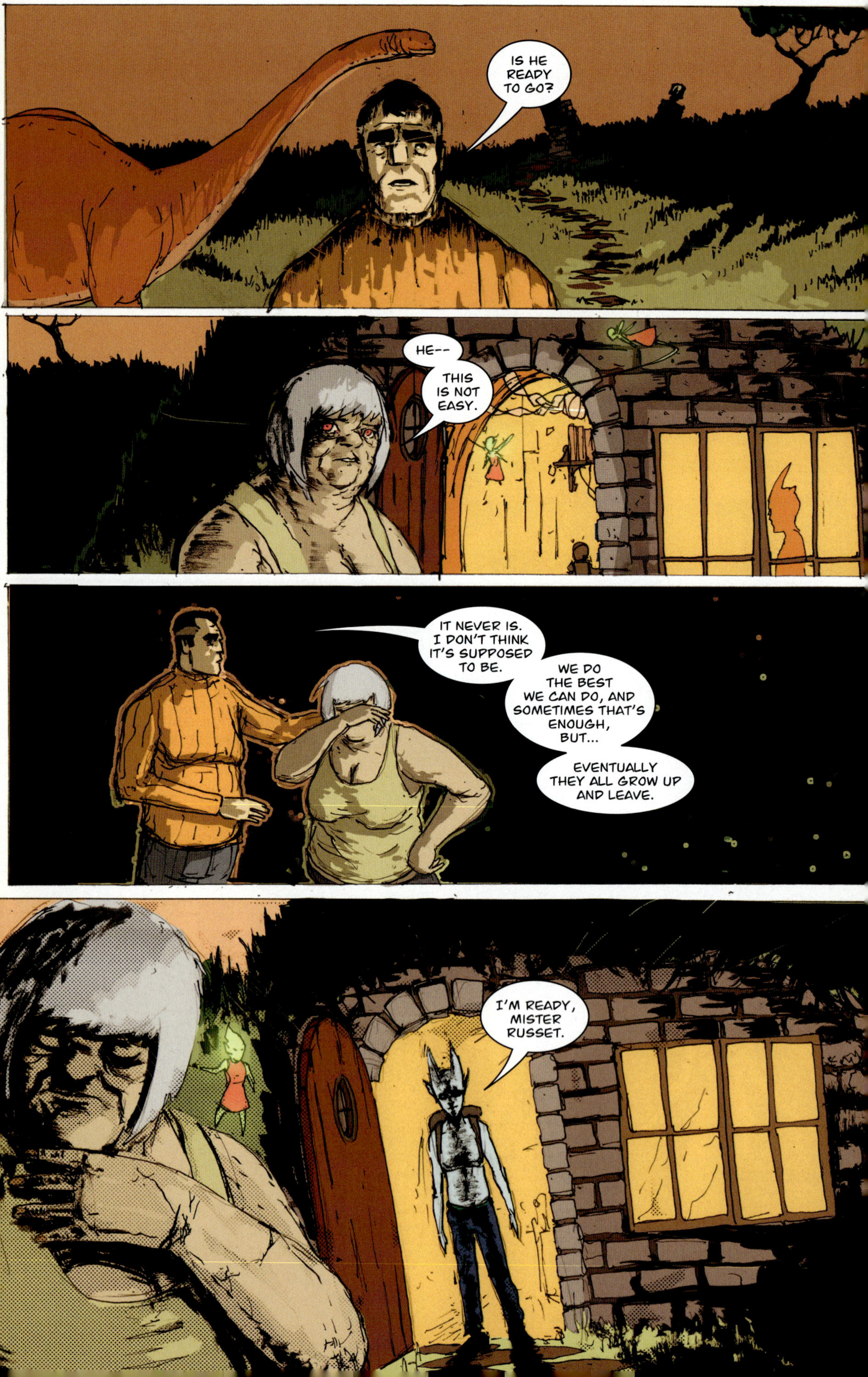
IS HE READY TO GO?
HE--
THIS IS NOT EASY.
IT NEVER IS. I DON'T THINK IT'S SUPPOSED TO BE.
WE DO THE BEST WE CAN DO, AND SOMETIMES THAT'S ENOUGH, BUT...
EVENTUALLY THEY ALL GROW UP AND LEAVE.
I'M READY, MISTER RUSSET.

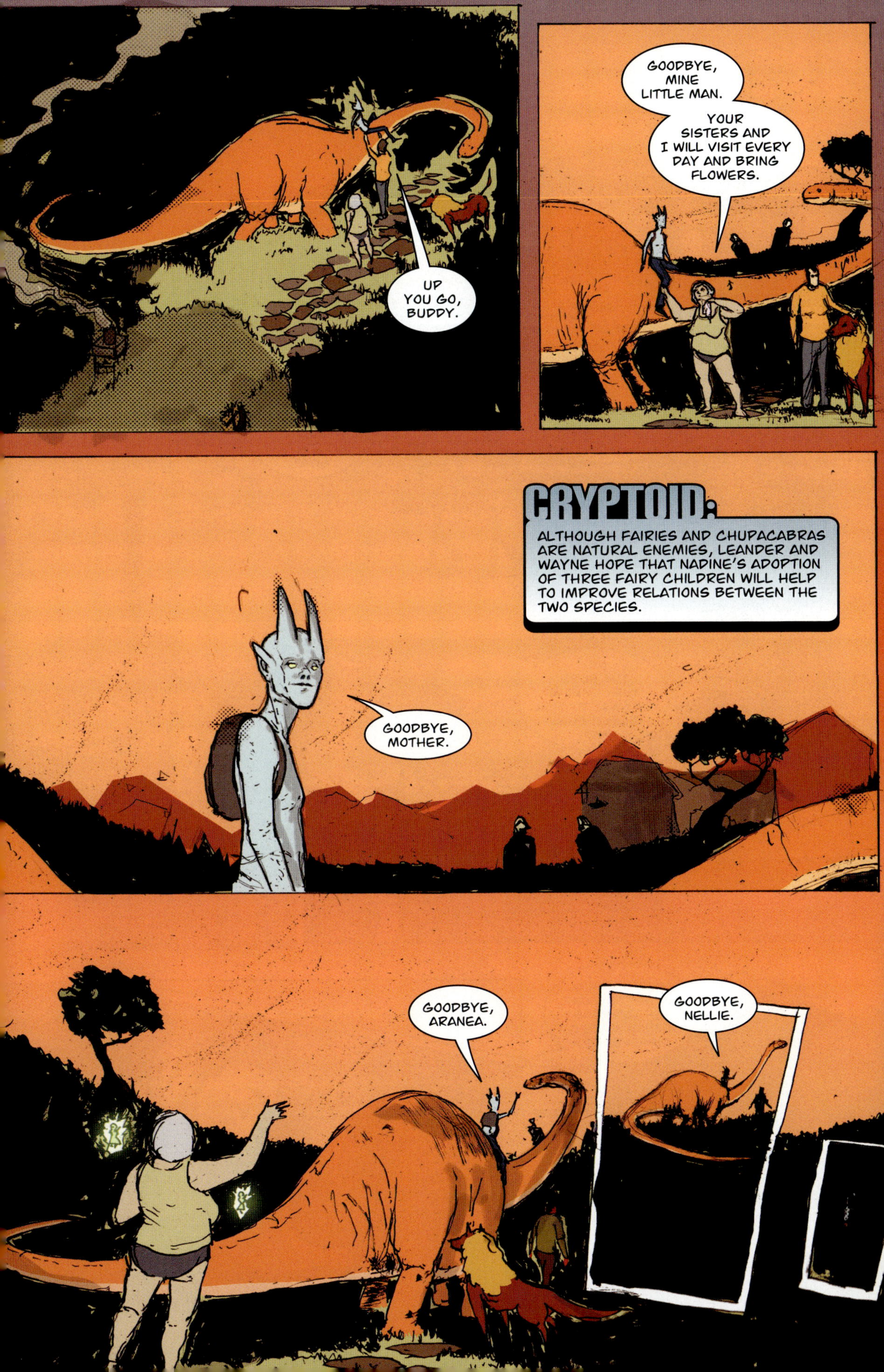
UP YOU GO, BUDDY.
GOODBYE, MINE LITTLE MAN.
YOUR SISTERS AND I WILL VISIT EVERY DAY AND BRING FLOWERS.
CRYPTOID:
ALTHOUGH FAIRIES AND CHUPACABRAS ARE NATURAL ENEMIES, LEANDER AND WAYNE HOPE THAT NADINE'S ADOPTION OF THREE FAIRY CHILDREN WILL HELP TO IMPROVE RELATIONS BETWEEN THE TWO SPECIES.
GOODBYE, MOTHER.
GOODBYE, ARANEA.
GOODBYE, NELLIE.

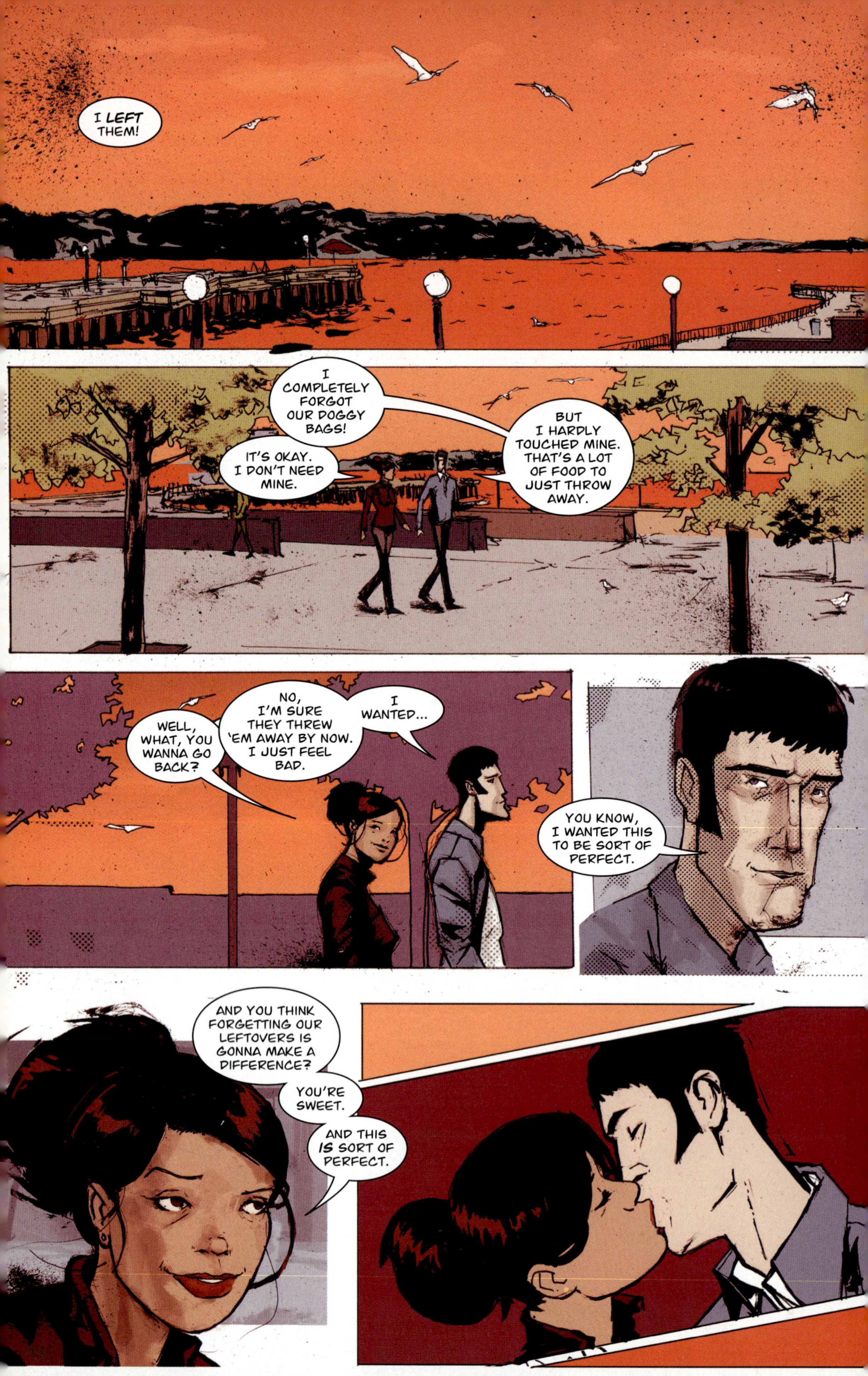
I LEFT THEM!
I COMPLETELY FORGOT OUR DOGGY BAGS!
IT'S OKAY. I DON'T NEED MINE.
BUT I HARDLY TOUCHED MINE. THAT'S A LOT OF FOOD TO JUST THROW AWAY.
WELL, WHAT, YOU WANNA GO BACK?
NO, I'M SURE THEY THREW 'EM AWAY BY NOW. I JUST FEEL BAD.
I WANTED...
YOU KNOW, I WANTED THIS TO BE SORT OF PERFECT.
AND YOU THINK FORGETTING OUR LEFTOVERS IS GONNA MAKE A DIFFERENCE?
YOU'RE SWEET.
AND THIS *IS* SORT OF PERFECT.

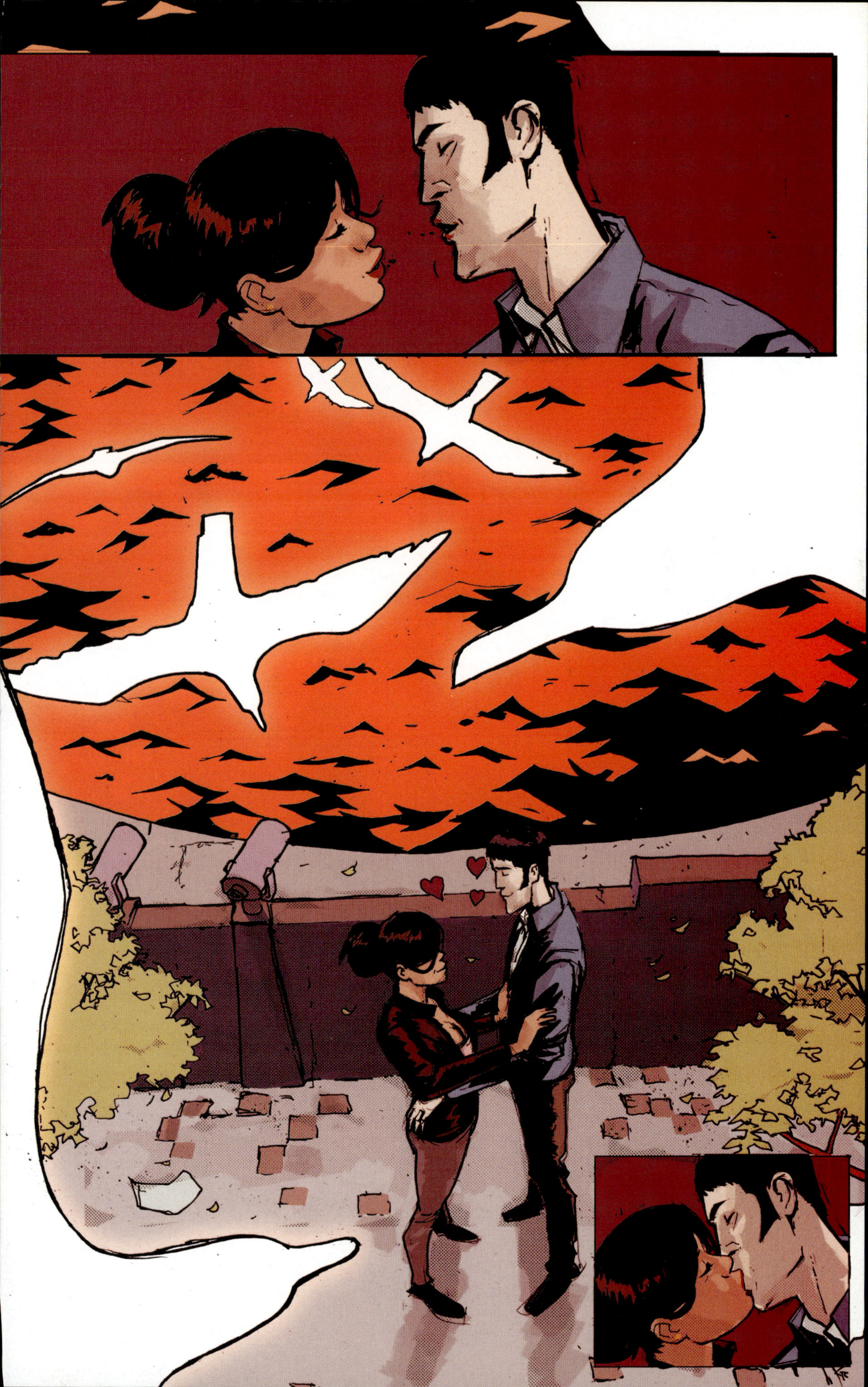

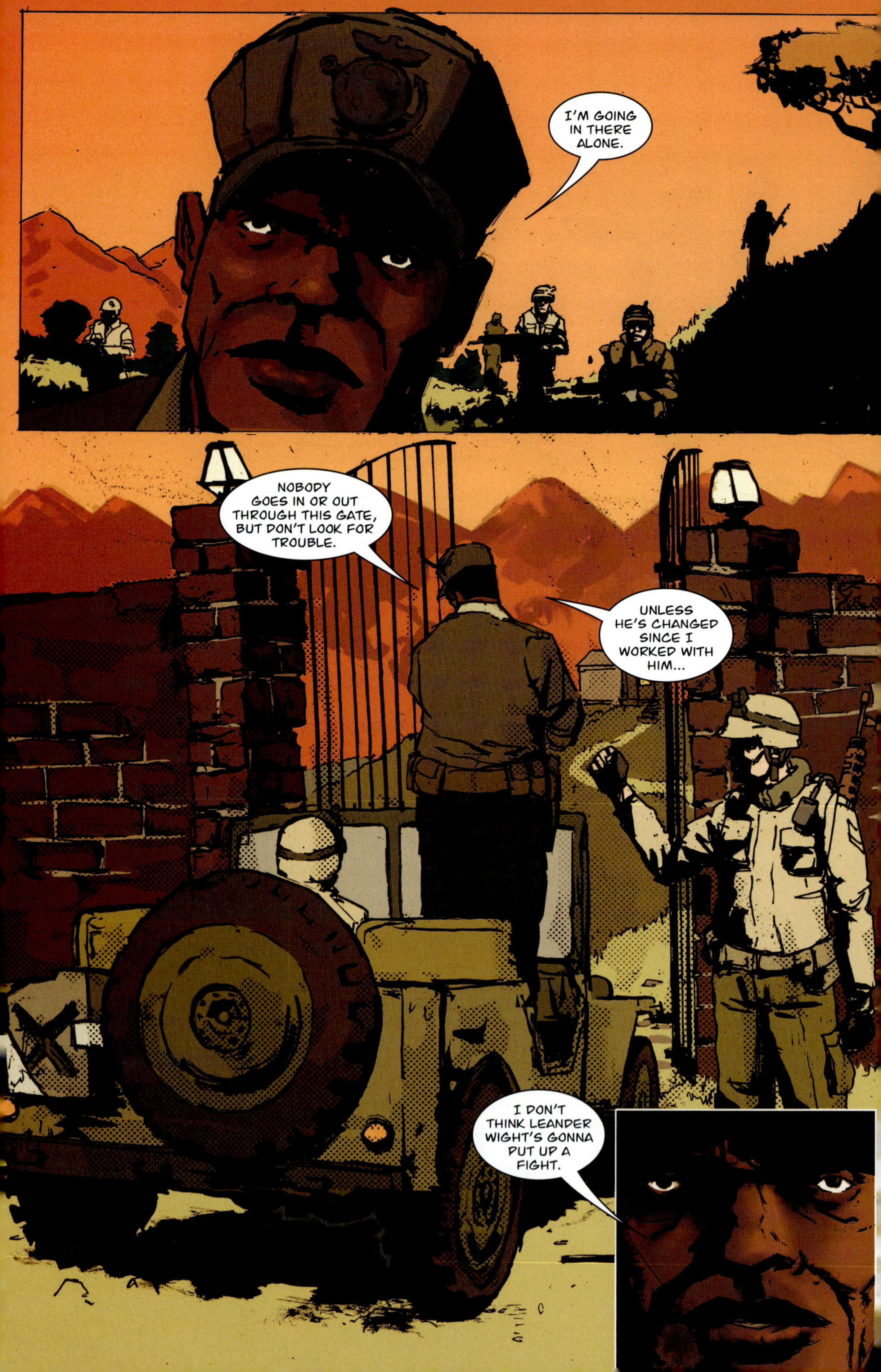
I'M GOING IN THERE ALONE.
NOBODY GOES IN OR OUT THROUGH THIS GATE, BUT DON'T LOOK FOR TROUBLE.
UNLESS HE'S CHANGED SINCE I WORKED WITH HIM...
I DON'T THINK LEANDER WIGHT'S GONNA PUT UP A FIGHT.

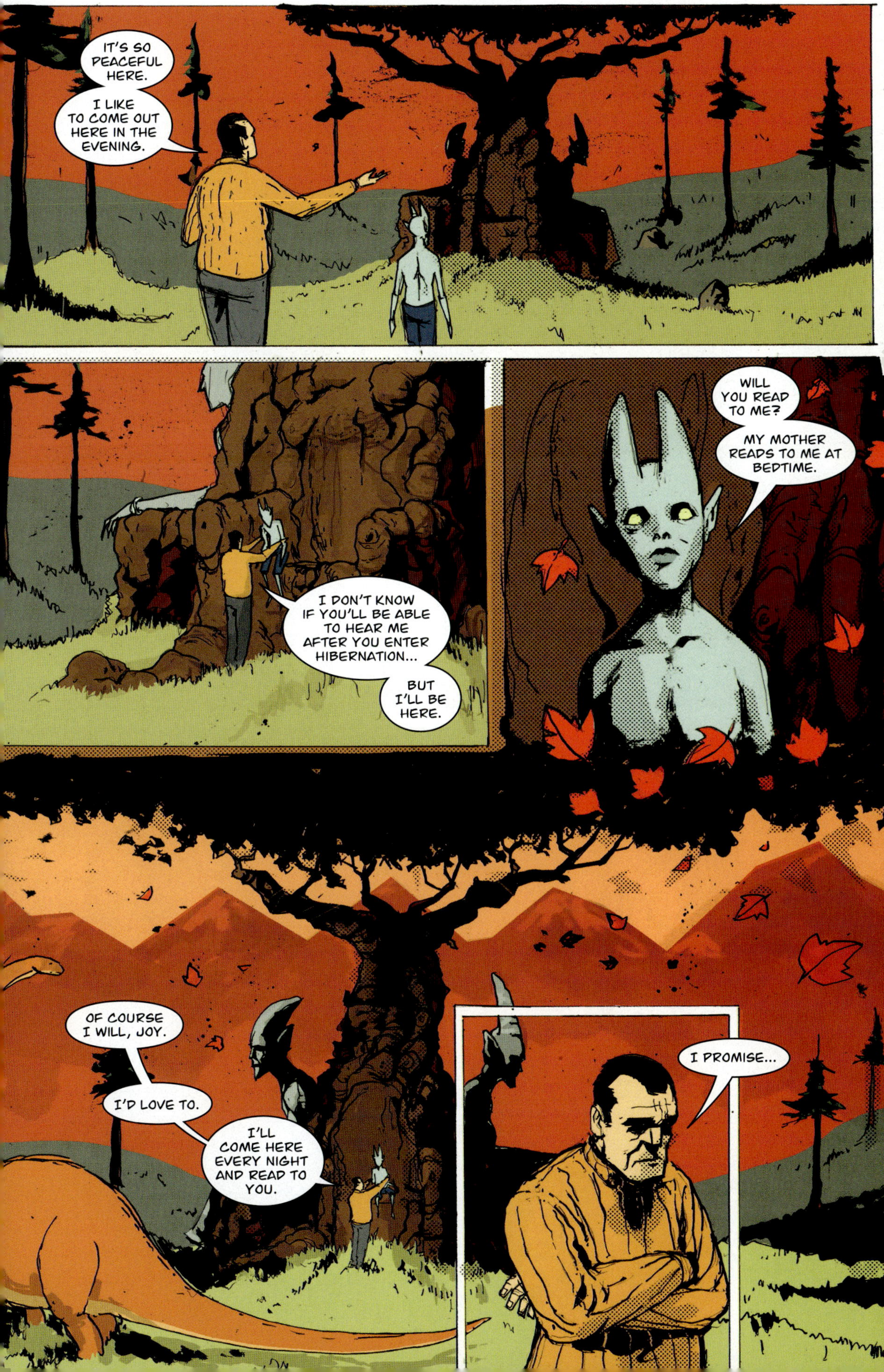
IT'S SO PEACEFUL HERE.
I LIKE TO COME OUT HERE IN THE EVENING.
I DON'T KNOW IF YOU'LL BE ABLE TO HEAR ME AFTER YOU ENTER HIBERNATION...
BUT I'LL BE HERE.
WILL YOU READ TO ME?
MY MOTHER READS TO ME AT BEDTIME.
OF COURSE I WILL, JOY.
I'D LOVE TO.
I'LL COME HERE EVERY NIGHT AND READ TO YOU.
I PROMISE...

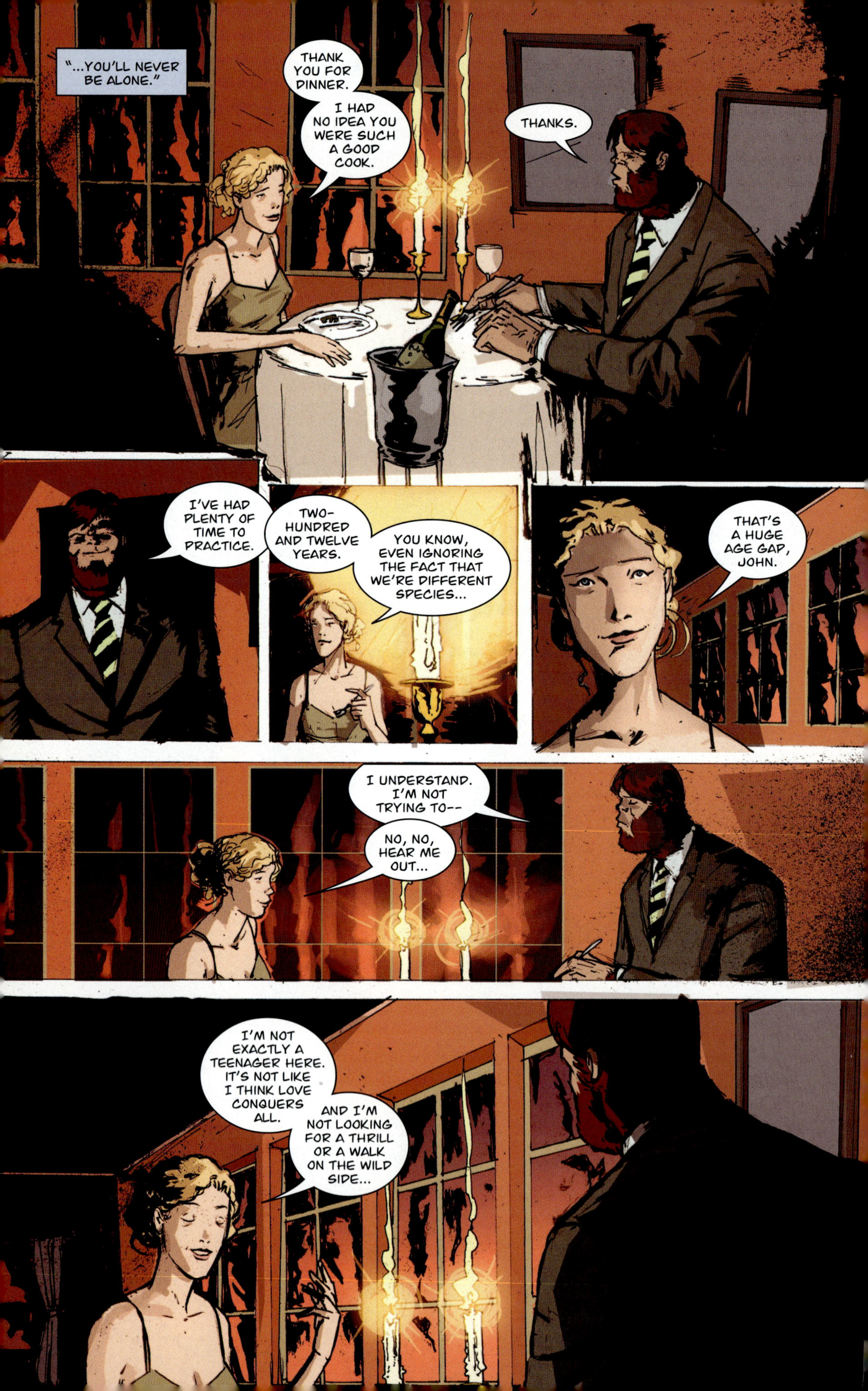
"...YOU'LL NEVER BE ALONE."
THANK YOU FOR DINNER.
I HAD NO IDEA YOU WERE SUCH A GOOD COOK.
THANKS.
I'VE HAD PLENTY OF TIME TO PRACTICE.
TWO-HUNDRED AND TWELVE YEARS.
YOU KNOW, EVEN IGNORING THE FACT THAT WE'RE DIFFERENT SPECIES...
THAT'S A HUGE AGE GAP, JOHN.
I UNDERSTAND. I'M NOT TRYING TO--
NO, NO, HEAR ME OUT...
I'M NOT EXACTLY A TEENAGER HERE. IT'S NOT LIKE I THINK LOVE CONQUERS ALL.
AND I'M NOT LOOKING FOR A THRILL OR A WALK ON THE WILD SIDE...

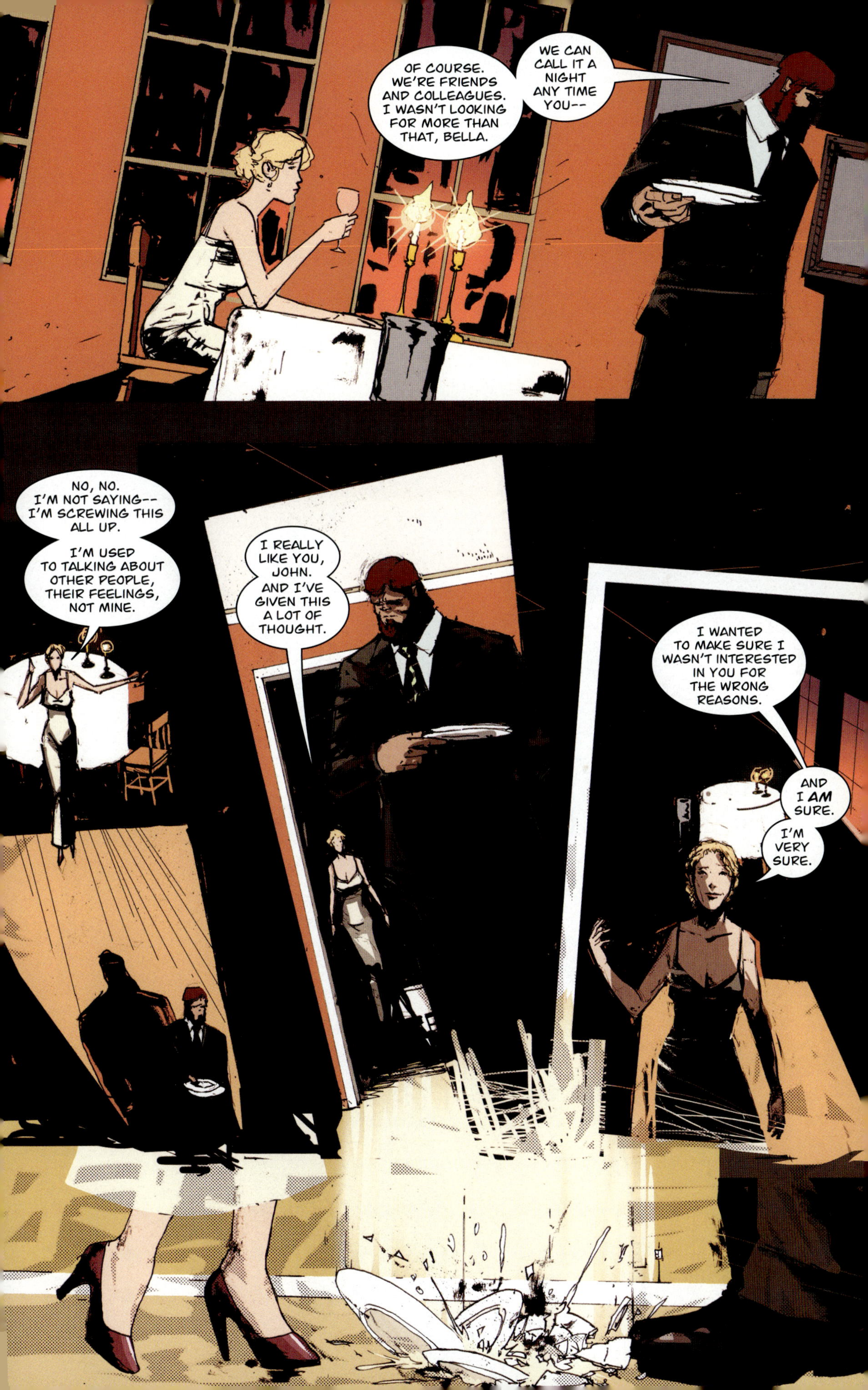
OF COURSE. WE'RE FRIENDS AND COLLEAGUES. I WASN'T LOOKING FOR MORE THAN THAT, BELLA.
WE CAN CALL IT A NIGHT ANY TIME YOU--
NO, NO. I'M NOT SAYING-- I'M SCREWING THIS ALL UP.
I'M USED TO TALKING ABOUT OTHER PEOPLE, THEIR FEELINGS, NOT MINE.
I REALLY LIKE YOU, JOHN. AND I'VE GIVEN THIS A LOT OF THOUGHT.
I WANTED TO MAKE SURE I WASN'T INTERESTED IN YOU FOR THE WRONG REASONS.
AND I **AM** SURE.
I'M VERY SURE.

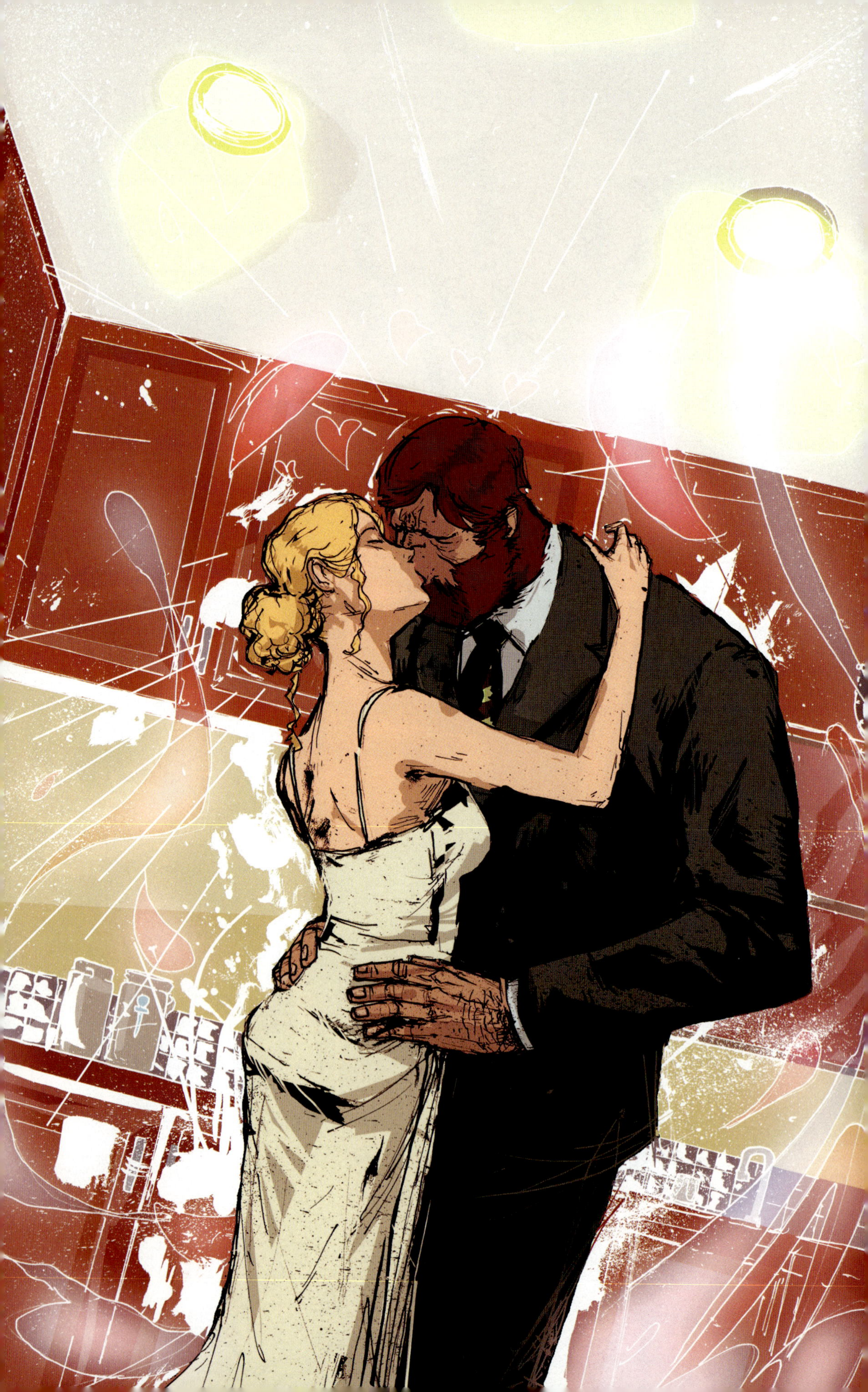

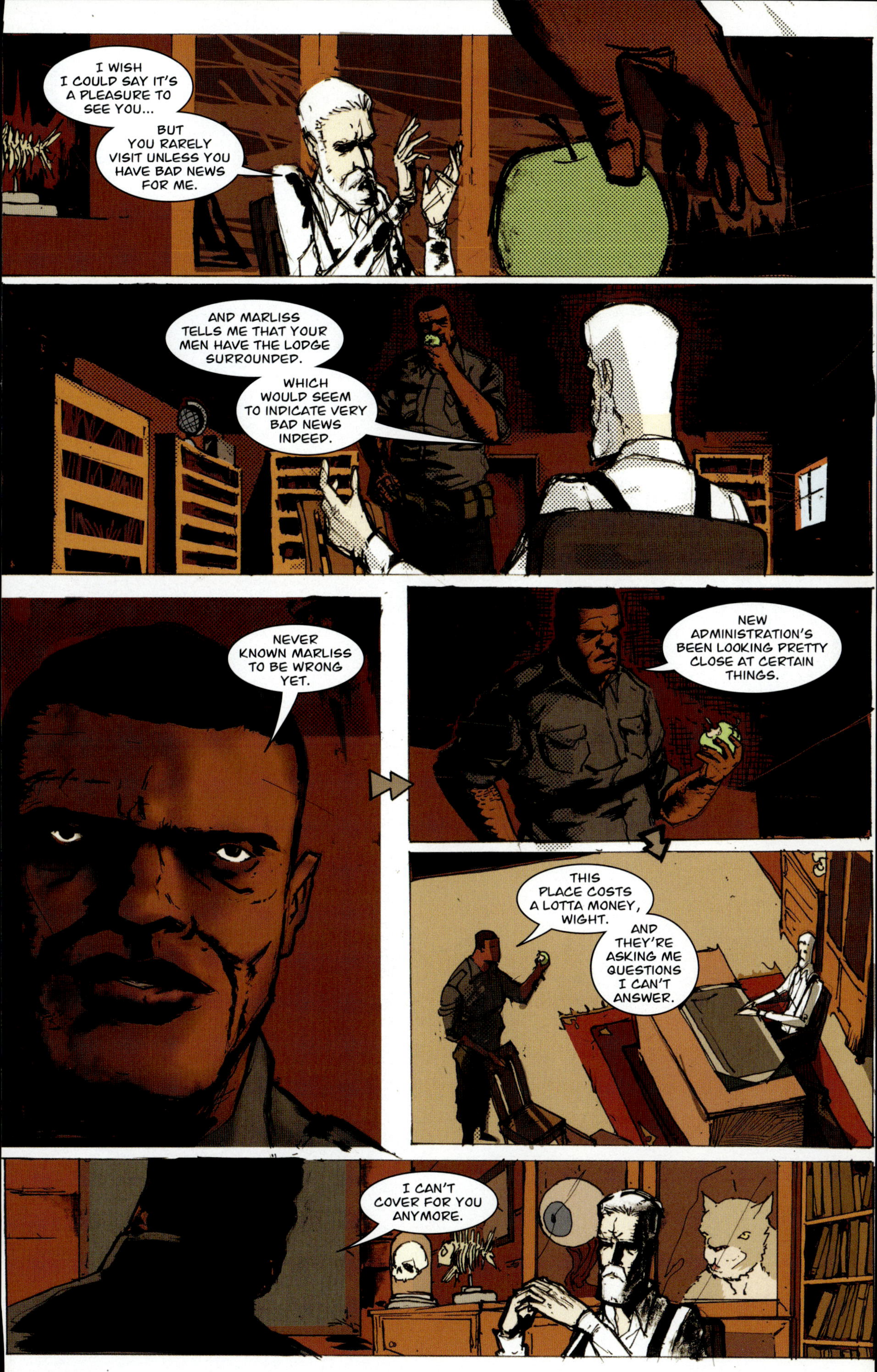
I WISH I COULD SAY IT'S A PLEASURE TO SEE YOU...
BUT YOU RARELY VISIT UNLESS YOU HAVE BAD NEWS FOR ME.
AND MARLISS TELLS ME THAT YOUR MEN HAVE THE LODGE SURROUNDED.
WHICH WOULD SEEM TO INDICATE VERY BAD NEWS INDEED.
NEVER KNOWN MARLISS TO BE WRONG YET.
NEW ADMINISTRATION'S BEEN LOOKING PRETTY CLOSE AT CERTAIN THINGS.
THIS PLACE COSTS A LOTTA MONEY, WIGHT.
AND THEY'RE ASKING ME QUESTIONS I CAN'T ANSWER.
I CAN'T COVER FOR YOU ANYMORE.

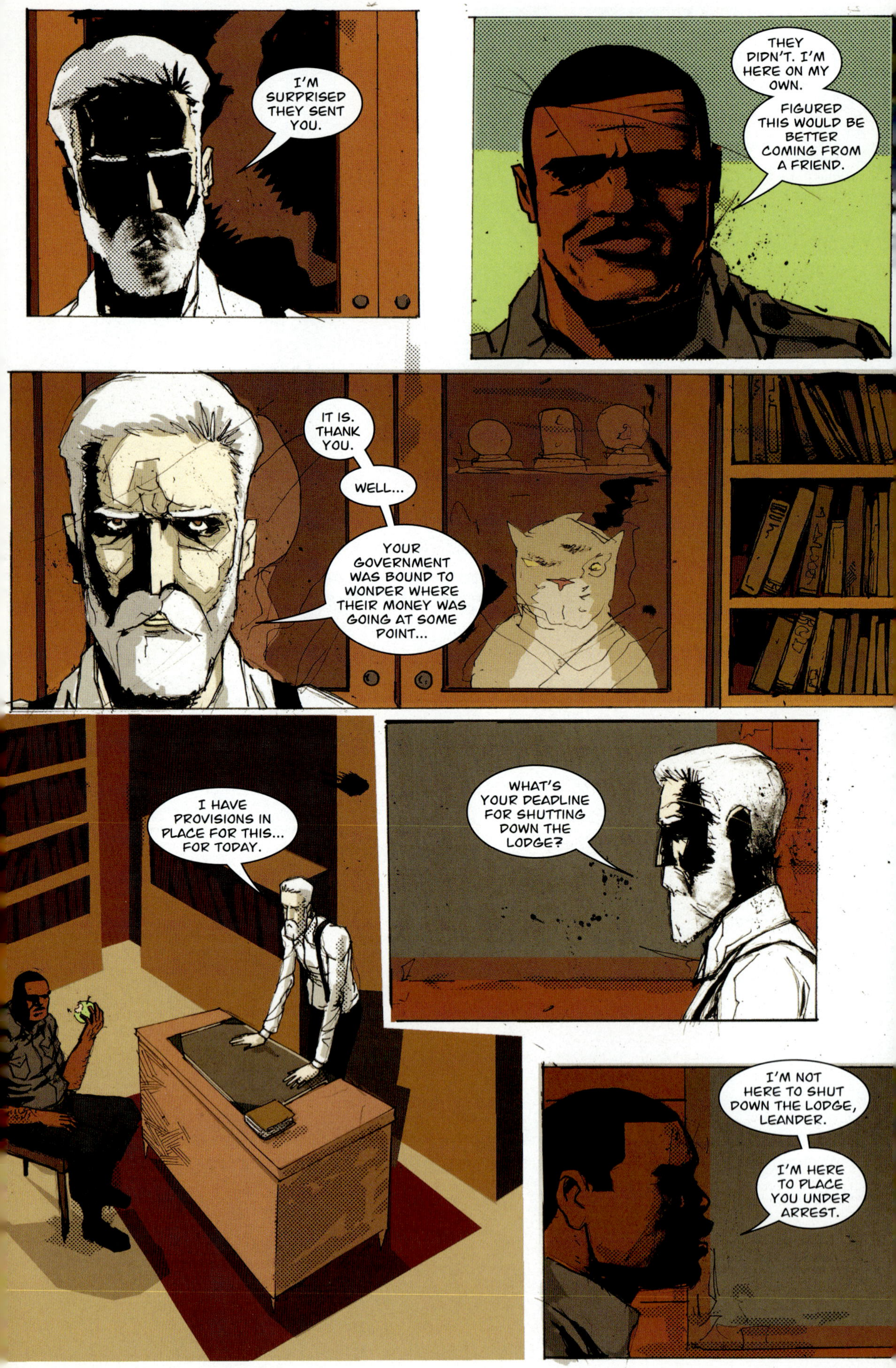
I'M SURPRISED THEY SENT YOU.
THEY DIDN'T. I'M HERE ON MY OWN.
FIGURED THIS WOULD BE BETTER COMING FROM A FRIEND.
IT IS. THANK YOU.
WELL...
YOUR GOVERNMENT WAS BOUND TO WONDER WHERE THEIR MONEY WAS GOING AT SOME POINT...
I HAVE PROVISIONS IN PLACE FOR THIS... FOR TODAY.
WHAT'S YOUR DEADLINE FOR SHUTTING DOWN THE LODGE?
I'M NOT HERE TO SHUT DOWN THE LODGE, LEANDER.
I'M HERE TO PLACE YOU UNDER ARREST.

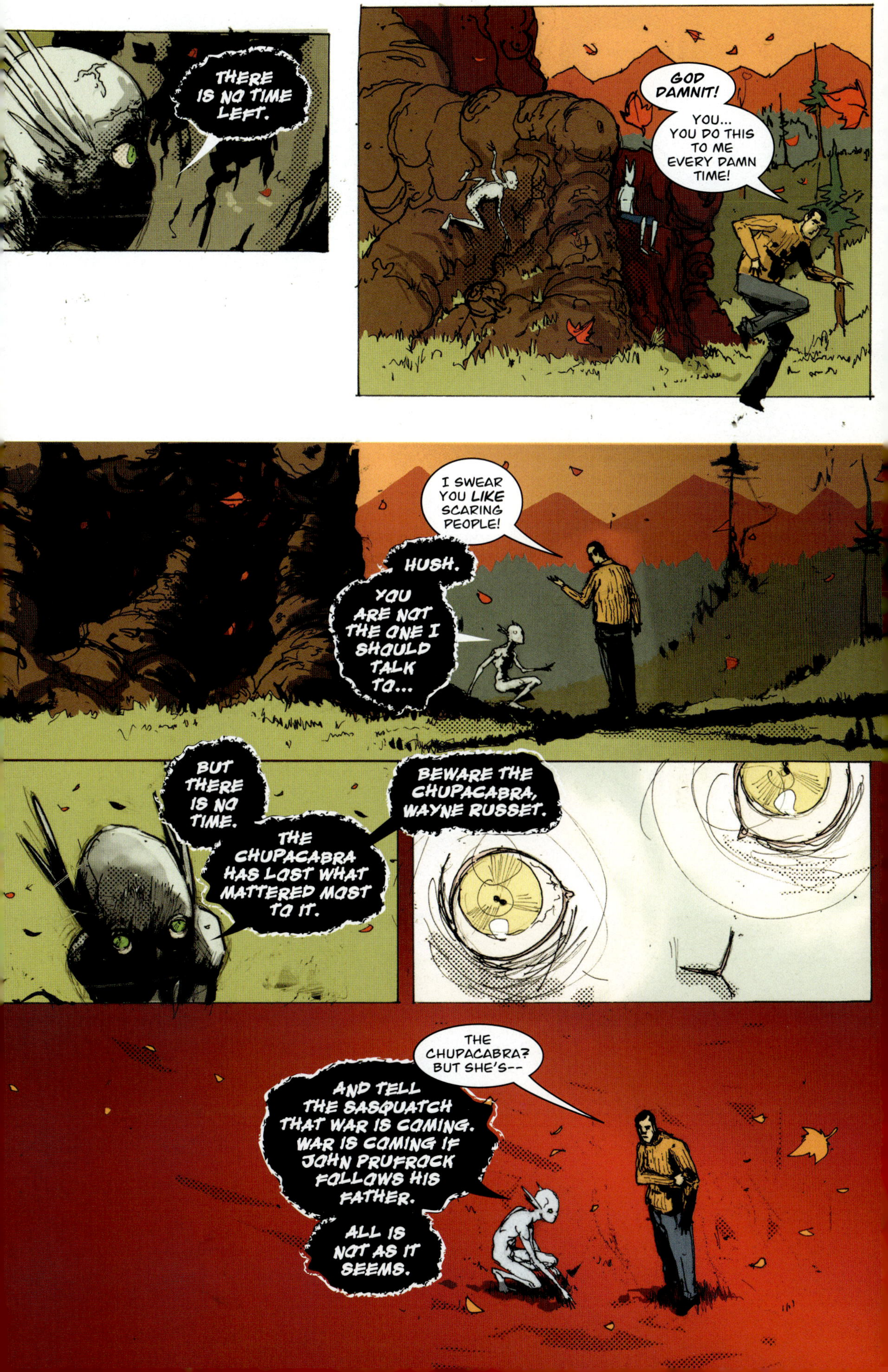
THERE IS NO TIME LEFT.
GOD DAMNIT!
YOU... YOU DO THIS TO ME EVERY DAMN TIME!
I SWEAR YOU LIKE SCARING PEOPLE!
HUSH.
YOU ARE NOT THE ONE I SHOULD TALK TO...
BUT THERE IS NO TIME.
THE CHUPACABRA HAS LOST WHAT MATTERED MOST TO IT.
BEWARE THE CHUPACABRA, WAYNE RUSSET.
THE CHUPACABRA? BUT SHE'S--
AND TELL THE SASQUATCH THAT WAR IS COMING. WAR IS COMING IF JOHN PRUFROCK FOLLOWS HIS FATHER.
ALL IS NOT AS IT SEEMS.

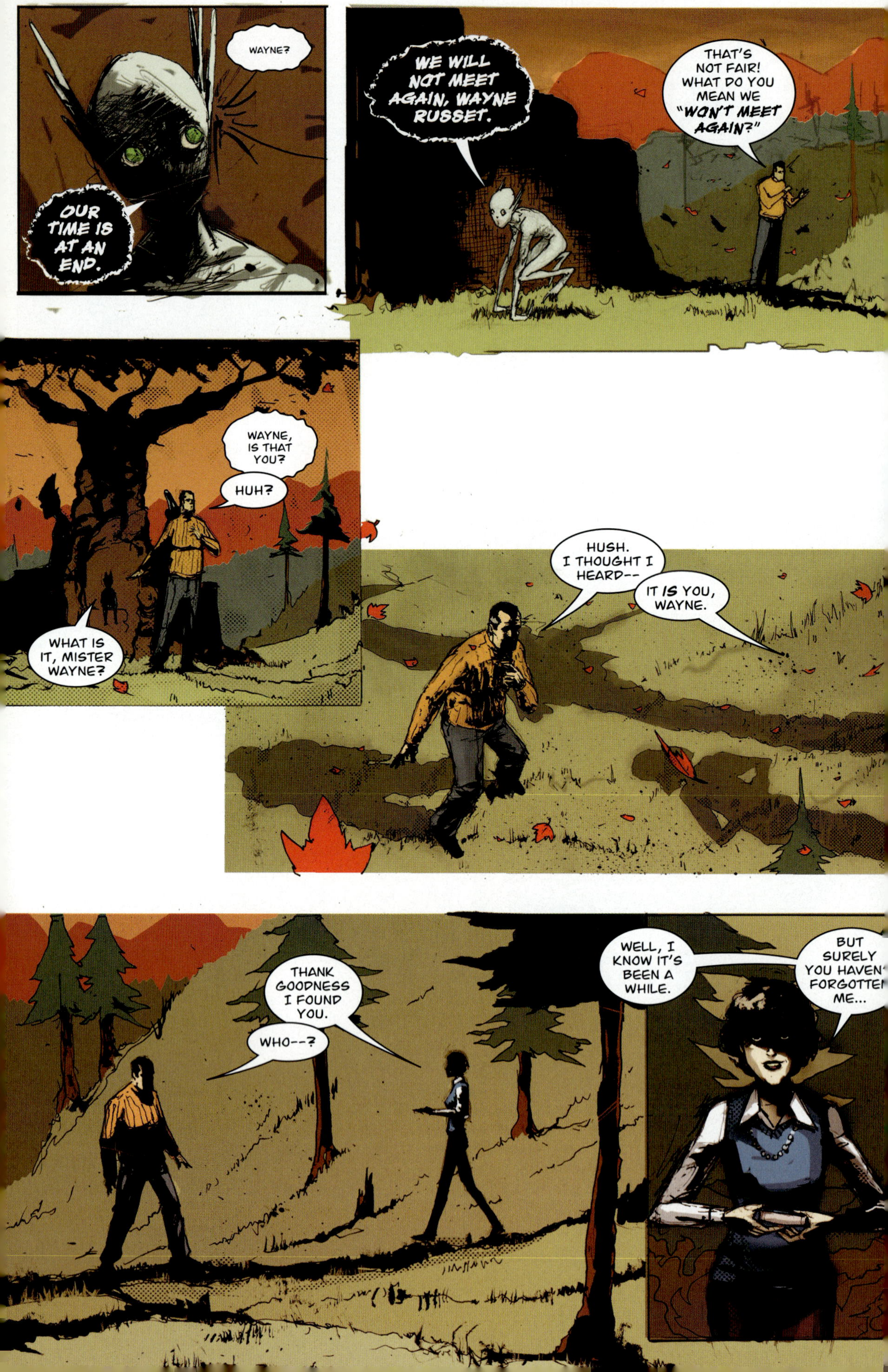
WAYNE?
OUR TIME IS AT AN END.
WE WILL NOT MEET AGAIN, WAYNE RUSSET.
THAT'S NOT FAIR! WHAT DO YOU MEAN WE "WON'T MEET AGAIN?"
WAYNE, IS THAT YOU?
HUH?
WHAT IS IT, MISTER WAYNE?
HUSH. I THOUGHT I HEARD--
IT IS YOU, WAYNE.
THANK GOODNESS I FOUND YOU.
WHO--?
WELL, I KNOW IT'S BEEN A WHILE.
BUT SURELY YOU HAVEN'T FORGOTTEN ME...

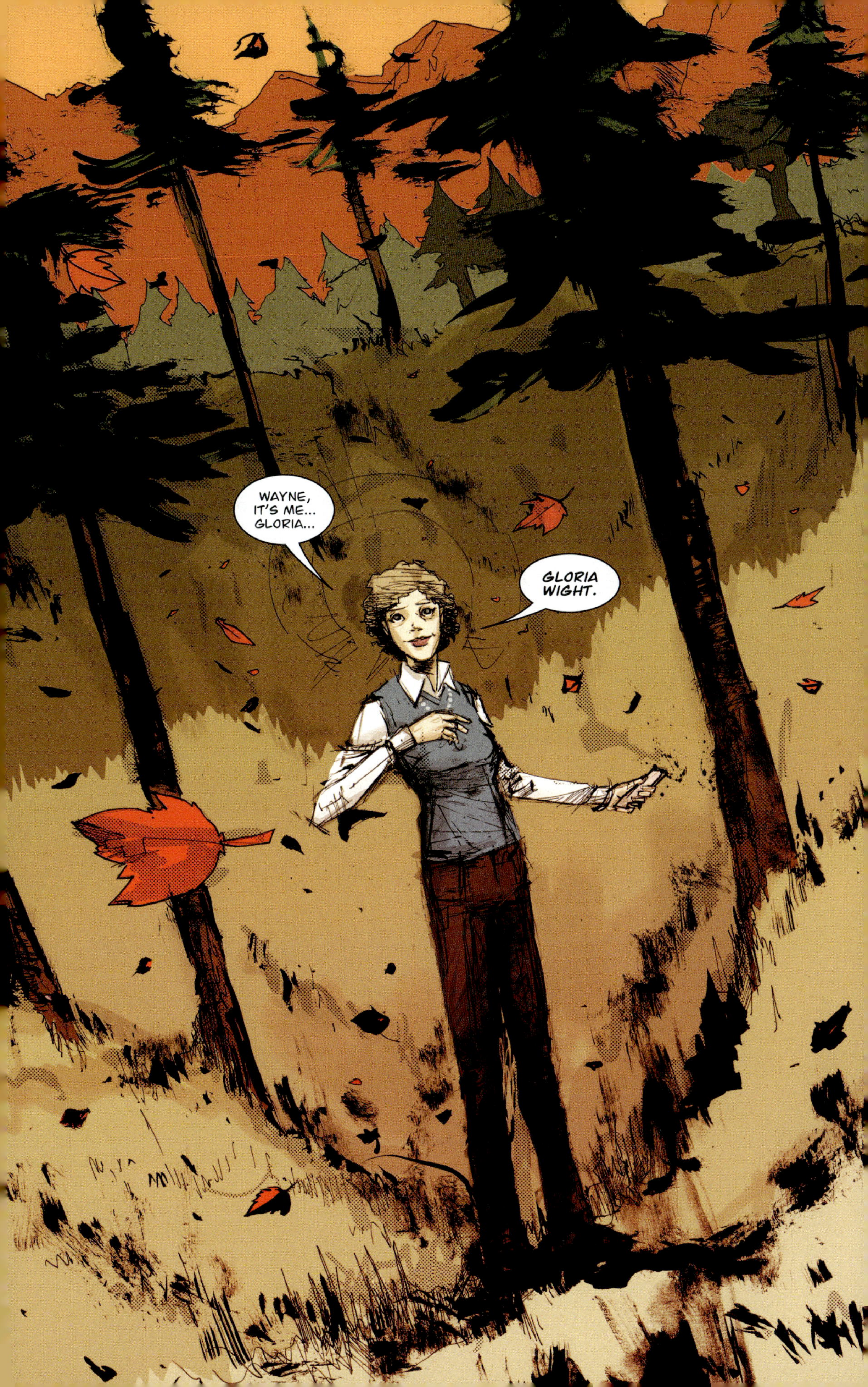
WAYNE, IT'S ME... GLORIA...
GLORIA WIGHT.

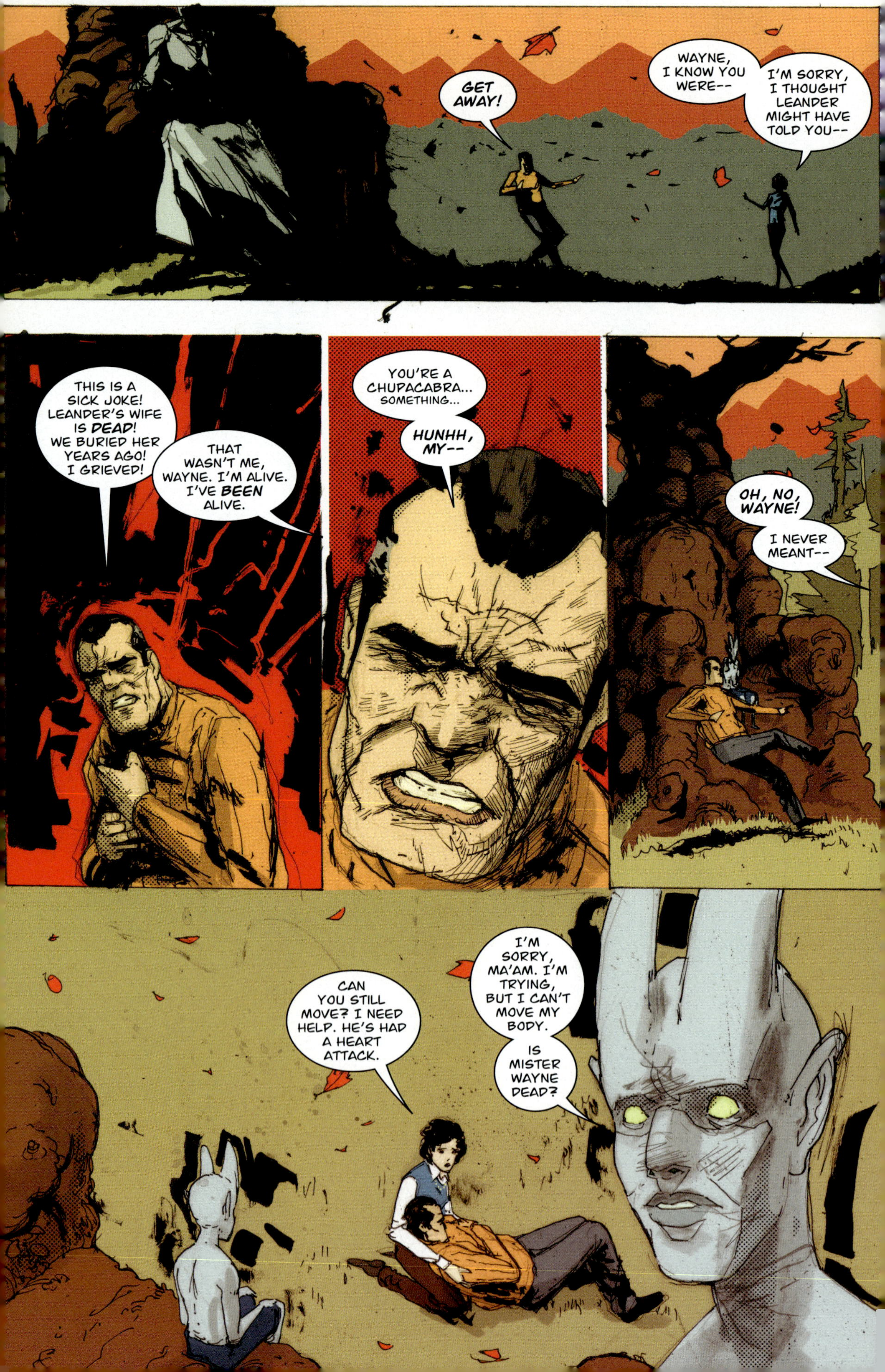
GET AWAY!
WAYNE, I KNOW YOU WERE--
I'M SORRY, I THOUGHT LEANDER MIGHT HAVE TOLD YOU--
THIS IS A SICK JOKE! LEANDER'S WIFE IS DEAD! WE BURIED HER YEARS AGO! I GRIEVED!
THAT WASN'T ME, WAYNE. I'M ALIVE. I'VE BEEN ALIVE.
YOU'RE A CHUPACABRA... SOMETHING...
HUNHH, MY--
OH, NO, WAYNE!
I NEVER MEANT--
CAN YOU STILL MOVE? I NEED HELP. HE'S HAD A HEART ATTACK.
I'M SORRY, MA'AM. I'M TRYING, BUT I CAN'T MOVE MY BODY.
IS MISTER WAYNE DEAD?

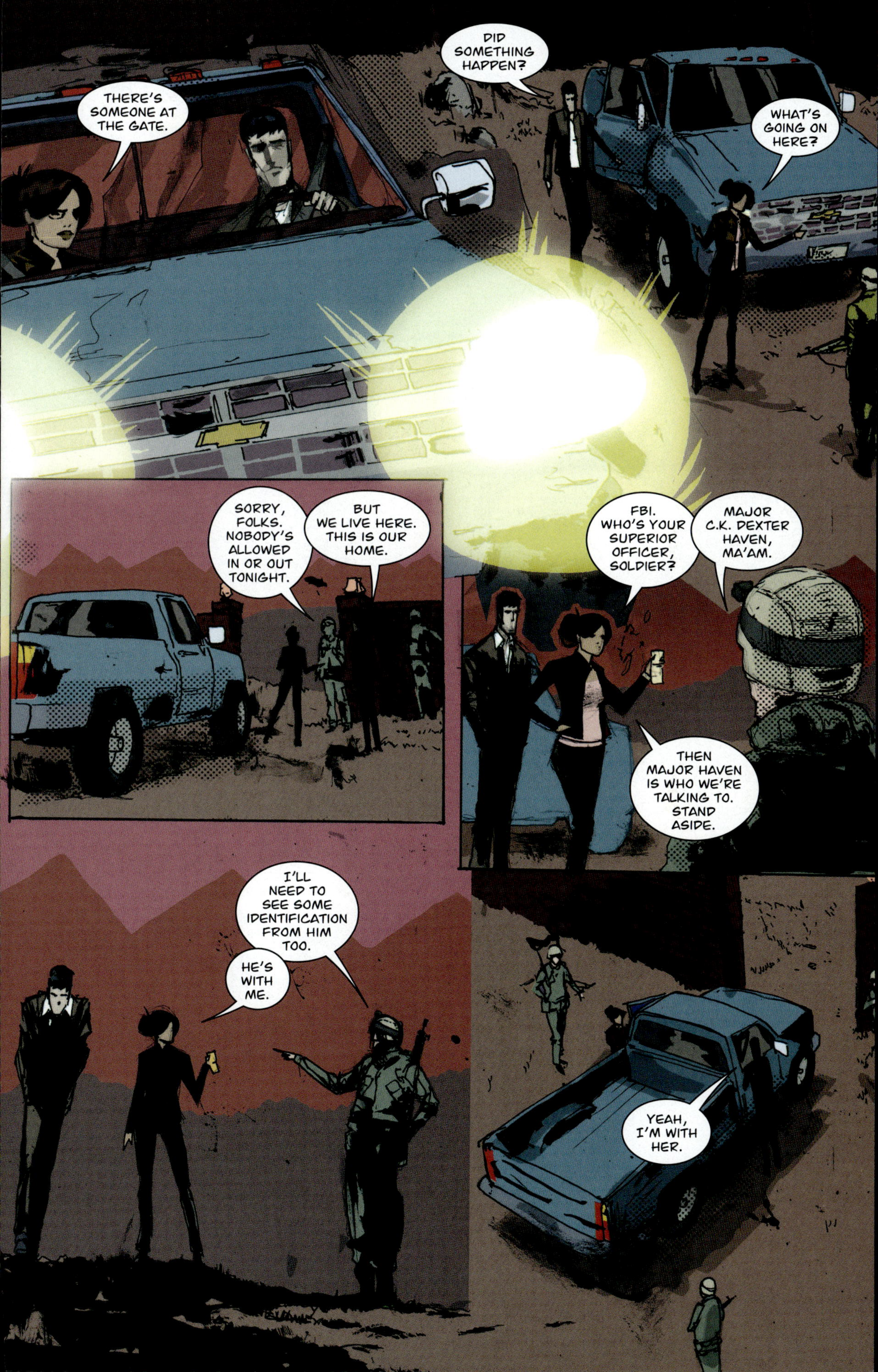
THERE'S SOMEONE AT THE GATE.
DID SOMETHING HAPPEN?
WHAT'S GOING ON HERE?
SORRY, FOLKS. NOBODY'S ALLOWED IN OR OUT TONIGHT.
BUT WE LIVE HERE. THIS IS OUR HOME.
FBI. WHO'S YOUR SUPERIOR OFFICER, SOLDIER?
MAJOR C.K. DEXTER HAVEN, MA'AM.
THEN MAJOR HAVEN IS WHO WE'RE TALKING TO. STAND ASIDE.
I'LL NEED TO SEE SOME IDENTIFICATION FROM HIM TOO.
HE'S WITH ME.
YEAH, I'M WITH HER.

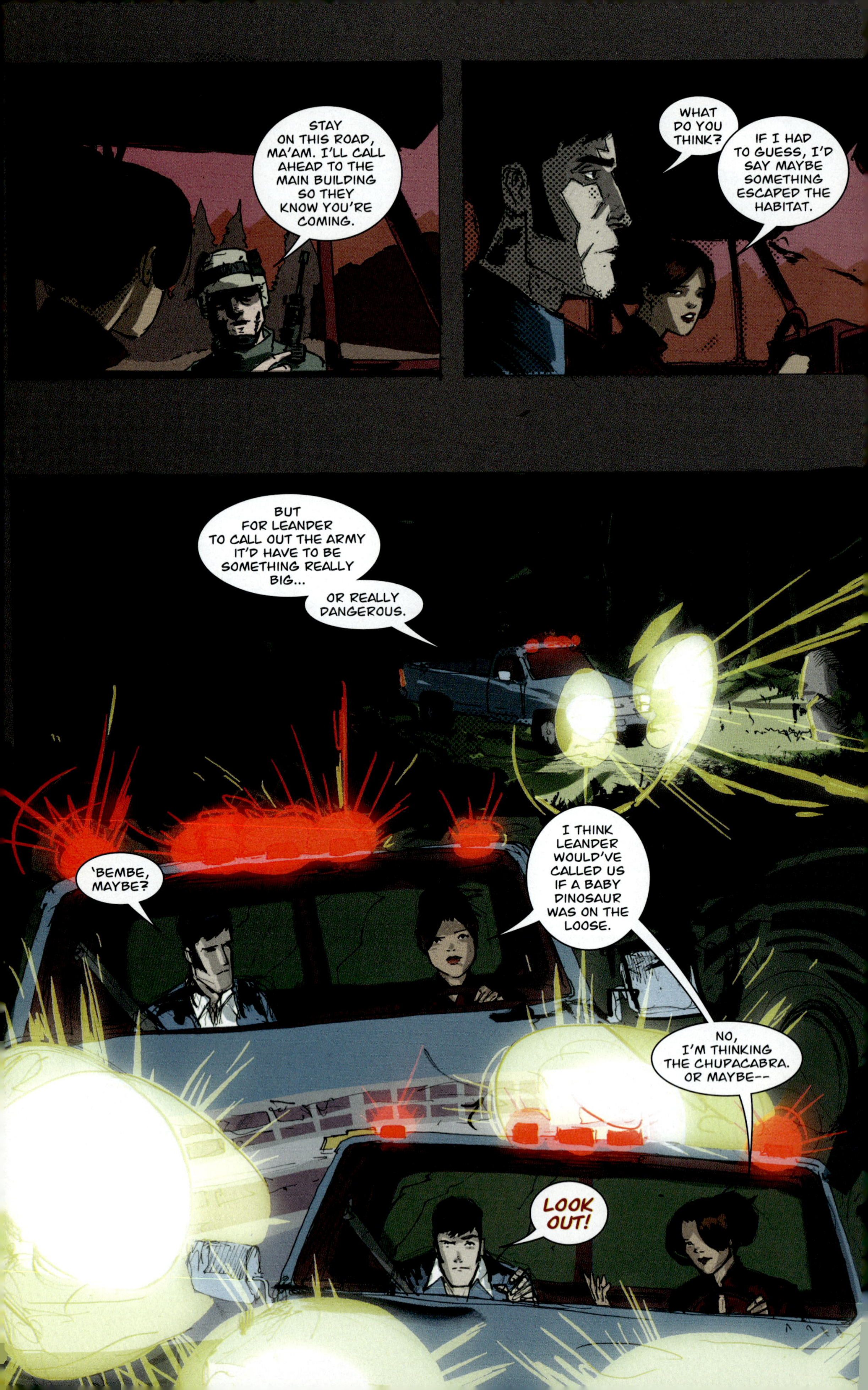
STAY ON THIS ROAD, MA'AM. I'LL CALL AHEAD TO THE MAIN BUILDING SO THEY KNOW YOU'RE COMING.
WHAT DO YOU THINK?
IF I HAD TO GUESS, I'D SAY MAYBE SOMETHING ESCAPED THE HABITAT.
BUT FOR LEANDER TO CALL OUT THE ARMY IT'D HAVE TO BE SOMETHING REALLY BIG...
OR REALLY DANGEROUS.
'BEMBE, MAYBE?
I THINK LEANDER WOULD'VE CALLED US IF A BABY DINOSAUR WAS ON THE LOOSE.
NO, I'M THINKING THE CHUPACABRA. OR MAYBE--
LOOK OUT!

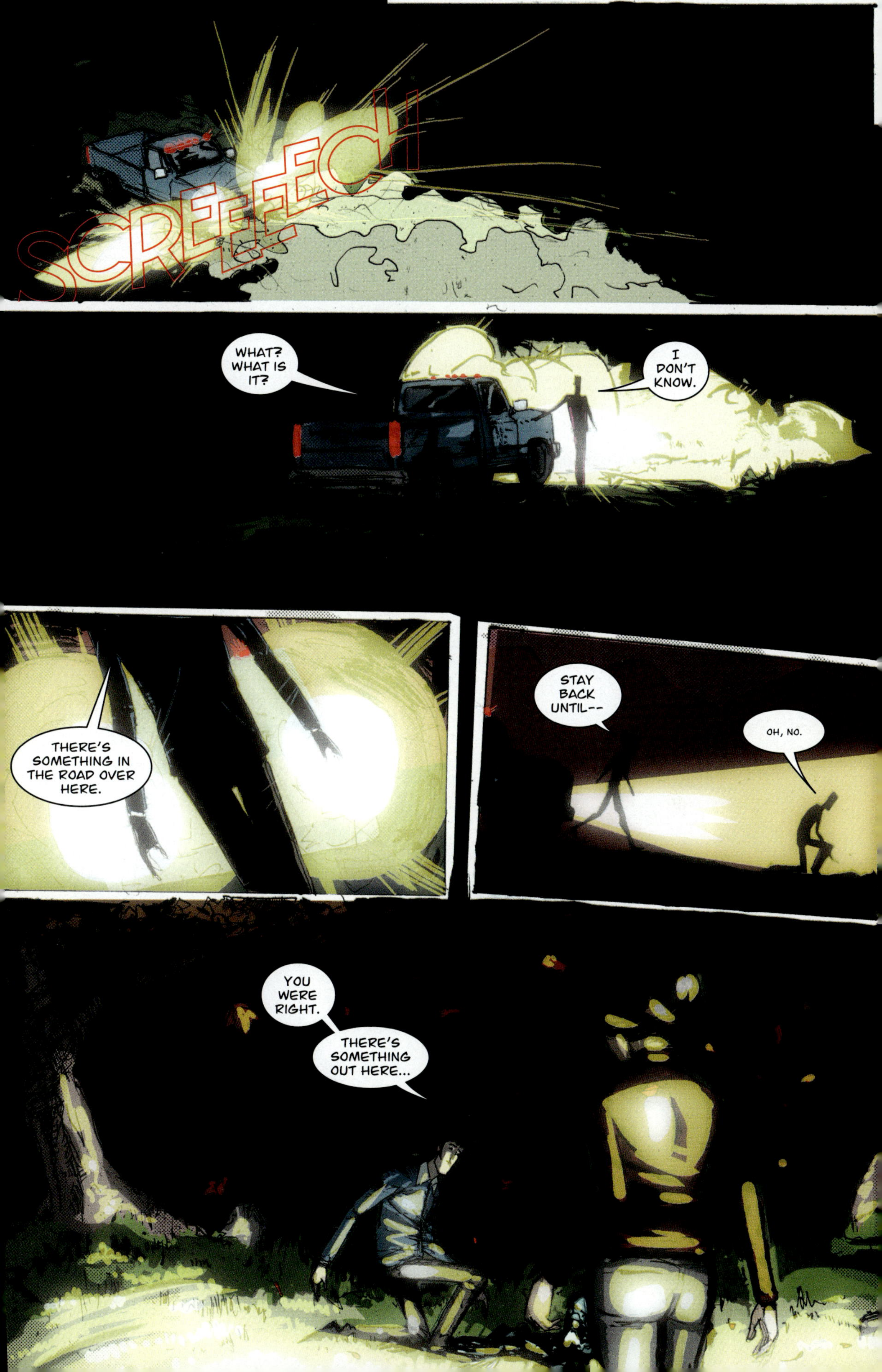
SCREEEECH
WHAT? WHAT IS IT?
I DON'T KNOW.
THERE'S SOMETHING IN THE ROAD OVER HERE.
STAY BACK UNTIL--
OH, NO.
YOU WERE RIGHT.
THERE'S SOMETHING OUT HERE...

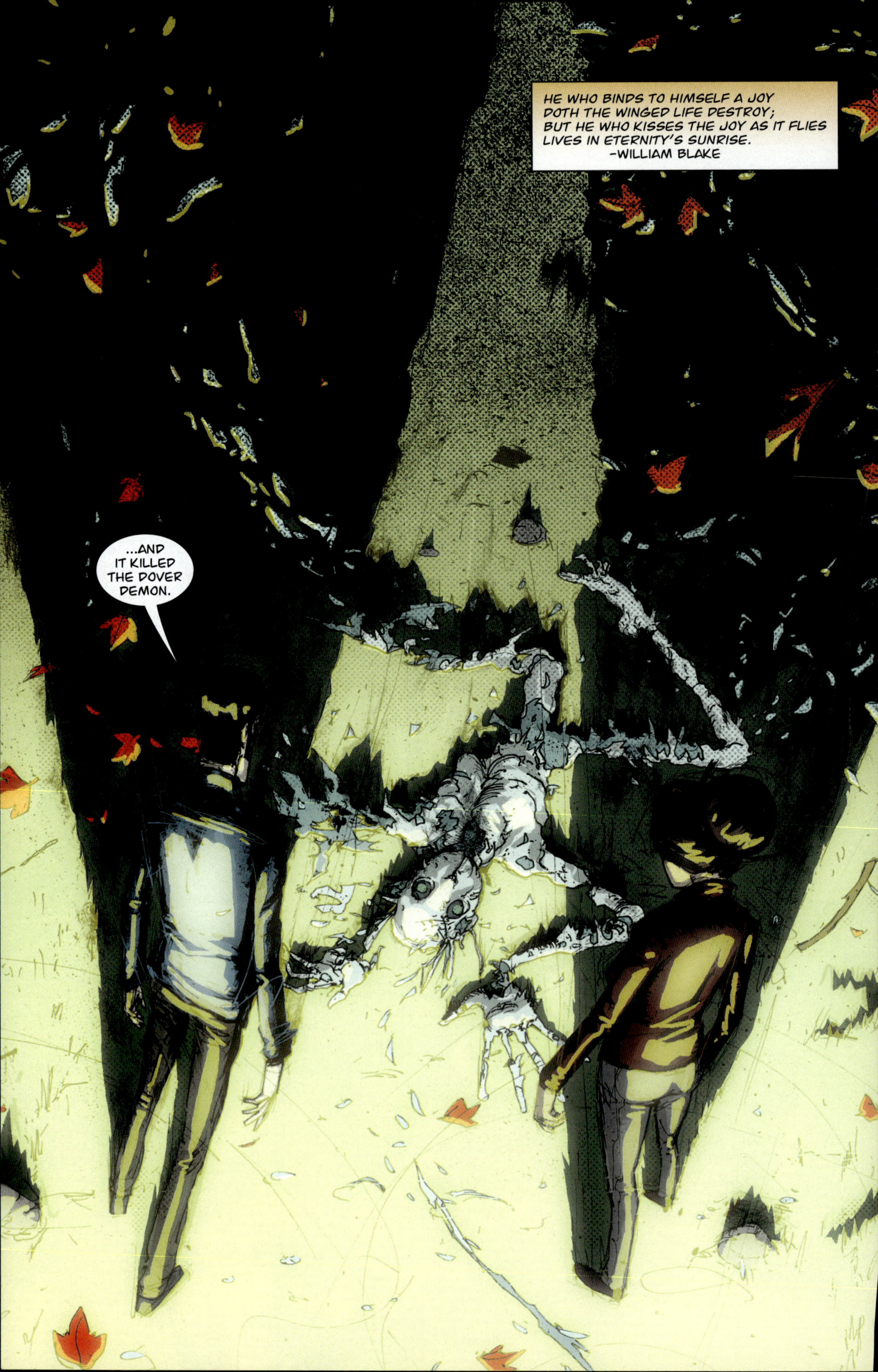
HE WHO BINDS TO HIMSELF A JOY
DOTH THE WINGED LIFE DESTROY;
BUT HE WHO KISSES THE JOY AS IT FLIES
LIVES IN ETERNITY'S SUNRISE.
-WILLIAM BLAKE
...AND IT KILLED THE DOVER DEMON.

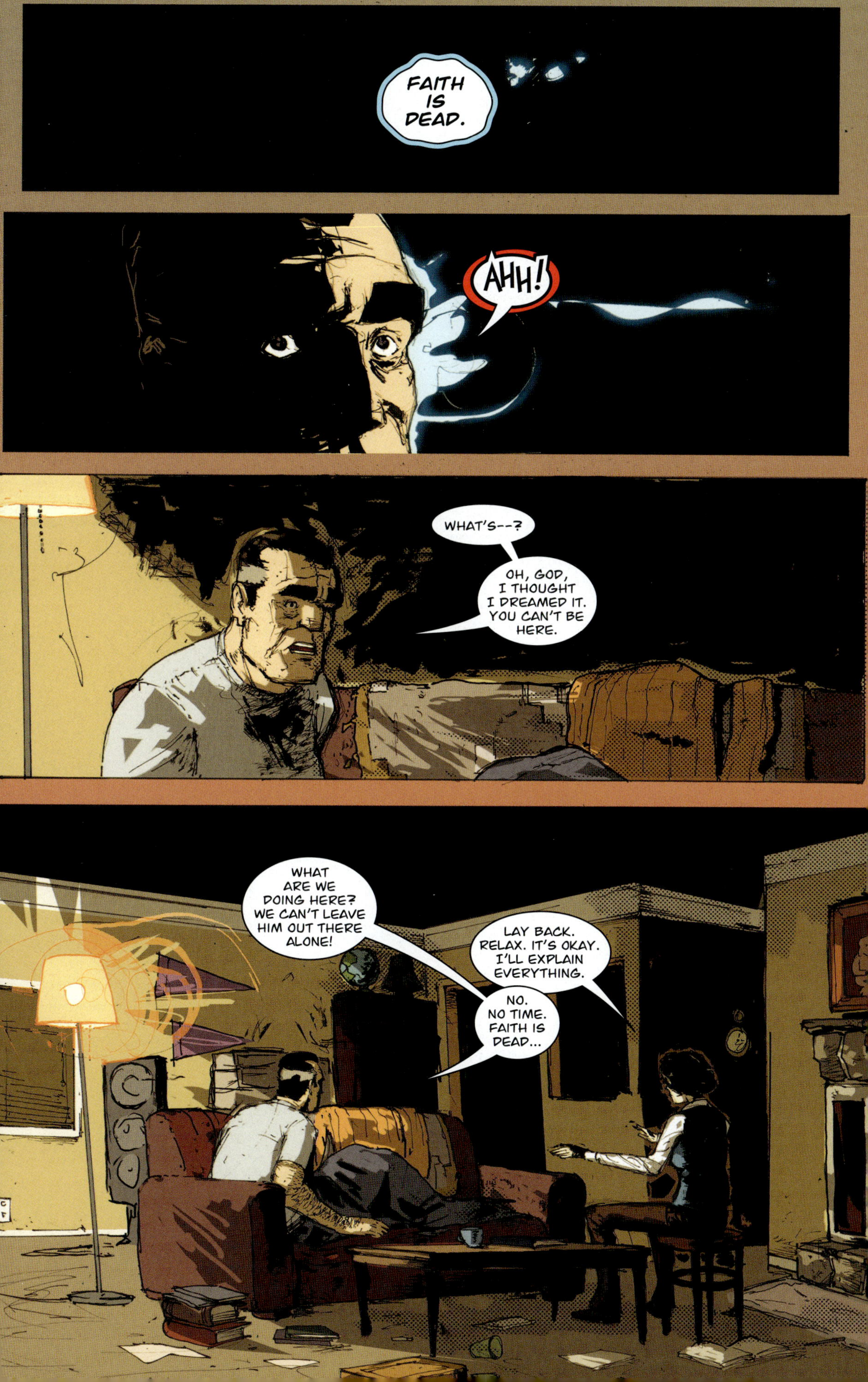
FAITH IS DEAD.
AHH!
WHAT'S--?
OH, GOD, I THOUGHT I DREAMED IT. YOU CAN'T BE HERE.
WHAT ARE WE DOING HERE? WE CAN'T LEAVE HIM OUT THERE ALONE!
LAY BACK. RELAX. IT'S OKAY. I'LL EXPLAIN EVERYTHING.
NO. NO TIME. FAITH IS DEAD...

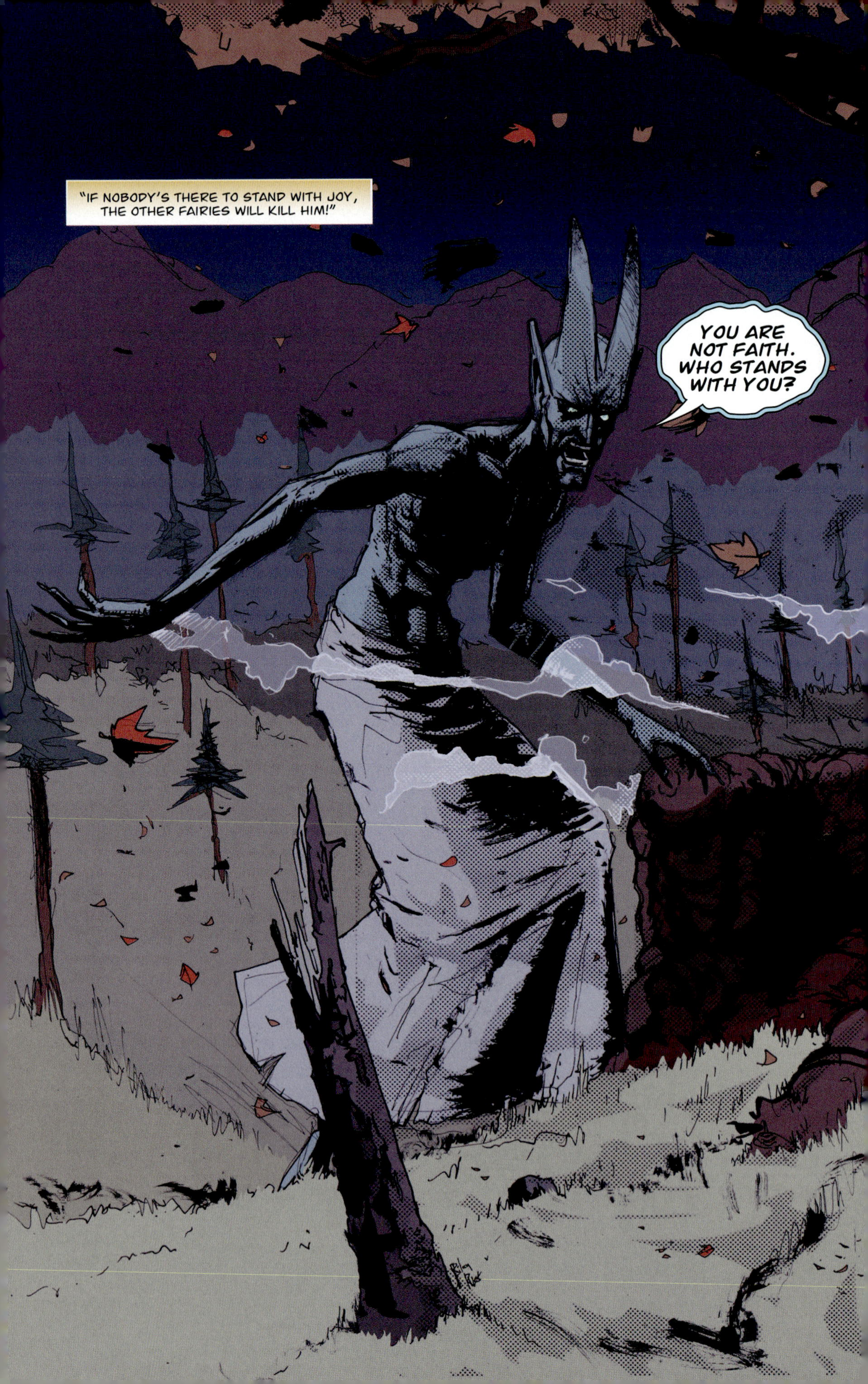
"IF NOBODY'S THERE TO STAND WITH JOY, THE OTHER FAIRIES WILL KILL HIM!"
YOU ARE NOT FAITH. WHO STANDS WITH YOU?

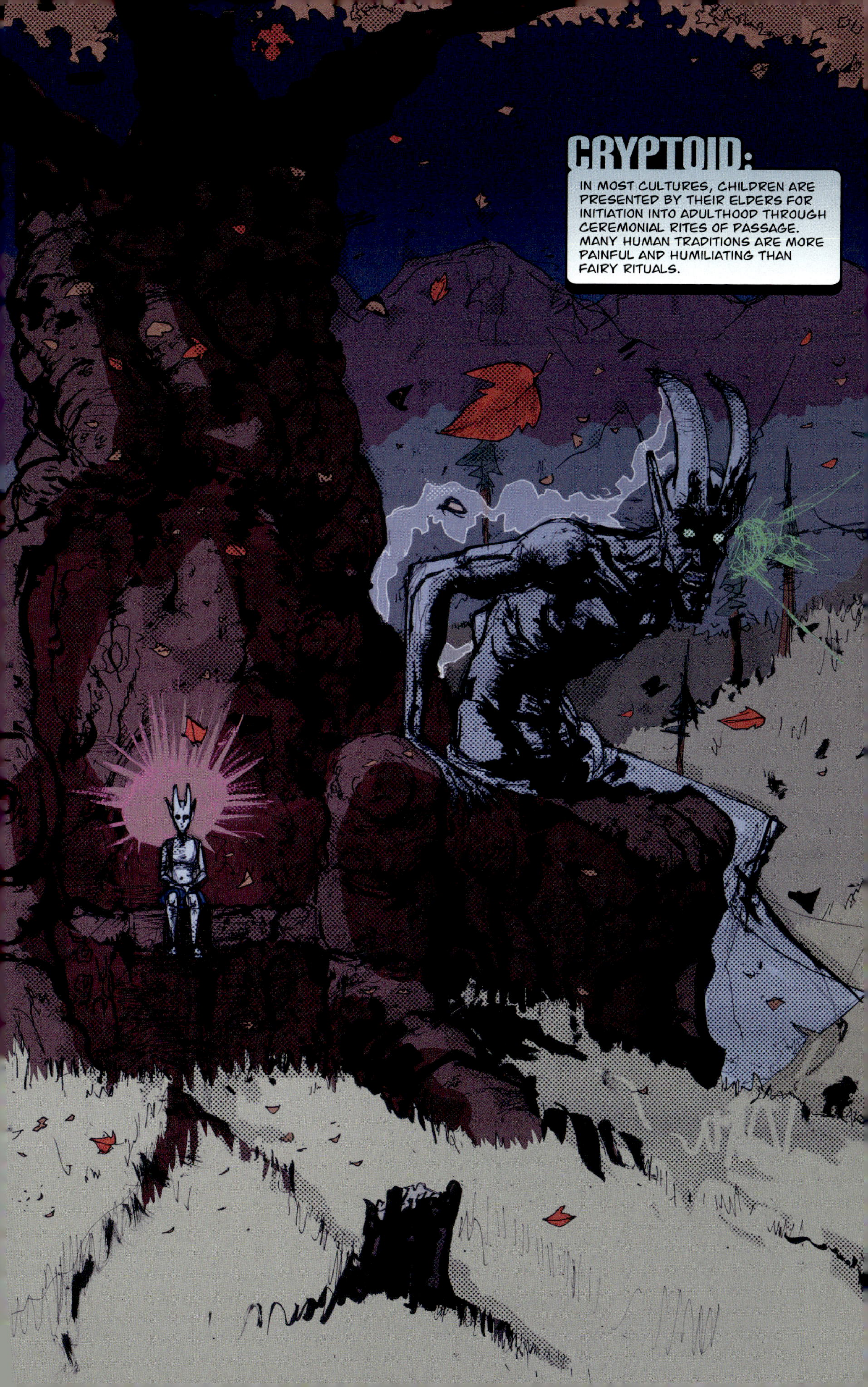
CRYPTOID:
IN MOST CULTURES, CHILDREN ARE PRESENTED BY THEIR ELDERS FOR INITIATION INTO ADULTHOOD THROUGH CEREMONIAL RITES OF PASSAGE. MANY HUMAN TRADITIONS ARE MORE PAINFUL AND HUMILIATING THAN FAIRY RITUALS.

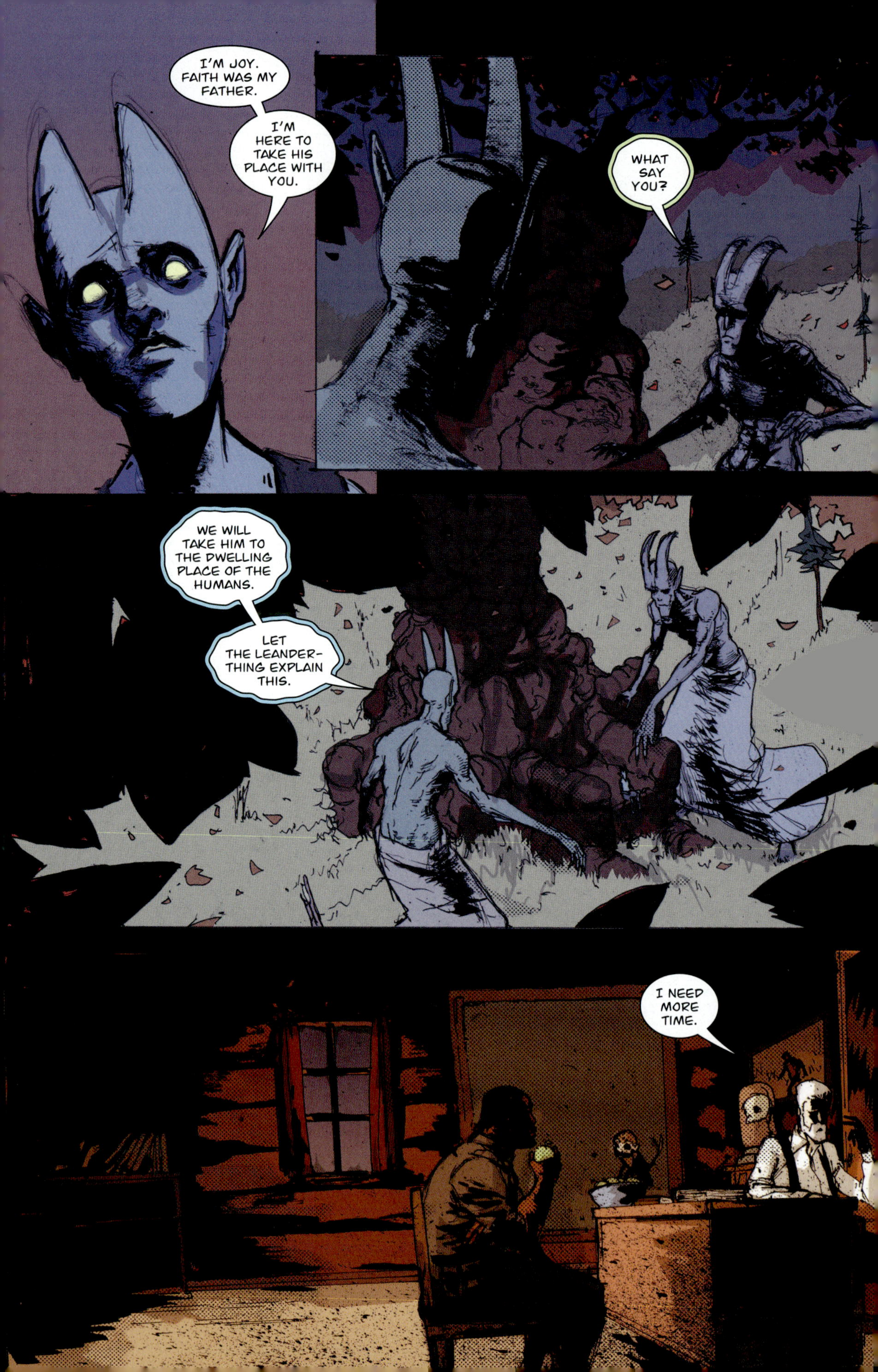
I'M JOY. FAITH WAS MY FATHER.
I'M HERE TO TAKE HIS PLACE WITH YOU.
WHAT SAY YOU?
WE WILL TAKE HIM TO THE DWELLING PLACE OF THE HUMANS.
LET THE LEANDER-THING EXPLAIN THIS.
I NEED MORE TIME.

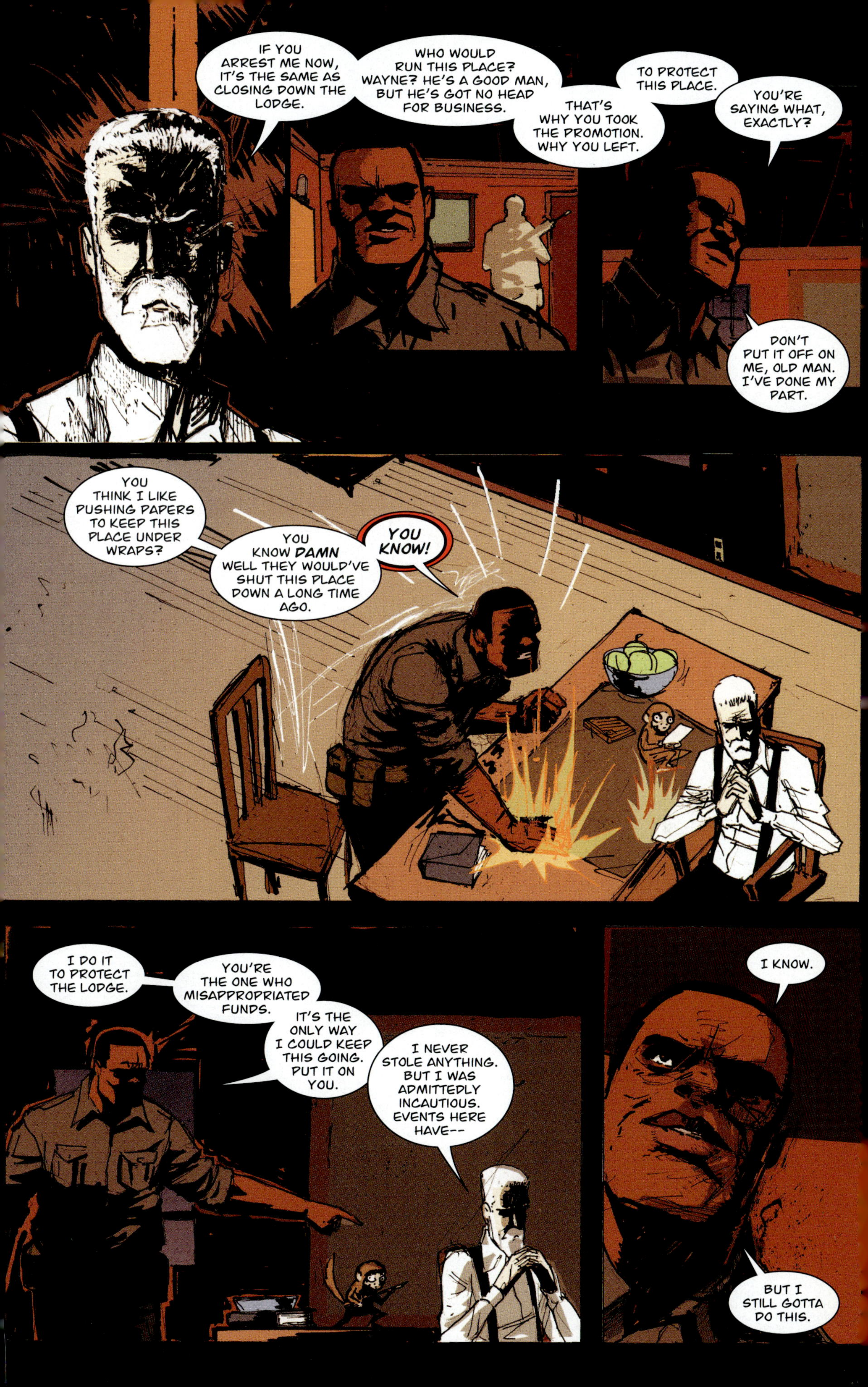
IF YOU ARREST ME NOW, IT'S THE SAME AS CLOSING DOWN THE LODGE.
WHO WOULD RUN THIS PLACE? WAYNE? HE'S A GOOD MAN, BUT HE'S GOT NO HEAD FOR BUSINESS.
THAT'S WHY YOU TOOK THE PROMOTION. WHY YOU LEFT.
TO PROTECT THIS PLACE.
YOU'RE SAYING WHAT, EXACTLY?
DON'T PUT IT OFF ON ME, OLD MAN. I'VE DONE MY PART.
YOU THINK I LIKE PUSHING PAPERS TO KEEP THIS PLACE UNDER WRAPS?
YOU KNOW **DAMN** WELL THEY WOULD'VE SHUT THIS PLACE DOWN A LONG TIME AGO.
YOU KNOW!
I DO IT TO PROTECT THE LODGE.
YOU'RE THE ONE WHO MISAPPROPRIATED FUNDS.
IT'S THE ONLY WAY I COULD KEEP THIS GOING. PUT IT ON YOU.
I NEVER STOLE ANYTHING. BUT I WAS ADMITTEDLY INCAUTIOUS. EVENTS HERE HAVE--
I KNOW.
BUT I STILL GOTTA DO THIS.

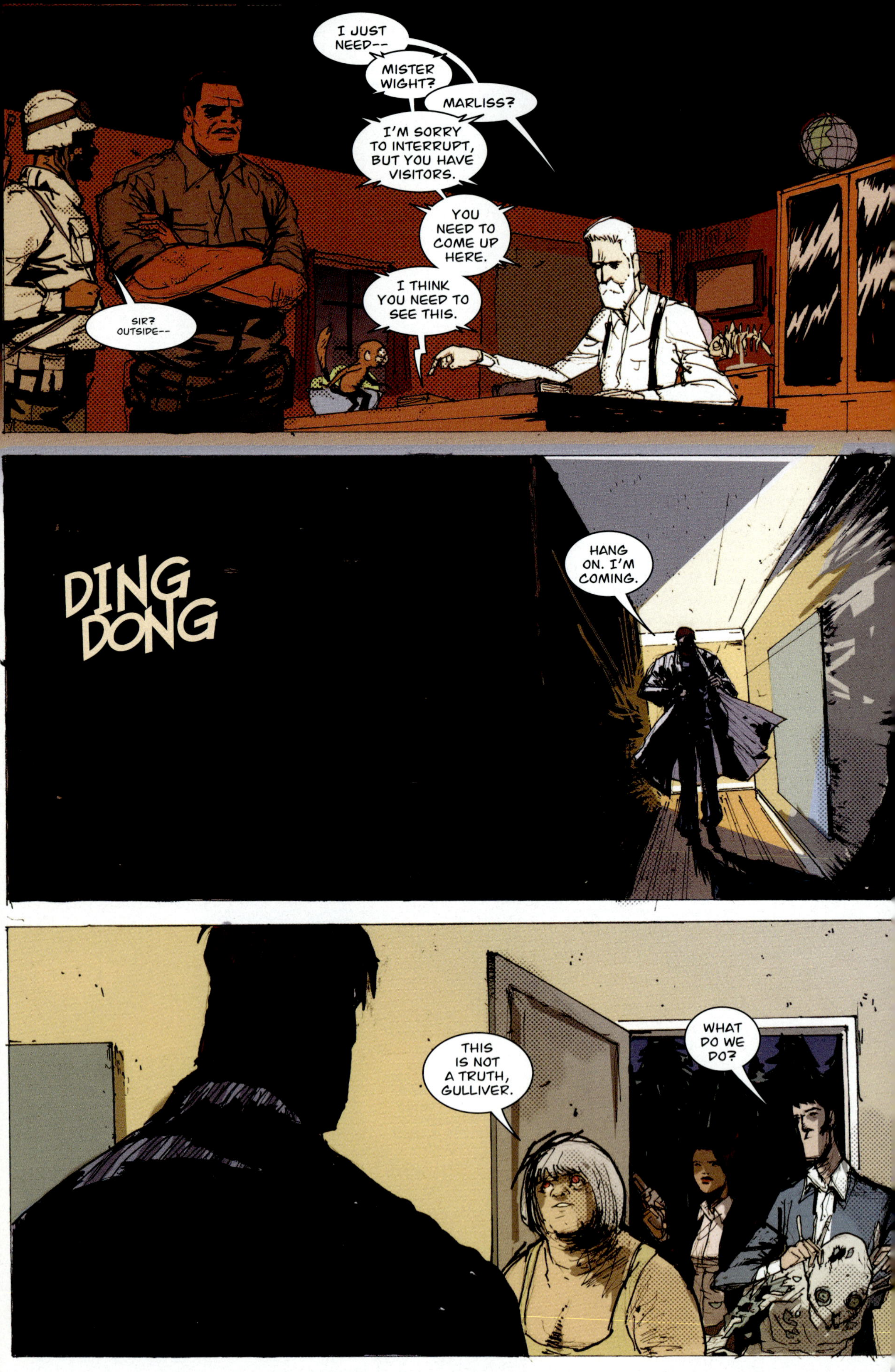
I JUST NEED--
MISTER WIGHT?
MARLISS?
I'M SORRY TO INTERRUPT, BUT YOU HAVE VISITORS.
YOU NEED TO COME UP HERE.
I THINK YOU NEED TO SEE THIS.
SIR? OUTSIDE--
DING DONG
HANG ON. I'M COMING.
THIS IS NOT A TRUTH, GULLIVER.
WHAT DO WE DO?

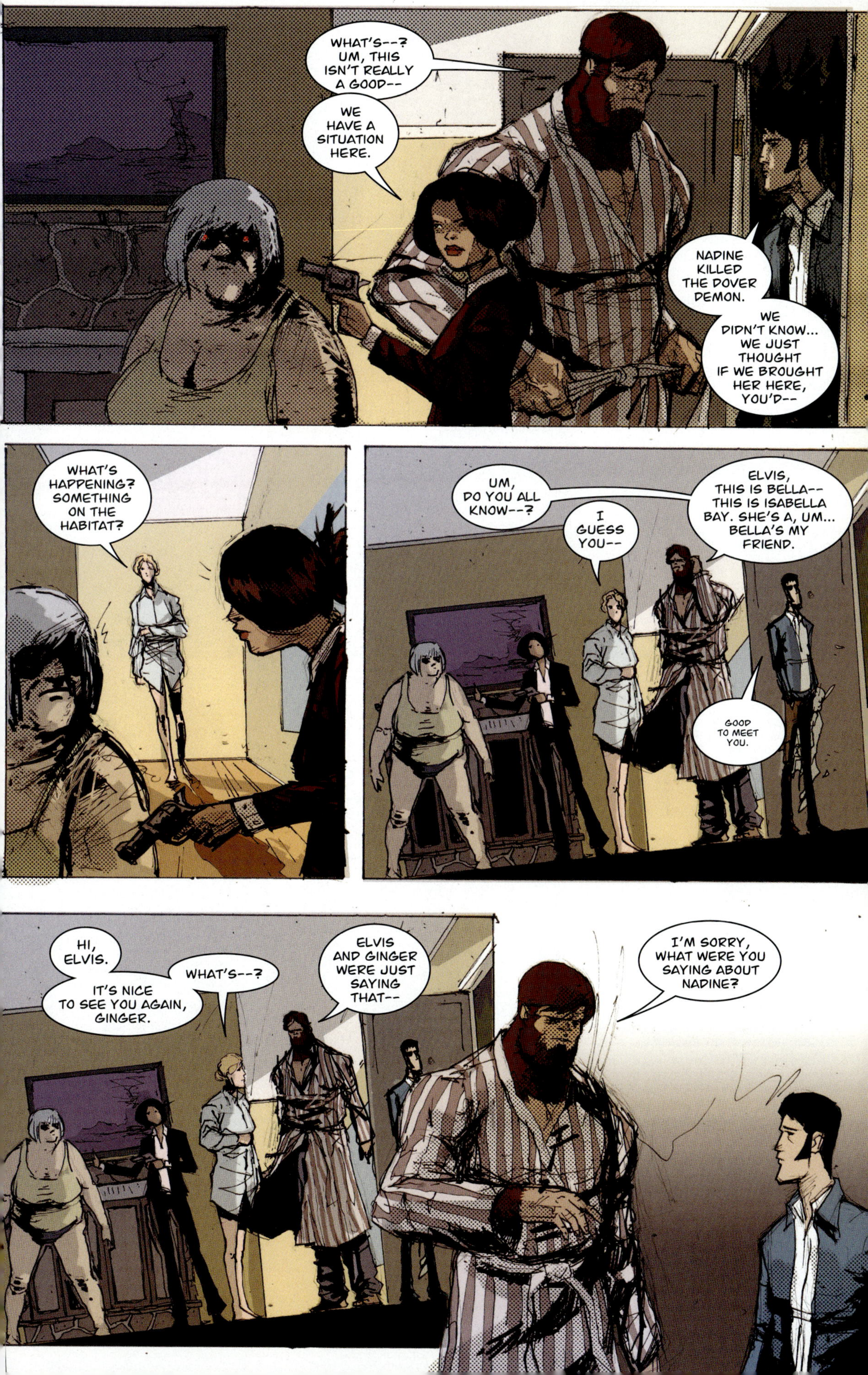
WHAT'S--? UM, THIS ISN'T REALLY A GOOD--
WE HAVE A SITUATION HERE.
NADINE KILLED THE DOVER DEMON.
WE DIDN'T KNOW... WE JUST THOUGHT IF WE BROUGHT HER HERE, YOU'D--
WHAT'S HAPPENING? SOMETHING ON THE HABITAT?
UM, DO YOU ALL KNOW--?
I GUESS YOU--
ELVIS, THIS IS BELLA-- THIS IS ISABELLA BAY. SHE'S A, UM... BELLA'S MY FRIEND.
GOOD TO MEET YOU.
HI, ELVIS.
IT'S NICE TO SEE YOU AGAIN, GINGER.
WHAT'S--?
ELVIS AND GINGER WERE JUST SAYING THAT--
I'M SORRY, WHAT WERE YOU SAYING ABOUT NADINE?

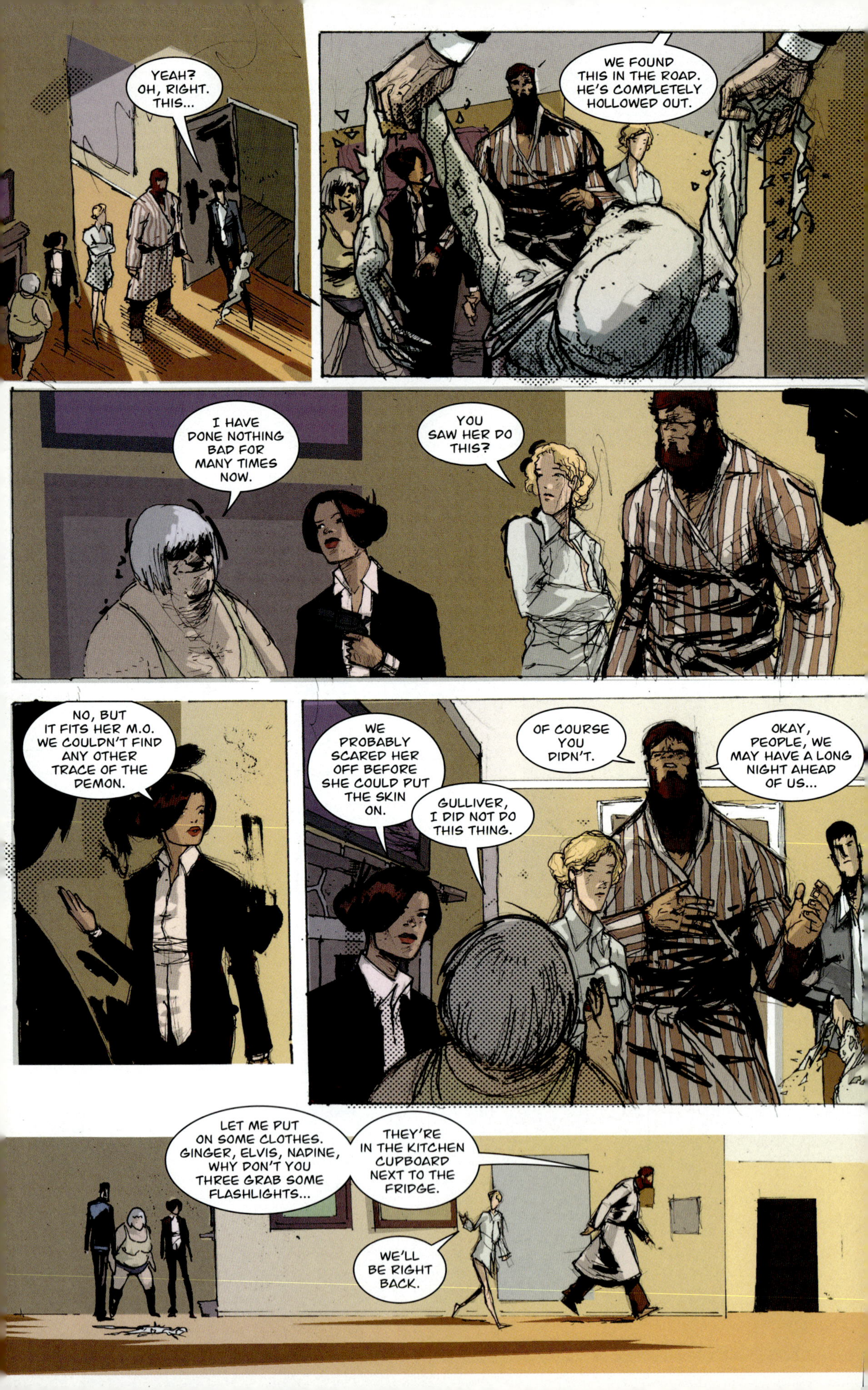
YEAH? OH, RIGHT. THIS...
WE FOUND THIS IN THE ROAD. HE'S COMPLETELY HOLLOWED OUT.
I HAVE DONE NOTHING BAD FOR MANY TIMES NOW.
YOU SAW HER DO THIS?
NO, BUT IT FITS HER M.O. WE COULDN'T FIND ANY OTHER TRACE OF THE DEMON.
WE PROBABLY SCARED HER OFF BEFORE SHE COULD PUT THE SKIN ON.
GULLIVER, I DID NOT DO THIS THING.
OF COURSE YOU DIDN'T.
OKAY, PEOPLE, WE MAY HAVE A LONG NIGHT AHEAD OF US...
LET ME PUT ON SOME CLOTHES. GINGER, ELVIS, NADINE, WHY DON'T YOU THREE GRAB SOME FLASHLIGHTS...
THEY'RE IN THE KITCHEN CUPBOARD NEXT TO THE FRIDGE.
WE'LL BE RIGHT BACK.

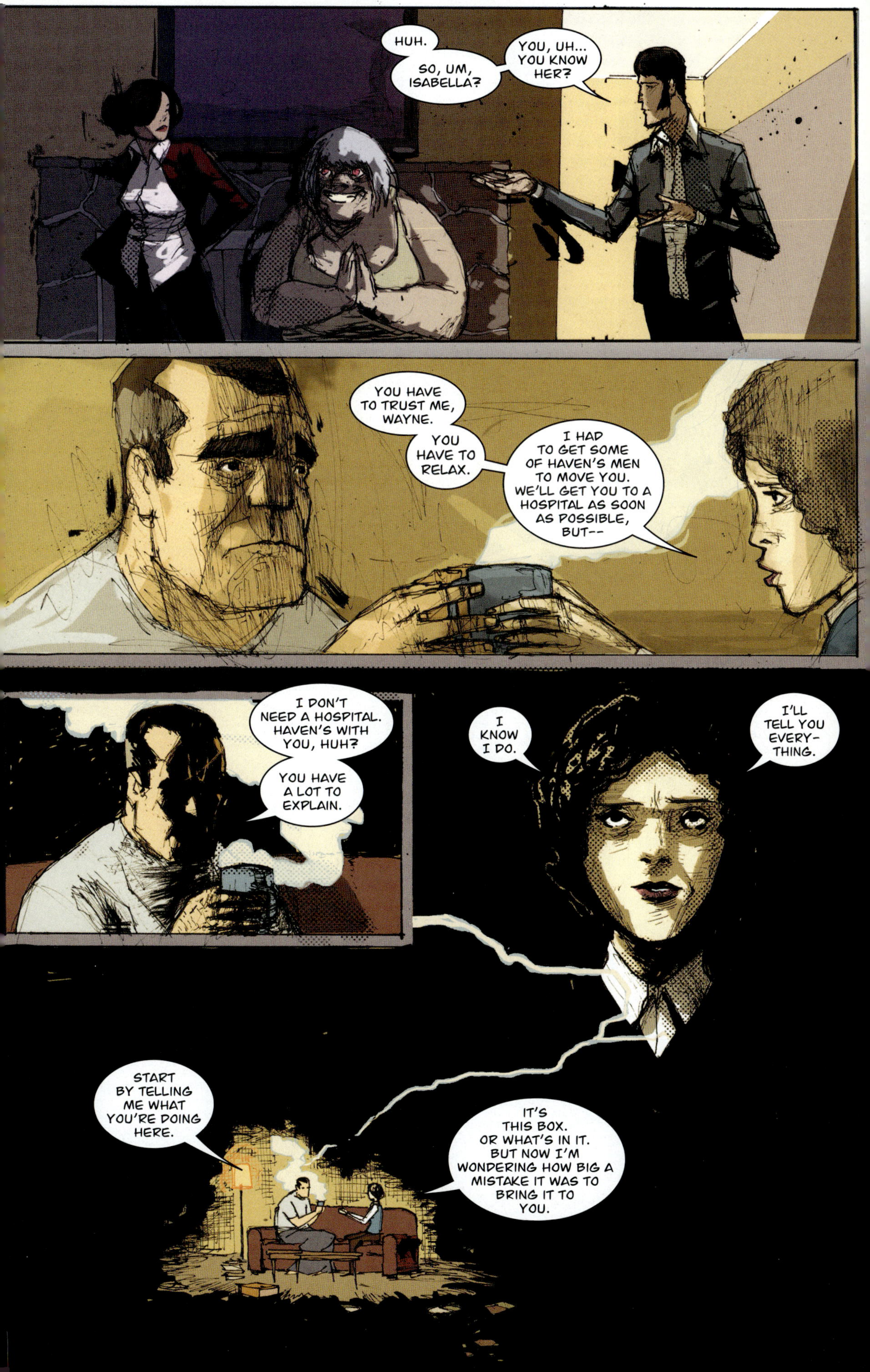
HUH.
SO, UM, ISABELLA?
YOU, UH... YOU KNOW HER?
YOU HAVE TO TRUST ME, WAYNE.
YOU HAVE TO RELAX.
I HAD TO GET SOME OF HAVEN'S MEN TO MOVE YOU. WE'LL GET YOU TO A HOSPITAL AS SOON AS POSSIBLE, BUT--
I DON'T NEED A HOSPITAL. HAVEN'S WITH YOU, HUH?
YOU HAVE A LOT TO EXPLAIN.
I KNOW I DO.
I'LL TELL YOU EVERY-THING.
START BY TELLING ME WHAT YOU'RE DOING HERE.
IT'S THIS BOX. OR WHAT'S IN IT. BUT NOW I'M WONDERING HOW BIG A MISTAKE IT WAS TO BRING IT TO YOU.

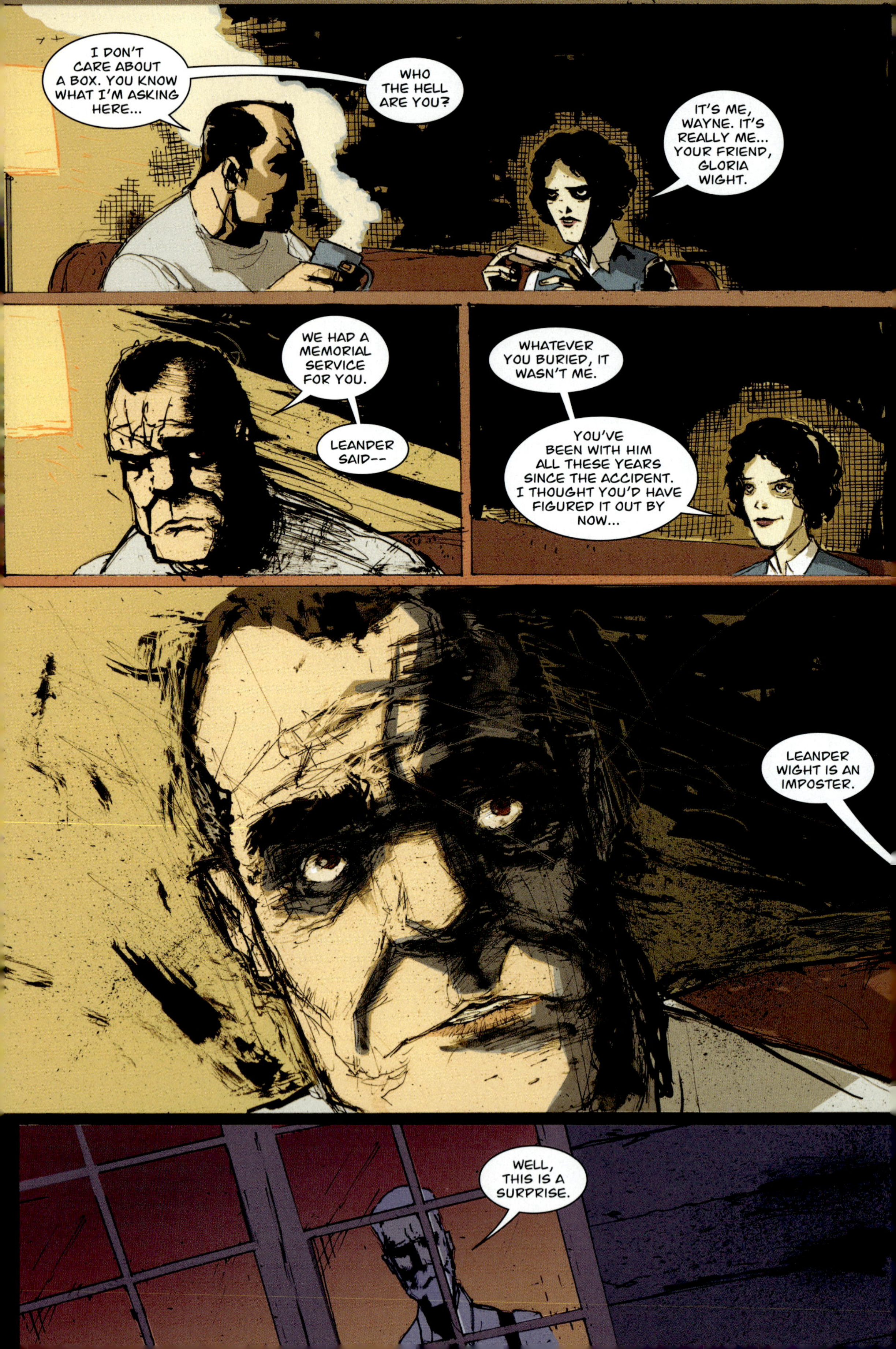
I DON'T CARE ABOUT A BOX. YOU KNOW WHAT I'M ASKING HERE...
WHO THE HELL ARE YOU?
IT'S ME, WAYNE. IT'S REALLY ME... YOUR FRIEND, GLORIA WIGHT.
WE HAD A MEMORIAL SERVICE FOR YOU.
LEANDER SAID--
WHATEVER YOU BURIED, IT WASN'T ME.
YOU'VE BEEN WITH HIM ALL THESE YEARS SINCE THE ACCIDENT. I THOUGHT YOU'D HAVE FIGURED IT OUT BY NOW...
LEANDER WIGHT IS AN IMPOSTER.
WELL, THIS IS A SURPRISE.

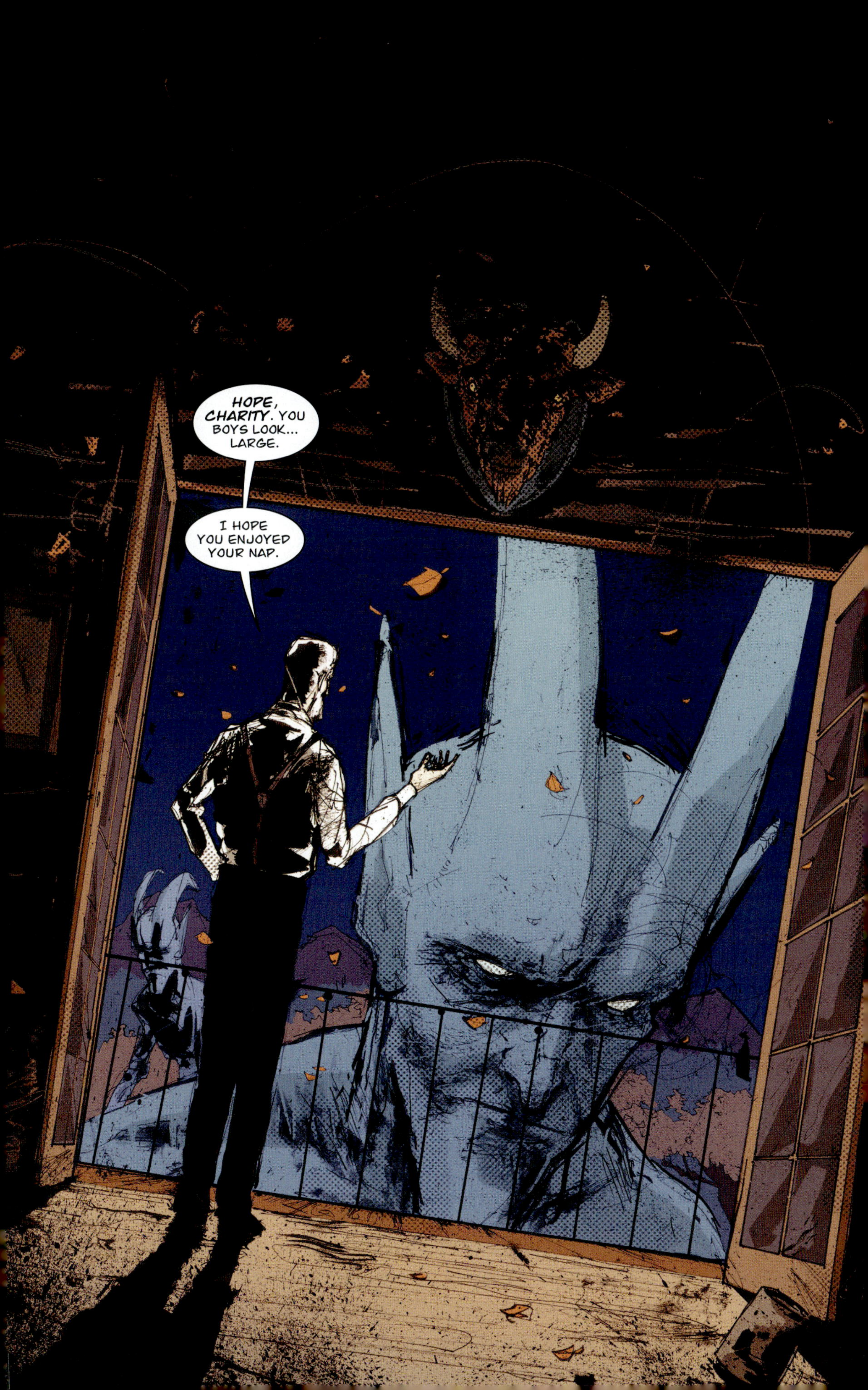
HOPE, CHARITY. YOU BOYS LOOK... LARGE.
I HOPE YOU ENJOYED YOUR NAP.

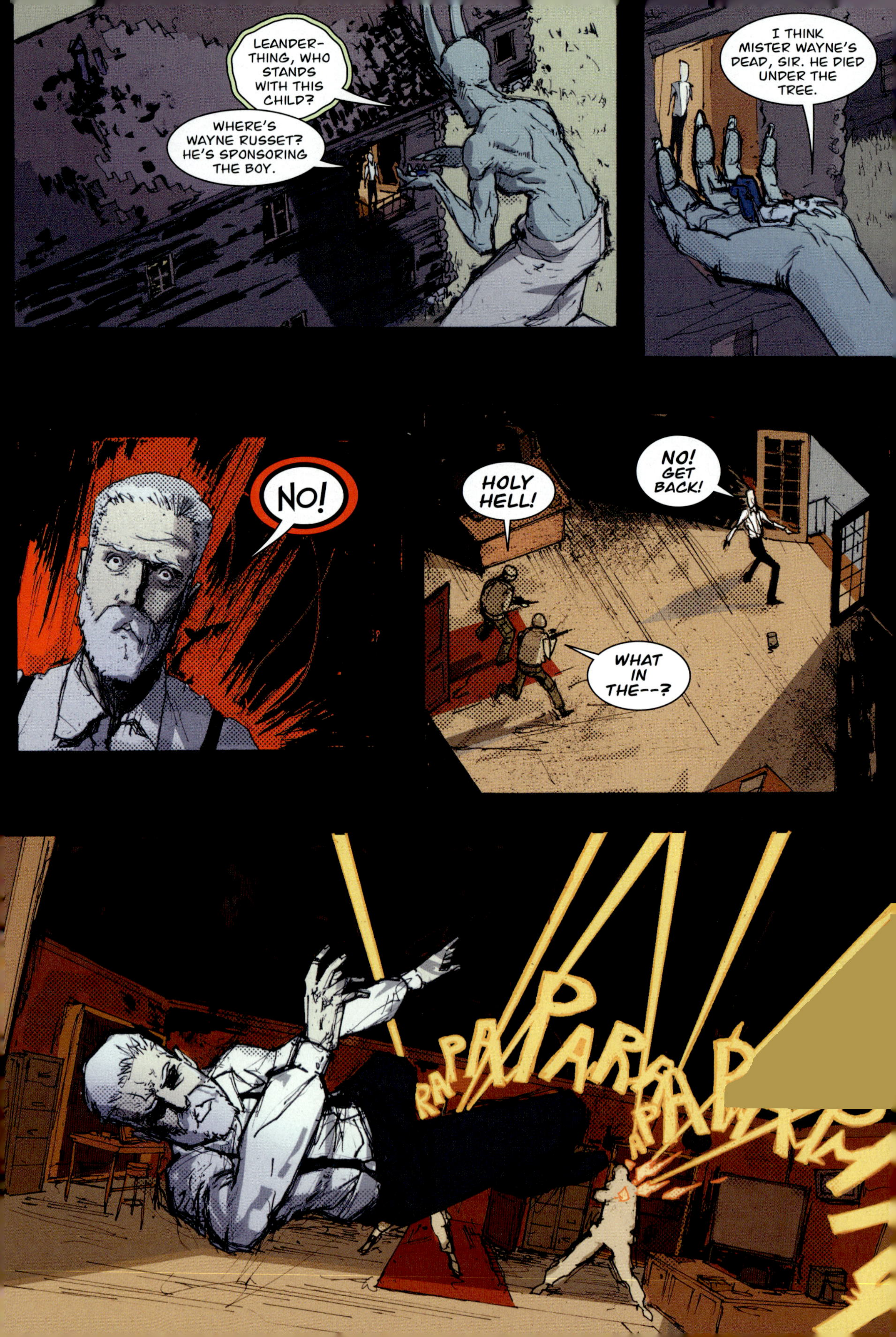
LEANDER-THING, WHO STANDS WITH THIS CHILD?
WHERE'S WAYNE RUSSET? HE'S SPONSORING THE BOY.
I THINK MISTER WAYNE'S DEAD, SIR. HE DIED UNDER THE TREE.
NO!
HOLY HELL!
NO! GET BACK!
WHAT IN THE--?

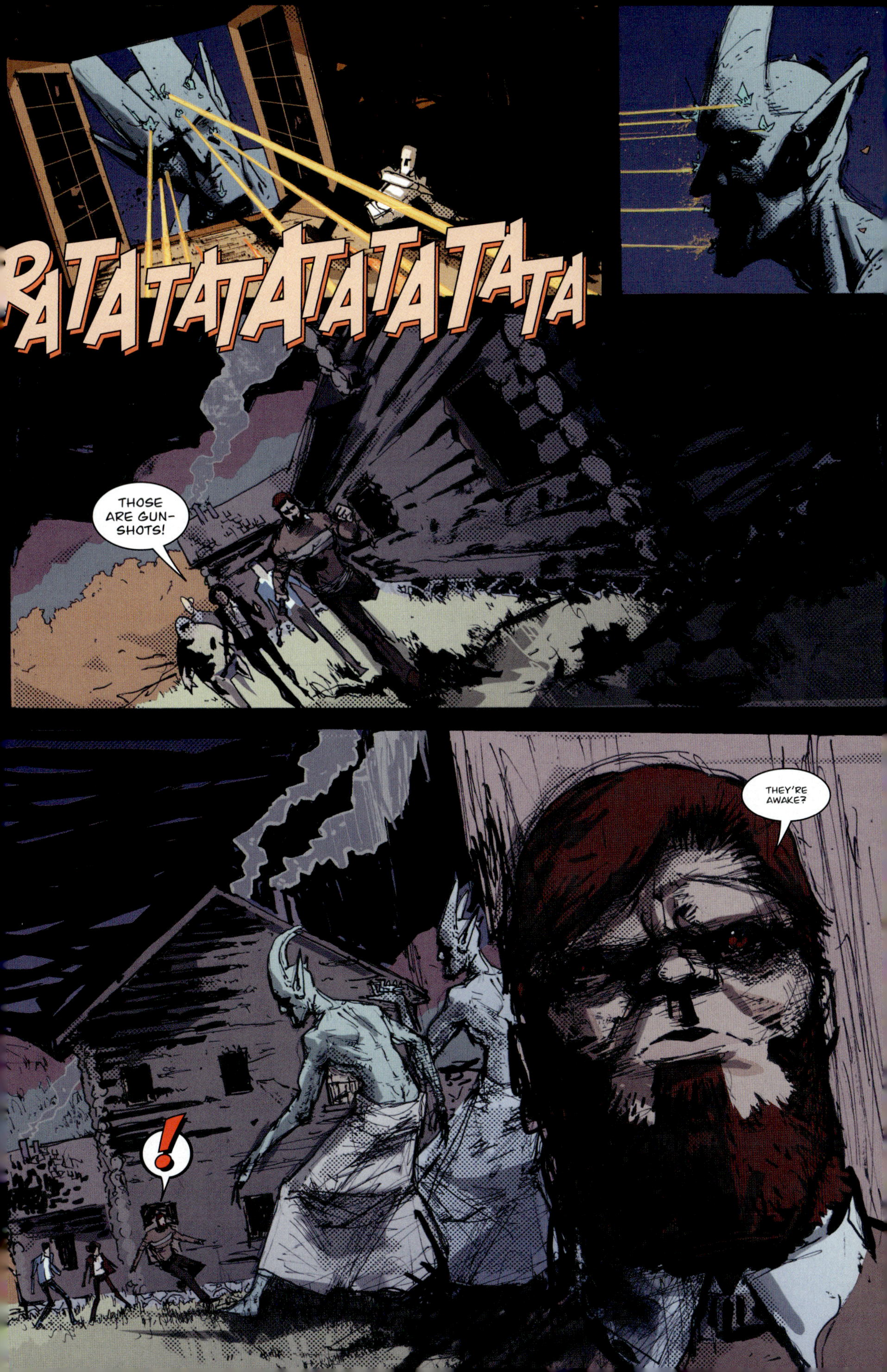
RATATATATATATATATA
THOSE ARE GUN-SHOTS!
THEY'RE AWAKE?
!

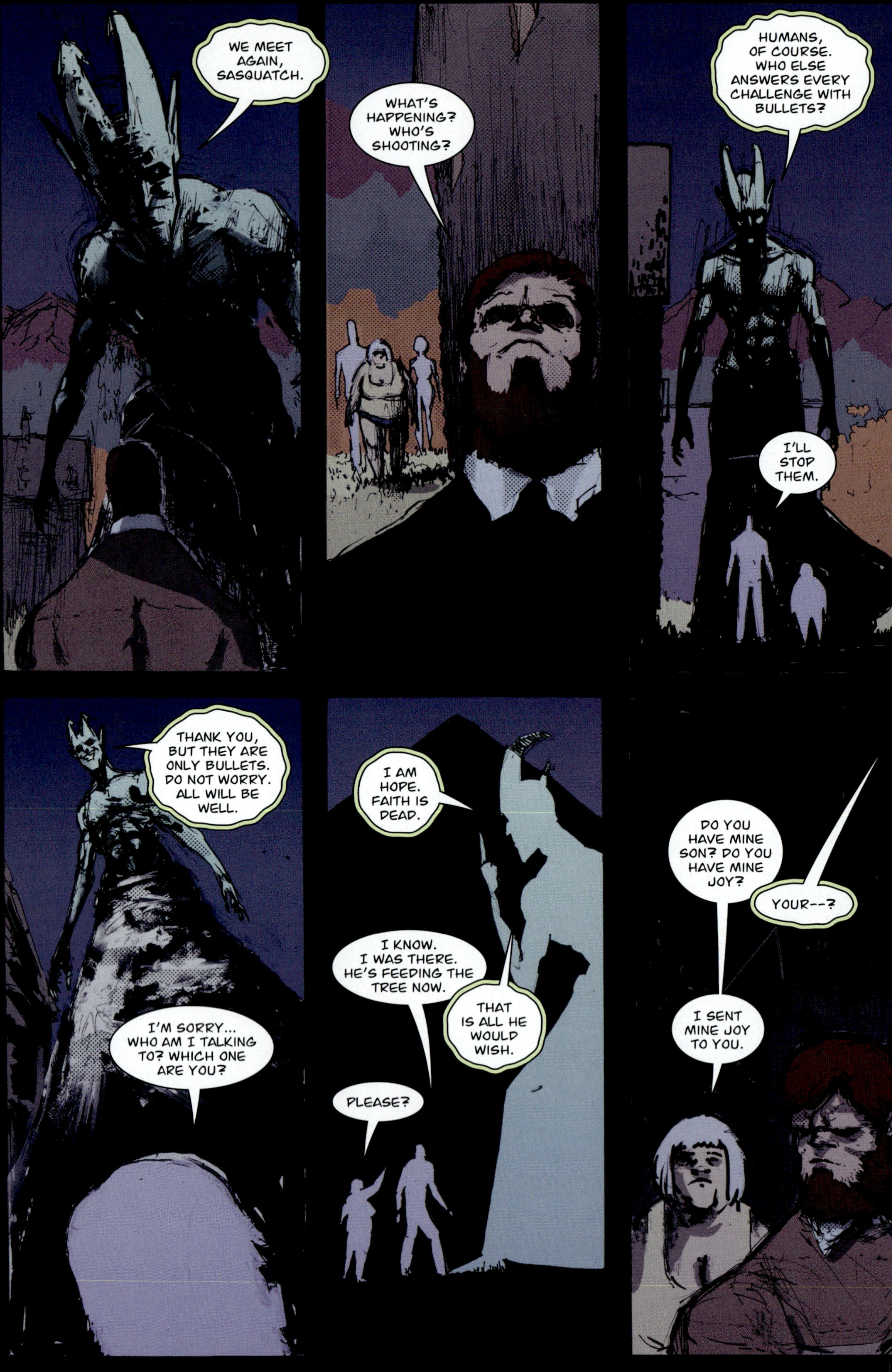
WE MEET AGAIN, SASQUATCH.
WHAT'S HAPPENING? WHO'S SHOOTING?
HUMANS, OF COURSE. WHO ELSE ANSWERS EVERY CHALLENGE WITH BULLETS?
I'LL STOP THEM.
THANK YOU, BUT THEY ARE ONLY BULLETS. DO NOT WORRY. ALL WILL BE WELL.
I'M SORRY... WHO AM I TALKING TO? WHICH ONE ARE YOU?
I AM HOPE. FAITH IS DEAD.
I KNOW. I WAS THERE. HE'S FEEDING THE TREE NOW.
THAT IS ALL HE WOULD WISH.
PLEASE?
DO YOU HAVE MINE SON? DO YOU HAVE MINE JOY?
YOUR--?
I SENT MINE JOY TO YOU.

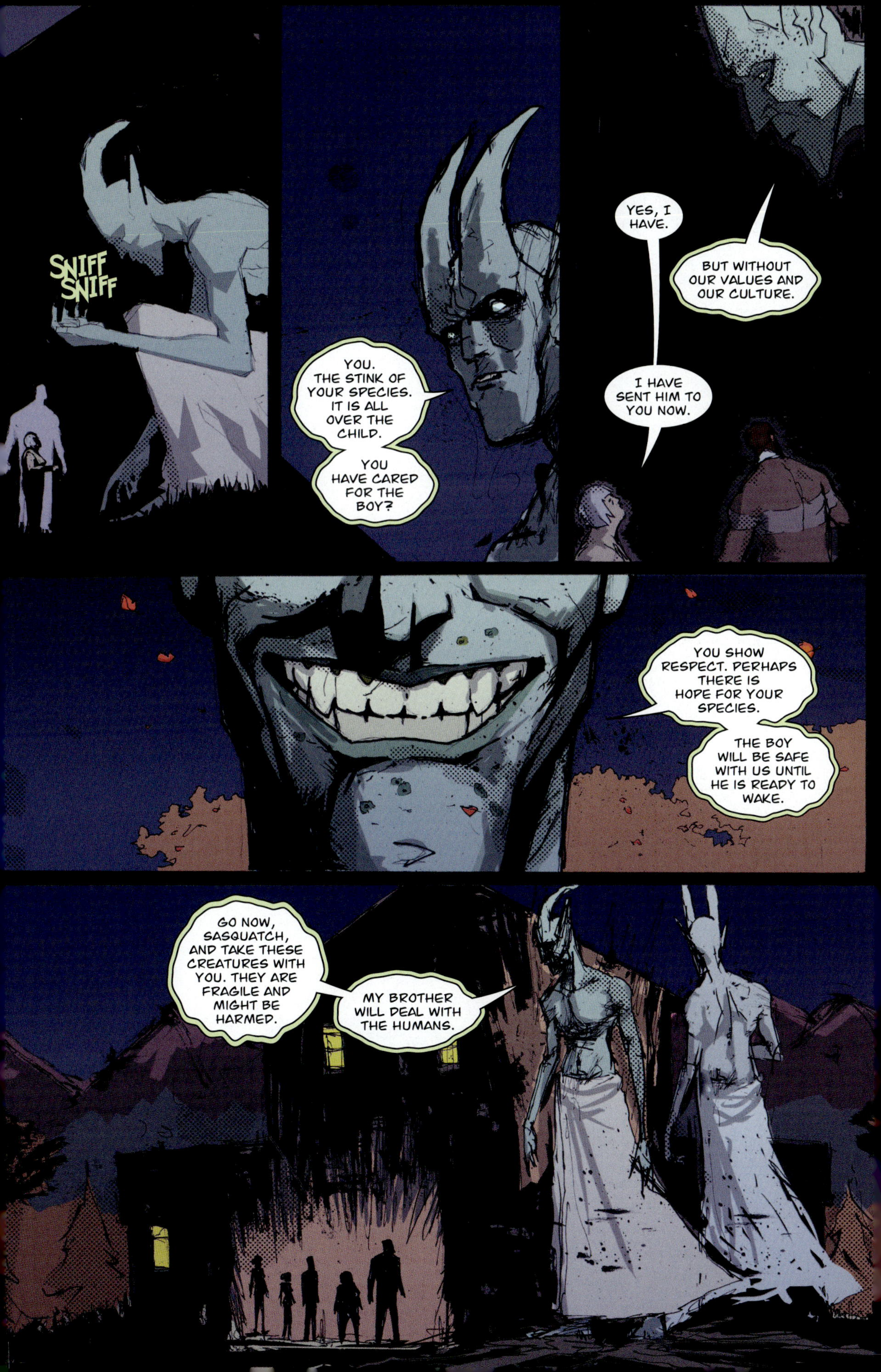
SNIFF SNIFF
YOU. THE STINK OF YOUR SPECIES. IT IS ALL OVER THE CHILD.
YOU HAVE CARED FOR THE BOY?
YES, I HAVE.
I HAVE SENT HIM TO YOU NOW.
BUT WITHOUT OUR VALUES AND OUR CULTURE.
YOU SHOW RESPECT. PERHAPS THERE IS HOPE FOR YOUR SPECIES.
THE BOY WILL BE SAFE WITH US UNTIL HE IS READY TO WAKE.
GO NOW, SASQUATCH, AND TAKE THESE CREATURES WITH YOU. THEY ARE FRAGILE AND MIGHT BE HARMED.
MY BROTHER WILL DEAL WITH THE HUMANS.

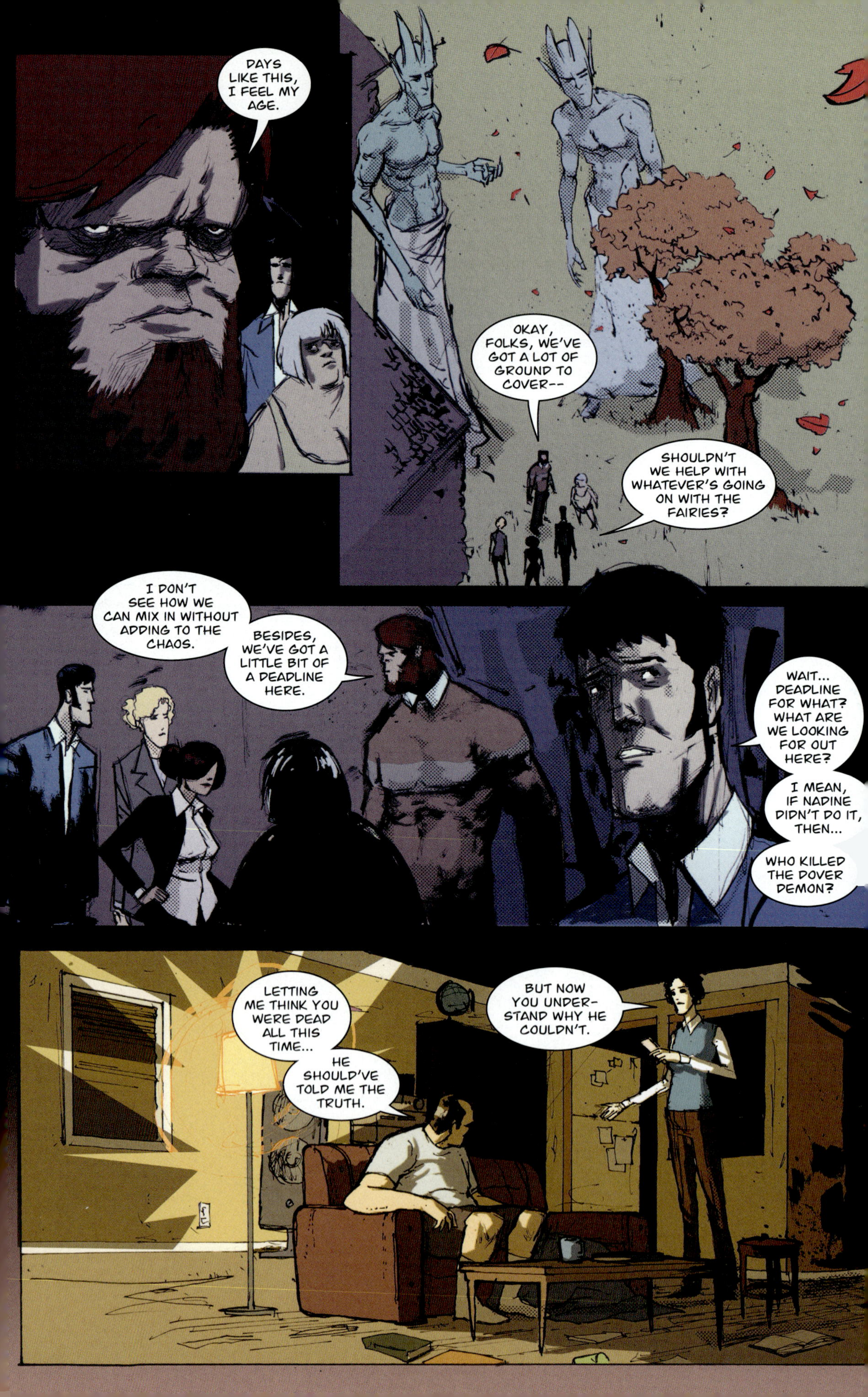
DAYS LIKE THIS, I FEEL MY AGE.
OKAY, FOLKS, WE'VE GOT A LOT OF GROUND TO COVER--
SHOULDN'T WE HELP WITH WHATEVER'S GOING ON WITH THE FAIRIES?
I DON'T SEE HOW WE CAN MIX IN WITHOUT ADDING TO THE CHAOS.
BESIDES, WE'VE GOT A LITTLE BIT OF A DEADLINE HERE.
WAIT... DEADLINE FOR WHAT? WHAT ARE WE LOOKING FOR OUT HERE?
I MEAN, IF NADINE DIDN'T DO IT, THEN...
WHO KILLED THE DOVER DEMON?
LETTING ME THINK YOU WERE DEAD ALL THIS TIME...
HE SHOULD'VE TOLD ME THE TRUTH.
BUT NOW YOU UNDERSTAND WHY HE COULDN'T.

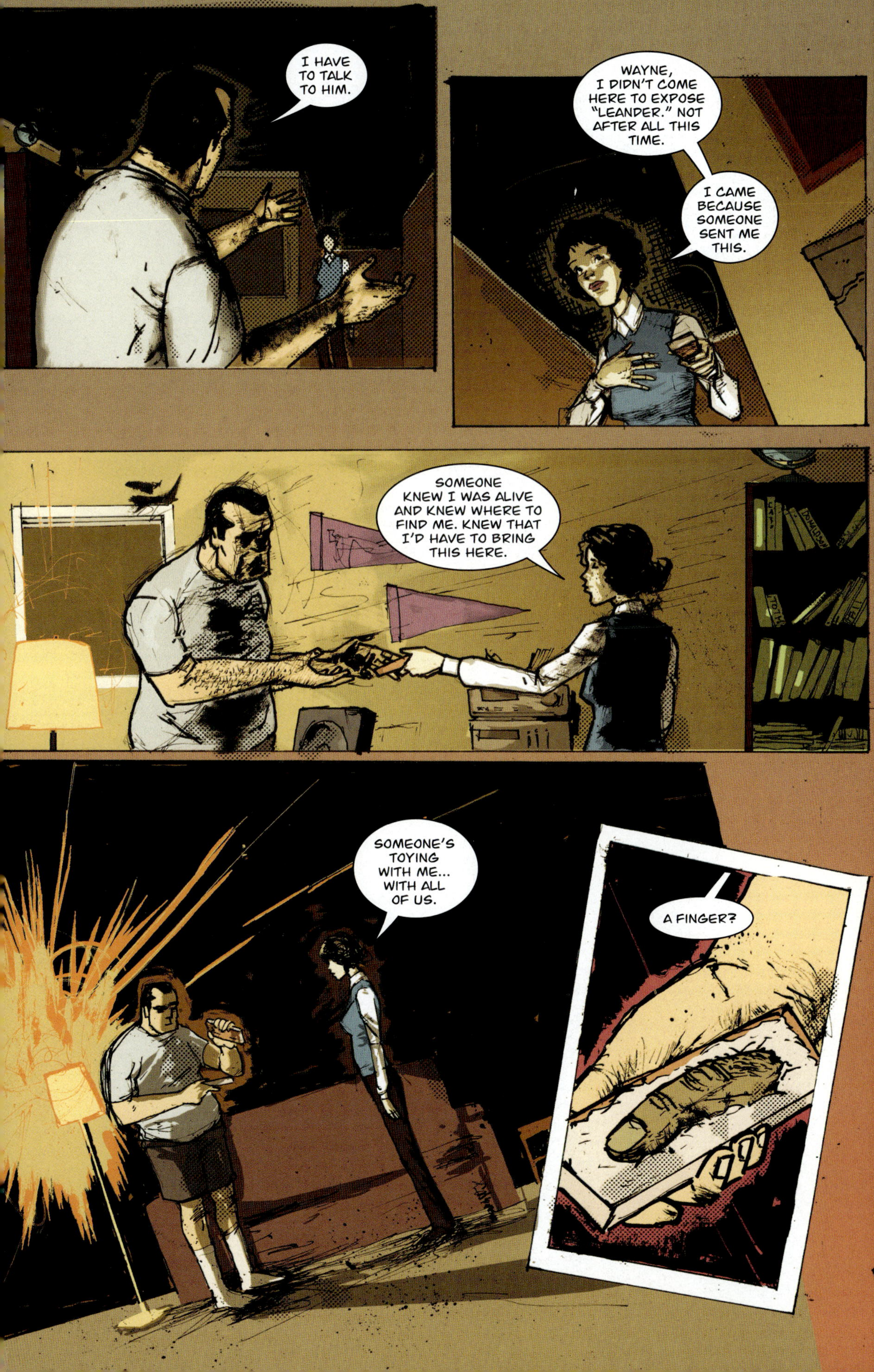
I HAVE TO TALK TO HIM.
WAYNE, I DIDN'T COME HERE TO EXPOSE "LEANDER." NOT AFTER ALL THIS TIME.
I CAME BECAUSE SOMEONE SENT ME THIS.
SOMEONE KNEW I WAS ALIVE AND KNEW WHERE TO FIND ME. KNEW THAT I'D HAVE TO BRING THIS HERE.
SOMEONE'S TOYING WITH ME... WITH ALL OF US.
A FINGER?

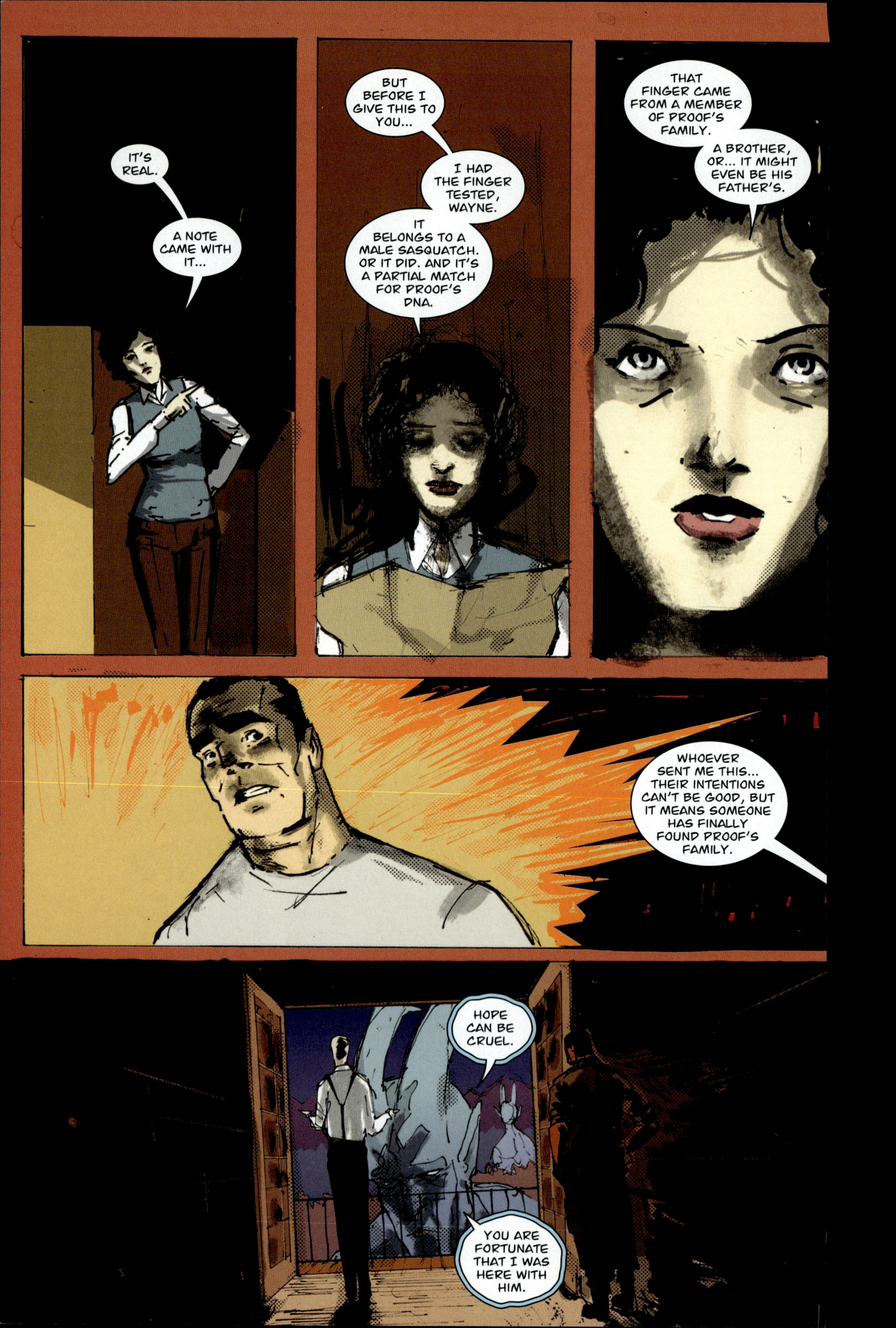
IT'S REAL.
A NOTE CAME WITH IT...
BUT BEFORE I GIVE THIS TO YOU...
I HAD THE FINGER TESTED, WAYNE.
IT BELONGS TO A MALE SASQUATCH. OR IT DID. AND IT'S A PARTIAL MATCH FOR PROOF'S DNA.
THAT FINGER CAME FROM A MEMBER OF PROOF'S FAMILY.
A BROTHER, OR... IT MIGHT EVEN BE HIS FATHER'S.
WHOEVER SENT ME THIS... THEIR INTENTIONS CAN'T BE GOOD, BUT IT MEANS SOMEONE HAS FINALLY FOUND PROOF'S FAMILY.
HOPE CAN BE CRUEL.
YOU ARE FORTUNATE THAT I WAS HERE WITH HIM.

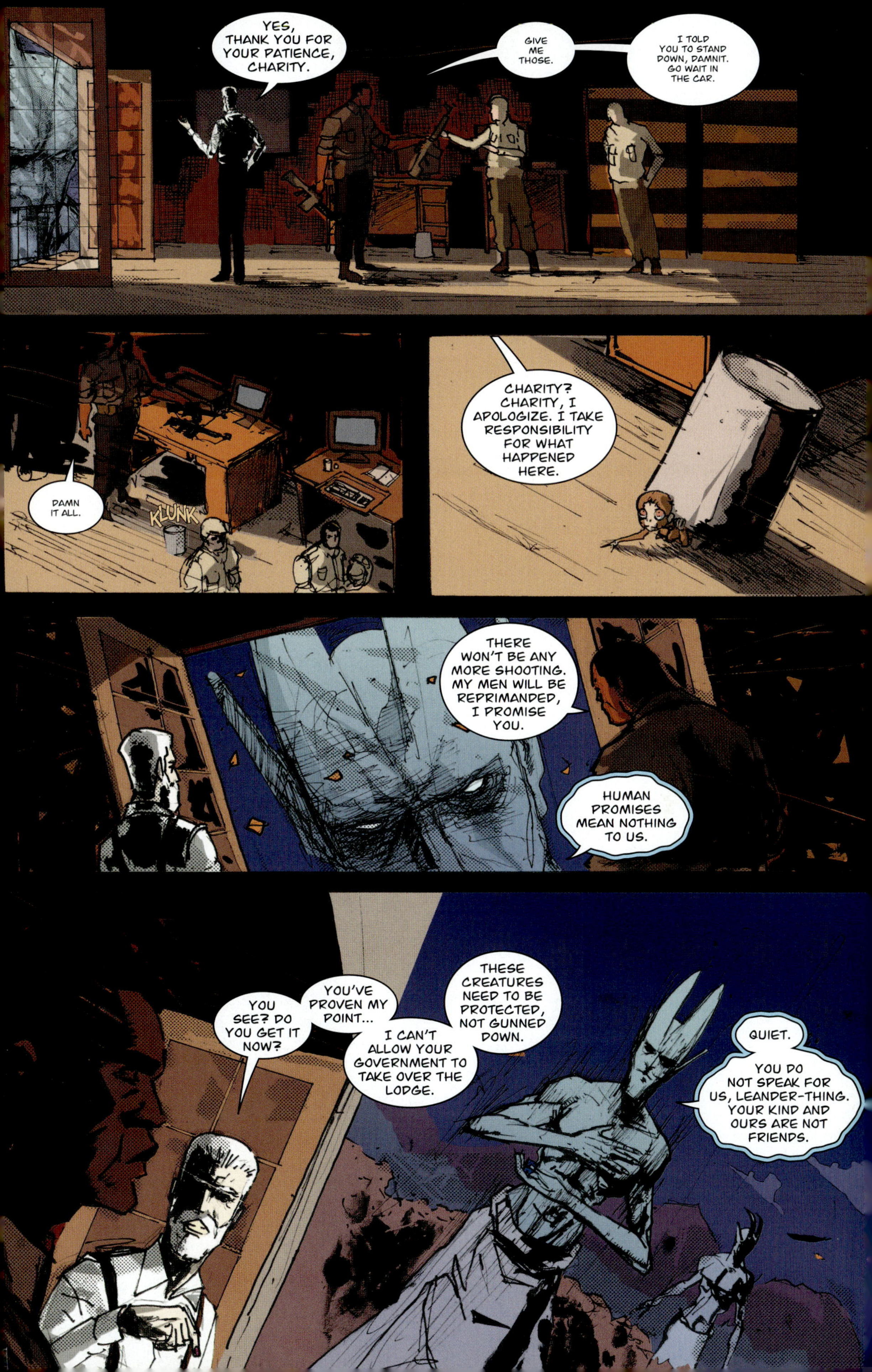

YES, THANK YOU FOR YOUR PATIENCE, CHARITY.
GIVE ME THOSE.
I TOLD YOU TO STAND DOWN, DAMNIT. GO WAIT IN THE CAR.
DAMN IT ALL.
KLUNK
CHARITY? CHARITY, I APOLOGIZE. I TAKE RESPONSIBILITY FOR WHAT HAPPENED HERE.
THERE WON'T BE ANY MORE SHOOTING. MY MEN WILL BE REPRIMANDED, I PROMISE YOU.
HUMAN PROMISES MEAN NOTHING TO US.
YOU SEE? DO YOU GET IT NOW?
YOU'VE PROVEN MY POINT...
I CAN'T ALLOW YOUR GOVERNMENT TO TAKE OVER THE LODGE.
THESE CREATURES NEED TO BE PROTECTED, NOT GUNNED DOWN.
QUIET.
YOU DO NOT SPEAK FOR US, LEANDER-THING. YOUR KIND AND OURS ARE NOT FRIENDS.

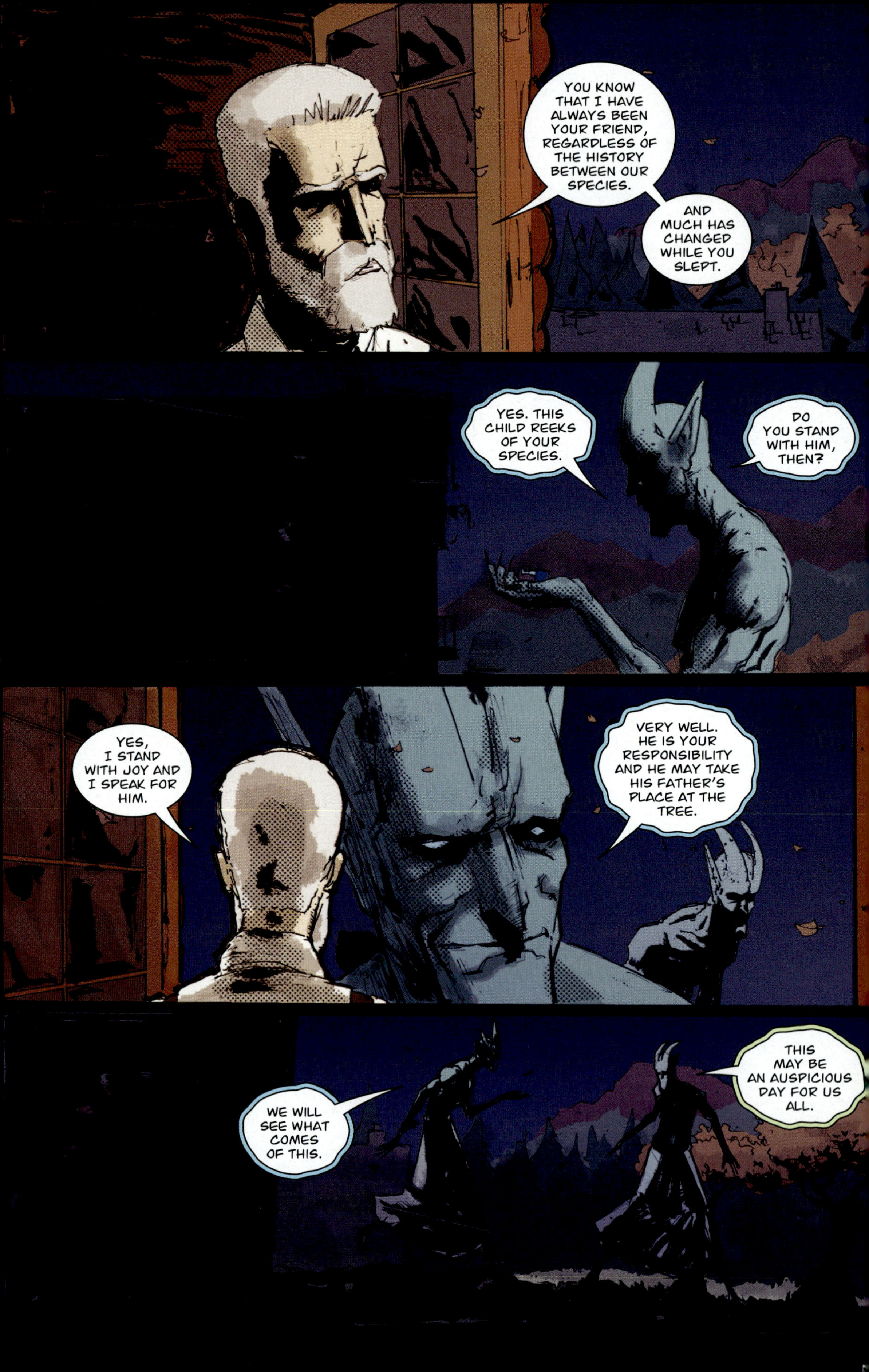
YOU KNOW THAT I HAVE ALWAYS BEEN YOUR FRIEND, REGARDLESS OF THE HISTORY BETWEEN OUR SPECIES.
AND MUCH HAS CHANGED WHILE YOU SLEPT.
YES. THIS CHILD REEKS OF YOUR SPECIES.
DO YOU STAND WITH HIM, THEN?
YES, I STAND WITH JOY AND I SPEAK FOR HIM.
VERY WELL. HE IS YOUR RESPONSIBILITY AND HE MAY TAKE HIS FATHER'S PLACE AT THE TREE.
THIS MAY BE AN AUSPICIOUS DAY FOR US ALL.
WE WILL SEE WHAT COMES OF THIS.

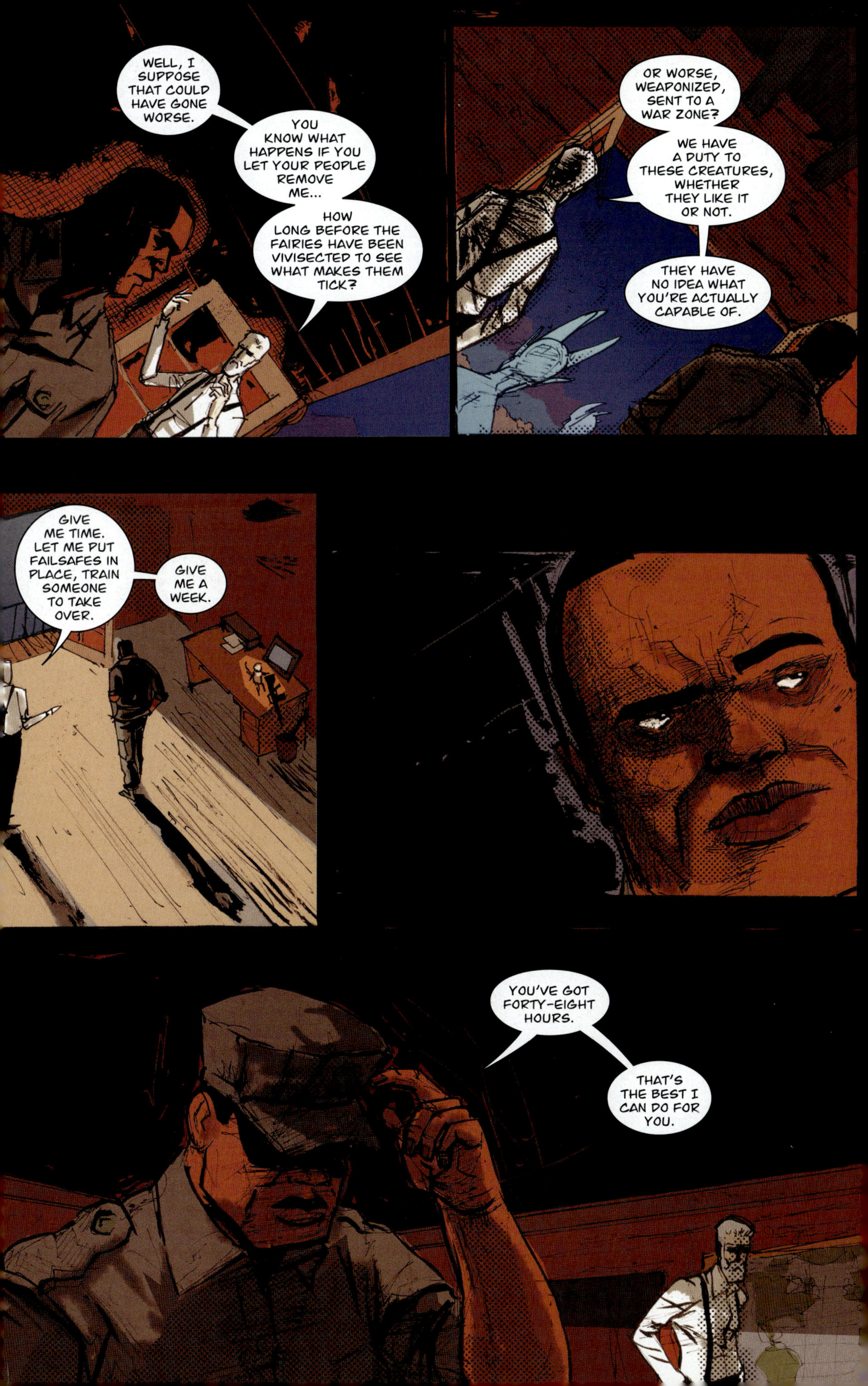
WELL, I SUPPOSE THAT COULD HAVE GONE WORSE.
YOU KNOW WHAT HAPPENS IF YOU LET YOUR PEOPLE REMOVE ME...
HOW LONG BEFORE THE FAIRIES HAVE BEEN VIVISECTED TO SEE WHAT MAKES THEM TICK?
OR WORSE, WEAPONIZED, SENT TO A WAR ZONE?
WE HAVE A DUTY TO THESE CREATURES, WHETHER THEY LIKE IT OR NOT.
THEY HAVE NO IDEA WHAT YOU'RE ACTUALLY CAPABLE OF.
GIVE ME TIME. LET ME PUT FAILSAFES IN PLACE, TRAIN SOMEONE TO TAKE OVER.
GIVE ME A WEEK.
YOU'VE GOT FORTY-EIGHT HOURS.
THAT'S THE BEST I CAN DO FOR YOU.

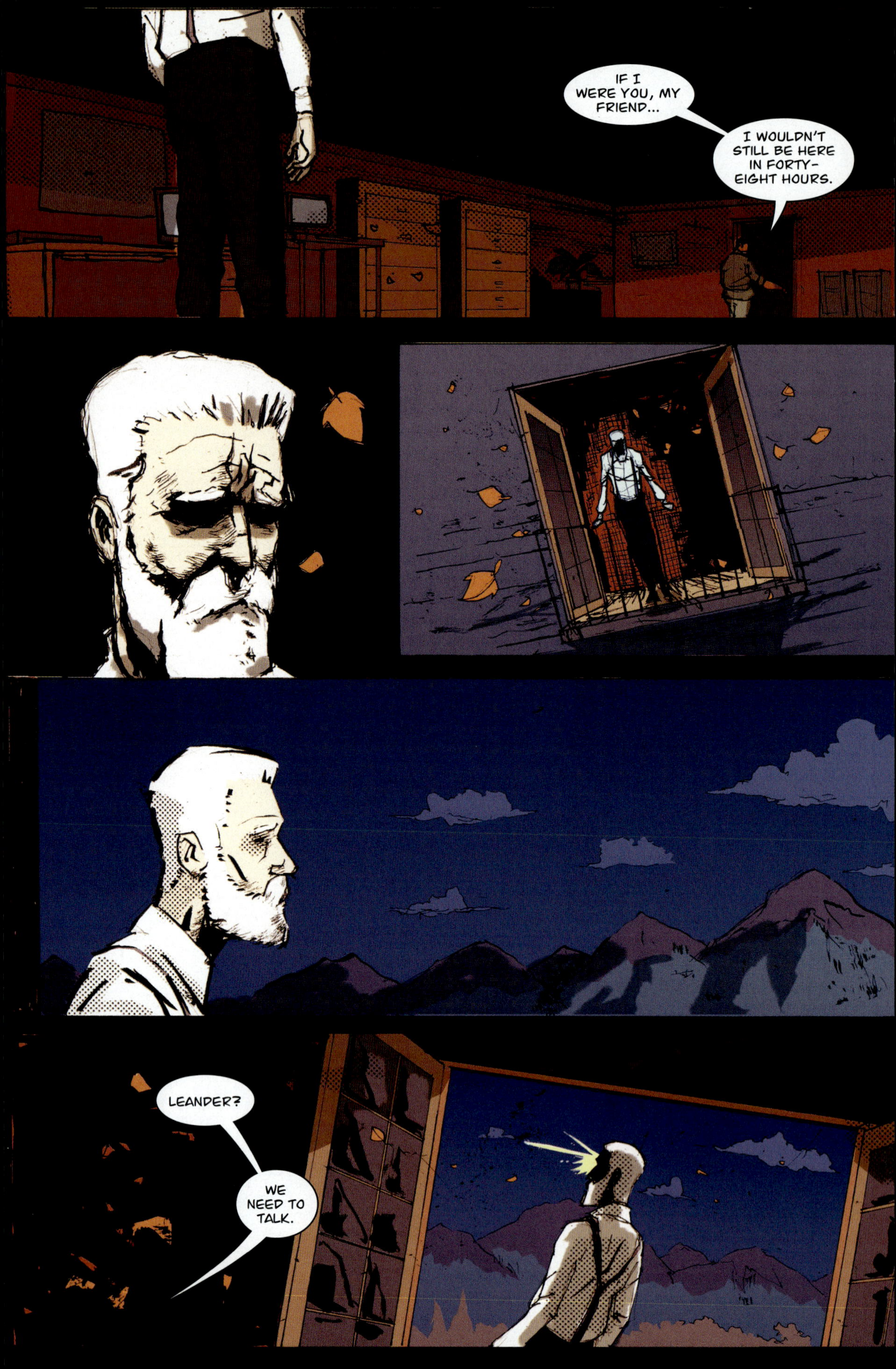
IF I WERE YOU, MY FRIEND...
I WOULDN'T STILL BE HERE IN FORTY-EIGHT HOURS.
LEANDER?
WE NEED TO TALK.

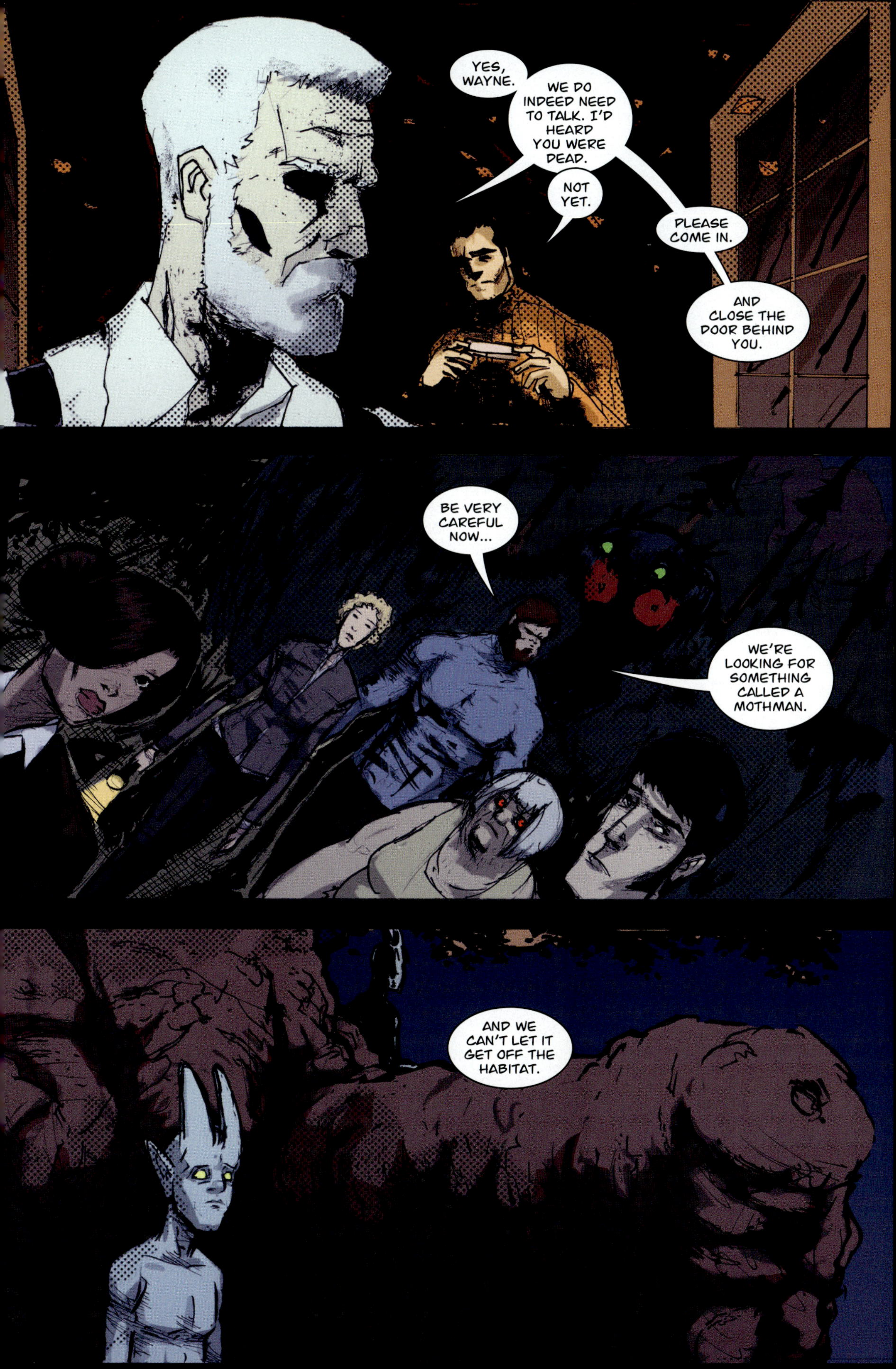
YES, WAYNE.
WE DO INDEED NEED TO TALK. I'D HEARD YOU WERE DEAD.
NOT YET.
PLEASE COME IN.
AND CLOSE THE DOOR BEHIND YOU.
BE VERY CAREFUL NOW...
WE'RE LOOKING FOR SOMETHING CALLED A MOTHMAN.
AND WE CAN'T LET IT GET OFF THE HABITAT.

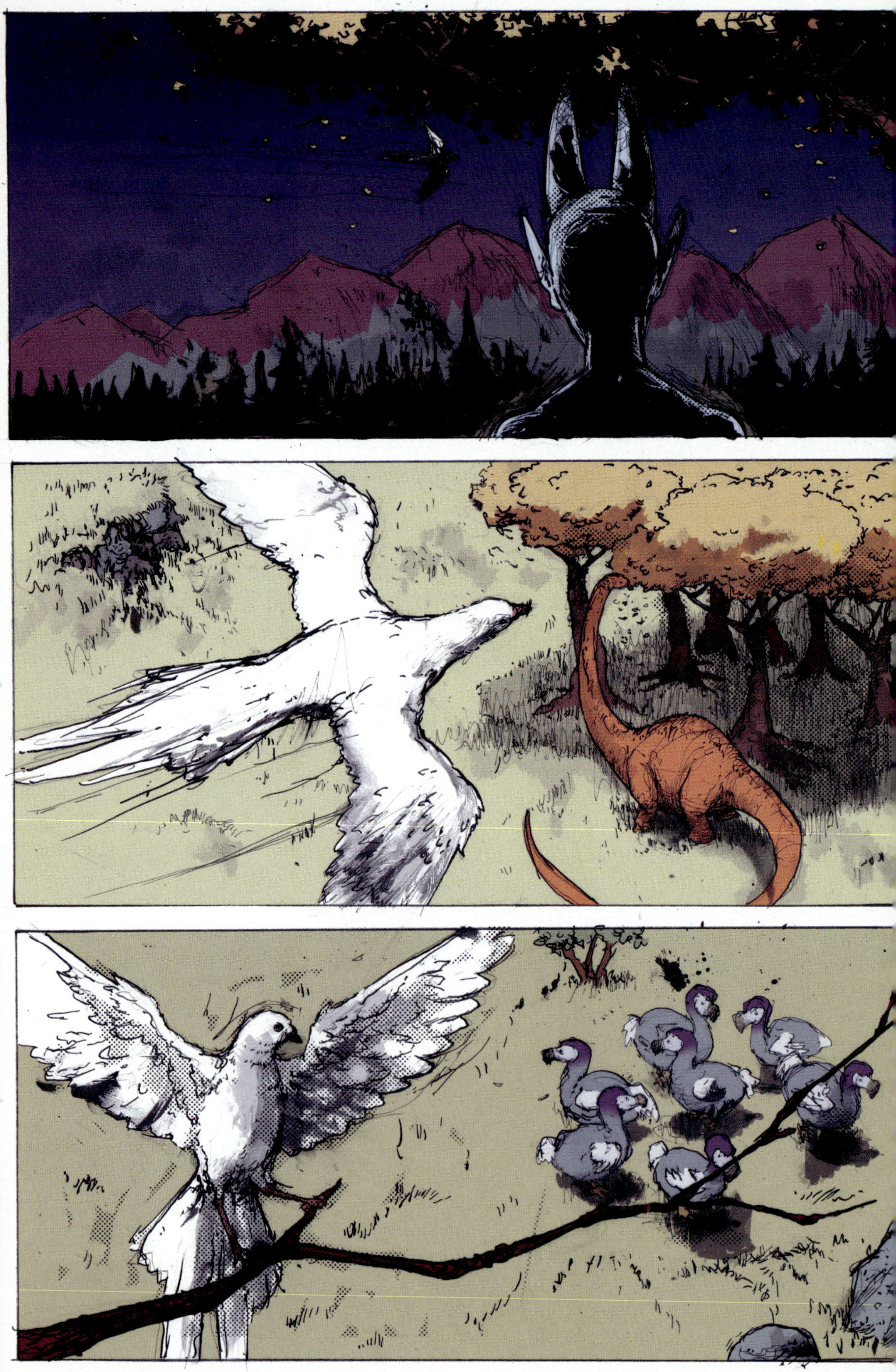

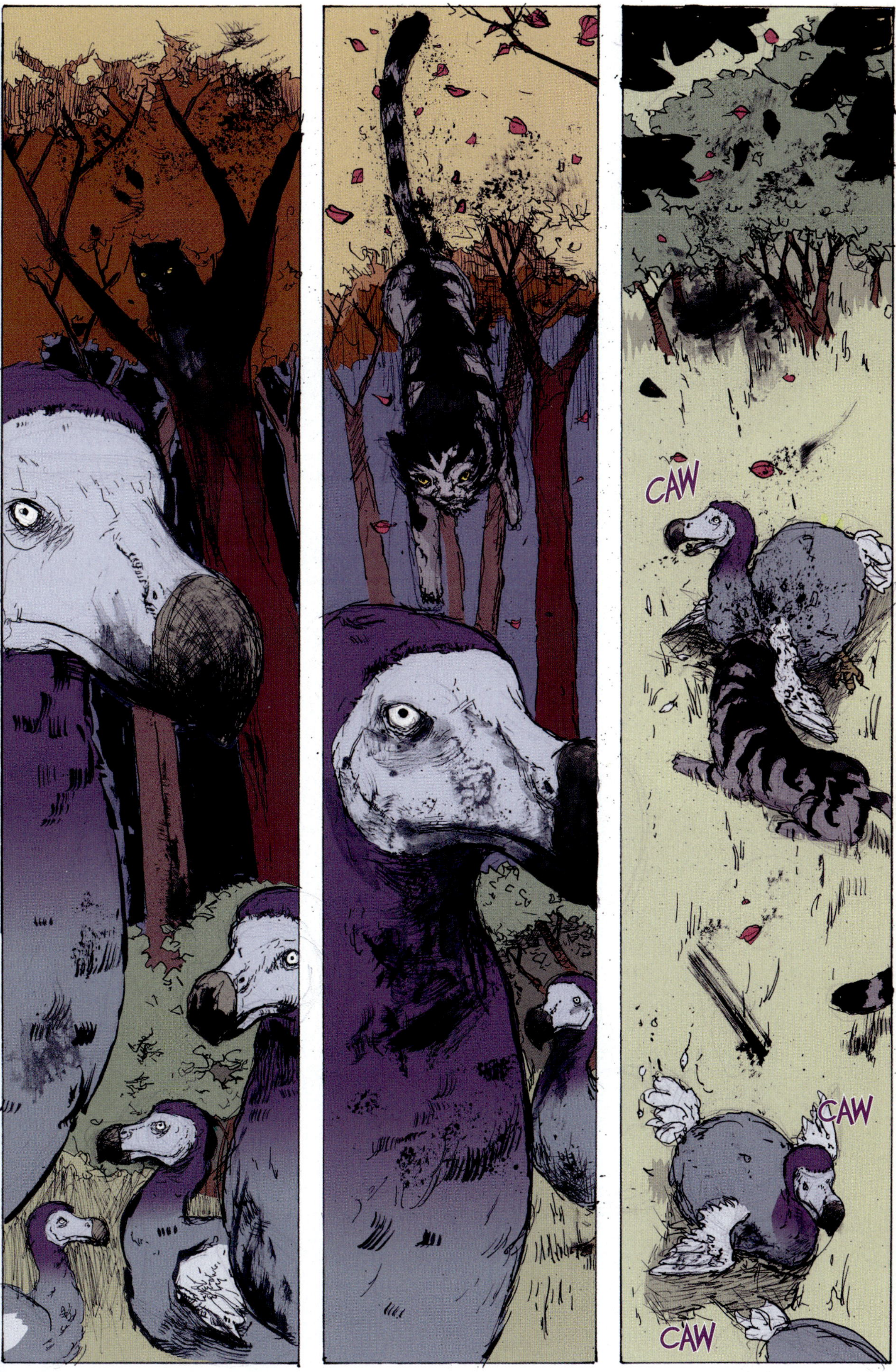
CAW
CAW
CAW

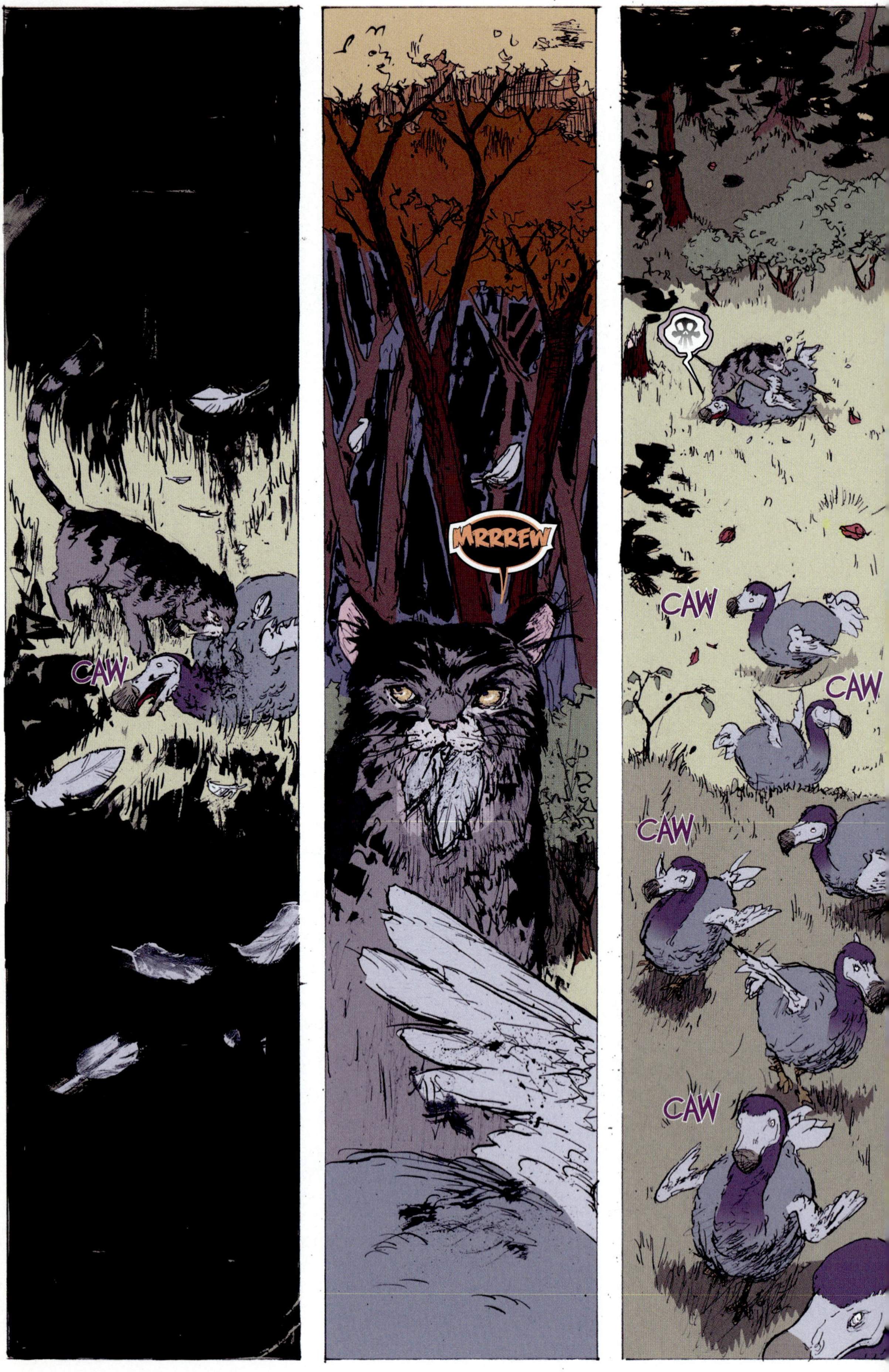
CAW
MRRREW
CAW
CAW
CAW
CAW

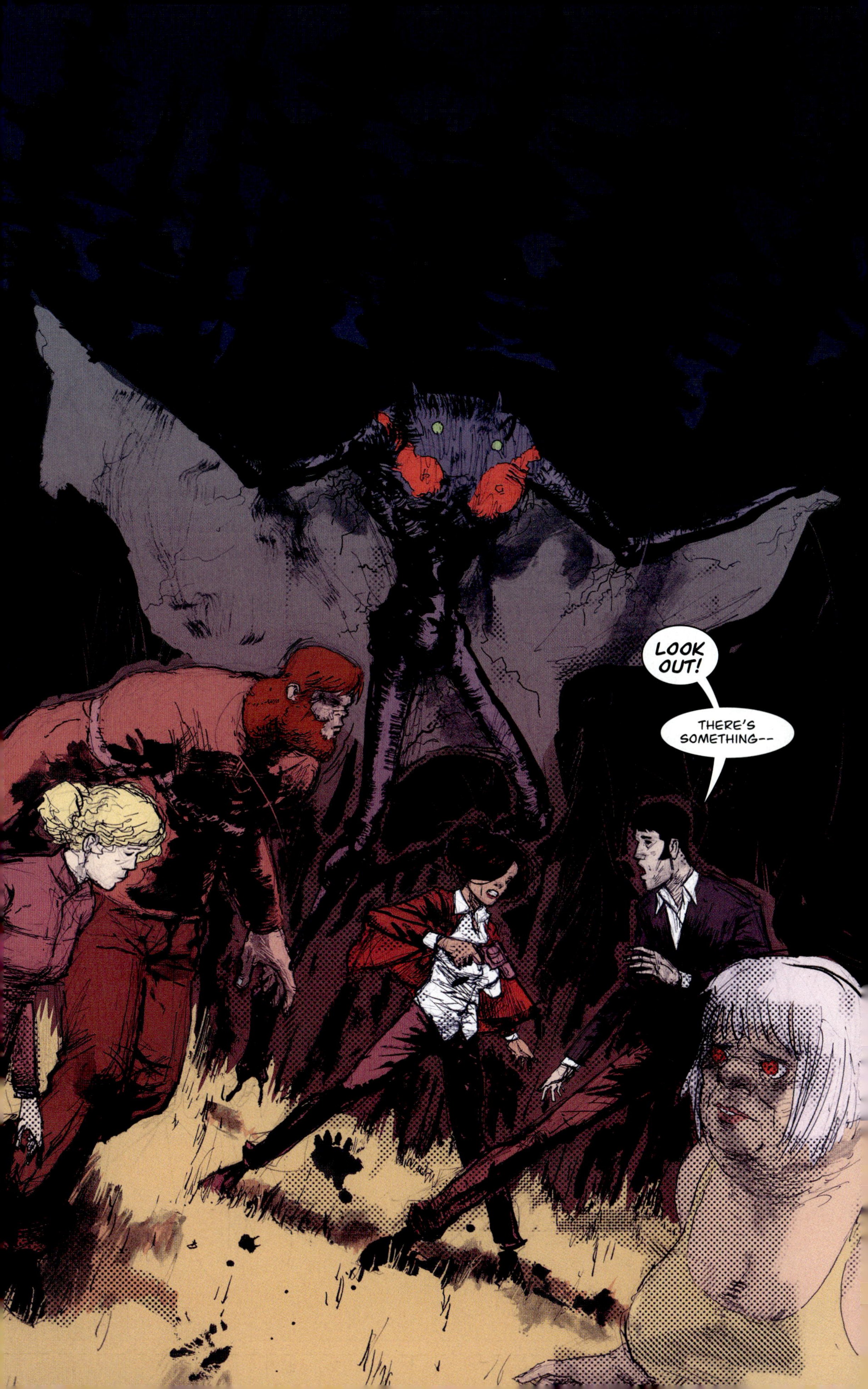
LOOK OUT!
THERE'S SOMETHING--

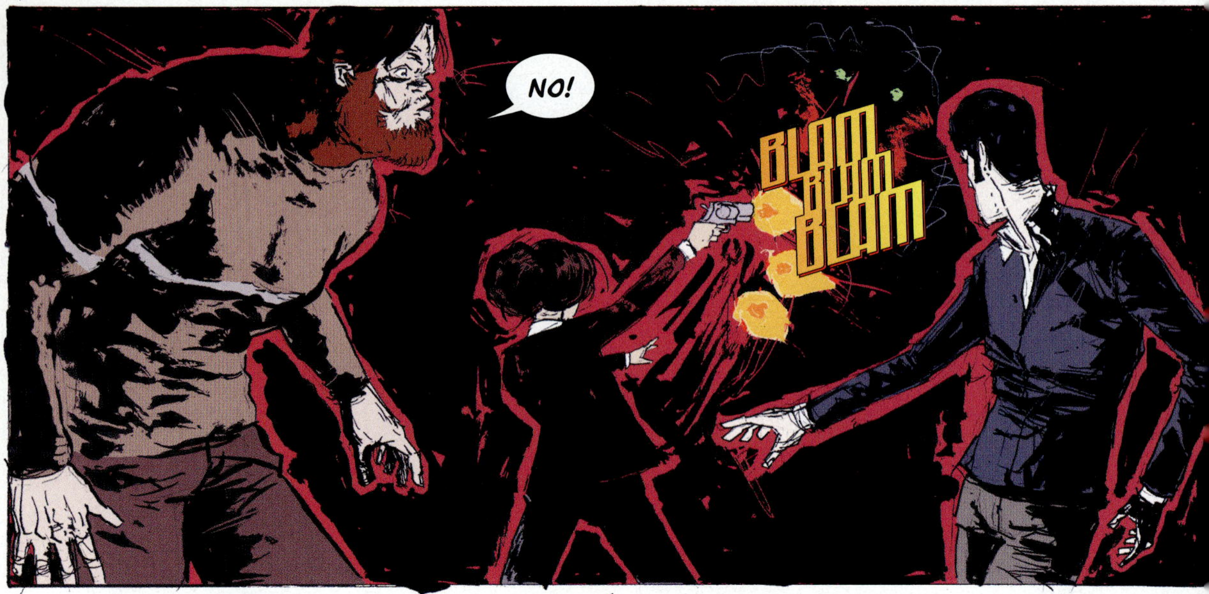
NO!
BLAM BLAM BLAM

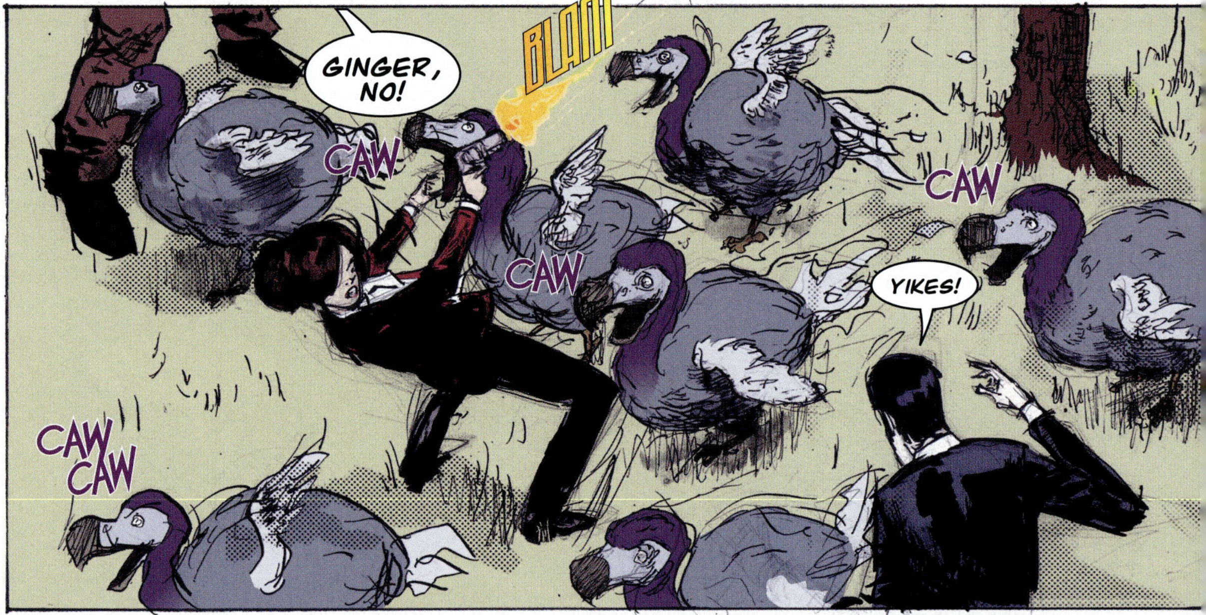
GINGER, NO!
BLAM
CAW
CAW
CAW
YIKES!
CAW CAW

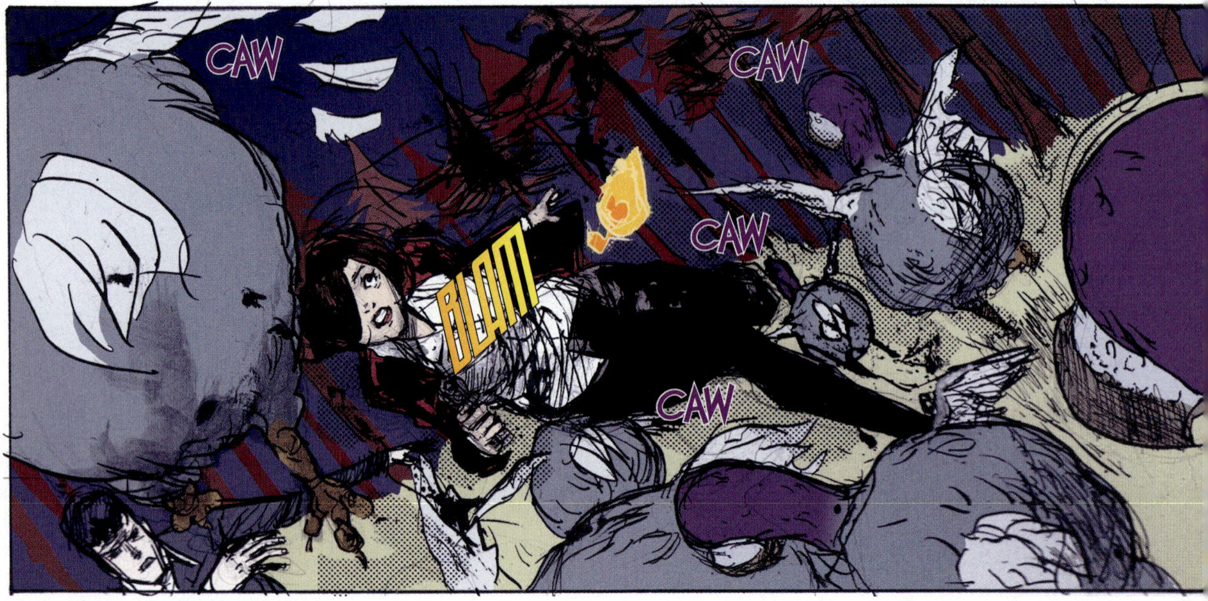
CAW
CAW
CAW
BLAM
CAW

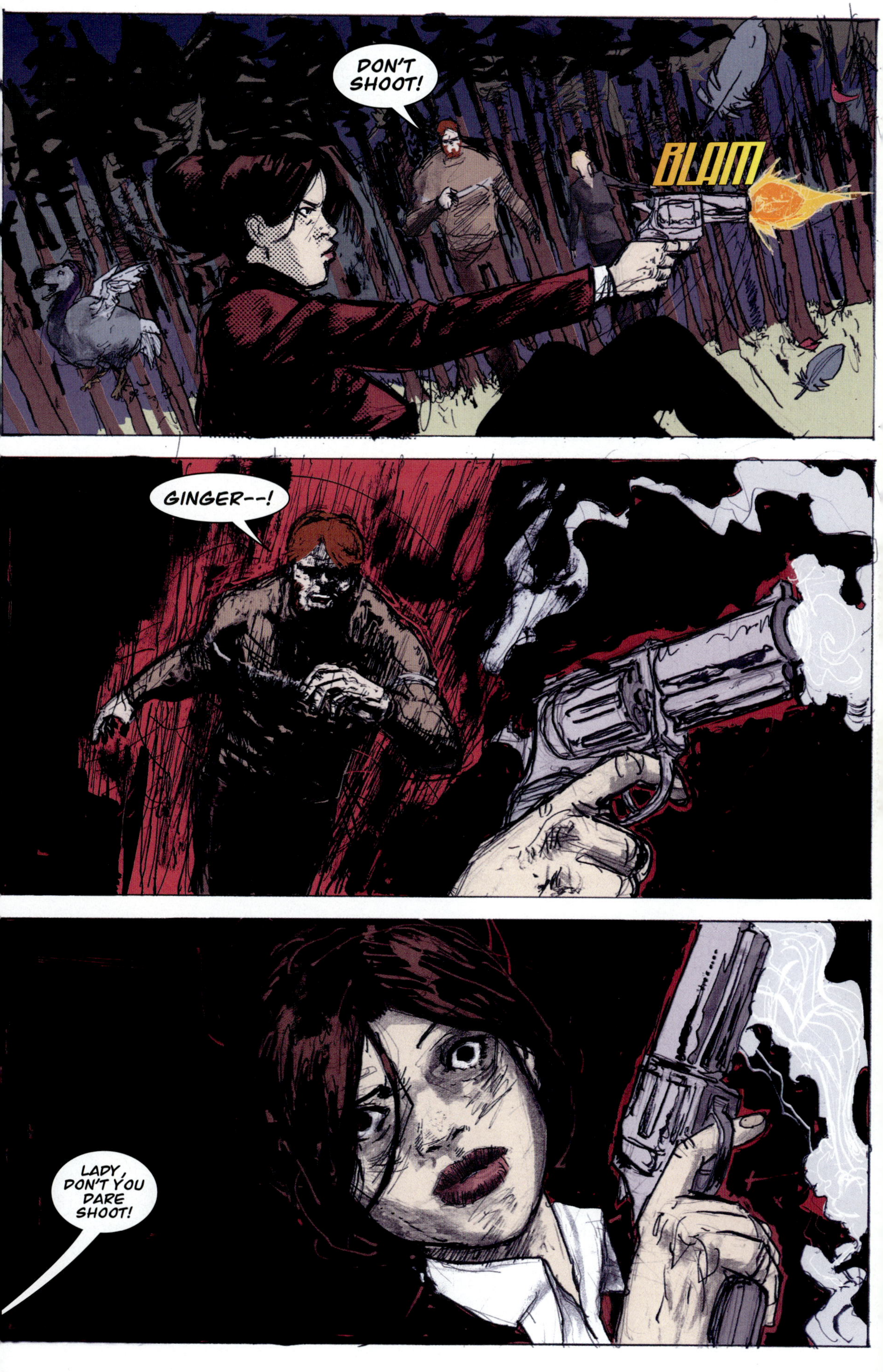
DON'T SHOOT!
BLAM
GINGER--!
LADY, DON'T YOU DARE SHOOT!

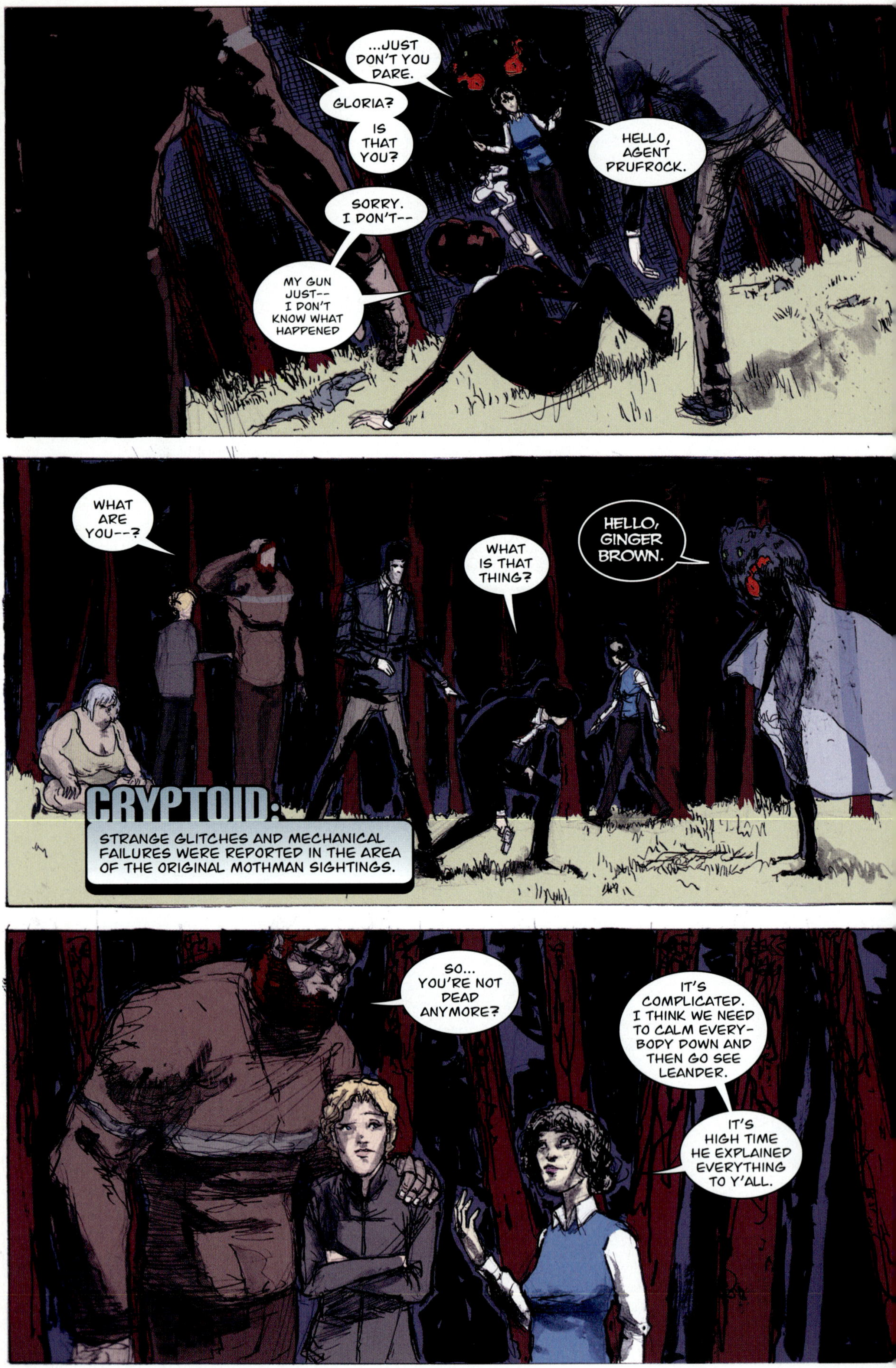
...JUST DON'T YOU DARE.
GLORIA?
IS THAT YOU?
HELLO, AGENT PRUFROCK.
SORRY. I DON'T--
MY GUN JUST-- I DON'T KNOW WHAT HAPPENED
WHAT ARE YOU--?
WHAT IS THAT THING?
HELLO, GINGER BROWN.
CRYPTOID:
STRANGE GLITCHES AND MECHANICAL FAILURES WERE REPORTED IN THE AREA OF THE ORIGINAL MOTHMAN SIGHTINGS.
SO... YOU'RE NOT DEAD ANYMORE?
IT'S COMPLICATED. I THINK WE NEED TO CALM EVERY-BODY DOWN AND THEN GO SEE LEANDER.
IT'S HIGH TIME HE EXPLAINED EVERYTHING TO Y'ALL.

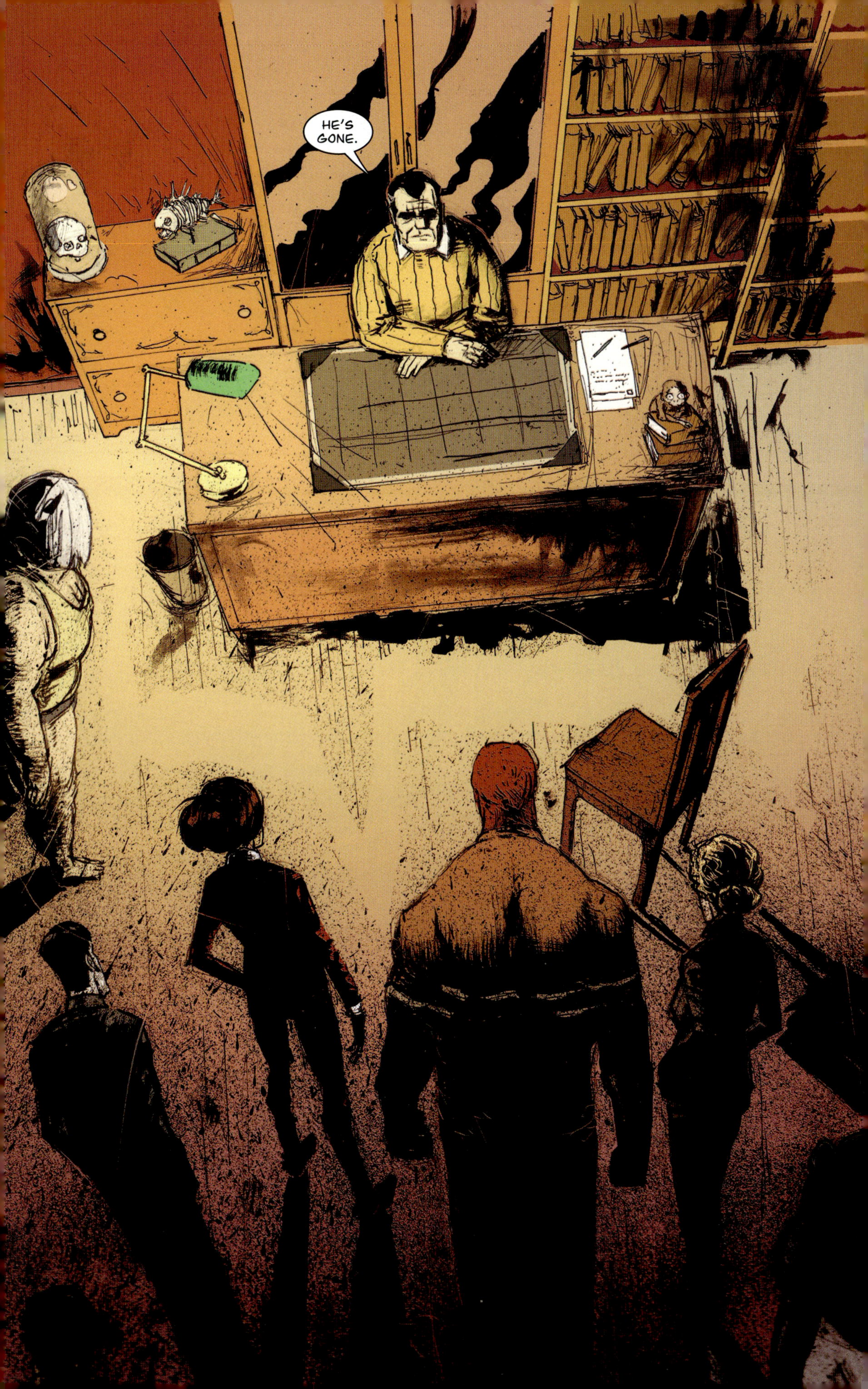
HE'S GONE.

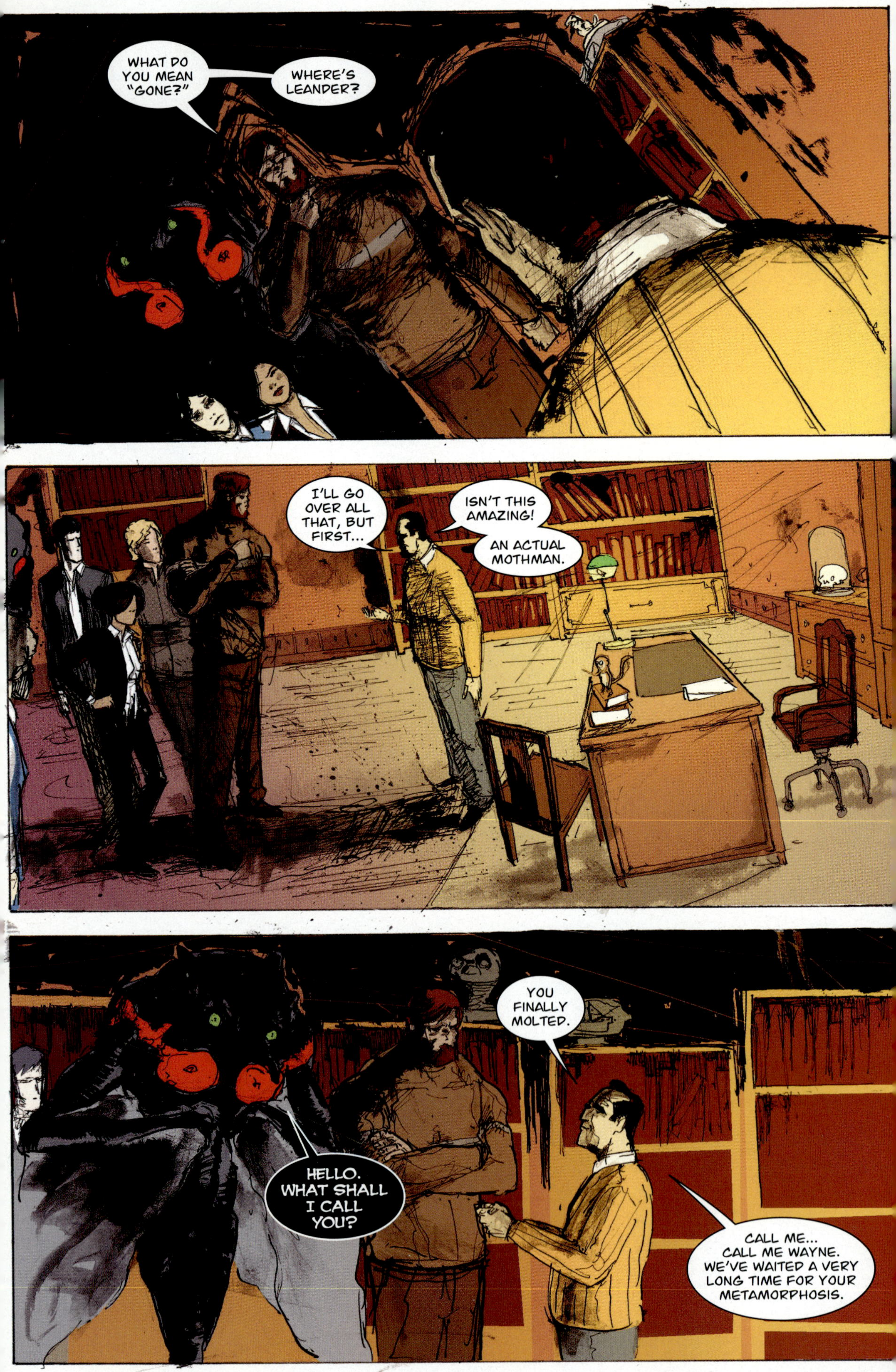
WHERE'S LEANDER?
WHAT DO YOU MEAN "GONE?"
I'LL GO OVER ALL THAT, BUT FIRST...
ISN'T THIS AMAZING!
AN ACTUAL MOTHMAN.
YOU FINALLY MOLTED.
HELLO. WHAT SHALL I CALL YOU?
CALL ME... CALL ME WAYNE. WE'VE WAITED A VERY LONG TIME FOR YOUR METAMORPHOSIS.

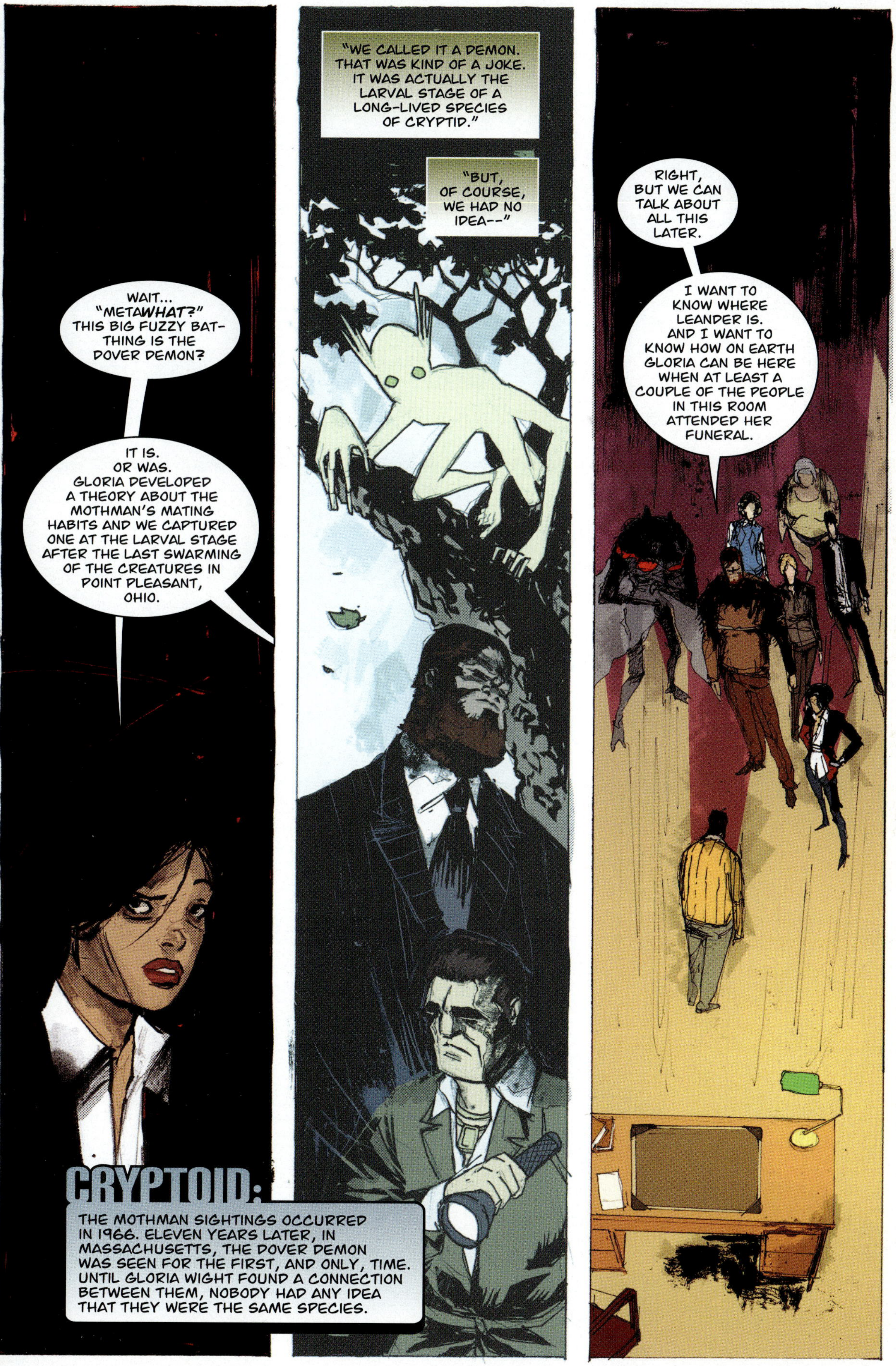
WAIT... "METAWHAT?" THIS BIG FUZZY BAT-THING IS THE DOVER DEMON?
IT IS. OR WAS. GLORIA DEVELOPED A THEORY ABOUT THE MOTHMAN'S MATING HABITS AND WE CAPTURED ONE AT THE LARVAL STAGE AFTER THE LAST SWARMING OF THE CREATURES IN POINT PLEASANT, OHIO.
"WE CALLED IT A DEMON. THAT WAS KIND OF A JOKE. IT WAS ACTUALLY THE LARVAL STAGE OF A LONG-LIVED SPECIES OF CRYPTID."
"BUT, OF COURSE, WE HAD NO IDEA--"
RIGHT, BUT WE CAN TALK ABOUT ALL THIS LATER.
I WANT TO KNOW WHERE LEANDER IS. AND I WANT TO KNOW HOW ON EARTH GLORIA CAN BE HERE WHEN AT LEAST A COUPLE OF THE PEOPLE IN THIS ROOM ATTENDED HER FUNERAL.
CRYPTOID:
THE MOTHMAN SIGHTINGS OCCURRED IN 1966. ELEVEN YEARS LATER, IN MASSACHUSETTS, THE DOVER DEMON WAS SEEN FOR THE FIRST, AND ONLY, TIME. UNTIL GLORIA WIGHT FOUND A CONNECTION BETWEEN THEM, NOBODY HAD ANY IDEA THAT THEY WERE THE SAME SPECIES.

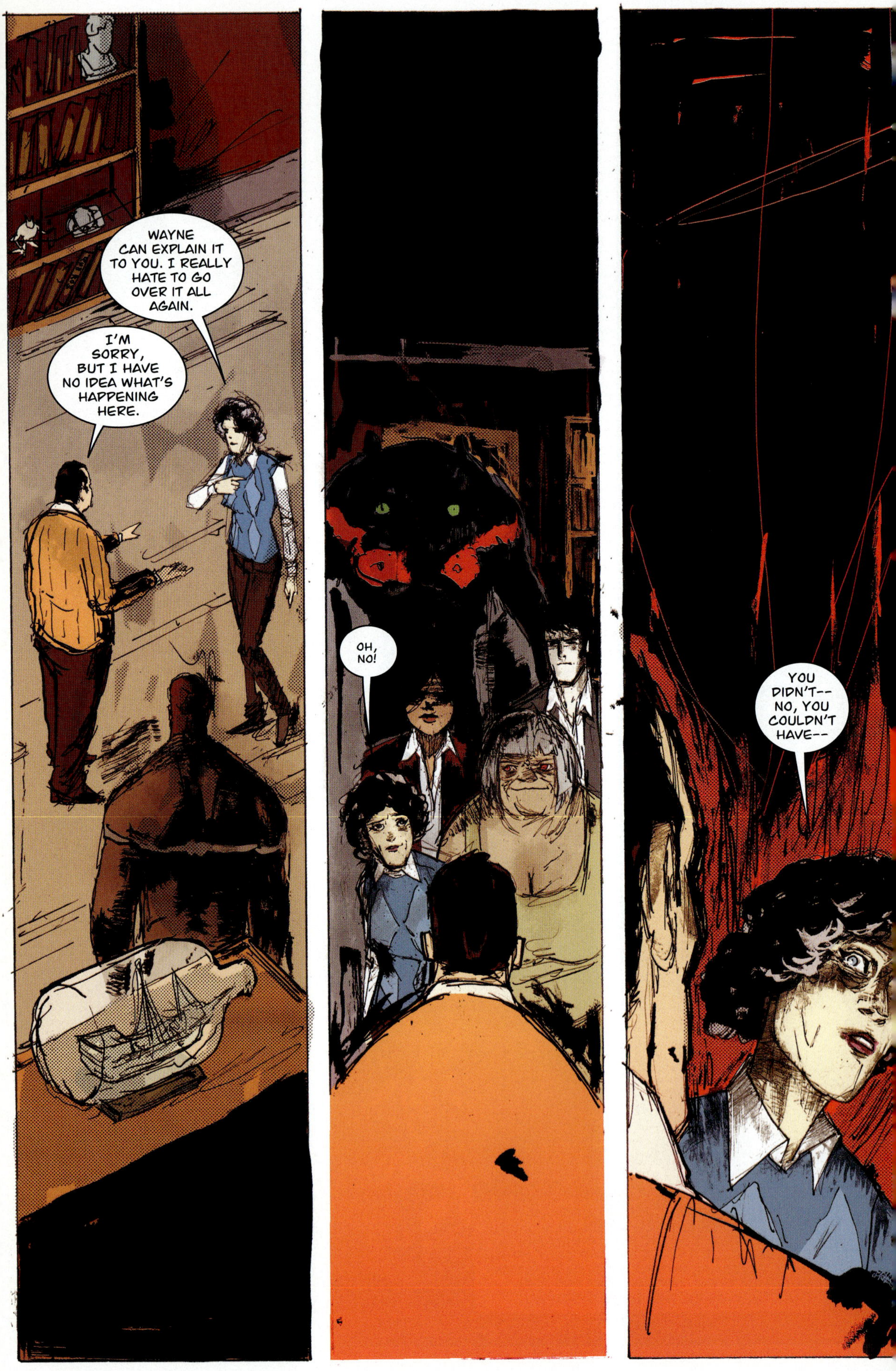
WAYNE CAN EXPLAIN IT TO YOU. I REALLY HATE TO GO OVER IT ALL AGAIN.
I'M SORRY, BUT I HAVE NO IDEA WHAT'S HAPPENING HERE.
OH, NO!
YOU DIDN'T-- NO, YOU COULDN'T HAVE--

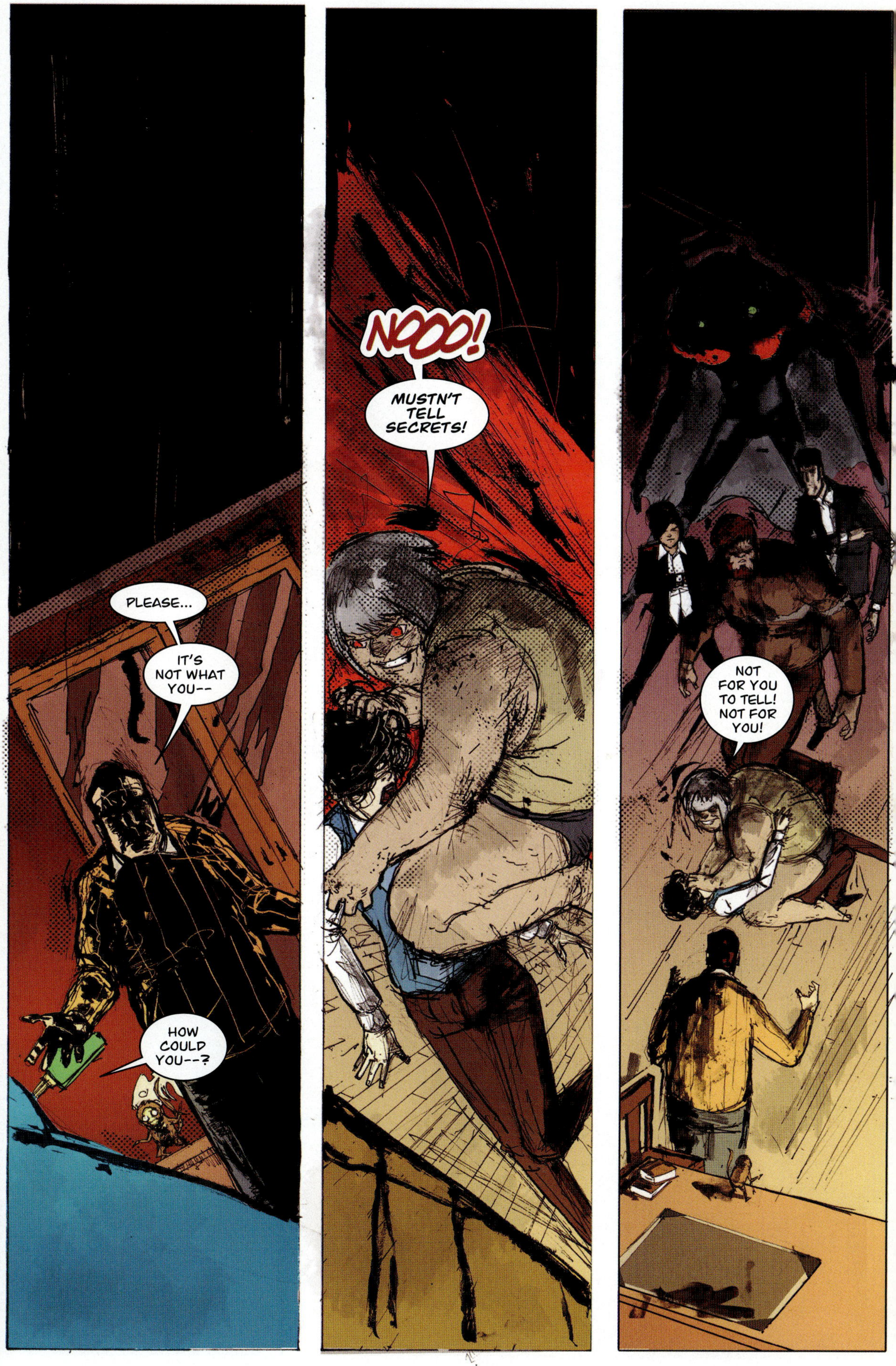
PLEASE...
IT'S NOT WHAT YOU--
HOW COULD YOU--?
NOOO!
MUSTN'T TELL SECRETS!
NOT FOR YOU TO TELL! NOT FOR YOU!

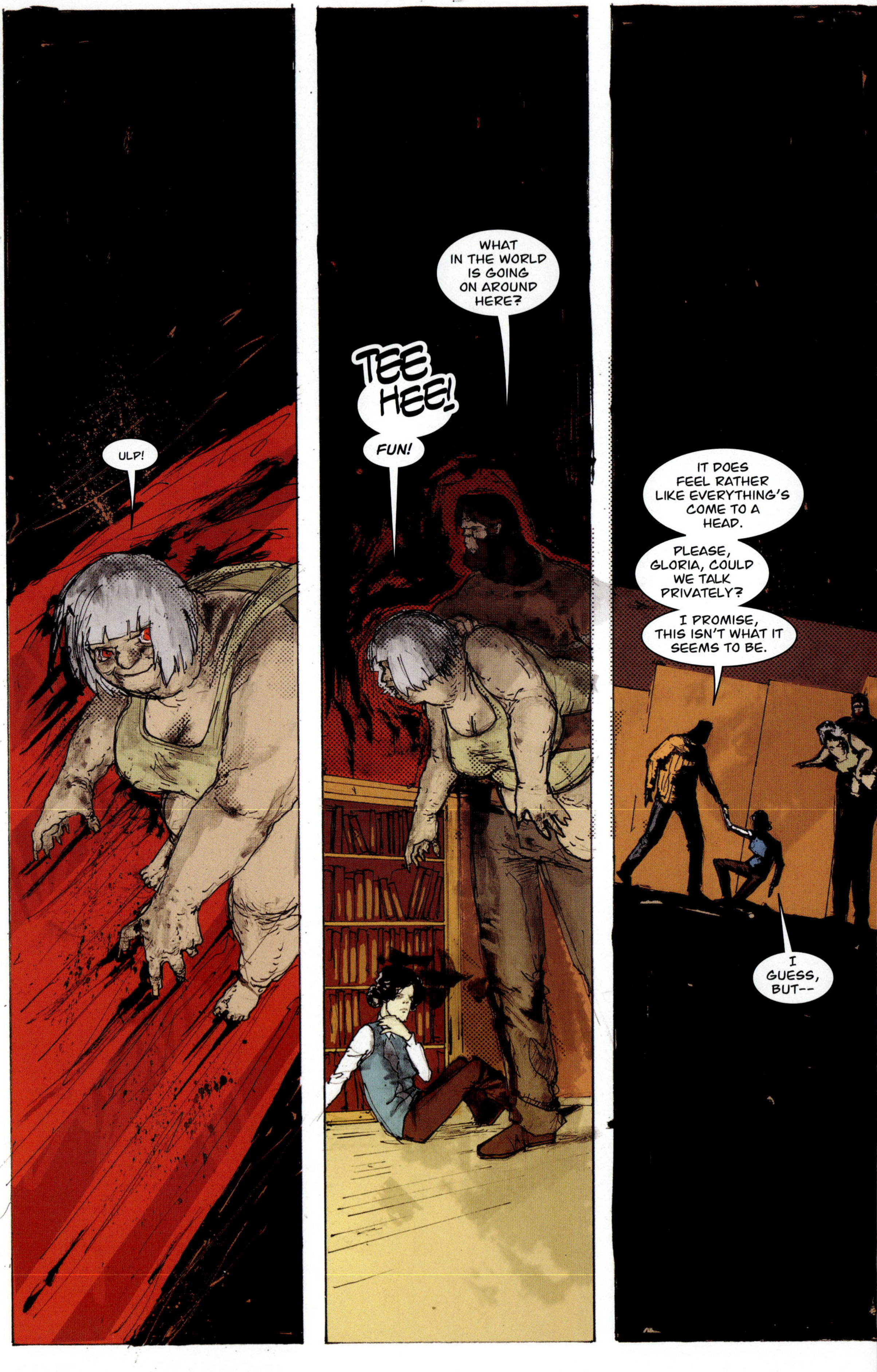
ULP!
WHAT IN THE WORLD IS GOING ON AROUND HERE?
TEE HEE!
FUN!
IT DOES FEEL RATHER LIKE EVERYTHING'S COME TO A HEAD.
PLEASE, GLORIA, COULD WE TALK PRIVATELY?
I PROMISE, THIS ISN'T WHAT IT SEEMS TO BE.
I GUESS, BUT--

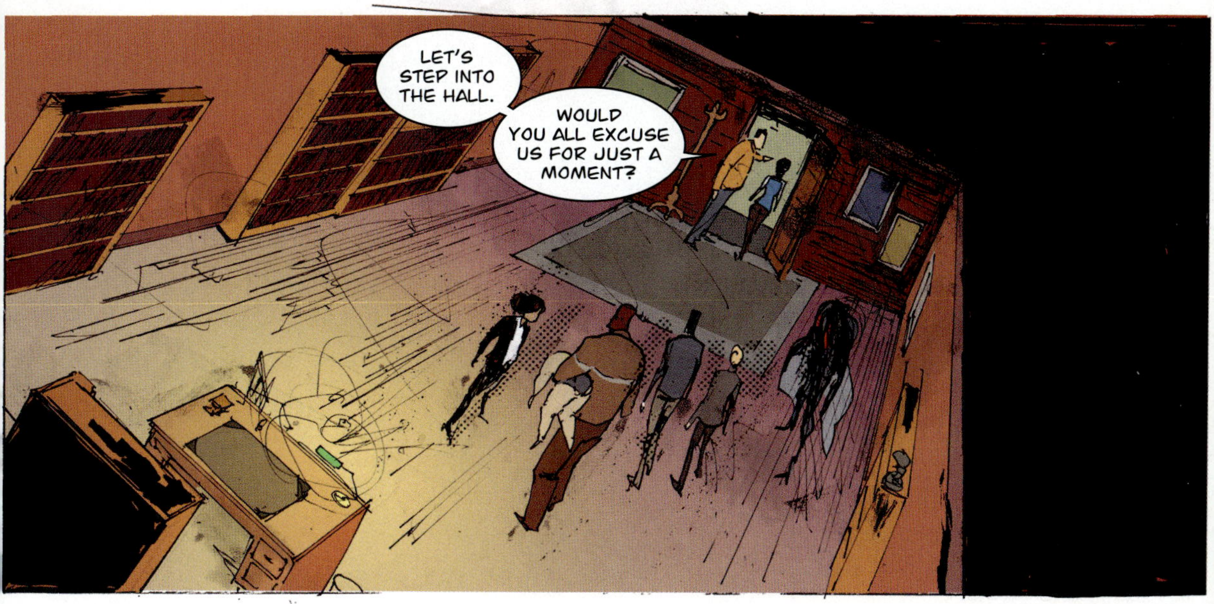
LET'S STEP INTO THE HALL.
WOULD YOU ALL EXCUSE US FOR JUST A MOMENT?

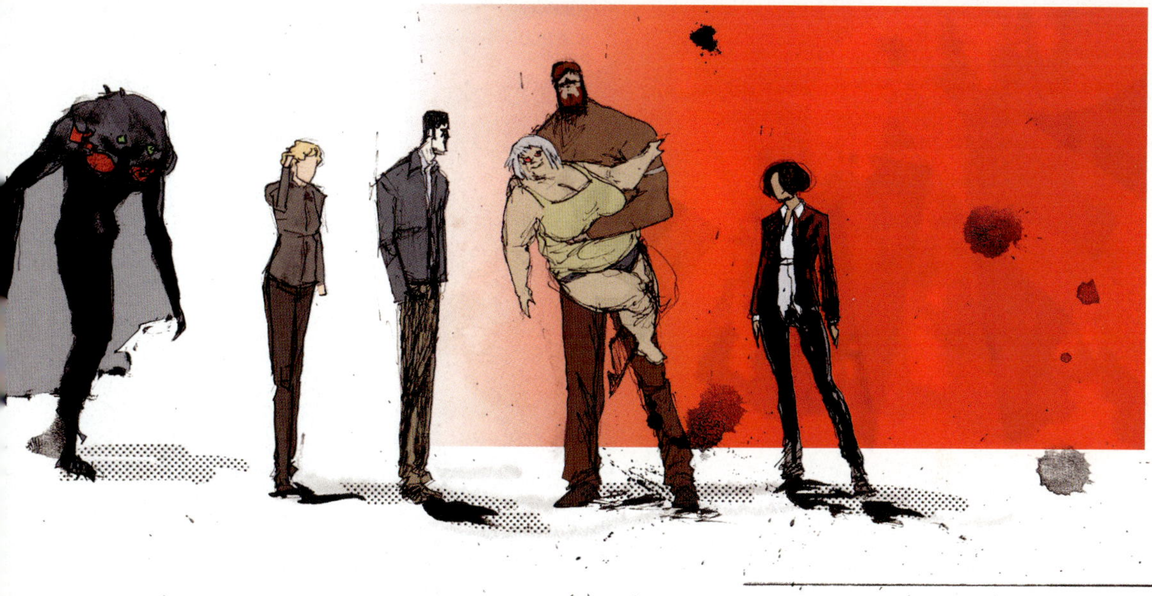

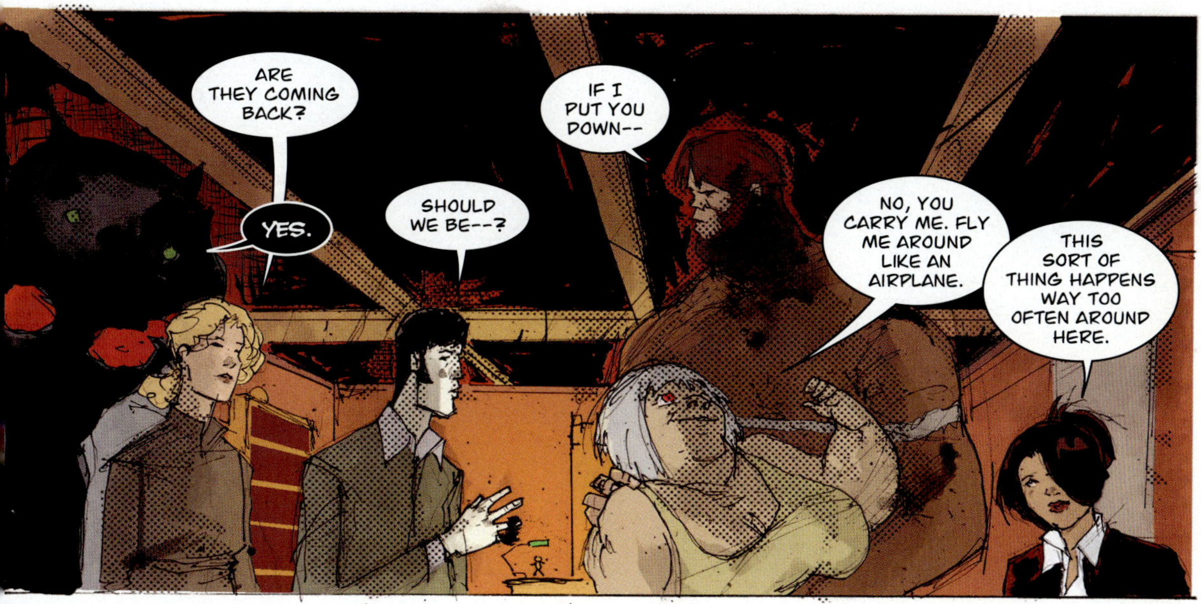
ARE THEY COMING BACK?
YES.
SHOULD WE BE--?
IF I PUT YOU DOWN--
NO, YOU CARRY ME. FLY ME AROUND LIKE AN AIRPLANE.
THIS SORT OF THING HAPPENS WAY TOO OFTEN AROUND HERE.

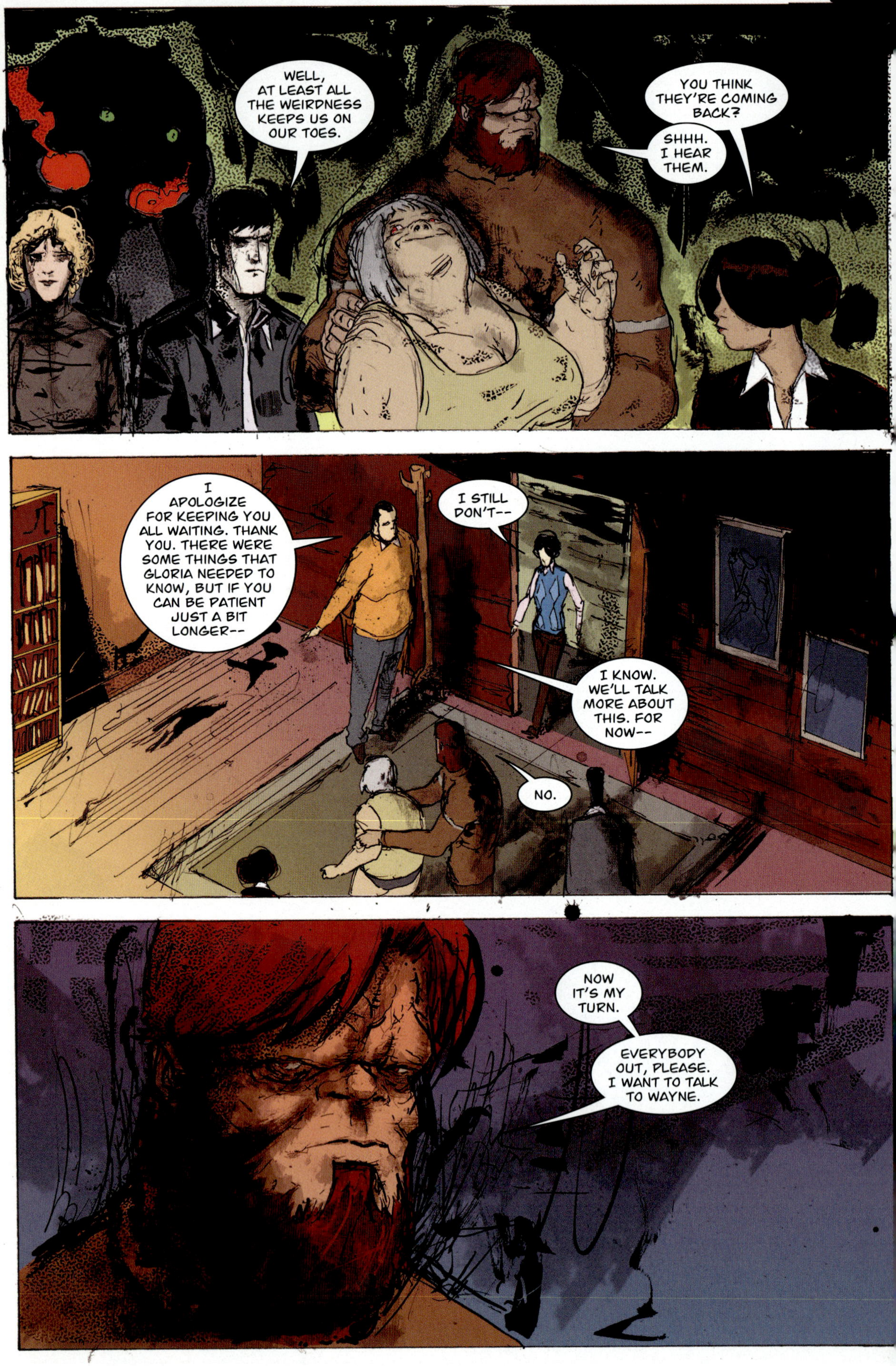
WELL, AT LEAST ALL THE WEIRDNESS KEEPS US ON OUR TOES.
YOU THINK THEY'RE COMING BACK?
SHHH. I HEAR THEM.
I APOLOGIZE FOR KEEPING YOU ALL WAITING. THANK YOU. THERE WERE SOME THINGS THAT GLORIA NEEDED TO KNOW, BUT IF YOU CAN BE PATIENT JUST A BIT LONGER--
I STILL DON'T--
I KNOW. WE'LL TALK MORE ABOUT THIS. FOR NOW--
NO.
NOW IT'S MY TURN.
EVERYBODY OUT, PLEASE. I WANT TO TALK TO WAYNE.

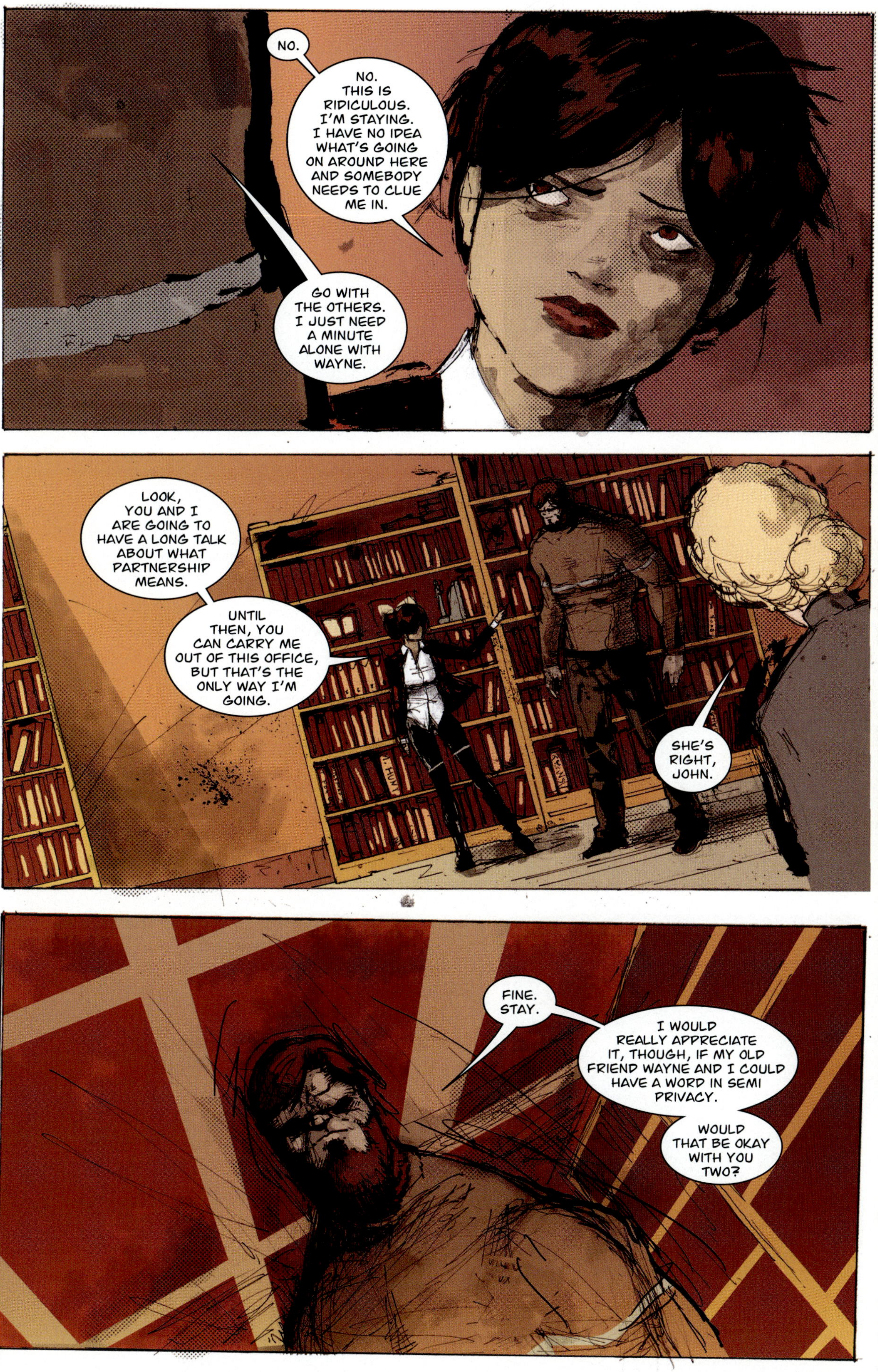
NO.
NO. THIS IS RIDICULOUS. I'M STAYING. I HAVE NO IDEA WHAT'S GOING ON AROUND HERE AND SOMEBODY NEEDS TO CLUE ME IN.
GO WITH THE OTHERS. I JUST NEED A MINUTE ALONE WITH WAYNE.
LOOK, YOU AND I ARE GOING TO HAVE A LONG TALK ABOUT WHAT PARTNERSHIP MEANS.
UNTIL THEN, YOU CAN CARRY ME OUT OF THIS OFFICE, BUT THAT'S THE ONLY WAY I'M GOING.
SHE'S RIGHT, JOHN.
FINE. STAY.
I WOULD REALLY APPRECIATE IT, THOUGH, IF MY OLD FRIEND WAYNE AND I COULD HAVE A WORD IN SEMI PRIVACY.
WOULD THAT BE OKAY WITH YOU TWO?

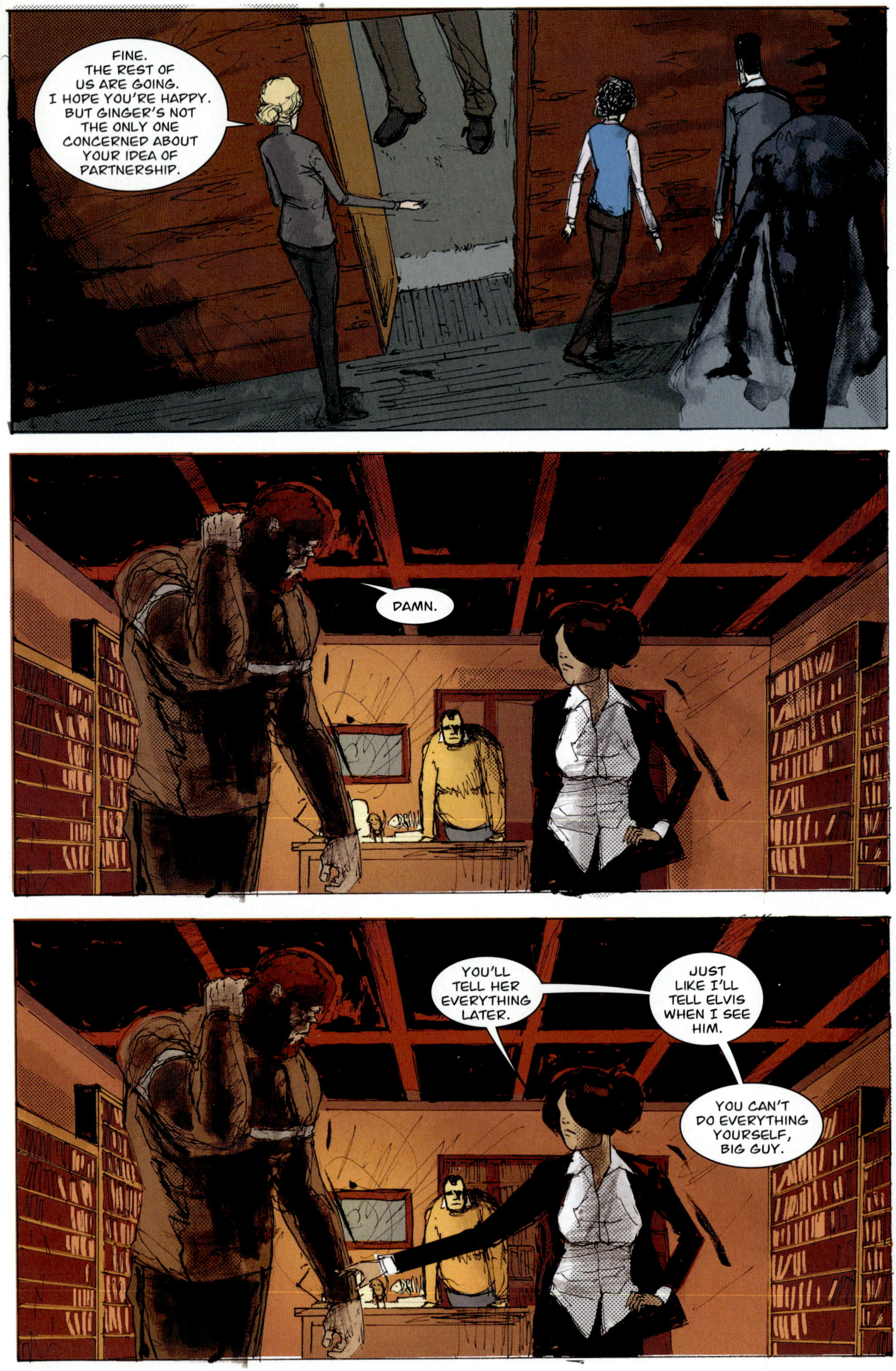
FINE. THE REST OF US ARE GOING. I HOPE YOU'RE HAPPY. BUT GINGER'S NOT THE ONLY ONE CONCERNED ABOUT YOUR IDEA OF PARTNERSHIP.
DAMN.
YOU'LL TELL HER EVERYTHING LATER.
JUST LIKE I'LL TELL ELVIS WHEN I SEE HIM.
YOU CAN'T DO EVERYTHING YOURSELF, BIG GUY.

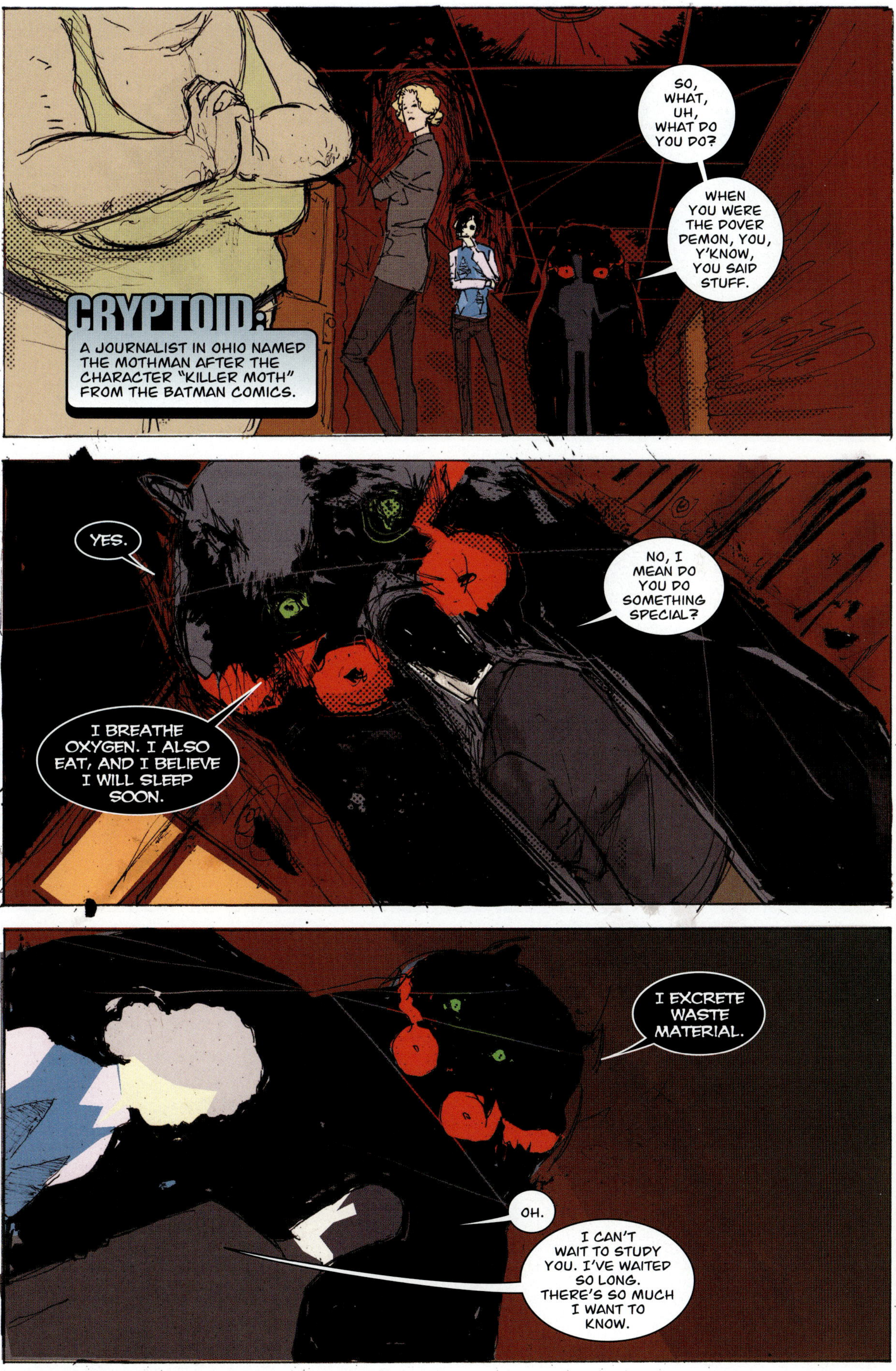
SO, WHAT, UH, WHAT DO YOU DO?
WHEN YOU WERE THE DOVER DEMON, YOU, Y'KNOW, YOU SAID STUFF.
CRYPTOID:
A JOURNALIST IN OHIO NAMED THE MOTHMAN AFTER THE CHARACTER "KILLER MOTH" FROM THE BATMAN COMICS.
YES.
NO, I MEAN DO YOU DO SOMETHING SPECIAL?
I BREATHE OXYGEN. I ALSO EAT, AND I BELIEVE I WILL SLEEP SOON.
I EXCRETE WASTE MATERIAL.
OH.
I CAN'T WAIT TO STUDY YOU. I'VE WAITED SO LONG. THERE'S SO MUCH I WANT TO KNOW.

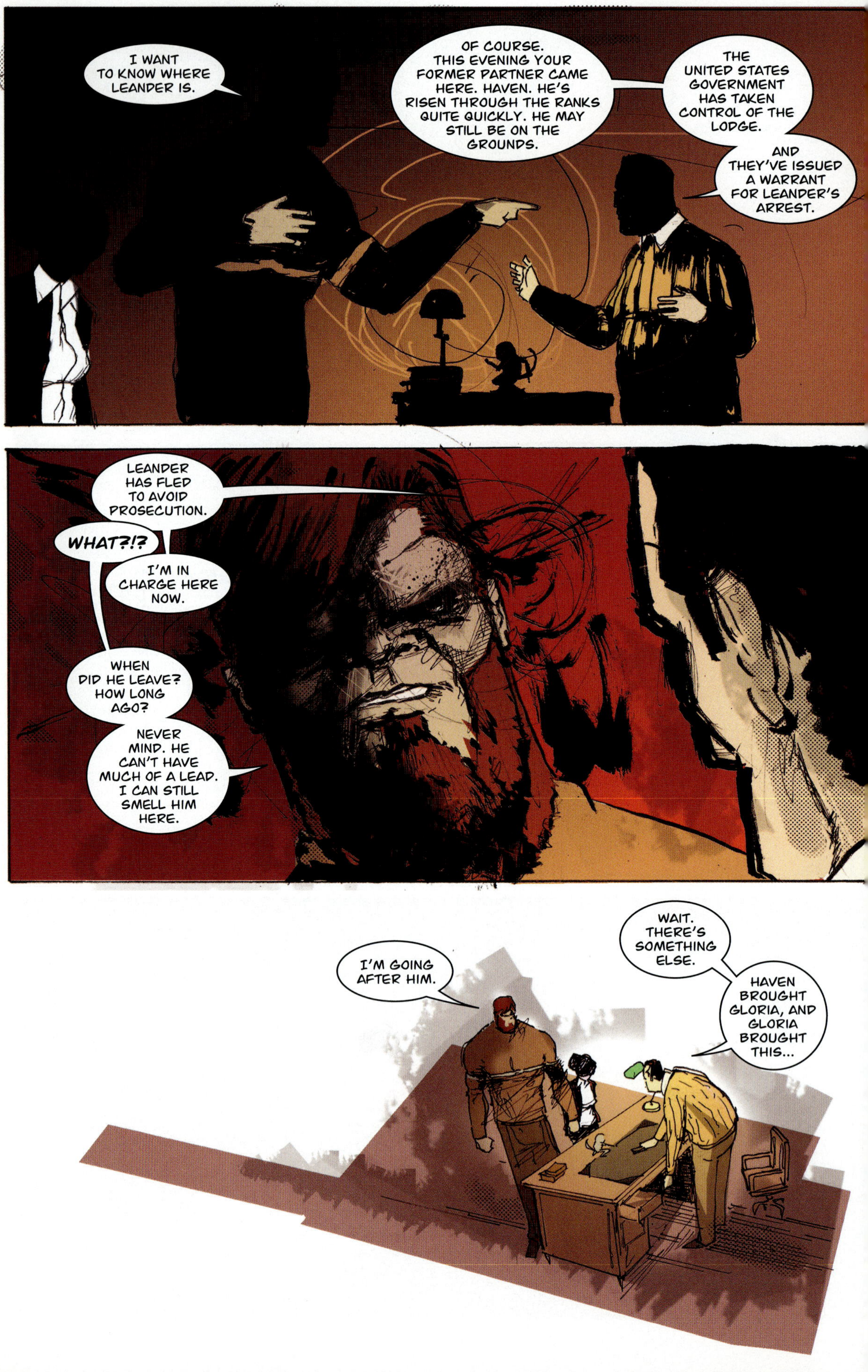
I WANT TO KNOW WHERE LEANDER IS.
OF COURSE. THIS EVENING YOUR FORMER PARTNER CAME HERE. HAVEN. HE'S RISEN THROUGH THE RANKS QUITE QUICKLY. HE MAY STILL BE ON THE GROUNDS.
THE UNITED STATES GOVERNMENT HAS TAKEN CONTROL OF THE LODGE.
AND THEY'VE ISSUED A WARRANT FOR LEANDER'S ARREST.
LEANDER HAS FLED TO AVOID PROSECUTION.
WHAT?!?
I'M IN CHARGE HERE NOW.
WHEN DID HE LEAVE? HOW LONG AGO?
NEVER MIND. HE CAN'T HAVE MUCH OF A LEAD. I CAN STILL SMELL HIM HERE.
I'M GOING AFTER HIM.
WAIT. THERE'S SOMETHING ELSE.
HAVEN BROUGHT GLORIA, AND GLORIA BROUGHT THIS...

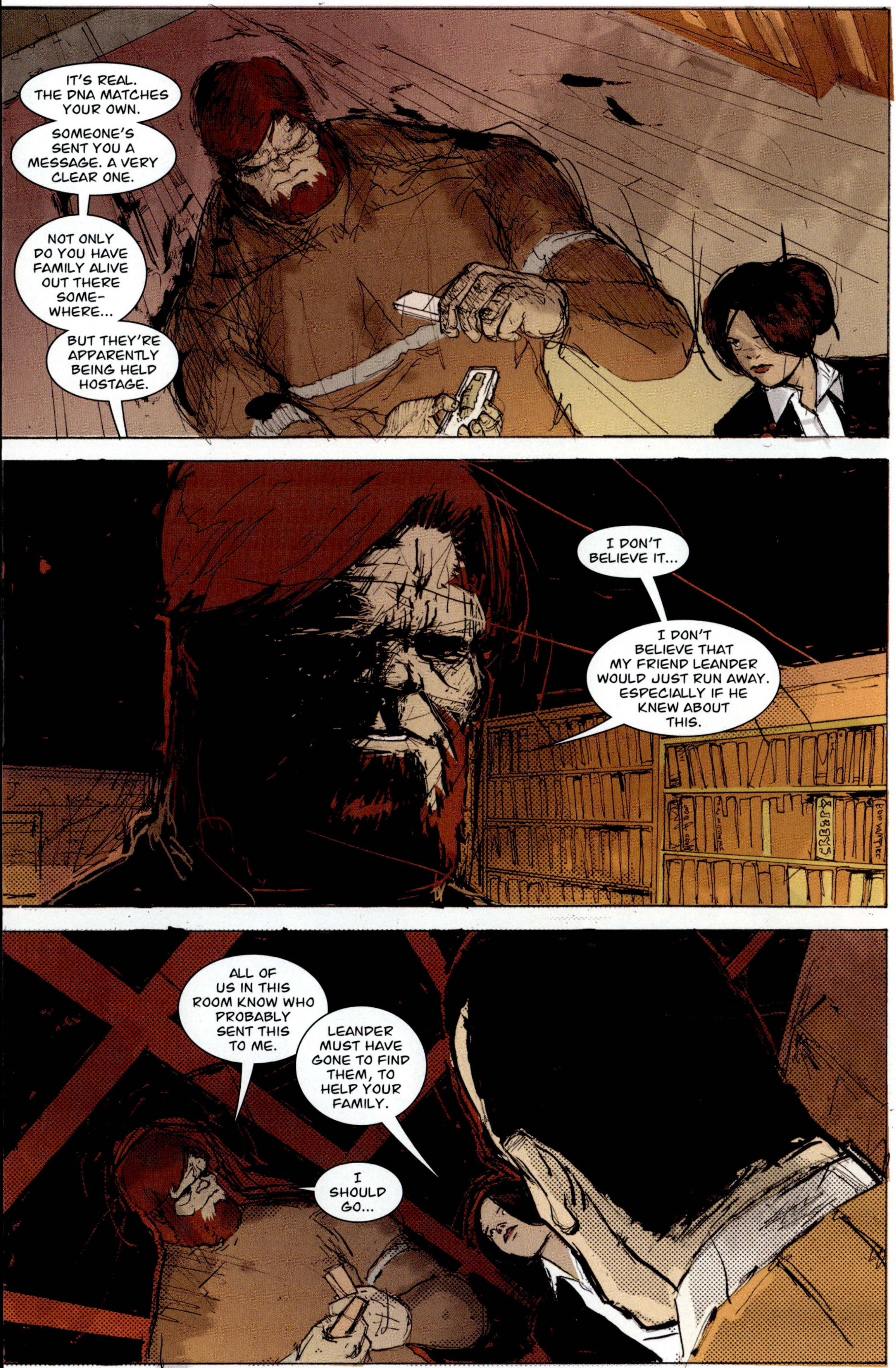
IT'S REAL. THE DNA MATCHES YOUR OWN.
SOMEONE'S SENT YOU A MESSAGE. A VERY CLEAR ONE.
NOT ONLY DO YOU HAVE FAMILY ALIVE OUT THERE SOME-WHERE...
BUT THEY'RE APPARENTLY BEING HELD HOSTAGE.
I DON'T BELIEVE IT...
I DON'T BELIEVE THAT MY FRIEND LEANDER WOULD JUST RUN AWAY. ESPECIALLY IF HE KNEW ABOUT THIS.
ALL OF US IN THIS ROOM KNOW WHO PROBABLY SENT THIS TO ME.
LEANDER MUST HAVE GONE TO FIND THEM, TO HELP YOUR FAMILY.
I SHOULD GO...

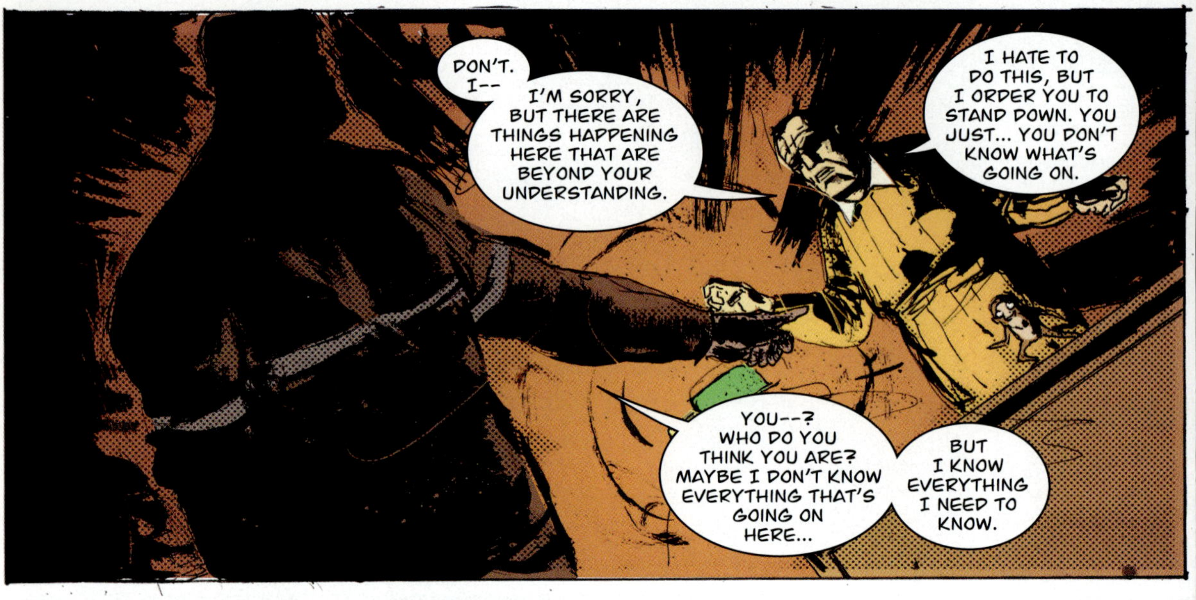
DON'T. I--
I'M SORRY, BUT THERE ARE THINGS HAPPENING HERE THAT ARE BEYOND YOUR UNDERSTANDING.
I HATE TO DO THIS, BUT I ORDER YOU TO STAND DOWN. YOU JUST... YOU DON'T KNOW WHAT'S GOING ON.
YOU--? WHO DO YOU THINK YOU ARE? MAYBE I DON'T KNOW EVERYTHING THAT'S GOING ON HERE...
BUT I KNOW EVERYTHING I NEED TO KNOW.

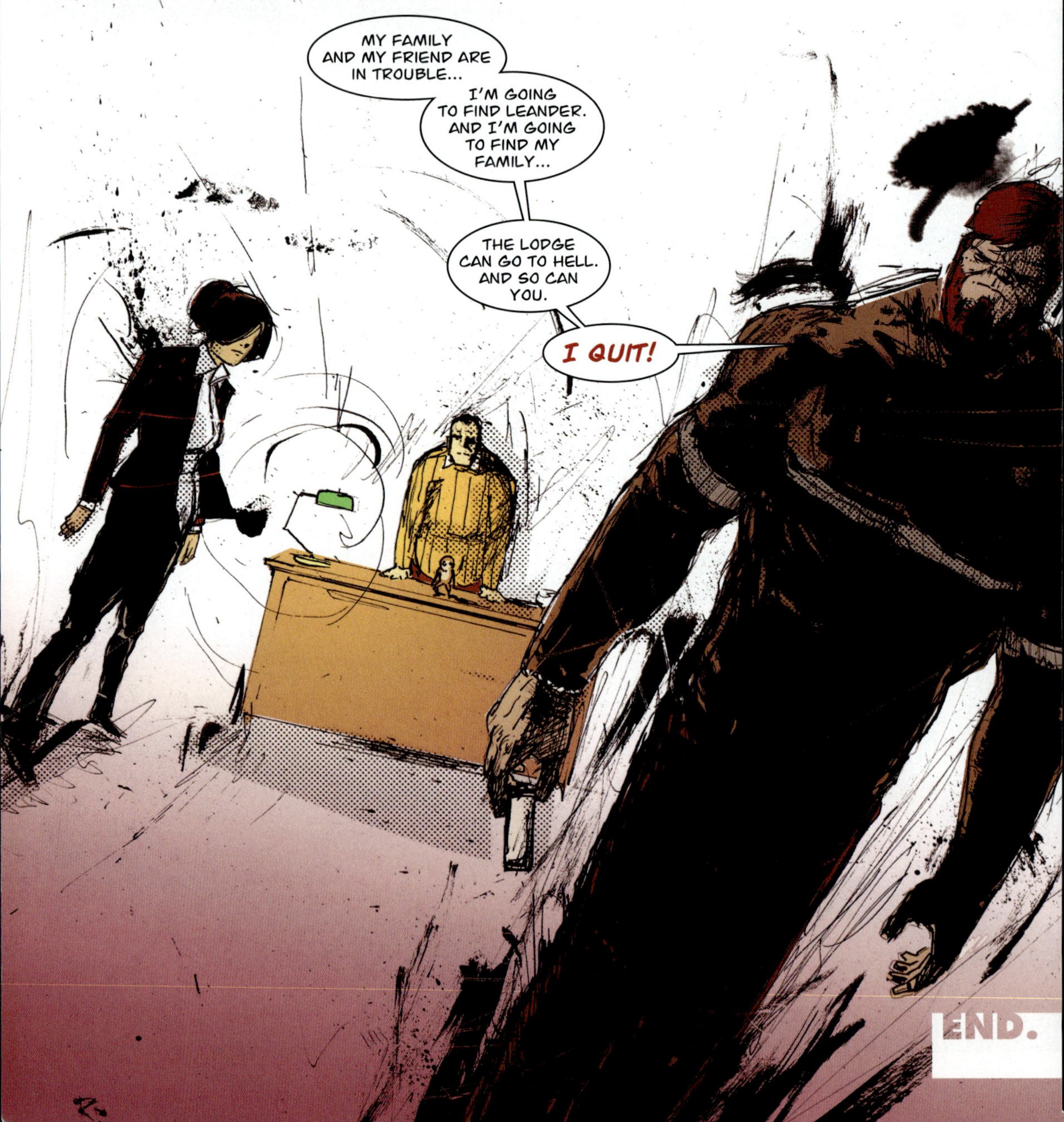
MY FAMILY AND MY FRIEND ARE IN TROUBLE...
I'M GOING TO FIND LEANDER. AND I'M GOING TO FIND MY FAMILY...
THE LODGE CAN GO TO HELL. AND SO CAN YOU.
I QUIT!
END.

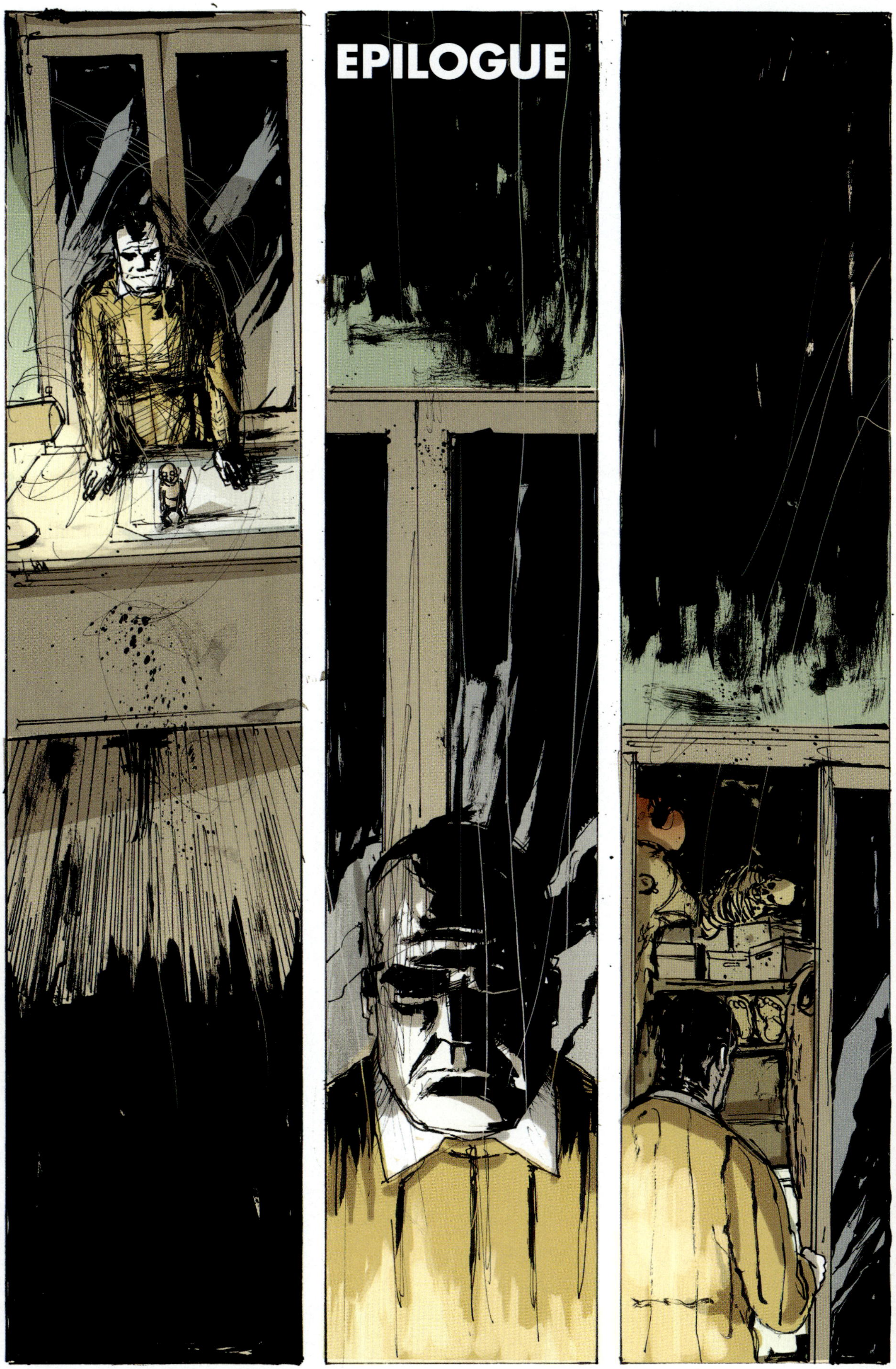
EPILOGUE

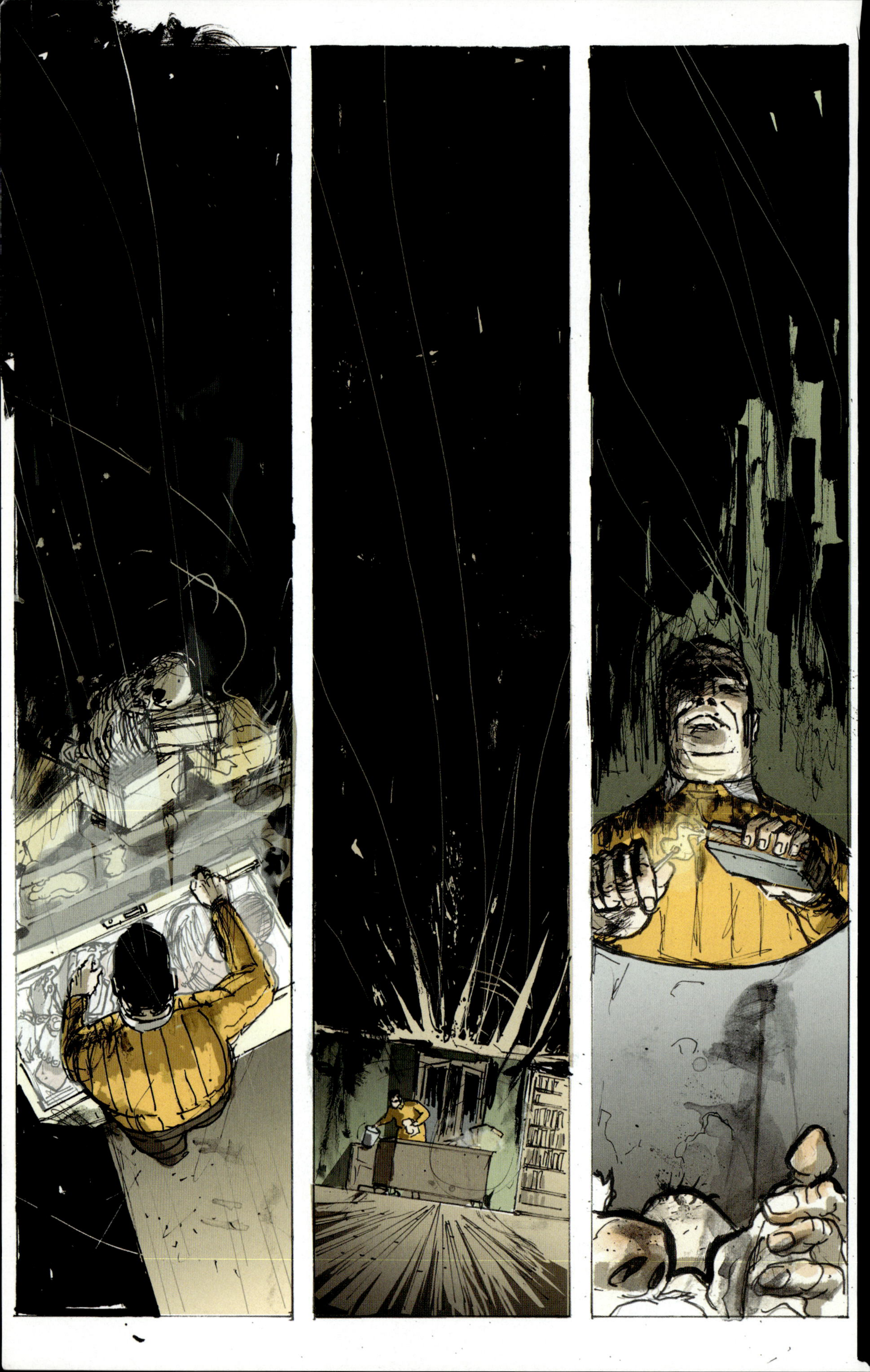

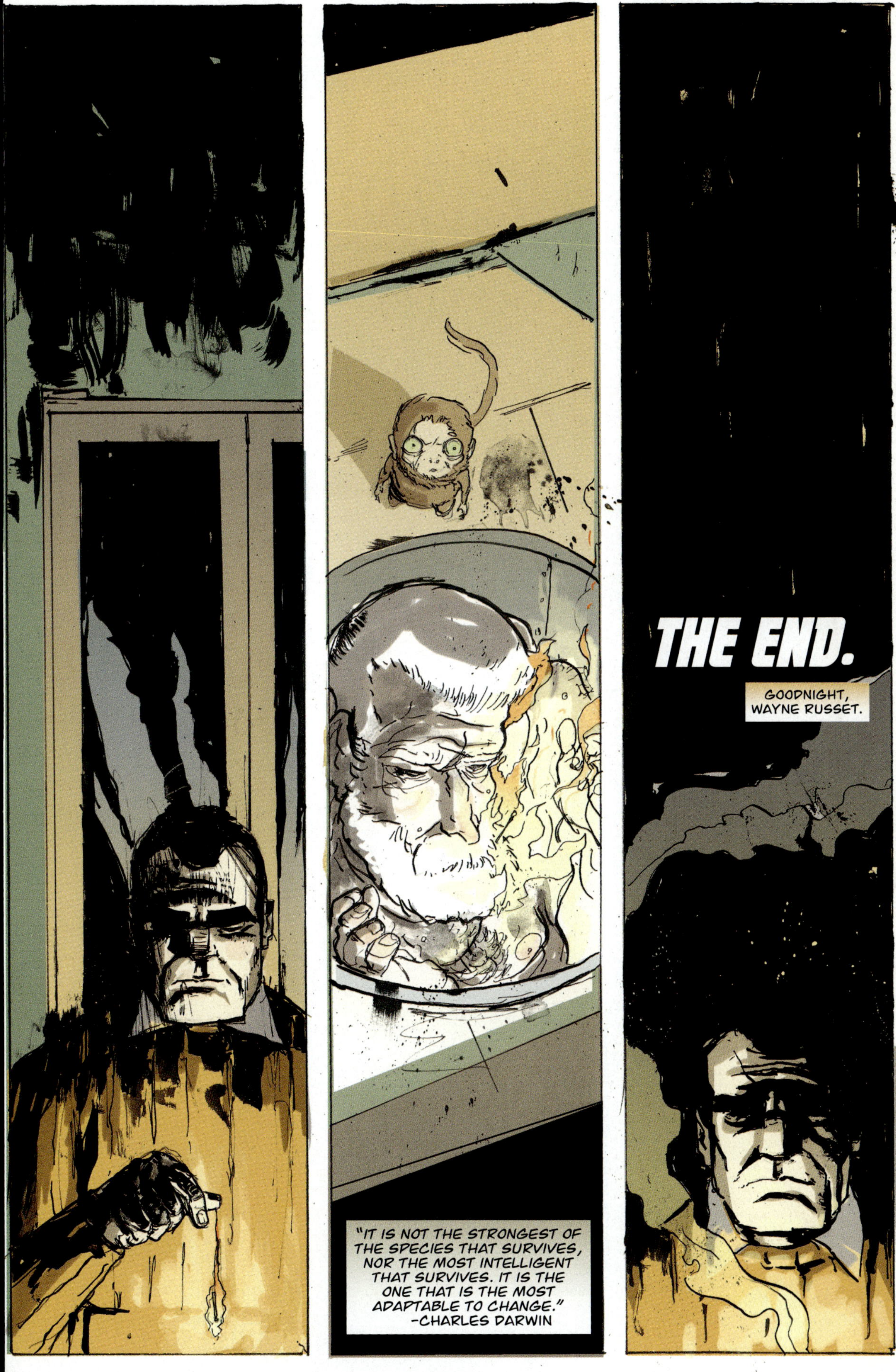
"IT IS NOT THE STRONGEST OF THE SPECIES THAT SURVIVES, NOR THE MOST INTELLIGENT THAT SURVIVES. IT IS THE ONE THAT IS THE MOST ADAPTABLE TO CHANGE."
-CHARLES DARWIN
THE END.
GOODNIGHT, WAYNE RUSSET.

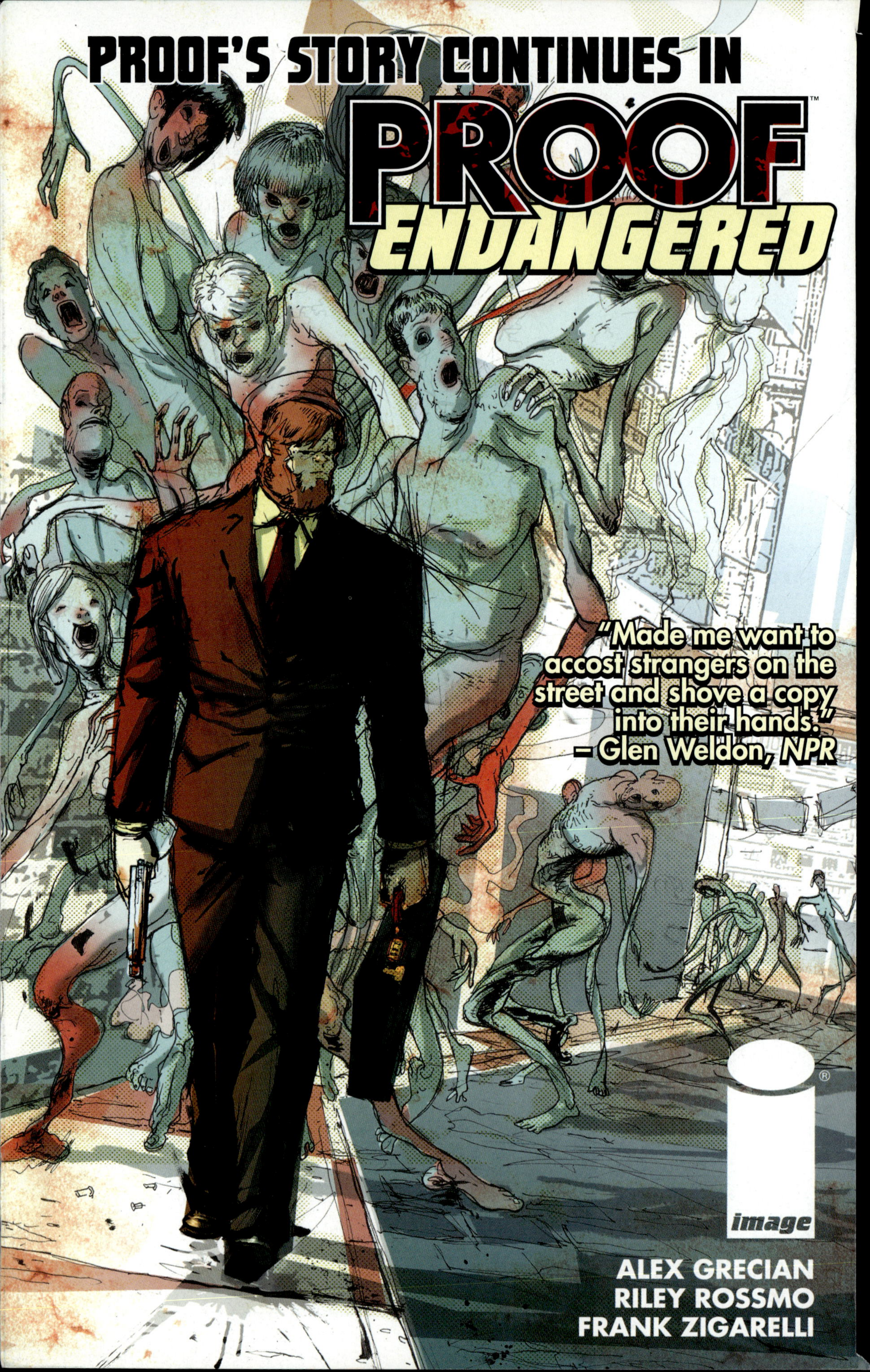
PROOF'S STORY CONTINUES IN
PROOF™
ENDANGERED
"Made me want to accost strangers on the street and shove a copy into their hands."
– Glen Weldon, NPR
image
ALEX GRECIAN
RILEY ROSSMO
FRANK ZIGARELLI